TO LORNA

Ordering Information: For quantity sales details and orders by U.S. trade bookstores and wholesalers, please contact Novabook Publishing at info@novabook.us or 323-871-0889.

First published in the United States by Novabook Publishing 2014.
10 9 8 7 6 5 4 3 2 1

NOVABOOK

Novabook Publishing
Los Angeles
www.novabook.us

ISBN 978-0-9894896-6-9

Sudden Rivers

A Novel by

Michael Jeffery Blair

Aslo by Michael Jeffery Blair

EXIT POINT

THE ARCHITECT OF LAW

CONTENTS

There are many Arabic terms used throughout essential to the story, most of which are well defined in the text. I have put together a glossary so that any unfamiliar ones can be clarified since it has been found passing a word that is not understood will cause one to have trouble reading.

There is a far off storm
Where it is night

Where the moon has slipped off
Into extreme distances
Falling deftly to the sea below
Leaving its ivory image
Seared into the self as beauty's imprint

Where haze and restlessness mingle
With waters constantly migrating
Neither destination nor origin known
Eternal. Vigilant. Only to move on
Here is where purpose lies

Purpose and redemption
Motive and alibi

I | The Light of Stars

The crumpled white paper was still in the pocket of his coat. A child lay dying in his arms. "Not me!" he whispered as eyes like arctic seas darted into the desert night. "I'm not the one!" His protest was muted by brittle wind. Lights flared in the distance. The air smelled of dust and sage and saffron. Words seethed through clenched teeth. "...damn message!" Circumstances had escalated beyond his control. Regret gripped him. He felt sick. The decision made by some faceless entity mired in the government office...he would never forget. Never. If that other man, the nameless one, had been able to cut it this would not have happened and life would not have changed—it would be like it was. Erskine Parrish MacKenzie thought of it all as he plunged into the vortex and through the events that followed he would remember one thing forever: how brilliant the light of stars that night.

White sands had drawn a pale windy scythe against the azure sea. Not a soul was visible. He had been silent witness to the great curve of Africa pounded by white cap waves under relentless sun as he descended for the final approach. Jet engines whined. It had only been three days ago.

His destination, the yacht, lie in the warm sanguine waters—tinted by a red tide—off Safi, Al Maghrib, two hundred miles south of the nearest airport at Casablanca. A sirocco had been up for a week and left the region desiccated. He had tumbled down the chuck-holed two-lane highway that wound along the coast with hot air blasting out the vents. The Arab had promised cool relief of air conditioning when he first rented the car. Nothing outside the cities was in good repair. He should have known better. Blue phosphorous white water reflected brightly when headlights, the surf, and the shore collided. The ship, his destination, was a ghost. It had undergone an expensive retrofit to preserve its life. Once it had been used to transport bullion by German socialists and then had been the private yacht of a Turkish businessman who spent his final years plying the Dardanelles. The South American mahogany in which its bridge, dining, and first class staterooms were trimmed was no longer available; the brass fittings were a luxurious anachronism, and the teak decks from Indonesia that ran seamlessly up against iron bulkheads were irreplaceable treasures from a vanished era. The vessel had lain in dry dock at Istanbul for twenty-five years as a sort of shrine until it was bought by Muhammad Abd al' Rashid.

It was much later when perspiration and spice had wafted through the bus mixed with strong odors of gasoline and exhaust from the open windows—by which fiery gusts raced never seeming to penetrate the interior. The noise of the highway ran uninterrupted. Each passenger a refugee from devastating defeats clinging to destinations up ahead—landmarks in the mind. Salvations. Unmistakable wonder filled their eyes. Their faces were bathed by tiny amber running lights that glowed in the cabin against a landscape of rushing distances.

During the journey he could not have imagined that it was possible: having been lulled by the rhythm of the tires, mesmerized by the spectacle of starlight stretching out over the desert for what seemed like thousands of miles, and being confidant that terrible things only happened to others. The mob. But they, the faceless proselytes of terror of whom there is an endless stream, had materialized in the road as if chimera flitting by in the deep cobalt of night, which at first Parrish thought they were. That morning he had unwisely consumed two whiskeys and a croissant—a rare event instigated by some overwhelming need—and had not eaten again all day. He had placed his hands flat against the white marble top to the bar to feel its coolness in the restrained heat of morning and had looked at his ring whose inscription read, "St. Eustatius College", where he had taken his degree in theology. They came later. It was much later that they appeared. Long after the meeting on the yacht where the sea was pregnant with sweetness and after his car had died ignobly on a bleak stretch leaving him stranded with a pressing itinerary and running behind the time. They had swept across the headlights of the lumbering bus as apparitions in flaming scarves painting the shadows with terror and uncertainty. The light of the full moon washed over them. The frenzy of the wind whipped their rage. The windshield shattered. Harsh staccato cracks punctuated the serenity of the desert nightfall. Shots fired seemed unreal. Echoes. Reflections. Memories. Blood. But that was later.

Earlier, when he had arrived, children scurried at his heels. They followed him all the way out to the rock jetty that ran up from the quay where the yacht was moored. The air was thick and still in between gusts, pungent with the smell of fish and seabirds. Grimy fingers pulled at his elbows and chattering mouths mechanically chanted the incantations that had worked before, that had paid off in cash. But Parrish could see immediately what their eyes revealed: they were elsewhere—not begging, not doing what had to be done, but instead dreaming of the future like all children. No different than it had always been except for the huge desalinization plant that loomed over the ancient harbor at Safi as a reminder of which century they walked through.

Earlier still it all began. The day before Parrish arrived it had snowed. Washington DC was cold—far into its winter. The last thing he had wanted was an unexpected assignment. Once again he scanned the white paper trying to read meaning into it that was not there. The sheet was frayed where it had been folded and unfolded so many times. Finally, he stuffed it back into his pocket and disappeared inside a massive post-modern building of chiseled, red-flecked, matched granite stone. He had been greeted by a city of white where for an instant the crush of poverty and the soot of a crumbling social infrastructure was suspended by nature's hand and faces radiated with a fragile hope. He hated the cold now that he'd become acclimated to the Nile delta and missed the early suppers sipping Pernot in outdoor cafes and haggling over prices with the unlicensed antiquities dealers who inhabited the fringe between the legitimate and the black market.

Outside his hotel traffic snarled. Voices were chilled with frosty breath. Tempers radiated. He remembered the rasping black man with no legs holding out a cup with his hand in a fingerless knit glove spouting off to no one, "...fine lookin' pussy, fine lookin' pussy I'd ever seen..." Parrish knew it was a religious question rife with the moral ambiguities that had finally gotten to him, but he had left all that behind. So he thought. Lingering memories make people cling to a home–he had none except adopted places. They require the bitter of the street to be harsher and the disenfranchised to rage at the world in which they have no voice more voraciously for their permanence. He forced his eyes ahead. The economy was strong however, the strongest in twenty-five years he was assured on the television news that morning as he watched ice crystals melt on the window of his room. He didn't care, didn't give a good goddamn. And what's more couldn't remember when he did, but he knew he had. Once.

"I don't give a shit." He sputtered into the mirror through the white lather on his face as he stood completely naked flexing all of his muscles until at last he relaxed and finished shaving.

Cold winds ended up here—made their homes in the vapor plains outside the tall buildings where humans cocooned themselves from the real. Hawks rested beneath the overhangs targeting unwary pigeons passing from one plaza to the next seeking a handout. Zeroing in on these fat trawlers was effortless. The sprawling city below seethed under its coat of white. Pedestrians in the street left their marks, each one a story untold, and automobile tracks drew stripes across them in turn racing to mysterious destinations until through the falling snow a vision of migration became etched in wildly animated lines leaving a tattooed impression of the human symphony that boiled all around. Soon it was lost in the flurries only to begin again a mirror of the reaching and the departures, triumphs and defeat. Life was fleeting and it made him anxious.

Parrish had been summoned from the embassy in Cairo to the offices in Washington. His ire was raised by this act that he considered a blow to his personal sovereignty. The Deputy Chief of Mission for the Central Middle East, known by the acronym DCM, was the perpetrator. No one can argue with an acronym. That was five days before his unexpected jaunt down the North African coast. He glanced one more time at the full wall-sized iridescent television screen in the hotel room where in frustration he had hoped to get some current news. Evening prayers were on. The anchorman could be seen bowing his head piously beseeching the Almighty to cleanse him of sin in silent exaltation. Hymnal music droned in the background. Key lights shone off his balding summit. Suddenly white noise and static ripped across the screen as Parrish climbed into his overcoat and threw a scarf around his neck clicking the remote off and tossing it down in disgust as he slammed the door.

* * * *

"al' Rashid is just like all the rest of us," the woman chortled while leafing through a file, "except, of course, he's filthy rich."

"Entertains women on that yacht…and drinks." A man interjected.

"Can't blame him. There's not even any liquor on Middle East bound flights now."

"That's right. Everyone was getting so stink-assed…couldn't disembark without help."

"…storing it up I guess." A chuckle rippled through the room. "Squirrels!" Secret knowing looks passed between them.

"Faith doesn't deny…in moderation." A heavy man responded through his teeth. The effort to keep a friendly smile betrayed an undercurrent of hostility behind his sated eyes. "Praise Jesus."

"I'll never forget his handshake!" The woman pursed up her mouth until light sparkled off her dark lipstick. "Never." The little shudder of sexual energy she kept to herself.

They moved incessantly. Restlessly. The four men and three women that waited stiffly in the conference room trussed up in business suits of grays, blues, and charcoals with tight collars and ill fitting jackets that pulled under the arms and back off their necks. It was warm—stuffy. There was a slight sweet scent of humus in the air. Recessed lights beamed low across a long table of briar wood veneer casting subtle shadows on faces. On the wall outside was inscribed, "U.S. State Department Office of the Under Secretary for Political Affairs".

She in her late forties with an unwavering perspective paced. The muscles of her legs rippled with each step—blonde hair was sculpted back off her face in waves. Stray wisps floated past clear eyes in the air. The outline of her was painted against a wall of windows through which the last glow of the sun could be seen searing tempestuous clouds above the skyline of the capital. She was the Crisis Manager.

After three years acting as Under Secretary without official congressional sanction, a ceremony that was indefinitely postponed, Karine Russo was imperturbable. When asked at her first confirmation hearing how she could perform in a position she could be relieved of at any time she replied, "Life perpetually straddles extinction." So deep were her sanctuaries that light could not penetrate. Often she would drift into sleep dreaming of ringed mountains rising far beyond the tree line whose immutable rock faces were scarred by tiny lichen beneath ice and snow and of ceaseless winds that blew dual symphonic refrains off the crags. Her breast would rise and fall with the rhythm of night. It was the only way. She could not sleep without these visions. Perhaps it was the drone of the expressways: the ten gridlocked lanes of glittering lights undulating off in all directions for as far as anyone could see, or the air tainted with soot and poison gasses. Stories were all she had because the forests had vanished. They lived in memory now to help men sleep.

"Touch me, will you?" The encroaching cold permeated the warm room. A night shiver danced along her spine. Without preamble she had spoken to the man who was standing next to her at the window watching the eventide. Her voice was intensely private. She did not raise her eyes from the blank stare that could not have penetrated the glass.

Collin Murdoch, a man to whom the foibles of others was an anathema, frowned. It was not the thought of touching that offended him. He was, after all, a global traveler and had spent a decade in the Middle East rubbing elbows with the conflux of humanity: his robustness was a matter of pride and he based his self concept on the image of physical ability, even though somewhere in his mid-fifties his center of gravity had shifted. The ultimate truth was that he had a great disdain for most people. They simply failed to meet his expectations. Nature, however, had compensated for this blemished character by omitting certain details in his make up; one of which was the ability to truly grasp the seriousness of a situation. Accordingly, he had a reputation as a consummate diplomat by reason of unflappable handlings of the most delicate matters—circumstances that bypassed any deeper understanding by him. Being the Chief of Mission for the Central Middle East—an Ambassador for Christ's sake—he did not think it correct to be addressed so intimately but he reached out and touched Karine Russo's shoulder as if an addict reaching for a fix yet consumed with apprehension at such a personal gesture towards his superior. She was a complex and private woman who so carefully guarded her own individuality that he had trouble recognizing the true significance of her request.

"Are you alright?" He offered as she grasped his hand and pressed it against her bosom.

"For a moment…" He felt her shudder—it made him embarrassed. He shifted his weight and glanced around the room. Collin faced her. She did not move but stood clasping his hand to her warm breast and he prayed none of the others were looking. She breathed heavily and a single tear materialized in the corner of her eye. "…for a moment I felt dizzy. Actually I…" turning abruptly to him without releasing his hand, "it's all the voices."

At that moment he remembered the scent of musty roses and the thought rushed by of taking back his hand, but the intimacy of her look paralyzed him. "And here I thought it was serious," he stammered.

"Of course I'm alright!" She looked at him with incredulity and dropped his hand.

A fury blustered in him but dissipated almost immediately its intensity quickly spent. "Nervous energy I guess." When he was younger he would not have stood for such affront, but now—middle age allowed him to forgive whole categories of insults. The spirit was there but not the energy anymore.

She imagined the bull-necked man with his Gallic profile and swarthy complexion standing across from her at one of the five-star restaurants he was always raving about robotically swirling over-priced Bordeaux under his nose, ("It releases the keytones!"), preparing to satisfy every sensation and longing he had ever known at one sitting. For him she could imagine no tomorrow; everything was right now, immediate. She, on the other hand, was never satisfied. The contempt she felt for self-centered men knew no bounds. It was the crux of the problem between them.

Karine swiveled on one heel to the window absorbing waves of scintillating lights sounding off the city night. In her mind boiled thoughts of the young Saudi PETEC minister who was the cause of her anxiety. OPEC had ceased as an effective producers' consortium shortly after the last war being riddled with internal squabbles over politics and religion. Its progeny was PETEC—*Petroleum Exporters Technology and Energy Cell*. Commodities traders coined it *The Cell*.

"He is not within our reach at the moment," she stated as if continuing an interrupted dialogue to Collin's surprise as he was expecting something deeply personal to be revealed, "...even managed to disappear during *Ramadan*...and for three days of the *Hajj*, but since his return to the yacht...after such pious abstinence can we be sure he'll stay put for a while?" She spoke to the Ambassador without the slightest regard for his opinion.

"He does like the company of women I understand," toasting the air with his glass knowing immediately of whom she spoke, "not one of the pillars of the faith."

"Rumors." Her eyes narrowed at the thought of the Arab's infidelity. *"For a cause men have laid down their tools and left their home..."* she murmured to herself some long ago verse that once had meant something. "He is a man with no moral essence and cannot be trusted."

"Perhaps." Collin Murdoch sipped from the rim of his glass. "But also a highly regarded strategist—PETEC members put their decisions largely in his hands. He has played a key role in reducing the bickering among his fellow oil ministers. A major cause of OPEC's demise if you recall."

"Did you know that the share of total financial wealth held by the bottom eighty percent of the families in this country has declined to below five percent? And the top one percent increased their share to nearly sixty percent? Compounding this, the globalization of capital has aggravated tax avoidance by the arbitrage of funds between countries. Mr. al'Rashid and colleagues are obsessed with maximizing the return on capital without regard to national identity, political, social or religious consequences. He's a vulture: no restraint, no sense of propriety between profit and nature. A danger—Muhammad Abd al' Rashid," she rolled the name on her tongue, "a threat to us and a risk to regional economics." She faced the Ambassador with an exasperated look and hung there suspended as if a bird in mid air with no legs to land on. "We must do something," then added with no attempt to hide her disdain, *"you* must do something."

"He should be here any moment." The Chief of Mission replied somewhat belligerently despite himself and appeared to be on the verge of laughter, but as anyone knows who has suffered grief or any of the darker emotions it was only the turbulence being held back. The sense of failure that had dogged him all his professional life welled inside. Vodka slid soothingly down his throat and helped numb the futile weakness. It had begun slowly, but then as he felt the nihilistic grip of defeat grasp him he discovered that alcohol helped him hover above it—supported his self-respect. Never mind that it left him dull witted, slow to decide, and with a headache most of the time...except when he was drinking of course. He would handle his responsibilities here in Washington and as soon as possible return to the villa in the Azores where some minor officials of the Arab League were in conference. In the company of equals he could be understood. "I spoke to Erskine last night at his hotel." *You bitch*, he thought as his eyes blazed hatred toward the woman who stood before him unmoved.

Parrish entered the building shivering. Angry. Detached. The blast of warm air that greeted him did nothing to take away the chill. Even in the cramped elevator that soared so rapidly it made his ears pop—where the breath of people lingered—the heat did not dispel the cold winter that lie outside. He had lost his resistance to low temperatures and shuddered. The doors to the conference room burst open.

"I'm not late?" Parrish yanked up the sleeve of his coat and glared at his watch. "I'm not late."

The meeting in Washington seemed lifetimes ago viewed through the blur of kaleidoscopic images that had led him to this moment. The hot wind. Kneeling on the sand. The old bus back in a ditch somewhere its tires shot out. The crumpled landscape of a young girl lying in his arms bleeding crimson. In his memory was the constant of the seeking, the pursuit of the indefinable—neither love nor conversation, riches nor excitement—nothing in the end had more to give than simply a long embrace. Until now. Everything pivoted on this moment and time held it all in the future. Held its breath. Waiting. Until now. Moments that overlapped like scales cascading down a Mexican blue lizard's spine each one filled with perceptions of the chase; like sequins sewn one by one onto a beautiful woman's evening gown, undulating when she walked, clouding the absolute continuity of events as they may have occurred; like swells out across the white water sea blowing fury with a gale each folding one into the other eternally—instant upon instant, multitudes of instants all compounded to the infinite degree and then still more would be needed to make up all the time he had lived. When he was centered he remembered the longing, reaching never touching, streets without names, alleys, great brawling cities rising up out of nowhere as huge dusty behemoths shaking the earth beneath them with the power of men. The men who built cities. Other men whose quest had been somehow fulfilled. Yet he was left with just the burning. It gave him only enough impulse to move forward in life when reason failed.

"Can't you stop that damn wailing!?" He spat into the wind rocking the unconscious girl—frantically searching—knowing that inexplicably the others crowded around him in the desert night were looking to him. "I'm not the one." He beseeched them silently.

"The girl's mother..."

"What?!"

"It's the girls mother..." the man with near ebony skin jerked his thumb in the general direction of the sounds, "the one who's crying..." He shook his head compulsively unable to bear the tragedy. "God is merciful. God is good." Moonlight shown off his oily forehead and his teeth glinted bright ivory next to the gaping hole where one was missing.

The girl's mother began the high trilling with her tongue and the keening rose in the air and was carried off by the sirocco. From the distance, came an answer—a kindred survivor of the attack was also stranded alone—and then another, like wolves. Their grief and terror found voice intertwining above them sailing into the ether. Parrish looked down at the anguished girl. She could not have been more than ten and her skin was flawless in the starlight free from the wrinkles that years of injustice gave and she lie still, breathing laboriously with a slight sweet scowl on her face. A bullet had found her abdomen where now it was burning poison and though he pressed his hand firmly over the wound the flow of blood would not be stanched. It was certain she would die, and yet expectancy bristled in the air with the desperate pleas to turn back time. There it was. He could not stanch the flow of moments. Surely they knew this, he thought in panic, yet they looked to him.

"Not me." He whispered violently.

Until that instant he had not realized the meaning of true fear. Now it settled upon him as if fog upon a sodden bay. Coldness hurried in, though the night wind was still aflame, and he was mysteriously shivering with a torrent of energy. His life appeared devoid of purpose as it was reflected from the tender embrace and he recoiled from it sensing an abyss too near—one in his arms and one in his mind. Out across sage into the obscure distances where his eyes burned with the injustice of mortality, with the injustice of his own failures, where the only light was that of stars, were the fevered young men. That was when it occurred to him they might be watching, they might be—suddenly he scoured the shadows for any flicker of movement and every sound was amplified into a thousand different nuances each one setting him off causing his eyes to search frantically. He was seized by anxiousness and an overwhelming need to survive, which was something he had not felt in a very long time.

Parrish was looking at the girl sprawled in his arms. "Do you hear anything?"

The man with the missing tooth whose head was cocked back scanning the night replied instantly as if they were of one mind. "Nothing."

"Will they return?"

"*In-sha Allah,*" the man said, "If God wills."

II

A FAR OFF STORM

IN THE DESERT PARRISH HALF REMEMBERED THE HUSH THAT HAD FALLEN over the meeting as the Crisis Manager began to speak. He had felt oddly out of place—a misfit. His hands had rested palms down on the table reminding him how earlier he had done exactly the same thing on the marble bar at Safi—both times it helped center him. Outside the window snow had been drifting by the glass in huge white flakes as they caught the light from the room and then vanished into the dark. He could not shake the cold. They had gone for three interminable hours and it was obvious there would be no consensus soon. *That's the trouble with democracy*, he thought, *everyone's equal.*

"Clear enough." Karine Russo declared. "Clear enough. Per-barrel too low… glut on the market, as we have all observed, and…correct me, but there's no evidence of production slow downs? No evidence at all is there?"

"No." Viktor retaliated. He had been raw with attentive energy nodding his head robotically to every word spoken. "Outside of labor disputes in Venezuela causing a distribution bottleneck." The inflexible scowl permanently scarring his angelic face hid the smugness he felt in

15

the glow of his own brilliance. "Which analysts believe have nothing to do with the cartel management; and a shipping strike in the Bafra fields on the Black Sea; pipeline breakdowns between platforms off Acaba and Djibouti—pump problems we suspect from surplus unloaded on them— then there was that refinery fire in Qatar...but no, nothing to indicate there will be any slowdowns from PETEC. Not even a whimper despite the short-term adverse economic effects to member countries."

The Operations Center, known in the Department as" The Watch", was an information service open around the clock to brief State Department officials on overseas news and events and to coordinate the Department's response to emergency situations. It also provided selected communications support. Its mandate had been elevated however, and roiling beneath its facade nothing worth knowing was held back from its inner circle. Victor Jaraslav, Chief of the Watch, operated directly under the Secretary of State and in an effort to ingratiate himself was fond of saying, "The secret is...there is no secret." It was because he was responsible to no one else and privy to such in depth information, which inspired wild animal reactions in those who had something to hide and introspection in those who wondered if they should, that he was a man with many enemies.

"Feedback!" Karine drew her eyes tight and ground her back teeth. "I've got your reports. I've read them and now after listening to you explain...without the insight I expected...I am compelled to ask what you really think. I'm just not getting the picture here!" She sighed with infinite tiredness. "What the hell's going on?"

"All the indicators are present..." He conveyed the faint impression of a half-breed, Javanese hairless cat. Something about the eyes...the man from the Bureau of Economic and Business Affairs. He swiped moisture from his face with a large handkerchief, stuffed it back into his breast pocket and spoke to Karine with a belligerent self-importance that rendered other comments superfluous. "…to think we've spent a century pouring capital into the region…they're going to turn off the flow. There is no doubt. And when they do, they're going to dump in the money markets and devaluate the Dollar, the Euro, the Yen, the Renminbi, the Deutsche Mark…and god knows what other currencies." Darkness ringed his eyes. The white oxford cloth shirt he wore was enveloped with wrinkles, but his blue, striped, synthetic, tie was stiff as plastic. A slight odor of perspiration lingered around him.

"We'll just watch and see if someone cheats." Viktor interjected, "It's clearly not a popular strategy, though the temptation is much greater when the price per barrel is $245 or more rather than under $160…having said that however," shaking his leg under the table with great impatience at having to explain things that he felt people should already know, "usually when the price is high and production is severely curtailed only the Saudis have a surplus, but now all the members have a surplus. Even London Brent from the North Sea"

"Green Technology was supposed to handle all this."

"Green technology has nearly doubled the use of foreign petroleum as we are all aware." Viktor went on to recite obscure statistics in a staccato disdain. "Once the West Texas Intermediate and Arab Light reserves ran dry anything that hit the market sold at exorbitant prices: Saharan Blend, Minas, Dubai, Tijuana Light and even Isthmus…I've got reports, spreadsheets…accountings…"

"That's it…the big money," the man from the Bureau of Economic and Business Affairs continued struggling to illuminate his inner thoughts. "They're gonna screw us!"

"Granted," Collin replied sardonically, "it's been their weapon." He too exhibited little patience with those he considered not politically savvy enough to grasp the relative significance of obvious things and felt that many people, in fact many at that very table, were just too slow witted for their own good and, what really infuriated him, they embraced each other in their dullness. "But it's not money, you can see that of course? No!" He proclaimed, "It's not money at all."

"You can't expect much more from people who have not accepted the Savior." The military attaché pronounced from the far right corner of the table. His epaulets were trimmed with a thin line of gold that shimmered on his dark uniform like iridescent chameleons. His blue lips were drawn tight. His white officers cap sat on the table nearby at an exact ninety-degree angle to its edge. Only he had a firm grasp on the complex regional strategy, only he had full military intelligence briefings unlike the watered down renditions at State. Leaning forward to speak in confidence, "It's not coincidental that PETEC members are all agreed; obviously they've devised this market saturation as a strategic move." He was conscious not to reveal too much to the table of civilians keeping his face completely devoid of any emotion. "What I mean is, prices can't get much lower…some of our own petro-companies are starting to go. Stock is plummeting…below junk…"

"Now *what if*…and I'm not saying take this at face value, but *what if*, as a hypothesis…" another man raised his finger in the air and held it relishing the moment. "What if it's not all the PETEC members? Now just think about that. They don't all have the same agenda?" He paused and scanned the table. "Other than being profitable certainly, but there again, I don't think so. I have to agree, it's not the money. I believe," he nodded, "personally, it's the brotherhood manipulating the price index or something of that nature. A damn *jihad* or something!"

"Perhaps." Karine interjected. "But we'll need to have a more fundamental basis than your opinion to substantiate that suspicion if we are to act rationally. Facts people! Intelligence! I feel, as Viktor pointed out, that since all member countries are adhering to these quotas that most will have stockpiled reserves. It will be interesting to see how they all toe the line now since each could cheat if they got greedier than usual. It's happened more often than not. It only takes one to raise the price. Meantime we'll wait. Gather information. Action may be warranted, but we must know precisely!"

Silence descended. Each present secretly felt they alone already knew and was only waiting for his turn in the sun.

*　*　*　*

He recalled their last conversation, one that had occurred on the occasion of an earlier trip to Washington, in the warmth of a spring when cherry trees were aflame with blooms against a seamless blue sky. It was during one of those innocuous social functions designed to integrate the Washington community into State Department agendas and ultimately secure annual budgets. The confinement and compulsory social graces made him long for the melodious corridors of Cairo's slums where the hopeless humanity made music with their voices.

She had stood close to him, too close as was her habit. Chamber music wafted above their heads being pounded out by four bony women borrowed for the night from the Boston Conservatory to be flown back in the morning all expenses paid. They were playing modern works— beyond Bartok—rhythmic, discordant, blind. Parrish sweated beneath his close white collar. He watched beads of perspiration form between Karine Russo's breasts above the top of her tight navy silk suit and it gave him disturbingly erotic thoughts. Parrish attributed it to the wine, even though there was something vaguely sexual about her, as if a lingering emotion from a former lifetime. He frowned at his glass. The pungent scent of her met his nostrils. Alcohol was on her breath. Her voice husky.

"You're too sensitive," she said bluntly, "You lack people skills." Lifting the crystal glass to her lips, "I think you're intelligent, very bright as a matter of fact…we need people like you. But certain staff need nurturing, support…they're looking to you for leadership."

"That's not the way it is."

"Give them the benefit of your experience."

"Nobody wants my experience," he drank and added quietly, "not even me."

"Look, you're frustrated. I know that. Use me. Let me be a buffer. You've got complete authority over your section."

"I am my section."

"See what I mean? You're tense. Everyone knows you're unhappy. How do you expect promotion if you're not with the program? You're bright, we need people like you. I don't know why everybody thinks you're the problem; personally I've always enjoyed working with you, I feel we're all going the same way… just a lack of communication, that's all."

"Who is 'everybody'?"

Karine smiled in the overbearing way she had of wrinkling up her brow quickly making it seem she was more concerned than she was. "You don't really want to know do you? It's nothing."

"Christ. As I suspected."

"Come on Erskine…" her warm hand clasped his arm, "you need a drink…" she leaned even closer to him and spoke confidentially, "and don't blaspheme. What if a Homeland Religious Officer heard you?"

Everyone called him Parrish except those who called him Erskine in a divine effort to patronize. He had been Assistant Foreign Service Officer for Political Affairs Central Middle Eastern Mission at Cairo for nearly his entire career. His upward mobility had died, buried in a performance evaluation report somewhere along the line and he had just begun to realize the futility of his position now that he was past forty. The mission had been established in Cairo as an administrative center for the region after the series of wars when the Western coalition had redrawn the map— and then green technology had generated an addictive dependence on Middle East oil reserves. The same dependence it was supposed to have been a resolution to. Now the West and the Middle East were inexorably linked by greed and hatred of each other's way of life, but neither economy was able to exist without the other.

A career in the diplomatic service had never been in the master plan. It was an accident. Distinct from the clear-eyed yearlings that came trooping into the department with each graduating class from the Ivy League he had not been recruited from a university, but rather applied himself out of an irrational surge of responsibility. Most of his associates had studied law or international relations. His degree in theology had been driven by something more intrinsic to his nature. Unfortunately, he soon discovered money and religion are in the end incompatible. Business did not suit him either for as much as he desired wealth he was by reason of his basic purpose and restless nature a driven intense man, which made him unpopular and misunderstood by the kind of person who felt secure in a static office where the slightest shift of routine was debated interminably in a series of supportive group meetings. It was during a stint working in the public relations department of an oil drilling company based in Texas that a career in the foreign service had first occurred to him and after several years in the Middle East—where he had learned to speak conversationally in Arabic, Farsi and Swahili—he discovered the one thing he was truly good at. Dealing with difficult people face to face. It was this native ability coupled with the barely passing marks on the public service exams that secured him an entry position with the State Department, and of course those crucial contacts in the oil industry. But he had neither the school ties nor the Kissingerian indoctrination for success, though he could not have understood that at the time.

Later he would remember; it was later, after the men and women had filed out of the conference room with dour important looks upon their faces, when he was collecting his scribbled notes, scraping them up off the table and stuffing them into his worn leather brief. Already the chill of the street was intruding with tiny fingers causing him to turn up the collar of his mackintosh until it touched his ears. His long, dark hair tumbled over brooding eyes. The fury of uselessness nearly overtook him with the feeling that he had been ordered all the way to the meeting for nothing. He looked down the table at Karine Russo talking with Collin Murdoch as he was about to leave and heard her emotional reference to Muhammad Abd al' Rashid. It wasn't as if they didn't recognize him, it was the fact they refused to acknowledge him the way it was with an old soldier in a time of peace. Parrish slipped out the door without anyone noticing. On the night flight back to Cairo the anger and waste at his being summoned to the meeting without reason festered under the duress of five whiskeys from a flask he smuggled on board, five over the airline's limit, as he worked on getting so stink-assed that someone would have to help him off the plane.

Three days after he'd returned, the dispatch came. It was waiting on his desk that morning when he arrived. The taste of the thick Turkish coffee that he bought first thing at a street vendor's stall—where pastries and other sweet things were sold, where old men sallied their memories and imagined glories that would never happen in the clouds of smoke from their water pipes—lingered on his tongue. He recalled exactly how he felt the moment he tore open the envelope and unfolded the white paper to read the words over the creases. It was an unreasonable sense of flight and his hand had trembled slightly as if a great shift in time and space were occurring far across the universe.

The man who was supposed to take on the mission could not now do it, no reason given. He was indisposed, vanished, replaced, gone. Mysteriously disabled. Perhaps he had received a better offer. Maybe he'd been assassinated, or was just being irascible and sat in some contemptible flop house with a fleshy prostitute drinking beer and watching sports on the television in his underwear. It could have been that his wife had begged him to stay home from fear of middle age, or his child had taken ill, or the plumbing had backed up, or the bank called to inform him he was overdrawn once too often and they were going to have him arrested. There was no reason given.

In his stead, Parrish was ordered to keep the rendezvous on a yacht off the Moroccan coastal city of Safi and meet with Muhammad Abd al' Rashid, the young Saudi oil minister. The cryptic note instructed him to discover the full meaning of al' Rashid's intentions in maintaining high crude oil production and ascertain if any U.S. interests were being intentionally compromised. It was one of those communiqués that otherwise rational people issue only when their bonding with a group was complete, as if the work experience dulled their wits and they assumed others were either unsound or inexplicably naive. Parrish knew everyone in Washington, with few exceptions, was certain the situation existed as a part of a calculated economic strategy. He searched for hidden meanings unable to grasp the oblique instructions at face value. The note was unsigned except for the DCMs initials—Karine's hieroglyphic "KR" that looked like one chicken-scratched letter enclosed in a circle. Businesses were failing, he knew that, the unprecedented oil supply was driving consumer prices down to nearly nothing and engendered a demand that could never be met under normal circumstances and an economic panic would almost certainly ensue once production was cut back. The scenario, he sighed with disdain, was too familiar; he had heard it his entire stint in the Middle East starting with the oil company. The Islamic manifesto! Finally, Washington bureaucrats must have shuddered ecstatically, the time had arrived and they were the ones to reveal it to the world. Another justified war in its embryonic form.

"I'm not for this," he said aloud to himself in his office. The last thing he wanted was another mission.

The evening flight soared out over the thermals rising up from the greatest expanse of desert on earth: a landscape so gigantic, so unearthly its single rival was the vast plains of the Mediterranean sea—the only barrier immense enough to stop the sand's terrible race to the North else it would have consumed Europe long ago just as the Phoenicians dreamed of doing as they plied its coast; where whole cities were built, lived their life and then were devoured by sands that roiled like churning oceans depending only on winds and tides. Men have never had much effect here. The falling sun tore the sky with crimson fingers.

That night he could not sleep. Waves of clouds lofted above in long thin rows breaking against the shore of a luminous twilight until finally they dissipated. He sat naked in his caftan on the cramped balcony of the mud brick hotel smoking small aromatic cigars and watching the celestial thunder swirl above him as he imagined the billions of civilizations that lie in the warp of the ether each pregnant with hopes unrealized. Were they of the blood like him, people with names and histories? Was life as much of a struggle for them? The universe, he thought, was full of tears.

At first light he walked down to the street and found a sidewalk bar that catered to Europeans where he ate a croissant accompanied by two whiskeys. His hands lie flat before him on the marble counter and he absorbed the slight coolness seeking a refuge from the heat, which lingered from the day before and was being rapidly fed by the all consuming sun flaming into the morning sky. The tile rooftops began to shimmer. He had not looked forward to this trip.

Parrish had made the swarthy man get in the rental car and test the air conditioning. He sat in the drivers seat and begrudgingly raced the engine winnowing the last squealing bit of exhaust from it with a solemn distingué face, dark lugubrious eyebrows and thin lips drawn tight in resignation at the humiliation of having to perform a menial service. "See…?" He insisted without the courtesy of looking holding his hand up to the vent, "See…? Air! Air! What more air could you want. See? Air!" Parrish feebly held his hand out and felt the coursing across his moist skin and out of sheer mental hypocrisy let the subject drop. He did not want to argue. He didn't care. Winding out of the city towards the chuckholed highway that snaked down the coast to Safi he drove with his hand next to the vent waiting for the air to cool off. It never did, and finally he gave up feeling cheated. Betrayed. The day was brittle in its intensity. The heat shattered the sweltering sky. He cursed the Arab man for lying. The inferno parched his throat and he scowled as the automobile bore down on the asphalt only then realizing he had forgotten to bring bottled water.

On the deck of the yacht, he was greeted by a crushing handshake. The Arab was vibrantly alive. Scintillating. He exuded a flush of energy that splashed into the panorama of light streaming across the restless tattered sea behind him and made his face appear holy. From his eyes came the unmistakable Bedouin glare.

"I am Muhammad Abd al' Rashid." He spoke in a clear smooth voice.

After six hours on the road there was no smile. Perhaps he wouldn't have smiled anyway as he'd passed the point of trying to hide his bitterness some time ago. "Erskine Parrish MacKenzie," he replied formally pausing a moment at finally meeting the man and returning the strong handclasp. "Parrish," he relented, "call me Parrish…" he squinted up his eyes suddenly in exhaustion, " I must ask you for some water, I forgot to bring it…"

"Of course…" The man snapped in Arabic to one of his servants as they moved into the shade of the cabin. "al' Rashid," he glanced back over his shoulder, "that's what my friends call me." Out of the corner of his eye Parrish glimpsed the unmistakable flash of smooth, white skin. A rustle of fabric. A rush and it vanished. The scent of henna lingered in the room along with an indescribable sweetness.

He could not ignore a perception of the man's dark nature, which al' Rashid seemed completely unashamed of exuding, an aura of danger like smoke from flames. He did not smile, but was inordinately gracious, a fact which Parrish had always watched for as ingenuous. But to compare him with the ordinary mongrelized civil servant, of which the Middle East was luxuriant, would have been a criminal act; for he was lucid, refined to an excruciating degree and to Parrish's amazement possessed of a crisp, biting intelligence that at once took his mind off the long unpleasant trip if for no other reason than to defend his viewpoint. It all seemed so incongruous with the man's physical presence: eyes set deep into a darkened mask clarifying their brightness; jaw squared and skin like sandalwood; the curve of his lips perfectly symmetrical behind the black Van Dyke. People with perfect biological gifts were supposed to be dull, or carnal, or sophomoric and self absorbed, or insecure and neurotic; but al' Rashid was none of these things and Parrish was pressed to use reservoirs of intellectual capabilities he had thought abandoned.

"There are certain things I am obliged to do by my faith."

Parrish was hot. The wind on the water had ceased and the yacht was perfectly still in the becalmed seas up against the jetty where children scurried in the dust. The air was so dry that there was no smell of fish but instead one of wild aloe. Out the port side he could remember seeing the laboring dhows with their triangular sails hanging in limp disarray on the yards as the tillermen frenetically tried to bring them into the harbor against the tide. He felt their frustration.

"Of course. I understand that. As you know, the Christian Coalition is the strongest political party in the United States. We are a religious nation."

al' Rashid's eyes glimmered, "You are a Christian then?"

A beat. Coldness permeated his stomach. "Like anything one is raised into," he replied against his best judgment looking at his shoes. Unexpectedly, he was no longer cautious but antagonistic. "Truth is, I don't think much about it."

Eyes bore into him. "But you understand faith?"

"That's something else, isn't it?"

"I cannot separate them," the Arab replied with a shrug.

Parrish had had this conversation before but smiled politely. Al' Rashid was a Sufi and so he prepared himself against the evangelizing of Islam with all its political rhetoric—to which he had inured himself as a result of experiences from his tenure in Cairo—and the onslaught of the true way which was nearly as certain as death. But it never came, and to his surprise he found himself a bit disappointed. Instead the man fell silent as three dark Berber servants entered the aft cabin with austere formality covered head to foot in deep indigo robes each holding a golden tray. On the first was a single tall glass of sparkling water so cold that its sides glistened with melting frost. Curiously three kumquats lie undisturbed beneath the ice. On the second tray were two exquisite cups and saucers of bone china holding the thick black mixture of coffee laced with butter he had developed a taste for. On the third tray were etched crystal glasses and a squat bottle of very old cognac beside which lay two thin hand rolled cigars that looked like bent twigs inside a pearlescent abalone shell. The alcohol and tobacco confirmed the rumors Parrish had heard; he still perceived the scent of henna lingering and was watchful for signs of al' Rashid's illicit mistress.

The difference between the two of them was immediately apparent. Parrish wondered what it must be like to have no restraint upon one's life; he, for instance, was always up against it—cornered—especially now that his future was as ambiguous as the blue cigar smoke that rose while they finished their cognac accompanied by stilted conversation.

"Water." al' Rashid intoned after they had talked at length, "Water is the millennial element." He was unconcerned about the details of life and showing neglect as only the very rich can do. "The future is water…and it's vanishing." Animated strokes of his long brown fingers detailed the technical fundamentals of the latest desalinization technology—which in case Parrish had forgotten was pioneered by the Saudis, keepers of the two holy shrines—which left him dizzy with misunderstandings of the terminology. "I feel exhilarated to think of it," he rejoiced, "the only true power is water. Consider, because of seas and rivers all great civilizations evolved! Now they are vanishing; dissipating into nothing, into the air as cloud vapor. There are people even today, many people, who have no fresh water…and isn't that the essence, the primal brine out of which creatures emerged? The ribbon of breath? How can so many organisms exist that the environment cannot support them? It seems the whole balance of life on this planet has lost its moral basis…and, don't you suppose," his eyes were bright with nervous energy, "that all our economies would suffer if that were not the case and nature had provided for all these shortcomings? Surely you agree with that?" al' Rashid urged him to invest, sink any excess funds he could spare into the Saudi water projects, spoke to him as if he were an equal, as if he sailed on yachts and bought expensive automobiles for his friends and kept an illegal mistress. "…a twenty-thirty percent yield. Easily." The man wore a starched white shirt beneath his robes and even in the sweltering heat appeared absolutely composed. "Water," he said. "is power." Then repeated it once more in spontaneous self-affirmation.

Parrish wrung his hands nervously. They were damp with perspiration. He felt patronized. "You knew I was coming?"

"Of course."

"My government is concerned." He spoke perfunctorily hating himself for the way the dry words dribbled from him, without the glamour of al' Rashid's magnificent water projects, without the sheen of immense nearly inconceivable wealth easing his troubles.

Al' Rashid nodded. "...enough to send you... I see that." He sipped from the small crystal glass.

Parrish tapped a finger on his knee and tried to focus through the underlying contempt that had festered unabated over the past few years. "al' Rashid," he struggled, "I'd like to be completely honest with you...".

"Certainly."

"There is uneasiness over the price of crude." He began in the droll cadence of international diplomacy, "You can understand...with the per barrel price still plummeting...we're surprised, frankly al' Rashid, anxious there haven't been production cut-backs."

"Yes."

Silence. He waited, but there was no further comment. "Perhaps," his voice cracked hoarsely, ill at ease in the presence of a man he knew would not be forthright, "we are witnessing some long term strategic initiative?"

The same obsidian eyes leered at him concealing machinery that whirred in perpetual motion. "In any organization complete accord is impossible to attain," came the reply. Indifferent, inhuman, relentless. Al' Rashid had an agenda that existed between himself and his God only. Parrish was an interloper.

"Regions are setting their own price policies? You mean it's competitive pricing?"

"Business." The Arab tilted his head slightly to the right smiling pleasantly and raised his hands in a universal gesture of frustration. "We are not autocrats...just business."

Parrish observed everything intently trying to wear him down, get to the elemental man and reveal the motivation of his actions, his words, his behavior. To the nub. Truth, however simple, is elusive. "The situation is delicate," he sipped affectedly at his cognac. "They say you're the perfect business man you know...the markets are nervous"

Al' Rashid was amused and his face melted into an uncharacteristic softness. "Really?" He lowered his eyes enjoying some private compensation, but to Parrish he was simply smug. "I've never thought of myself as a business man, or perfect. Only Allah is perfect. While I, though a man of the straight path, can only emulate His word. Perhaps a nationalist...but a businessman...no. Not in the Western sense."

There was a far off storm: Where it was night: Where the moon slipped off into extreme distances falling deftly to the sea below sliding silently beneath the waves leaving its ivory image impressed on the senses for untold years—seared into the self as beauty's imprint. Where haze and restlessness mingled with waters constantly in motion—migrating—coming from nowhere, going somewhere else neither destination nor origin known. Eternal. Only to move on. Here is where purpose lies, purpose and redemption. Motive and alibi. Suddenly Parrish was graced with the knowledge of the air and breathed deeply, gasped to confirm his mortal existence as he slipped from the body's clutches and viewed things more clearly with his spirit eyes. He walked the length of the aft cabin and gazed across the North African blue.

"Are you alright?" al' Rashid asked.

"Yes. Fine." Was the reply as he struggled to become grounded and fought against complete disillusionment overtaking him right there and then in that exact space in time, trembling slightly with back turned to al' Rashid who sat sagaciously in his chair enjoying the sin of alcohol and the small crooked cigar and perhaps in the afterglow of a tryst with his forbidden mistress of the smooth white flesh. Parrish, who could only suspect, no longer had the compulsion to chase the truth as the obvious masquerade had collapsed. While another might view it as a challenge, he would rather go around or flee into the expanse that raced away from him to the far thin horizon line. He did not know at that moment it was a choice each man is faced with at some point in his existence, which runs silently parallel to turbulent lives and can scarcely be perceived above the din that surviving makes. It is shrugged off—merely a longing or a wanting. One moves on. Don't look back. The past is a bucket of ashes. But what of the casualties, those of little faith?

Parrish turned to face al' Rashid. In his eyes was the raw, unembraceable turmoil that is the sign of men on the edge, the rage that came from confronting the abyss where spirits without voices tumble endlessly. The Arab recognized this at once for even though he had not experienced it himself he was a deeply religious man despite slight peccadilloes of sex and drink—it stunned him momentarily as if he was a bird who had flown into a window thinking it was free air. The truth burned between them for that one brief instant.

"What is the forecast?" Parrish asked adding to the stillness.

"There is a storm far off." Al' Rashid replied.

Now it churned up around him and he remembered what the Arab had said. The grasses bristled beside him. The hot wind roared in his ears nearly drowning out the wailing keening sounds of the girl's mother gone wild with grief. The toothless man prostrating himself to Allah in supplications for pity the real being too much for him to shoulder. Everyone knew a child's death is a tragedy beyond those things with which to compare it, beyond the things of magnitude people use to make suffering more bearable.

Without hope he sat hard on the sand cradling the dying girl in his arms. He felt her pain and it mingled indiscriminately with his own. He felt the weak pulsing of her heart each moment expecting it would cease and yet completely unable to grasp the finality of the instant. His own heart boomed. Her body burned in fever. Her eyelids fluttered in unknown dreams. He felt useless. Waif like. Without place in the world. Without sense or purpose or anything of worth to hold onto. It had been a long time since he had possessed any sense of value and the violence of the night had shaken whatever delicate web he had been clinging to until now all that remained was the hollow wind off the desert blowing through him as if he was not there. He would have given his existence if the bullet had found him instead of the girl. It would have been a favor. Yet he could not cry for her and instead of apathy anger churned in him, boiled and seethed and frothed and spat until he could hardly contain its vehemence.

And so it was at that moment the significance of life struck Parrish with its full impact. And he shattered in great resounding crescendos. Now he had arrived at the foul end of the earth. It was clear to him after all his searching that hell had finally opened up and consumed every effort he had ever made until at last his final failure lay sprawled before him as a ten year old girl with the face of an angel soaked in blood. His heart thundered, and then it was silent, altogether silent; not even the rush of wind could interrupt the profound silence of that moment. His demise was complete and he could only wait for death. He had reached the point in the abyss when he looked, no one looked back.

Yet the girl still breathed. He stared resolutely into her face. Through the tips of his fingers against her fevered flesh Parrish could just perceive the pale flutter of her heartbeat. It was precisely then the thought came to him—burst upon him without consent. It was beyond words and, as he perceived it then, more than human: He suddenly realized that the only value he had or will ever have was in his ability to help others. His worth lay completely in the eyes of others. His life depended on their life. Rivers and tributaries of life. Cascades of life. Ringing storms of life. He trembled at the power. The incredible lightness.

He would come to know that it was fully human and not as he suspected, but that was later. For now he breathed deep as before, but saw everything quite differently.

Parrish looked at the girl. For the first time since the incident he was able to face her anguish without feeling the terrible grief or shaking uncontrollably with rage, which had nearly debilitated him. As if by witchcraft now he could clearly see the child as a spirit apart from the body; and the injured vessel that lie sprawled across his lap appeared, to his surprise, so insignificant, so utterly unessential that for an instant he could hardly imagine people needed them to live, to speak, to be. And then as if it had always been his nature he laid his hands upon the girl. The structure of her body was too familiar: so simple, so primitive. Parrish closed his eyes and traced its routes and channels by permeating the flesh; feeling its bone and sinew, nerve and tissue. In an instant, he contacted where the bullet had torn its way through the child's abdomen and now lay inches from her spinal cord. Slowly a hand was raised and he discarded the spent lead hollow point—mangled and flattened out from its sudden impact—into the sand and bush nearby. Again he laid his hands upon the girl. The flesh and vessels and cartilage and membranes knit together instantly as if by a sorcerer's spell and full life was restored once more. The girl shuddered. She heaved a breath; gasped and convulsed as with a newborn finally delivered from the purgatory womb into this world of force and life, beauty and danger. And then she cried. Cried in storms as if her heart was breaking. She let the grief run from her a torrential river. Parrish knew her trauma, perceived the mental images clinging to her soul as black clouds of pain, unconsciousness, loss, and sorrow. He saw the impressions of other traumas, of earlier lifetimes. Of infinite lives. Of eons. These he eased away from her with a sweeping gesture and the girl immediately was quiet and at peace. It was as it had been.

He sweated profusely, his eyes haggard and ringed with red. His breath was shallow and rasping in the dry air. His heart beat wildly. Only then he noticed that the others had crept close. Startled, he jerked his head up from the girl and realized the women had stopped their wailing. Everyone was quiet. Except the wind made its sound again and came in gusts to whisper in his ears. The hot night once more embraced him and wicked perspiration from his forehead and caressed his cheeks. He raced inside. The girl's astonished mother struggled over to them in disbelief and pressed her palm against her daughter's face. She pulled back the torn, bloody garment to reveal the smooth, flawless belly. Finally, the woman collapsed and held her daughter tearfully in her arms overcome, rocking back and forth where she knelt looking with fear and wonder at Parrish. "*Mahdi!*" She gasped sobbing, "*Mahdi.*" He could not understand her. Then the dark skinned man took up the refrain. "*Mahdi!*" He repeated quietly, and then with more conviction as if all doubt had been a violation of the faith. "*Mahdi!* The will of Allah."

III Moon and Tide

In time, the opus of the streets brought him around. Humanity revealed itself as a cyclone of dust and smells and confusion and tumbled into the future bearing great bundles of grief. It gave him solace. He was beginning to find meaning in the struggle—hidden truths. The richness of the fabric eased staccato memories: the blinding lights of helicopters in the desert, the cries, wind whispers, questions he could not answer that left him confused, smells of burning kerosene. Once more he could sleep, though fitfully, but it was the cradle of voices that gave him refuge, the throb of humans pulsing through the city as one living mass driven by many vectors pulling itself apart but drawn together by the one shared impulse: To survive. They gave him continuity and expectations for the future.

He had glared down at them from the window of his flat leaning with arms against the sill and the thin cigar clenched in his teeth with blue smoke curling in the heat before the day.

"They say you healed her…" the man in a crisp uniform had quipped sardonically.

"Not me," came the reply, "they are mistaken…" Parrish hypothesized the blood to be someone else's, perhaps the bus driver who had the top of his head blown off by the first salvo "...she was never hurt." He had abandoned hope some time back, he dared not reach again—he dared not—and so could not bring even himself to believe. "I'm not the one you're looking for."

The line that divided the past from the future was like wire pulled taut. Parrish liked to roam that path, it was his domain. Each time he left Cairo the substance to his life was wrenched from him leaving a hollow he could not fill until he returned. Like departing lovers, he mused: skirts tossed in late summer breezes. Hair flying. Faceless figures. Ephemeral images. Lost moments. Familiarity more than anything was to blame, for he was certain that his existence once had meaning outside the context of the sweltering Al-Qāhirah even though now it was only the city that infused him with promise and gave him reason where his own had failed.

"So you've got something...ehhh?" He pushed the cup of sweet dark coffee across the table toward the enigmatic Egyptian who sat opposite him in the outdoor cafe. The unwavering eyes of Ali Fakeih Aissa fell on Parrish. The man struggled to suppress an ungainly grin perhaps because of unhealthy teeth or just the subtle understanding that it was bad business. The resulting grimace made his weathered features screw up like an old shoe and gave Erskine Parrish MacKenzie comfort. "What is it, what is it you've got that was so damned important?"

Flames rose up inside as they often had threatening to consume the small dark man. That morning, just past the dusty buildings where men in flowing robes paid the equivalent of fifty cents to share a one room flat without water or electricity, Ali Fakeih Aissa had awakened to subterranean murmurs of the far off Nile. It brought messages from beyond the hills and he had listened. A deceiving coolness lingered. The fabric of voices had barely been stilled but for the one brief moment before night had pivoted into a transcendent dawn and all was abated in breathlessness, poised in an equilibrium of forces between one day and the next. Even the river's mists hung suspended. It was precisely when his revelations had always come before and so he had sat in reverent expectation on his small cramped balcony, which doubled as a laundry, surrounded by the odor of sour linen listening—always listening. The city was breathing and he heard its breath rushing, its whispers almost understood, its soul and substance nearly touched—but nothing came to him. Nothing. Even though he focused all his energies gritting his teeth so hard they almost chipped. The silence was most profound just before first light.

But then, as if a phoenix arising from his sense of abandonment, the dawn exploded in a storm of voices that thundered from mosques and shook the great city to its foundations. Clarions of Allah were summoning the faithful as they had for fifteen fleeting centuries. He could easily count twenty minarets silhouetted against the pre-dawn light from where he sat—pillars of the faith.

"God is most great…" The muezzin's call came in dream-speak. "I testify there is no God but God…" Smoke like voices moved through doorways and windows as desert wind. He poured into the half-light with the others having chosen long ago to hide his Coptic Christian origins to be absorbed by his beloved city. Later, as he prostrated himself in ritual, it occurred to him that the thousand-year-old Cairo—which perched as fragile dew at the edge of the Sahara, stretching from the Mars Atlantic well into Asia—had another name: Al-Qāhirah. It meant victorious.

Now he raced through the streets to meet the American from the embassy: his heels echoing determined tattoos, sweat bathed his nut-brown face. He had his revelation. It had come after all. And it was a great relief to him for on his side of the Nile few dreams were ever realized and the ground was too agonizingly near. Ali Fakeih needed a lift from victory.

Today it would happen.

He had been born in a nameless village on the Muqattam hills, a barren plateau that rose above Cairo's eastern perimeter. The dirt track that lead to it wound endlessly up the slow bluff and strained the legs and backs of those who hauled their priceless burdens into the nightmarish world of the *Zabbaleen*. He had been cursed from birth and could not purge himself of the memories and, though luck had given him escape as a child, he would never admit to his history. Still he violently cursed the *wahiya*, the street bosses, and vowed that until his own crossing into paradise he would seek vengeance on one exceptionally evil man for his father's death. "It was a massacre!" He spat out venomously if ever the subject came up, which it rarely had except in angry dialogues within his own mind. He regarded the *wahiya* as snakes, vermin he would just as soon shoot as allow to pass by in the street undisturbed.

The *Zabbaleen* were rubbish barons. They alone had rights to the garbage of Cairo. Blood rights. Inalienable rights. Contested rights. Early in the twentieth century, Muslims swept in from the Western Sahara and had developed a profitable business collecting the city's trash. Decades later when Coptic Christians arrived from the South the Muslims sold the Zabbaleen the privilege to their collection routes charging both the new arrivals and their old tenants simultaneously. The system endured. Still palls of smoke float eternally over villages of roofless huts in the Muqattam hills where there is no electricity or water or sanitation, nor schools or clinics and only one great old Coptic basilica to whose doorstep the rubble brews. Clouds—as clouds once hovered in an earlier age over areas where the rubbish was burned to heat Turkish baths.

Forty percent of the children die their first year, but not Ali Fakeih Aissa and it was his indelible curse to bear. Memories still scalded him of clambering up spiral staircases that clung precariously to the sides of ancient buildings and retrieving the garbage left there to the little cart waiting below. If there were servants, anything of value had already been removed leaving his family to eke out a living from the rest. It was chance that elected who would survive and who would not played out across the dirt floor of a hovel shared by family members, chickens, pigs and goats where the haul, a thousand tons a day, was sorted by hand. Soggy paper in one pile, which sold for seven dollars a ton; metal, computer parts, household items to be repaired or used and other things—anything without worth was burned as fuel. Over the years garbage swelled and cascaded down towards Cairo in an ineffable flow. It had always been that way. Whole communities had evolved on top of trash. Seven or eight steps had to be descended to reach the once street level entrances of some Cairo buildings as civilization's waste accumulated. Anyone who has spent time living knows the fundamentals never change. Children and scrawny dogs danced amid the dark piles.

Everywhere else the night was effervescent with prospects for the future. Overhead a thin golden line was etched into the firmament as the first globally functioning commercial space station caught the rays of a sun slumbering behind the horizon. A hundred men lived inside all sweaty and suffering from the same hungers and moral weaknesses earthmen complain of. It was humanity's needle piercing the unattainable. A man named Castogan had ultimately designed it in a fit of brilliance unmatched thus far. It was one of the high moments of life that was trumpeted across the globe in luminous press accolades. Ali Fakeih Aissa, however, had never heard the name and if he had, and if the small pin of light had been pointed out in the sky accompanied by the fact of men living there in space just as he did in the swelter of Cairo, it would have meant nothing to him. Nothing at all. He had been overcome with bitterness from his first breath and consequently expected nothing better.

Stories had circulated through the lower rungs of Cairo's social hierarchy for generations that the Zabbaleen had become rich from mistakenly discarded treasures and hoarded their wealth out of sight of the *wahiya* in fear of reprisals. However, brutal tradition had taught them that if they failed to pay their rents or if they tried to collect from the tenants themselves or in any way attempted to better their condition they would be roughed up—men would bloody their faces and smash their carts scattering a days work to the street. How these rumors were started was a mystery. Father Ghazali, the young bearded Coptic priest who was the only civilizing element in all the villages of the Zabbaleen, attributed them to "weak brains".

The rumor was exactly the reason Fakeih's father became the accused. As a small child scampering through the trash—already deeply embittered and plotting his impossible flight from the wretchedness of the Muqattam hills—little Ali Fakeih Aissa did not pay close attention to the details. One day his father came home without a thumb. Dried blood covered his leg. That was the first time he heard the utterance *Shari'ah*. Only later did he learn that it was the word for the Islamic legal code employed in its entirety only by fundamentalists. His father had been branded a thief by a *wahiya* who, driven to it by jealousy of the Zabbaleen's imagined wealth, denounced the man publicly and produced a small, insignificant item from his trash cart he claimed had been stolen. All things considered the minor Imam who determined the case showed mercy and considerable restraint by only severing his father's thumb contemplating the fact that he had been driven to the act by desperation. Compassion, the Imam knew well, was the one thing that would assure him a place in paradise. Later he cursed himself for wavering in his rendering of the *Shari'ah* when Fakeih's father was accused again and this time had him imprisoned to await judgment as an habitual thief. He knew well personal interpretation was the one thing that could destroy Islam.

Ali Fakeih Aissa had yet to be truly tested. The pivotal moment in his young life was to come later. It was, he decided afterward, by divine intervention that he had been guided to that exact spot in the city as a spiritual lesson. Suddenly a squall of people arose from the hot winds that swept up the dust from the streets and there were crowds. Shifting. Pushing. Wiping their gritty brown necks. Heated multitudes that towered over his small frame and were packed shoulder to shoulder. He squeezed through their legs propelled forward by an unquenchable curiosity. As he reached the center around which all were gathered he saw a huge Ethiopian man with glistening skin. A deep foreboding embraced him. The giant black man stood with his weight squarely distributed on both legs, his muscles were flexed and he exuded an animalistic power. From his clenched hands hung a three-foot sword.

The Ethiopian would earn about two hundred piasters that day, more money than Fakeih had ever imagined. On a piece of cardboard before the man the boy was shocked to see his father trussed up and splayed out in a curiously awkward manner. It was as if he had expected to see him there in complete humiliation, as if the fates had hold of him and so he numbly took in the sight yet it was dreamlike and unreal. Then a flash. A glint from the sun. A whoosh. Then once again. Quicker than the eye. Quicker than a breath. Infinite. Inexorable. An act that could only be regretted in old age but never undone. It was the sort of act that changed the course of civilizations and catalyzed wars and great migrations. A soldier held up the severed hand and leg in the air brandishing them in sacred victory.

Although his father survived the sentence of double amputation, he died a week later from infection.

It was perhaps that traumatic moment which caused Ali Fakeih Aissa's later conversion to Islam. For the day after his father's death when by rights the trash route fell to him as the oldest, and indeed only male, he came into possession of the very item that was to be the key to his escape from misery and introduce him to a completely new existence. It was a change as complete as from black to white, in one instant he was a Zabbaleen and then he wasn't. Simple. How else could he attribute this miracle except to the will of God. From then on the phrase *In-sha Allah* took on meaning where it had none before and he lavished it on everyone he met.

His hands had been sunk to the elbows in the muck he had collected that day long ago when he felt something hard, solid, rock like. Its surface was smooth and irregularly shaped yet even with his fingers he felt the design. He yanked it out but it was so soiled and caked with sediment what it was remained a mystery even under close inspection. With a strange excitement he ran to wash it in a nearby bucket and soon in his hand, glistening from the water as if newborn, lie a small figurine unlike anything he had ever seen before. A horse, yes a horse, but not a horse... something else, more ancient, a conduit perhaps through which his soul could travel into lives past. The fat perfectly arched neck crowned by a neatly cropped line of mane that culminated in a small graceful equine head. The body obese, legs impossibly short so that it could never run—out of its back rose a round fluted opening with a lip. No, he knew immediately this horse was never meant for the real world, it was spirit horse. A painted saddle decorated with leaping greyhounds and partridges and other symbols too, beautiful and mysterious, figures which he could not fathom although he tried taking long meditative moments to run his small fingers over the smooth, cool ceramic horse. It electrified him. The past reared and swirled about him in double spinning whirlpools until he became dizzy and euphoric with wonder. Here was something he had never dreamed of, never thought of, and now he held it in his hand. It was the first time in his life he had ever felt the true weight of something, the pressure and the substance all at once. It unleashed a strange and wonderful fire in him and he imagined that he might posses something of his own someday, something of value.

Years later he was still imagining. The fire had dimmed and only flickered at full storm when the deal smacked of exceptional opportunity. At such times his eyes were luminous and one could never imagine the degradation out of which the man had drug himself.

"What've you got?" Parrish could not contain his excitement and was drumming his foot and his right index finger in unison. He smiled inwardly, but his face betrayed nothing.

Fakeih reached down with leathery fingers and nimbly grasped the bone white cup bringing it to his lips where he savored the thick brew. He exhaled. The moment was his. "I can only say one thing…", he sipped again from his coffee narrowing his eyes with a distant look, "I have had an offer from the Egyptian Museum already."

"Christ…" Parrish mumbled and sat forward tapping his fingers on the tabletop more deliberately. "Have you?" He hated competition, especially when it came to things nearly out of reach anyway.

"This very morning."

"I'm not a foundation," he raised his hands and glanced sideways under hooded lids, "just your underpaid public servant. Why do you come to me with something I can't afford?" Of course he knew why—it was stolen. All of it was stolen. Collections around the world were filled with stolen artifacts. Museums, mansions, ateliers of the rich. Perhaps this time the Department of Antiquities was under pressure and it was not worth the risk for the institution. Even the excess of PhDs couldn't justify certain acts. All those driven men were the same as he was. The illicit quality made them want the treasures all the more, their pedigrees impelled them forward and tantalized with the spice of resistance. But ultimately it was the inner need drawing others as he knew he was lured toward the ancient by a sublime desire to unravel the outstanding questions of existence and redemption. Assyrian monuments standing still stark and grand upon breathless shimmering plains gave testimony. Who was not challenged to learn what these ancient men knew, what advantage might it bring? Each artifact a piece of the puzzle, fragments making their way through the black market. Parrish was suddenly anxious with longing. "I'd like to touch it," he said, "just touch it."

Ali Fakeih Aissa smiled more broadly than before recklessly betraying his hand and the bad teeth he had been so careful to hide. "I don't have it."

"You don't have it?"

"What I mean is, it's not with me."

Parrish fondled the pocket full of money he had brought just in case wishing now that he had left it in the bank. "Then where is it?" The streets of Cairo were not a safe place to carry cash.

"In a house that we will go to."

"Damn! A house? …close?"

"Yes." Fakeih replied already up from the table without looking back knowing that the discontented American would follow unquestioningly. "Yes. It's close."

They flew on rays of light from Egypt's eternal sun. Glittering rainbows reflecting off shop windows, cars and passing busses. Radiating back from asphalt streets. Penetrating everything. Their footsteps became lost in the clutter. The sweat. The clamber. The jumble. The shuffle. Echoes absorbed by a million voices all talking—all at once: in the bargain, the grift, the hustle. The jazz of their voices lofted on searing thermal winds so that desert travelers have reported hearing them a hundred miles out while viewing a mirage of the ancient skyline scintillating over the horizon as indistinct waverings. The labyrinth of Cairo—heat and brick, wrought iron and stucco nested alongside towering glass stilettos that reflected the Nile in their gut. Smells hovered from the night before, stenches advancing from gutters and dumpsters into the unclear air made foul with exhaust and industrial pollution that never seemed to dissipate. It was only nine O'clock and already ninety-seven degrees. Mid-morning radiance—it was neither pure yellow nor cream nor ivory nor white, yet it purified with hot blasts of sirocco gone too far east, as if by the breath of some fuming spirit.

In the streets, Ali Fakeih Aissa blended to within one degree of invisibility as he led the way into the maze. As far as Parrish could judge, sweating heavily now just keeping up, they were still close to the American mission where they had begun in the Garden City district and were heading south toward Old Cairo.

Streets soon narrowed and above hovered ghosts of British imperial mansions laden with overhanging, latticework balconies called *mashrabiya*—haven for the reclusive colonialists and only inadvertently shade for Egyptians in the streets. Old homes nearly touched leaning with age across to each other as if to exchange tainted memories of bombing raids ordered across the Sudan and Egyptian badlands whenever a brown skinned nationalist became too insolent. Those structures that had survived the riots of 1952 and again in 2011 were in shambles except a few renovated by wealthy locals and wired with the latest technology. It was their best revenge. Egyptian petty bourgeois occupied what the Europeans left and in turn the rural poor took up their places.

Even the City of the Dead—the vast complex of thousand-year-old cemeteries outside the old city—became a link between the traditions of the land and the urban elite. Men without voices had no recourse but prayer and so their cemeteries had grown vast. Now migrants had taken up residence in the old tombs, often paying rent to the interred's family, stringing in electricity for televisions and stoves. Ritual *Qawwali* music blended with the *muezzin's* call from tinny sounding radios as people sat on grave markers cooking a meal. They have been here for over eight hundred years looking for a better life or waiting for redemption.

A thousand new babies a day come into Cairo. Immigrants too come in streams seeking unnamed conquests: What is another face? The veiled slow walking women in black flowing robes pass alleys strewn with trash and goats and yellow light. People carry on their business in biblical tableaus: timeless, enduring. They are oblivious to the huge, gleaming desalinization plants that recently began to dot the North African and Arabian coasts and had brought down the cost of purified drinking water from being more expensive than gasoline to one affordable by common people. Before that, even into the millennium, many were without fresh water. The lush stands of banyan trees that once lined the Nile had given way completely to massive apartment complexes that spewed raw sewage unabated into the river. Water came from wells, sources that were targets with each era of civil unrest. Easily blown, their walls were often collapsed into a tumble of stone and gravel that polluted them. Corpses were even thrown in to contaminate the drinking supply. Life at the Sahara's edge was fragile.

Parrish struggled to keep up. It was the Egyptian's turf. He had marked it with blood and tears as a boy. Parrish was the interloper. After many blocks he felt disoriented and lost—it was a feeling he welcomed, even longed for, and he drove himself willingly into it as refuge. Heat came in a full shimmering blast. The inch of annual rainfall had already come seven months ago. Parrish's breathing was labored, his mouth coated with fine sand, the way everything was coated with it. Electronics, computers, prized jewelry…all wrapped in plastic—shades were shuttered, doors insulated so that Cairenes could live in the hermetically sealed shadowlands. Only yellow light peeked through. There was no escape. Everything was victim. The crush of humanity in a city effervescent with life, overflowing with people, faces and voices, the eternal cacophony itself was coated with a fine layer of sand.

Dar al Imara was the last street sign he glimpsed before following Fakeih into a narrow passage. Light became dimmed, muted, and only a few shops were open—all other doors were closed, wrought iron shutters locked—though a throng of people jostled through. Smells of spice vied with the reek of urine for prominence. Abruptly Fakeih ducked into a shop and Parrish quickly followed. Inside the air was stale and old. Carpets hung from the ceiling and lay rolled and stacked on the floor. Dusty cases held merchandise which could only be imagined since the glass was so crusted with age and dirt nothing but blurred shapes could be seen inside. The main room was a large covered courtyard with a defunct fountain at its center filled with things: broken crates, straw and pottery shards. Beams from skylights transcended the space riding on dust making the center of the room brighter than the rest. A man stood unpacking boxes. A ring of light in his hair gave him a holy aura.

"My partner." Faheih announced breathlessly punctuating the last word with a sweep of his arm while the other man looked up disdainfully.

"That so." Parrish acknowledged sardonically and noted the fact he had a beard and wore little round glasses low on his nose that distorted his eyes and then surveyed the rest of the surroundings suspiciously.

"Ali bin Ahmed bin Saleh Al-Fulani." The man said.

"A Saudi?" Parrish asked wiping sweat from his face.

"Of course."

An awkward moment passed. Noise from the street drifted in on hot dry air bringing muted songs that murmured indistinctly from the distance.

"Well," he boomed apprehensively, "after that street marathon you led me on I hope it's worth it." A strange odor permeated the place; parched, desolate, ancient, and just slightly sour. Tile peeked from under dirt on the floor. He scrutinized the makeshift warehouse and at last began to distinguish form from shadow. Cheap clay sculpture, wood ornaments and brass, all done faithfully Egyptian—he supposed for tourists or unwitting seekers of relics. Things were stacked without foresight climbing the walls in snarled patterns where dust settled undisturbed. Its specter was eerie.

The Saudi looked quizzically at Fakeih who shrugged off Parrish's comment enthusiastically beckoning him to show something. "I couldn't carry it because it is so valuable."

A circle of winds twirled high above them spinning round lifting and roaring as if by flapping giant wings, rising, soaring, finding a place in the sky lofting on the flaming air into the distant cool altitudes. The great North African coast could be glimpsed mythically swinging round in an indefinably huge arch through Morocco past the Atlas Mountains then racing by turbulent Algeria, Tunisia, Libya, Egypt, Sudan—all one. Offshore the tattered sea lie ruffled frothing at the coast. The Sahara sprawled across a vastness of three thousand miles; its encroaching sands possessed infinite power as they reclaimed cities, routed migrations and defined life. To the south, the land's end could not be seen, its extent too immense: where the ocean has a tumbling, disorganized rage from Cape Agulhas to Antarctica. Great countries whose populations are four or five times that of Africa's could fit easily within its borders: China, India, Europe—all at once as if civilization had no meaning. No meaning at all. It was here where humanity's ancestors had been found. Three individuals' footprints fossilized in mud—a child, two adults. It would be millions of years before they existed anywhere else on earth. Perhaps it was kinship Parrish felt, a longing for a home he'd never had, roots that had eluded him. Or perhaps, as he himself thought, he was chasing an illusion of something that he knew with certainty could not exist in this harsh, force filled universe, but chose to believe in anyway. A man could not live without hope, even a fool's hope.

The Saudi lifted a dirty felt bag from behind the counter and set it down tilting his head back peering through glasses with eyebrows raised in disdain. A stained unfiltered cigarette hung from his lower lip, smoke curling into his nostrils. The object clanked impressively on the old glass and made Parrish's heart beat quickly. Of course it was unlikely that anything of true value would be found just like that after all the years of pilfering, but the excitement got him anyway. He moved closer where he could smell the body odors of the two men, the tobacco and coffee on their breath and the dust of the bag. He watched while weathered brown hands nimbly undid the tie that held the bag and expertly slid the fabric back revealing a tarnished, dull, oxidized and yet exquisitely sculpted statuette. Light seemed to fall on it from the ceiling windows. It stood nearly eight inches high and radiated with an inner vitality endowed by an anonymous artist obscured with time.

"It's Egyptian." The Saudi pronounced with authority. "Twelfth dynasty. Amenemhet's queen."

Though his finger had barely pressed against the surface, he felt he was trespassing against something sacred. Tombs should not be violated, he thought. A strange current passed through him making Parrish remember things of earlier lifetimes. People have had cause to escape life. There are reasons to seal up the past, to abandon it and move on. He would banish his own if he could.

He studied the sculpture closely for insight. It was a seated female figure with melon breasts exposed over the delicate folds of her wrap—carved out of a hard black stone with iridescent flecks of quartz. Hollow sockets where eyes should have been indicated there had once been gemstones inlaid there. Portions were inlaid with gold, he cold tell from the discoloration that he had seen before. The hair was exquisitely detailed in rings and curls each forming a perfect symmetry and the face, though corroded, was sublime and deftly proportioned. He caressed it for a long moment finally lifting it for closer inspection. Barely visible, so that he had to run his finger across to be sure, was an inscription. He did not know what it was but clearly not hieroglyphics. The statuette was from somewhere other than Egypt, he was certain of it. And it was old. Older than Giza—man fears time, yet time fears the pyramids. It was older than anything he'd ever touched before. He suddenly felt light headed.

Parrish scowled and shifted his eyes like a guilty dog. "Why didn't you take the offer from the museum?"

A musk like scent wafted through the open space and permeated the dry air making it brittle to the point of shattering. From behind the counter the Saudi looked at his shoes while leaning forward on both arms and drew his bluish lips tight across the cigarette puffing up great clouds of white smoke that threatened to envelop his head. There was a tension bordering on violence. Parrish didn't like it and wished he had never left the cafe.

"There's always a catch." The Saudi muttered. "No matter what they say…how good it seems. They'll tell you anything…there's always something." Fakeih stood by looking up painfully nodding his head.

"Probably not worth much then."

"'Course it is!" The Saudi shot back. "I told you, it's Twelfth Dynasty."

"Is that what they said?"

"Of course."

Not worth much, Parrish mused fondling the figure deliciously in his hands, *in the long run a lying man isn't worth much at all.* "What did they offer?"

"You…for instance…what will you offer?"

Desperate enough for Parrish to believe that the museum people hadn't even seen the damn sculpture, insistent enough for him to know their hunger. He pressed his hand against the hot money in his pocket. *Jesus Christ*, he cursed himself. Danger raced in his chest. "I'm interested," he confessed lured by the certainty that he could never afford the relic on the legitimate market, "it's an…interesting piece." He meant to say stunning, but thought again.

Poverty was inescapable in Cairo and he had grown callous to it the way a man becomes inured to the nagging of a venomous spouse: or constant pain, or a terminal illness. He knew he could never accept its presence because it was a desiccation of life. Only the dust of memories as a keepsake of what had once been. Sometimes not even that. Bleakness. It was the string that pulled taut, the balance, the counterweight to erudite thoughts. It was that invisible tension that held a ballerina's head impossibly high—her arms extended beyond the confines of the ceiling and legs reaching through the floor, the earth and into the space at the other side of the world. It was the dashing train upon which jazz men secretly rode riotous with motion clattering out rhythm, pounding out in steamy bursts, exploding in melodious, powerful, lyrical, cacophonous, riffs and storms and enchanting hollow sonnets to the black Diaspora vocalized. It was where one learned to make something out of nothing. It was where they all were waiting for something, every last grimy one of them. Waiting. Poverty was waiting. Once again Parrish offered up his plea; *not me*, he whispered shaking his head looking at the statue in the golden light coming down from the rafters, *not me*.

For the first few years he had been stationed in Cairo he locked his door securely. And then bought more locks adding one at a time for every fearful thought he had until the trouble of opening it forced him at last to throw caution to the wind in the name of physical convenience. He knew it must erupt, detonate in cataclysmic violence as the chain reaction of discontent reached an hysterical pitch with the realization that there is honestly nothing to lose, absolutely nothing and that all the mumbo-jumbo-bullshit they had been subservient to for their entire existence had not made their lives one bit better, not more worth living by a single degree. When the realization struck that nothing was working for them, that the words meant nothing, the people, the muscle, the economy, the market…and the sudden awareness that there were more have-nots than there were of the haves! Well…he had been waiting for that. He waited for a few years and then got thick skinned. It would still happen. The revolution. The explosion. But now it didn't matter. He removed the locks from his door. Breathed easier even though he drank a bit more and smoked more thin cigars. At last he could come and go easily. Parrish had become one of them in spirit.

The two men had been glad for his money. He had laid out the paper bills on the dirty glass one at a time, one upon the other and they greedily snatched them up like half-starved jackals. Afterward the realization came that he could have gotten it for less. *Malesh* he thought, *malesh*. A common phrase in Cairo that meant "never mind" in an effort to change the subject. He would have had it at any price.

* * * *

"Do you see them?" The sour stench of the Egyptian's shirt filled his nostrils. "Do you?" The money had weighed in his pocket before, but now, holding the ancient figurine wrapped in soiled cloth, Parrish felt all eyes focused on him. He pulled Fakeih up short and leaned back against dry brick holding him close enough to hear his breathing.

"Yes." Fakeih replied straightening himself with a lack of concern. "*Malesh*, they are nothing…curious, nothing more."

"Of what?"

"Your jacket, shoes…who knows?"

The disturbing events happened on the return trip to Garden City. He had disregarded as curiosity people watching when they hurried through the streets on the way to the warehouse, but now he realized it wasn't annoyance or fleeting greed. At one point he was convinced they were being followed. So he watched out. Curiously no one appeared. In a place as wretched as Cairo, where poverty rushed forth overwhelming everything, even Islam, in its power and fury, it wasn't hard to imagine the worst.

It was crumbling—all of it—deteriorating and calcifying like knit bone or coral or petrified wood in its fragile, formerly rich yet now aged and decrepit and strained-past-its-limits state. The once glittering held the indigent and centuries of desperate clawing had left marks. On one side of the Nile were oblivious starched white shirts and cocktail parties overlooking the shimmering water where two masted dhows still glided picturesquely by; on the other robes and prayers in dusty, crumbling buildings devoid of latrines or running water whose accumulated trash had to be shoveled from the hallways. In it's most populous areas two hundred and eighty thousand people crammed each square mile and the city had to import one seventh of all the world's surplus wheat to feed its minions. A baby is born every eleven seconds and every year sixty thousand students are graduated from universities and five hundred thousand enter the job market looking for employment that does not exist. Urban planning was irrelevant in a city that subsisted on hope alone.

They moved on. Eyes pursued as they retraced their path through the ancient labyrinth. Midday heat shimmered off tile roofs. Baked walls in narrow streets radiated. Men looked up at outdoor stalls, peered from under shop awnings. Loiterers stared. Women whispered to each other with veiled lips. Footsteps behind were muted by the cacophony.

"We are being followed!" Parrish insisted.

"Move faster!" Fakeih barked revealing concern for the first time as he quickened his pace. His eyes grew electric and darted wildly through the crowd ahead unsure of what he was looking for.

"How could they know?" He implored Fakeih, but there was no reply. It made Parrish angry. Suddenly a hand touched him. He glared back, but could not catch whoever it was. Then again. He clutched the small precious figurine pressing forward knowing that even at the price paid he should not have spent so much on it, which made him grip more tightly. Then something else occurred to him. The thought alone brought images of humiliation. An arrest for illegal concourse in artifacts. Dismissal from the Embassy staff. The coup de grâce, a final ignominious end. He spat contemptuously to the ground feeling he had nothing to lose. Then, unexpectedly, he pulled the small man up short again and pressed his face close shouting a whisper above the clatter of the street. "Do you think it's someone from the Department of Antiquities?"

The Egyptian's face grew pale for this was the one weakness to his enterprise. It was the one thing that could send him plummeting back down into the depths of the Muqattam Hills and the Zabbaleen—of whom he had banished the thought from his waking hours and only on occasion, in moments of severe tiredness did they intrude upon his dreams causing him to shudder at what might have been. Jail and then starting over again.

The *wahiya* to answer to. He had everything to lose. "No!" he said, "No..." looking sidelong his eyes mere slits in the bright sun, "it cannot be!"

"Maybe the museum people informed."

"No!"

"Maybe they did!" His voice rose in pitch. "How do you know?"

"They never did."

"What?"

Fakeih shrugged. "They never saw."

"Meaning what?"

"They never showed up."

"I knew it!" Parrish suddenly fumed. "I knew it."

Someone pulled at his coat from behind and mumbled weakly. He whirled and saw a man winnowing his way through the crowd. "What did he say?"

"Sounded like... "

Another man reached out and touched Parrish's arm and looked at him in a strangely vulnerable way, full faced and innocent and then slowly raised his hand over his head and mouthed a word without a sound. A child hung on his arm, men reached over shoulders and caressed his cheek, a hand gripped his wrist. The crowd pressed forward a breathing mass in the tight passage where pastel stucco buildings rose up above the street and electric wires doubled as clothes lines in the air.

"Let's get out of here..." Parrish muttered and struggled to push through the throng that had suddenly gathered. Hands reached out and pressed against him. He pushed them aside and tried to move. Everyone was speaking all at once. In the confusion, Fakeih disappeared and suddenly he was alone pressed by the heat of bodies, the odor of perspiration, the reek of sour linen from clothes left too long before drying. He stared into eyes unimaginable; ones in which the future and the past blended seamlessly into a monochromatic desert where hope was as meaningless as memory and desperation was the one continuous thread that held them together. It was utterly visceral. He shuddered and screamed silently.

A small hunched over old woman enveloped in black stood before him and spoke with an open heart ignoring any fear of disappointment—one more loss might be the final arbiter between life and death—finally giving voice to what was held close. She struggled to raise her arms higher towards Parrish and repeated as a vindication of her certainty. "Mahdi!" Then her expression froze and she seemed to fall away in a swoon.

Pain struck the back of his head as someone grabbed a tuft of hair and yanked it hard. A woman rushed off. Another was pulling on the side of his head. Parrish deflected the man's arm and pushed him away. People spoke with intensity, full of hope and desolation all wanting to touch him, to own a piece of him, as if he was a relic. The front of his shirt was ripped to shreds—hands grabbed for it, pieces torn from it—like they were praying, he thought. Praying.

Then he realized they were praying.

Parrish felt panic. He would be overwhelmed as he had been once before—once in his religious studies. The incident revivified in that moment with absolute clarity, the time he had abandoned himself to prayer and had been lifted by such euphoric ecstasy that he spun out of control for nearly ten days. They told him it was rapture—a divine state. Now it was all around him in a frenzy determined by unknown expectations. He desperately tried to escape, but everywhere people were waiting. Hope was driving them and when he moved through the street they flowed with him.

He the moon and they the tide.

Knocked to the ground, he covered his face. Feet and hands pummeled him. Clothing was shredded. Skin scratched. Their hot breath desperately pleading…*Let it be him.*

"I'm not the one!" Parrish finally shouted as he struggled to his feet, rising up against the press of bodies, punching and shoving until he broke free. Then, clutching the figurine, he ran. Ran as fast as he could.

Earlier, much earlier, a man had grappled with the belief that had possessed him like the others until, in a monumental feat of reason and faith, it had been exorcised. He had folded silently into the river of people following Parrish and Fakeih. He was a fervent believer in the crushing of blasphemy. He had certainty in his mission. He had not, however, anticipated the old woman in black—who now lay crumpled on the ground where a moment ago she was nearly touching Allah—getting in his way. Now too, he was running terrified by his own act gone awry.

At first, the police surmised just another old one expired from heat and too much excitement. It was later that they discovered the blood and the round wound in her back from a small caliber bullet. The incident caused disquiet among the local officers who sat up most of the night conjecturing why anyone would commit such an un-Islamic crime.

IV | Fingerprints of Spirits

"In this business, beauty fuels temptation." Ishaq Sadek rubbed the scar that ran across his cheek with his thumb as he looked at the photograph. "Beauty has many takers." His clients never gave him much information in the beginning afraid it might taint his observations–especially in these types of investigations where impartiality is vital. "Her eyes are beautiful." he intoned poetically, "It's always more interesting if they are beautiful."

Suddenly, she emerged from a building and lit for a long moment on the wide shoulder of the road as if absorbing radiation of the hot Egyptian sun like a Monarch butterfly moving its wings in gentle trance-like precision. Then she slid deftly into a car and was gone. Ishaq shoved the gas pedal to the floorboard of his dented silver compact and it lurched forward straining as the air conditioning siphoned off much needed power. She was a determined driver and though he sideswiped one vehicle with a gritty crunch and drove another off into the ditch raising plumes of dust miraculously avoiding a collision he finally managed to latch onto her tail unconcerned she would notice. No Egyptian looks in the rear view mirror. He snapped a cell phone photo with one hand for his report. She was driving a different car than yesterday and that made him suspicious.

It was earlier that the opportunity had fallen into his lap. Manna from heaven as they say. He remembered the deep relief when he received a first retainer and put it in the Banque du Caire replenishing an account that had become fossilized through neglect. It had been a long drought, but his will had ferried him bolstered by the knowledge of the many quality families he had helped avoid the pitfalls of matrimony.

"You don't always get what you see," Muhammad Abd al' Rashid had said, "everyone is like an onion."

He was not burning under the radiance of wealth. It was just clay and with it he sculpted what he wished. For it was a matter of confidence and that was worth all the endless desiccated moments of waiting and patronizing that it required to achieve. Once in hand, then it was another matter and his employers were only peripheral to his genius. In certain instances he'd even amazed himself with superhuman feats of intuition, or in the words of a Sufi mystic, divine epiphanies. Surely the Prophet was right, praise be to his name.

"I want you to handle this matter very delicately," the Saudi drew the long fingers of his right hand up before his face and gestured pointedly, "she is the daughter of a very powerful man and neither you nor I would want him to know about this."

"Then he is not aware of your intentions."

"I prefer to act only when fully informed, which is why I've come. You were recommended as a protector of my family name. Don't misunderstand me; she is very precious, a very precious creature, but women... can be a lot of trouble."

Ishaq Sadek mused silently. He had done his homework and knew the stories first hand, with some hard evidence even. al' Rashid spoke as if there were no women he had been with indiscreetly, as if his morals were beyond reproach, as if he were a *Sayyid*. A slight disgust filled him. The liquor and other Western habits he indulged in on that yacht… the detective's imagination began to percolate on what mischief he did when out of the country. He considered the Saudi in his starched white *thwab*, the fine cotton robe that never even made him sweat despite the 100-plus-degree heat and smiled.

"You can trust me."

" Her name is Azhara Binte Jibril Riyadh daughter of the great general."

He remembered now sucking in his breath cool even in the swelter of the day. Shocked, but silently. He knew better than to give away anything. In the end he had asked for more money attributing it to the risk. Al' Rashid had deep pockets.

Now dancing across potholed, two-laned city streets trying to keep the young woman in sight he wondered if it was worth it. This business did not allow for any slip-ups. Jibril Ben Jabbar Riyadh doted on his daughter and would do anything save blaspheme against the Qur'an to protect her, and perhaps even that in his private world. Ishaq Sadek would be erased from this word without a stain to show he had been here and the lovely young woman would never even have known he had breached her confidences. But worse, all his fine work would be without a witness.

Ivory aflame cast ultramarine eclipses upon the windowsill. The air was still then blustering. Dew escaped the astringent night. He remembered everything. Every word. Hakim's initial shock, amazement, yet in the end begrudging commitment of support. He had addressed the coiled insecurity within, the purpose, which could be sublimated, but never subdued. And fear. It was eternal.

"*Salaam aleikum.*"

"*Wa aleikin as-salaam.*"

"You are always rushing." He spoke frankly to the dark robed figure before him as the luminance from high windows pealed across the man's shoulders and brought a crown of light aglow in his hair. Abd al Hakim hunched forward with elbows resting on his knees to disguise the wildness coiled inside. Their voices echoed off the Tuscan red tile floor of the *majlis*, the main reception room adjacent a huge domed courtyard where pale stucco walls shot up three stories to triangular skylights that allowed the midnight blue to show.

"My nature, Ben Jabbar." Peering from under his brow, "Full of discontent. You know the type."

"Please…call me Jibril the way you used to…we're friends ehhh?" He gestured open handed with uncharacteristic kindness. They had been estranged for many years, but it was a crucial moment.

"Not discontent but fear, or perhaps greed…" Al Hakim sipped the steaming fresh cardamom spiced coffee. The knowing smile set Ben Jabbar's nerves on edge. The man knew something was wanted of him or he wouldn't be there, something only he could give. "I tell you these sins because…certain if I do not get there first it will all be gone. I've felt that way since I was a boy. Of course it's not true. With full repentance, I am impatient out of vanity. This flaw has served me well politically don't you think?"

How Jibril Ben Jabbar Riyadh hated politicians. Since the reinstatement of the *Shari'ah* a quarter of a century earlier they had been easier to bear—the Islamic legal code based entirely on the Qur'an and regarded as divine law gave them little room to maneuver—still not one of them spoke honestly. Consequently, he was convinced elected officials were inherently liars to gain popular support and each disguised a secret agenda to which every person addressed felt somehow used by. It was confirmation of democracy run amuck and an indication of how deeply Western influence had permeated in the faithful even after twenty-five years since the return to the fundamental tenets of Islam. His military life had been different, more orderly. Jibril pressed his hands together until he could feel the strength of his arms the way it used to be when he was young and full of spice.

"Chicago has over one hundred and fifty mosques and one point two million faithful." He shot back soberly. "It is part of the Islamic world, yet it is not." Other men were no longer large enough to embrace the demands of geopolitics and the truth of the revelation all at once, but he was. He had nothing but disgust for them, disgust and contempt. Yet empathy because they were, like him, common and of the earth; and if by chance they had followed the straight path as he had…but he among his fellows had always known his purpose was an incendiary. It was a terrible master and when he thought of the consequences of his past actions even he, "The Protector of Mosques", fluttered in the stomach. So, he was prone to act impulsively having ultimate faith in his own judgment and unwilling to look too closely at what he had already done. There was a thin line between megalomania and true power. It was familiar to him, he had walked both sides of it and in the end concluded that the final outcome really did justify the means.

"We must transform all unbelievers you see, or we have no right to live under the blessing of Islam."

"That is not a pillar of the faith." Abd al Hakim replied.

"We are compelled to do more…perhaps that is what I mean to say." A sudden surge of violent energy buoyed him on its river. In the beginning, when Jibril Ben Jabbar Riyadh was uninitiated he believed the faith lent him power. Now he was certain it was he who gave power to the faith. "We betray the revelation by not doing more." His voice edged cold. "I'm asking for your recommitment to Islam. That is all."

Nervously, Abd al Hakim contemplated the choice under unremitting glare mustering all his diplomatic skill, which was considerable. Death would follow if he disagreed too vehemently, sometime mid-stride when he least expected it. He pondered if religious ideas were worth dying for in this modern world—suddenly shocked at his lack of inner faith. Even he could be touched. Terror worked.

"Jibril..." he offered up cautiously and with good humor, "have I become that much more moderate? I am an elected representative of an entire region. My constituency gives me tremendous support, but somehow you make me question myself. You make me think about things I would rather not. Perhaps, it is as you say, I should recommit to Islam."

"We were radical in our youth," Jibril replied in a fleeting effort to humanize himself, "both of us—weren't we? But now...? " he gestured helplessly, "No one trusts a military man entirely. But I still have liberal attitudes. Listen! I will be 'The Believer' president. I will be the one. I am certain of it. Quite certain."

Later he stood like a captured force of nature in the arched window where the ivory light the moon made flecked his skin with shadow: cloaking his great arms and chest, his massive jaw, thick black mustache and funneled brows that poured emotion into the eyes—phosphorescent in the darkness, pools of fluorescence, beacons of intention. Away from people he did not have the same devastating effect on the universe and willingly swam in the feeling of humanness accepting it as a reprieve from responsibilities. With Abd al Hakim's help, much of the North African constituency would follow. He felt heady and wondered if al Hakim had any ideals at all worth dying for.

Distances embraced Jibril Ben Jabbar Riyadh. He soared in their expanses. He sought out deserts and wind and air and sea voyages and could not go for any length confined. On airliners, he stared enraptured at clouds for hours capturing the soaring viewpoint so that it would console him when earthbound again. Perhaps it was Bedouin blood, indelible maps on the genes, that compelled him to these spaces, or the frantic wanting of a spirit not finding all that he had assumed would come with an ardently religious life. The compound he kept in Cairo, even with slums encroaching nearby, gave him distance. He found he needed it more and more as he grew older just as his father had.

He knew well that if he had hesitated for an instant on his journey through life he would have been lost—as many have been never reaching their destinations. The reason for this chasm between himself and his fellows was his faith, which came naturally and without pretense, effort or bitterness; an event especially rare in an age of immediate fulfillment where everything one could possibly imagine was available for money. The fact of his unconditional belief had been testified to by his complete memorization of the Qur'an by the time he was seven years old. In an instant he could still recite any given line or verse in perfect rhythm and cadence maintaining the eloquence that differentiates the divine word from pagan Arabic with its poetry of love, camels, war and hunting. With a few simple answers he had accepted the revelation. There was no ceremony, no ritual. Even as a child he understood the implications and so came to be educated early at the famous al-Azhar mosque and theological college in Cairo—his parents believing he was a religious prodigy and would undoubtedly become a leading cleric in the *ulama* and perhaps a revered *mufti* to whom the experts would turn in order to clarify a point of Islamic law. This was not to be, but he remained devout throughout his entire life and his faith was unwavering even though he had become a military man and had been responsible for many atrocities in the eyes of Allah.

* * * *

"You may believe that wealth insulates me from people, but it's just not true. I've felt oppression, felt deprived even though I was not, lost even though I had found the straight path—I'm in touch with the woof and warp. Money will not buy paradise...it is as they say."

The man sat before him unconvinced. *Malesh*. It did not matter because Jibril had perfect insight into the psyche of Muhammad Abd al' Rashid. He was acutely aware of the man's sexual fancies and rumors of mistresses kept on his yacht, out of sight of the *mullahs*, that he supposed were brushed aside by those of lesser conviction as peccadilloes of an otherwise useful life. He had also been apprised of the young Saudi's reputation for drinking alcohol as any Westerner might. Jibril's sensibilities were offended at having to do business with this man, but there it was. He was essential to the plan.

His servants had spread out trays of elaborately prepared food as hospitality for the traveler. It was a gift. He had spent time in Damascus, Aleppo and Beirut to learn from the masters at the true source of Arabic cuisine–Lebanon. There he had been taught to blend baby okra and lamb, seminola and sesame paste, chickpeas with garlic, lemon, coriander, marjoram and sumac; and to cook the Red Sea fish *shaour* in a delicate spice for *sayyadiya*. Thousands of tastes were catalogued on his palate and he could improvise in the kitchen from this repertoire the way a *Sufi Qawwali* singer could elevate the spirit and bring listeners closer to Allah. He specialized in *mezze*, especially those with flaky pastry shells he had become known for among his friends and family. He surveyed the trays placed before them and was confident Al' Rashid, having some insight into his tastes, would be more pliable under the influence of delicious foods.

The spread was replete with some of his finest creations; *ataif*, small pancakes stuffed with nuts and cheese and doused with syrup; *mutabak*, savory turnovers with banana; *sambusek*, triangular pies filled with spiced meat, cheese and spinach; *kufta*, fingers of minced meat and spices charcoal-grilled on skewers; kunafi, shoelace pastry filled with sweet white cheese, and pita bread with *mouhammara*, a mixture of ground nuts, olive oil, cumin and chili to dip it in. There was aromatic coffee and a *sheesha*, the pipe he used to smoke dried fruit through a water filter after the meal. Tobacco he had given up as an act of conviction.

"As we both know, wealth is not a result of work." Al' Rashid replied flaunting a self-confidence bordering on arrogant and a darkly obscure intelligence. "People don't realize this and consequently are slaves to labor or schemes their whole lives." He picked absently at the painstakingly prepared delicacies set before him. "It gives men undue status."

Jibril wound his hand like a fan searching for the right word while resentment grew. "Try the *kunafi*, it's…" reaching for the word that would do justice to his exquisite cooking "…delicious!" He finally exclaimed for lack of anything better.

"For example, my father. Rich without effort." Al' Rashid looked at Jibril weighing in his mind whether he possessed enough strength to discuss the issue or if he was full of bluster like many others had been in his life quickly dissipating. "Perhaps there's nothing gained by an individual without reason, I'm not sure, perhaps it was an act of Allah. I'd like to think so, but I don't believe my faith is strong enough." He did not consider Jibril to be as devout as he liked to appear either. "Money doesn't account for character. Likewise it doesn't reflect it. A man cannot be judged by his wealth just as hard work or poverty does not make one oppressed."

"Yes…yes…but I can't agree completely." Jibril whisked one of the shoelace pastries filled with sweet white cheese off a tray and devoured it in one deft motion feeling contempt for the rhetoric that he'd heard often trying not to offend the young Saudi, whom he needed. But he could never pass an opportunity to make his opinion known, and if possible convert another's erroneous viewpoint to his. "I'd say it is the lack of money that's a basic motivation. And in that way reveals who a man is." It was such an obvious fact that he felt foolish having to comment on it. "We can't be so naive. Only after generations of wealth does knowledge of this fact cease to exist in the genetic makeup. For instance, you might say that the military produces nothing of value but lives off the economy of others, or is a luxury afforded by success. A matter of viewpoint. Money greases the wheel," he concluded licking his fingers. "It is the measure of a man whether we like to admit it or not."

"Nonsense. People don't even like to think about it. It upsets them except when it comes as a windfall…as in my father's case, otherwise…I don't think it has much relation to a man's purpose. Some things make money, some do not. Would you have everyone scrambling after wealth and leave, say…the *Ulama* without religious men? Factories without labor? What about women? Who repairs your shoes?"

"Of course. Some are more suited…"

"Preference. You can define a person by what they prefer in their lives."

"Or by what they are compelled to do to survive." The older man cupped his hands in front of his face and closed his elbows in tight to his body to suppress a sigh desperately trying to avoid a confrontation. Many times he had been criticized for being too emotional, too impulsive and it was true he possessed a fiery temper...*what of it*, he thought, *I may be old, but I'm not dead.* With his own actions he personally had been molded by the solidarity shown to the disenfranchised, the marginalized and had even chosen his vocation as a professional soldier with the tacit purpose to redistribute wealth and resources and try to make a level field out of the disparities of nature.

"Of course, as I'm sure is your intention, everyone is recipient to the revealed word and will be rich in heaven." Jibril offered covertly.

"Exactly so." Al' Rashid replied after a pregnant pause.

Jibril's was the task of removing distractions from the straight path, finding leverage when there was none. He couldn't expect this man to understand the concepts that had ruled his life. Al' Rashid was purely academic, a third generation, university educated businessman who was detached from life on the ground by those same intervening generations. Now he was more convinced than ever money revealed one of their characters and it certainly wasn't Al' Rashid's.

al' Rashid went on. "A strong market, production capacity not too far ahead of demand, balance of commodities, wages and prices in line...the optimum good of the system...that's what is best for people, and countries...and the world. When the economy is strong, so is the individual. When all the vital signs are positive it regulates itself..."

"Nonsense. Unregulated markets have shown absolutely no social conscience whatsoever and have only produced war when men finally came to realize it was the economy failing and not themselves..." Suddenly Jibril realized he had already gone too far. "Forgive me," he laughed sheepishly, "too many years on the campaign I suspect. I learned to make *sambusek* from a man who ran the best restaurant in Beirut. He is now in Los Angeles and owns a chain of them. Try one, I really think it's my best dish."

The Arab PETEC members were key to his strategy, and here was the one man who could help him. He thought now of money as water trickling through his fingers again realizing the validity of his mission before Allah. Al' Rashid, though a Saudi and not Egyptian, was an Arab. The borders to their lands had become indistinct with the flood of nationalism that had been concurrent with the revitalization of fundamental Islam. It was only feeding the West, this "balancing of the markets." It was un-Islamic. The world economy was not the way of the straight path. Divine law was not to be questioned. He had some responsibilities to keep for he was, after all, a man educated at Al-Azhar where he had learned to protect the *Qu'ran* from personal interpretation. That was the true way. The hidden pillar. *And when ye meet those who misbelieve, then strike off the heads until ye have massacred them, and bind fast the bonds.*

Later the men shook hands. Perhaps he had been too quick to take offense, Muhammad Abd al' Rashid thought as he departed through the high arched circular iwan to the courtyard and the muted light of early evening. Stars began to appear.

But it was fury that made Jibril shudder behind the closed door. He struggled with the dual nature of his life. He was rich and he was poor, filled yet so denied. It was something no one other than the women he had slept with and to whom he had murmured his most private interpretations of self could fully understand. Fingerprints of spirits were not meant for the daylight, it was best to whisper them dark and late where they would remain hidden from cynics. Those of little faith. Certain things remained indelible despite denial and they were etched on his psyche, though some chose to ignore them. Young al' Rashid for instance, had never felt the futility of living on the edge. He had missed the point entirely. Money was never an issue to men like that. The market could not support them all despite his evangelical enthusiasm, only those who fell within its margins.

For the rest, it was temptation beyond the ability to bear and distracted them from the real truths of life. Those of the *Qu'ran*. Jibril concluded that he lacked any kind of a spiritual life and was dangerous because of it. In the end the man had denied him, refuted all his overtures and some of his best cooking as well, an act alone that he would have difficulty forgiving.

He had counted on support from all the oil producing sectors of the Arab states—he counted on it—but now would have to rethink everything. Everything! The prospect made him storm about the courtyard seething with rage and violence and kick the door. He grimaced from the pain in his foot and all the noise made the servants peer out windows one by one as witnesses to the spectacle. It was the shock after all. The great Jibril Ben Jabbar Riyadh having this sheep, this dog of a man withhold his allegiance. He who had been pivotal in the second resurgence of Islam leading the military suppression of populist revolutions throughout the Arab world of the late twentieth century. He who crushed the backlash against clerical rule. He of the straight path who had always aligned himself with the marginalized and the disenfranchised out of charity and through him had given them voice. That was probably it, he thought, not of his cloth. "My disgust!" Jibril spewed. "The Protector of Mosques" he had been called by the *Ulama*.

"I am the one!" He committed himself again. The man was degenerate not to be able to just look and realize who he was dealing with.

Years ago he would have had swift vengeance, but in order to truly be "The Believer" president as Jibril desired he would not have the man killed, he would try to withold himself from doing that. Al' Rashid, he was certain, would hang himself, the evil always do. There was comfort in this thought. The man was un-Islamic. *In-sha Allah,* Jibril pondered with determination, *everything comes with faith.*

The pastel landscape of Ariel Addison's face was the first thing Parrish had seen when he finally looked up after returning to the embassy earlier that day.

"A few minutes ago," the trembling man began to rattle off in his own noxious way, "I received a call from a local police captain." His innocuous demeanor disguised longings that had become atrophied over the years from his own lack of initiative. Naturally, he blamed everyone else for his misfortunes until all ambition became petrified and consequently his face had a permanent scowl pressed into it like a musty rose suffocating between pages of a book so that even when he smiled there was something disquieting about it. And he was anemically pale. Once a promising academic who considered himself charismatic because of superior intellect, he was finally embittered by forgetting the life envisioned when younger until it was too late. Ariel Addison adopted arrogance to hide the sin of disappointment. As Deputy Chief of Mission he was Parrish's direct senior and in charge of embassy affairs on a day-to-day basis when Ambassador Murdoch was globetrotting or in Washington too drunk or hung over to function well.

"You did?" Parrish replied. Distracted. Shirt in tatters. Flushed and scratched. Eyes darting around the room. He rummaged through his desk drawers for a smoke. "Christ!" He steamed. A nervous Egyptian custodian who harbored a private jihad against nicotine had sanitized them of tobacco. "What the hell do you suppose he does with my cigars?"

Light that breached the floor to ceiling draperies softened shadows in the room with a pale yellow glow. Sounds were muted. The whole building rose from the ancient North African city as an affront to a culture that had its roots as far back as five thousand b.c.—one that had originated the idea of social justice by two thousand b.c. when the "God-intoxicated Man," Pharaoh Ikhnaton, tried to usher in an age of humanizing kindness in a sublimely tragic effort. It had been erected in the Federal style replete with red brick colonnades and fireplaces, never used, with alabaster mantles. Architecture as propaganda. There was a Bible prominently displayed in every public room, though Parrish had removed the one from his office and replaced it with a Qu'ran in a gesture of reconciliation.

"Yes, and don't…" he intoned reproachfully lowering his voice to just above a whisper, "…blaspheme! Do you want the religious officer to hear like last time?" "

"No. Of course not." He muttered stuffing a half smoked cigar, which he must have hidden from the custodian in the back of the drawer and forgotten, into his mouth and impatiently lighting it. "Hell no."

"Well…what's the matter with you anyway?" Pursing his bluish lips, "The captain relayed to me that a State Intelligence Officer no less had been following you this morning and reported a public disturbance." He tilted his head back slightly over his shallow rounded shoulders until it teetered like a billiard ball on the edge of a pocket. "I needn't ask if it's true."

"A misunderstanding, nothing more." Parrish slouched back in his chair. Tense fists unfurled with the first drag off the stale cigar until all his fingers were extended and trembled with relief accompanied by a shuddering sigh. "They thought I was somebody else." His mind raced trying in memory to identify the intelligence man in the blur of street faces wondering if he had been seen in his clandestine transaction. "Why do they set those sons of bitches on me?"

"It's not just you." Ariel shrugged awkwardly in an attempt to be sympathetic—walking further into the room, "They follow all of us.

Personally I'm flattered, makes me feel…" He stood staring for a moment waiting for Parrish to relax. "I'm going to put this in my report you know, better watch yourself."

He nodded with his hand curled up against his lower lip filled with contempt for the older man who had made a career out of keeping Parrish from promotion. "Thanks."

"You shouldn't smoke in the building." Ariel's ember eyes sparked desperately with the unexpected opportunity at self-righteousness. It was a windfall. "Ask God to help you quit." He added from the hallway.

In the nights that followed, Parrish began to dream. They were unlike anything he had ever experienced. Before this, he had tried to pull the significance out of real events so that by sheer reason he would understand existence. He had spent his whole life trying to figure out what to do next, weighing possibilities and consequences. Until now. Now there was focus, at least in the chimeras as day subsided in hushed retreat beyond the world of touch. An unnamed yet powerful purpose drew him into the future. This was not something he could easily assimilate into the dark nihilistic simmering of his own life where he perceived time running out and had abandoned patience long ago. It just didn't jive. Parrish kept going because there was nowhere left to turn. Simple. He knew that. Yet in his dreams existence was one long continuous track that inexplicably formed an absolute so complete that it had neither beginning nor end and lifetimes were held apart by only the thinnest membranes. It was through these he tumbled in the slipstream of time.

Over landscapes he could see a shimmering pearlescent glow as if moonlight had shattered into fine crystallized dust and covered everything. The hills, brushed by a gentle vermilion radiance of the last moment's light, stood out in the distance as sentries to the dark hours. Here there were voices, thousands and millions of voices and he heard them all—all at the same time ebbing and flowing in the great sweeping movement of men's souls.

Unable to sleep, he stood at the window sucking on one of his thin cigars. Even a whiskey couldn't help, though he splashed it down anyway in hope that it would at least make him sleepy. He had to smuggle it into the country and risked jail by keeping it. A minor sin. In the street below, a few anonymous figures crossed under the bright lunar light pursued by indistinct shadows. Parrish wondered who they were. He was restless. Disturbed. Something was happening that was beyond his understanding and it left him bewildered and furious. This was not how it was supposed to be.

Parrish didn't believe in love, though he had been brushed by its umbra and had desperately desired to taste from its cauldron no matter what price it extracted—devoting whole epochs of his young life in its pursuit trying to sort out the relationship between it and sex, between sex and spiritual hunger, between restraint and permissiveness—but it had mysteriously escaped his grasp. In the same way he wanted to believe, needed to have faith in something, but in the end could not. Yet he avoided becoming atrophied and filled with rage and discontent as might be imagined of a man to whom such elemental qualities were missing, for they had been replaced by an insatiable longing which was so intrusive and powerful that it determined the flow of his life. A tidal wave as yet undefined that propelled him blindly forward. Only hints of its existence such as his compulsive theological studies and his desire to be a public servant finally convinced him of its veracity and so he began to follow instinctive choices rather than trying to figure out the angle in everything. If it felt right, he went with it. But when even this didn't bring him closer to fulfillment, he scrambled for the logic in an effort to bring his life meaning—to bring it into perspective.

Finally, unexpectedly, it came to him.

He had been urgently dispatched to the ancient city of Al Iskandariyah, Alexandria by the sea, at the order of the Crisis Manager herself in an encrypted communiqué from Washington. The crumpled white paper was still in the pocket of his coat.

V | Silent Fire

It looked as if it should be cool. Indigo nightfall masked shadows and shutters were still drawn. The orb of the moon hovered a silent fire. Night rhythms were retreating, but those of day had yet to begin. Sea breath languished in empty streets. Cooking smells lingered. An impassioned muezzin's voice lofted out over fading stucco walls followed by a holy chorus from a hundred points across the city. Spirits were lost in transmigration.

Suddenly minarets cast long flaming shadows of cerulean blue as fire tore the horizon.

He fumbled with the enigmatic note from the Crisis Manager in the pocket of his coat and felt as if he were crumbling inside, deteriorating at the core from unrealized dreams. It was the way of icebergs. A thousand miles from the arctic when the great ice mountains rolled...that was the way of it. Neither Parrish nor they had a witness. Tinny music sounded from a street vendor's radio as he left Masr train station in a taxi.

"Can't smoke." The driver's dark eyes furled in the mirror.

"Why not?" Parrish shot back rolling the thin cigar between his teeth.

The driver huffed indignantly, "It's illegal."

"Not for me."

"What'ya mean!"

He flashed his embassy ID card. "Diplomatic immunity."

Sailors had spotted flickering lights out along this coast for as far back as memory goes. Yet only one great beacon ever reached completely across the impenetrable, out to where their boats hovered carrying cedar from Lebanon, long before its hills were denuded, or laden with amphorae of wine or olive oil. A likeness cast into the face of a Roman coin is all that is left now of the lighthouse—last of six vanished wonders—felled by massive earthquakes nearly nine hundred years ago. The majestic Pharos Light had risen forty stories from a small rocky island in the harbor at Alexandria for sixteen centuries. It was the tallest structure on earth for over a millennium rivaled only by the great pyramid at Giza. Sunlight by day and a blaze all night reflected off its mysterious mirror; seen, so stories tell, seventy miles out—when the enemy came it is said reflected rays burned the ships before they reached dry land. Stories of sailors. Sailors who rested on the strong back of the sea. Men roaming the decks rubbing their rope burned hands with oil. The sky was black and immutable. Tears sparked in heaven. The water was noiseless. The smell of the brine powerful in the still air. Brine and cumin. Sweat and diesel oil. Men out here sought nothing more than anonymity, nothing more than to turn their backs on where they'd been. And nothing can change that: not the immense desalinization plants looming over the coast; not the millions of electronic waves singing through the ether from wireless phones, satellites, television, radio, short wave and broad band; not the ubiquitous computer that had become an appendage to the human form; not the soft cry of the infant left behind; not the promise once believed in or the parting whisper. Out here men were pretty much the same as they always had been.

He checked in to the Cecil Hotel planning to stay only a night—maybe two. It had operated continuously since 1929, but here it barely had a history. The swarthy man who tended a horse and carriage for tourists before the pillared entrance lived in a building that dated from 1498, the same year the massive Qait-Bay fort was erected on the site of the fallen Pharos Light. Alexandria was flourishing when Amr Ibn-el-'Aas and his Arab forces entered the "city of four thousand palaces" in 641 AD and one of his soldiers recorded that reflected moonlight off white marble made the city so dazzling that a tailor could thread his needle by its light. Here at Raml Station Cleopatra had built the Casesarium to honor her passion for Mark Antony and where, so legend goes, she took her own life. Yet all Napoleon found in 1789 when he arrived was a fishing village and two red granite obelisks bearing the names of ancient kings: Tuthmosis III, Seti I and Ramsesses II. Cleopatra's Needles are gone now: One stands in Central Park in New York City and the other on the Embankment in London.

A wind whipped up from the sea. Parrish could have watched ships driven across the harbor in sheets of spray and loam if he had not been so consumed by his metamorphosis. As it was the whistle of air through a crack in the pane provoked a rage that climaxed with his slamming it twice in futile attempts to silence the annoyance. Glass shattered. The humid breath of nature flooded in. His suitcase lay askew across the bed where he had tossed it. A curtain fluttered boldly as if a battle flag. One hurried phone call and he was gone.

It was earlier that it had begun, a week earlier. A junior operations officer brought it to the attention of the Chief of the Watch.

"You'd better look at this." A young man with cool white skin appeared in a small video window on Viktor Jaraslav's monitor. A document popped up in another window and scrolled across the screen.

Viktor was not looking. "Speak," he said, and the computer drolly recited the report while he foraged through other papers.

"…document is the property of the U.S. Department of State and is classified under sections 708B and 8842.618." The machine's electronic speech suffered from inappropriate emphasis on certain syllables as a result of flawed programming that was supposed to make it sound more human and lively. "It has been reported by reliable sources in Al Mahallah Al Kubra that the outlawed opposition party Samūn will hold a mass demonstration on the week of the twenty-first. This demonstration coincides with the regional meeting of PETEC ministers in Alexandria. Any civil disturbance will have severe economic consequences on the Mideast Free Trade Alliance and…"

Viktor slammed his hand down on the computer keyboard. The voice ceased. He scanned the remainder of the report suppressing his annoyance at being interrupted.

"When did this come in?!"

"Just now."

Squinting up his eyes he peered closely at the type on the screen. "This report's a day old, you sure?"

"Of course!" He replied. Images of the girl fleeted through his head and the young man wondered if his flush was obvious on the Chief's monitor. It had only happened once. To be nearly found out infuriated him.

In his mind the feeling came again. Irresistible. He had leaned her back against the quietly whirring machines sorting incoming data and kissed her and been filled with an intoxicating scent. He remembered the impossible softness of her breast. It made him weak. Out of this weakness the act had come and from the act a demand for repentance. Later he would find many reasons: the unholy presence, the evil he had kept suppressed all his life, the unnatural sexuality of the girl who he should never have consented to working with alone in such a confined space for the long shift. Nothing helped. His sense of degradation was overpowering. It was there, in the heat, with the furnace of the girl's mouth roaring in his ear as she abandoned herself to the grip, at that moment when the report came to his mind. He had received it the preceding day and had forgotten to forward it.

"It may have been an oversight," the young man with cool white skin added as a conciliatory gesture between himself and his conscience.

Viktor Jaraslav acquired the skills of hypochondria one minutia at a time after years of focusing his attention on the infinitesimal details of the department. The obsession with all things biological raised hackles on medical doctors and dampened hopes for any love life whatsoever. His fundamental conflict was the dichotomy of living organisms: One must kill in order to survive. The concept failed to compute in his hyperwired intellectual freeways because of the conviction that man was purely of mind and that his substance lie in individual potential rather than within the elaborate biophysical mix known as "a human." He considered every physiological element of his existence under attack at any given moment by microbes making each day a battle from which he retreated at night exhausted and alone. It was a test of will.

He became a devotee of homeopathy regularly consuming dozens of remedies wrapped in milk sugar coating so that after a while the sweetness alone made him feel better. Stronger. He would hold vitamin tablets outstretched in his sweating palms and require any subordinate close by to press down on his arms…the one that held up best was the one with the element his body needed most to overcome the flood of germs. Soon, however, he began to worry about the air. It was at this phase that he met the Swedish architect.

Integral to the planning of the building was an elaborate air filtration system. It did not actually filter the air, but created it one molecule at a time. Conceived by Viktor Jaraslav as a final defense it was seized upon by the architect as a culmination of his life's work and from their cathartic meeting he labored under divine inspiration developing innovation after innovation until he had amassed sixty-seven patents and had created a building that was more a living organism than a material structure. The expense was justified as defense against biological terrorism. As the ventilation system expelled its synthetic air the building actually seemed to breathe. On quiet nights it could be heard quite plainly, as if a behemoth were hiding just out of sight.

Shortly after they had moved in to the new structure the rumors began. A few staff had fallen in fits of euphoric ecstasy at their workstations speaking in tongues only to be hurried away on stretchers so as not to enflame a delicate situation. Viktor Jaraslav stubbornly refused to admit there was any truth to the rumors and despite the protest of civil rights lawyers he immediately fired any employees of The Watch who intimated there was a presence within the building that caused the faithful mental disturbances. He had long since learned how to manipulate Christian fundamental jargon to his advantage, but he also knew how far he could go. He managed to keep a lid on the situation, but had accepted the Savior as part of his civil service oath and so was bound by a certain moral code himself. But undeniably, it was difficult for anyone of a spiritual nature to be so completely annulled by technology and as a result Viktor engendered a reputation as unpredictable with his staff and it made them feel insecure.

Implications were never lost on the Chief of the Watch. "Karine…" he had spoken casually over the phone, as a prelude, in such a way that his importance would take prominence over all other priorities and would leave the lasting impression of vital information withheld. Now they stood together huddled over the computer monitor their faces bathed in faint blue light while he slowly unraveled the report in its entirety, one screen at a time.

"That's it?"

"Yes."

She breathed silently, so quietly that Viktor kept looking out of the corner of his eye to make sure she was still there and was only certain because of the scent of blue gardenias from her perfume that hung in the air.

"What do you think?" Karine asked.

"Predictable. Destabilize the conference agenda and they'll have created an effect where we can't. But to what end? It's a matter of foreign policy."

"That may be, but I don't see that we have to do anything at this point." She had been waiting for him painted by the whispering light of a single lamp in the corner of her office. He sensed something from the ordered atmosphere and the slight aromatic smell in the air yet was completely surprised when he saw her. Astonished in fact though he suppressed it. Viktor had just assumed he would arrive first in the scenario created by his mind when he placed the call. The illusion of omnipresence was vital to his mantra. Karine, however, slept lightly. All at once she stood hushed before him at full power—thoughts racing from the day before—though it was past midnight she never ended the flow of hours and so each day overlapped one upon the other as a single continuous thread of existence, dates and specific times becoming blurred and superfluous unnecessary for her to resolve problems. She was gazing out the window over a nocturnal Washington glittering with tension and it gave her a hunted look. Even if she dreamt of the wilderness to find sleep, the city was where she always returned.

"You don't? I think it's in our interest..." Viktor sighed, his natural condescension assuming command "...our mandate."

"That's not how I see it Viktor."

"Well...ok...ok", frowning, mashing a lock of hair between thumb and forefinger, "explain it to me then. Perhaps if you explain."

His tone set her teeth on edge. "It's just that it's too obvious, too obvious...that's all."

"I wouldn't make any snap decisions." Viktor was unaccustomed to having his opinion brushed aside in such a casual manner. "Politics are obvious. You'll need to inspect this. You're missing the relative importance" A cloud crossed his face. His throat tightened and his left hand trembled slightly as he relinquished the lock of hair in an attempt to regain some composure.

"It's not that at all Viktor. I don't feel I'm missing anything. It's just that..." she sat down at the desk and folded her hands on the smooth pewter colored surface. "...all things have to be considered."

"Of course. Of course they do. I know that, you don't need to patronize me."

"This is a religious issue."

"No. Just politics. It's just politics!"

"That's not how I see it Viktor." Karine insisted in measured tones her eyes narrowing.

"There is going to be a confrontation and it is going to affect us. The markets will react. We can't ignore it. Better to take action preemptively. That's why I brought it to your attention. I know what's at stake here! Trust me. I can always go to the President."

She did not like to have her authority bucked and so glared at him, but this man was different from the others. He was autonomous in the department and could generate a lot of static and static was something she disliked more than having her authority bucked. "I don't agree with the idea of it."

"Is this crossing other missions?" Viktor demanded after a swirling moment of computation during which his eyes glowed.

"Perhaps."

"You've got to send someone in!"

"I don't have to do anything!" The air suddenly ozone. "And frankly, you scare me a little Viktor. I don't like that. Now listen! I will take this matter up in conference and that is the end of it! Do you understand?"

Viktor did understand, and without a word he spun on his heel and fumed from the office leaving the door wide open as the only insult he could muster in his offended state.

Karine was suddenly chilled. A wave of heat rolled across her body. She closed her eyes to better absorb all of it. A faint smile appeared. The indignation of the man evaporated in her mind. There were no religious ambiguities connected with power and she could indulge in it with complete impunity. She took a pen and began to write on a small sheet of dispatch paper that had the initials KR embossed on it. Not once had she used a computer to initiate a mission, instead something compelled her to set controversial orders down in her own hand. Whether it was an indelible mark of responsibility that she alone was ordering the action to happen or simple human rebellion, one thing was certain, somewhere in the process great tumults of sensuality existed—dangerous amounts—she instinctively knew there were no limits to what she might do to exercise her authority if she had the mandate from higher powers and was only waiting for the opportunity: the exact right moment—all the rest was foreplay.

Across the top of the note she scrawled the name Erskine MacKenzie, remembering her last conversation with him at the embassy dinner when she had been so hot in the stuffy room.

Now she shivered with a distant fury set in motion.

The driver provided by the embassy had taken Parrish east of the city through the old Gate of the Sun to the Al-Haramlek Palace at Moutazah where the government offices were. The building rose out of meticulous gardens and its nineteenth century architecture was an eclectic cross between Arabic and European with red colonial bricks boldly accented by alabaster ones. But despite earlier confirmation by mission staff in Cairo, the Governor declined to meet with him and so he spent a worthless two hours with the Minister of Parks and Public Works.

"I assure you Ambassador McKenzie…"

"Sorry…Assistant Political Officer. Erskine will do nicely."

"Alright…Erskine," he blithely continued, "I assure you no mass gatherings have been certified by my office and there is not the slightest indication of trouble. Not the slightest." He urged Parrish to return to Cairo, that afternoon if possible. A scenario that was later repeated in an audience with the Prefect of Police who even offered to have one of his men personally drive him—"Please, let me do this for you."

Clearly he was an interloper. No one wanted to talk to him.

By late afternoon a slivered moon was fully visible close to the planet Venus. The sky glowered a deep blue in anticipation of night as day held its dry breath when he had entered the Al-Qaed Mosque on his last appointment of an otherwise futile trip. He longed for a strong drink, to spit on the ground, to strike out and run feral in the streets—tired of the runaround, tired of getting no answers and of being spoken to like a sappy tourist he was determined to gain an audience with a powerful local leader of the Ulama. They were, after all, the arbiters of violence.

"*Salaam aleikum.*" The Imam had said.

"*Wa aleikin as-salaam,*" he had replied and began to breathe easier as he was led down a long corridor penetrated high above by shafts of dusky light from narrow windows. The air hung breathless. It smelled of sand. Shuffling feet echoed like murmuring voices. Voices entombed. Centuries of voices all beseeching the unseen power. Thousands of lives congregated here suspended by unfulfilled appeals. Parrish sensed the foreboding presence and it seeped past the ramparts he had erected against feeling. The Imam cast a pensive eye back over his shoulder and continued on without a word. The overwhelming thought of incalculable generations grappling with an elusive faith while caught in the desperation of survival was like searching for a handhold and slipping, like digging a hole in the sand—the multitude seeking yet not finding—the representatives of God wedged inextricably between crimes and perversity, inciting violence and hiding immoral acts. Why, he wondered suddenly, do people never give up, why do they keep on against these odds. And then, just as suddenly, it occurred to him that this was a place of expectation, nothing more than an oasis of hope.

It was faith that kept men going, faith alone.

"My name is Erskine McKenzie. I'm from the United States embassy in Cairo." His voice echoed. "I've come to speak with you."

"Of course." Eyes in turmoil, the Imam stroked his unkempt beard. "I am expecting you, but I'd nearly forgotten. This is official then?" He intoned in precisely elocuted English.

"Yes," Parrish nodded, "But..." he fumbled for a justification to be in the cleric's presence. "I'm really just looking for a dialogue with..."

"A man of God?"

"Exactly."

"You've come to the right place." The Imam's gaze penetrated all social veneers.

The room was warm yet Parrish shivered. He was caught in a slipstream as if all his life he had been destined for this refuge. The two men sat down in ornately crafted high-backed chairs in an office adjacent the mosque. An immense cedar desk lumbered between them on huge faded Turkish Kalims lain across each other—a wooden scent filled the room. Tender light splayed in between the slats of intricately carved screens through which Parrish glimpsed olive trees spreading across a courtyard in a flurry of sage green as shadows fell.

"The Christian Coalition is the largest political party in the United States," he stated frankly not in the mood for diplomacy. "We are a religious nation."

"And you?"

He felt as though he had been caught. The fact was he did not truly believe in anything, nothing at all, and Parrish knew that any religious man worth his salt could tell in an instant he was in self imposed exile.

"No one denies faith," he replied tactfully, "do they? We believe in order to continue. I suppose I'm too cynical for God. I am weak."

"You do remember though? We all experience Allah in our own way. There is no God but God."

"It's advice I'm after Imam. You are an influential man."

"Well then...that's different isn't it?" He smiled.

"We are concerned..." Parrish explained in his best diplomatic lingo that their peoples were strategic partners and, although not really the affair of the United States, "…that instability affects both of our economies especially within the Mideast Free Trade Zone and that any violated contracts involving foreign investment, on which the region has thrived, may result in international lawsuits brought by private companies"… *etcetera et al ad infinitum.* "But, you and I," he intoned anxious for a connection, "serve human need…in many ways we are similar. People rely on us for something they cannot find elsewhere. I've come to you because…"

"I understand perfectly," the man interjected, "no one else will talk to you." As he spoke, the Imam's dark and agitated eyes did not light on anything.

"The Governor…" Parrish ejaculated after a tense moment dreading how the interview might go.

"Ah yes, and the Prefect?"

"He did speak with me. Briefly." He wanted a smoke. God he wanted a smoke so badly his right hand began to shake, so he tapped it on his knee to hide the fact. "In Cairo, the embassy is close to the al-Azhar mosque." He rose and took a few steps across the kalims wishing he were somewhere else—somewhere distant. "I often go there to walk. An extraordinary place. Extraordinary to study there. It must be incredibly inspiring." He darted a look out the window to the enclosed courtyard and sucked in dry air. "I'm at the Cecil Hotel—you know it of course—across from where the great Library was. What have we lost twenty-one centuries ago?" He opened his hands and looked at them. "What wisdom are we missing? Anyway, I love to walk at al-Azhar because it gives me comfort to know someone is looking out for these things. Perhaps I've come to see you because I know you studied there. Perhaps I'm hoping you are a keeper of wisdom and that you can help me with my mission." The thick carpets immediately absorbed his words and silence ensued.

"Perhaps you expect too much."

"The Samūn will demonstrate tomorrow at the start of the PETEC conference," Parrish resolutely continued. "...it won't do any good to deny it like everyone else today. What I say and what you say make little difference to the facts. I am interested...my government is interested in avoiding a civil confrontation. People will have to work and live after tomorrow. We are a global economy. No one is separate any longer. Your problems are our problems. I am instructed to tell you we are prepared to offer concessions—substantial dispensation—I can say nothing within reason is out of the question...if we can come to an agreement. You are my last best hope. Only the Ulama has the clout at this late hour."

"If we agree to your terms."

Parrish nodded.

The Imam rubbed his fingertips together before his face. "You can't possibly understand the Arab unless you have studied the Qur'an. How could you?" He stared intently at Parrish. "You are not a believer. An essential element is missing. And you are not even doing anything about it. How can I accept your help seriously, in good faith—you don't know what we are doing!"

Parrish sighed deeply, so deep that his soul raked across the rocks that lie at the very bottom beneath which no mortal can go. He grasped for strength with the resolute muscularity of a great fish landed upon some deck somewhere dying breathless despite indomitable effort. In his mind, emerald islands glinted against a cool running deep green oxygen filled ocean with orcas and sea lions and cormorants dive-bombing the chop. Huge evergreens weeping with moss loomed out over the shoreline sheltering the tide pools where universes lie undiscovered. The smells of kelp and salt spray intruded: The sounds of Kittiwakes distracted him. He once dreamt of these things as Karine Russo did of mountains and they provided refuge. Now he questioned his own motives. What he was doing so far away from the things he loved roaming the fringe of the desiccated Sahara, where even color fell victim to the intensity of light, he no longer knew. Here where living things were tough and wiry and drawn where they existed at all. Years had evaporated and with each silenced vision it had become more difficult to continue the way he had been. When younger, it was only a matter of refocusing his attention, but at some undefined point he realized that the illusions were being revoked by what powers held sway over such things until at last he didn't even dream of them anymore and only in faint memories could he remember at all. Suddenly, in this old mosque, they had come roaring down to remind him of things he would never possess. He desperately wanted to run, but he sucked his breath in through his teeth and faced the Imam glaring at him from across the desk.

It was precisely then that the extraordinary thing happened and Parrish felt incredibly light. His rancor and disillusionment mysteriously dissipated as smoke and he suddenly bristled enlivened with exhilaration. It had happened so quickly that it left him breathless—beguiled. He gasped. Silently he moved out of his body to a point high in the room where he looked down and saw his mortal self and the Imam clearly facing each other. A dynamic yet subtle force wrenched him, one that he had never before experienced and one that humbled and made him feel meek. He then heard a distant rushing sound like the winds of space and immediately realized he was in the grip of power, true power that was beyond anything he had ever experienced. After the moment passed, things became clearer. Thoughts were more lucid and insightful, the problems of his life seemed to vanish into thin air and became virtually nothing: dark, fatalistic convictions that had dogged him his entire life disappeared. He felt a renewal. A lightness of being—vibrant and clarifying. And all he could do was smile peacefully.

"Do you ridicule the Qur'an!?" The Imam spewed venomously.

Parrish, by some incredible insight, understood the reaction. "You have something you need to tell someone, don't you?"

"What?! Not your business! Not your business at all! What do you mea…?!" The cleric fumed in outrage and rose up from his chair in a flurry of black robes and fury raising one hand above his head as if to strike with a sword. Suddenly he checked himself knowing he must never loose control and act foolishly, it was not the way of the straight path and was a bad example of the faith. So he regained composure by suppressing all emotion. Deeper still were the rivers that no one had ever visited so filled with furtive acts and clandestine meanings that it formed a web of impenetrable unconsciousness, which gave force to his venom and would not let him rest. "Forgive me." He exhorted as his heart beat wildly and his hands shook. "I should show you understanding, you who need faith! That is how we bring about the unseen, know the unknowable. Without it you are nothing. Faith is blood. We are in Allah's hands. He guides us."

"Men must guide themselves: *'Let anyone who will, believe. Let anyone who wishes, disbelieve.'*"

"In-sha Allah!!" The Imam cried out gathering echoes from the high arches glowering over Parrish like a reckless fisherman leaning into the wind above a raging brew of whitewater demanding the fishes come only because of his hunger, commanding obedience of those who by their nature would not obey. "Blasphemer!!" He gasped breathlessly. As he spoke, a look of pain enveloped his eyes and his forehead twisted into a map of wrinkles. Suddenly his lips turned blue and his face pale and with one final wheeze he collapsed on the floor.

The cleric's old secretary, startled by the cry, dropped his work scattering meticulously filed papers across the floor and ran the length of the hall to just outside the office where he hovered at a crack in the door. He could see the Imam lying crumpled on the ground. Everything was still. The American knelt over the body. He clapped his hand to his mouth to stifle a gasp—the old man could not bring himself to enter, but in a strange way it was comforting to see death, as it was something old men knew well. He watched the American, the one he had heard about, watched his every move.

Parrish placed the flat of his palm on the Imam's chest. He perceived nothing. Then he felt the forehead, pulled back the eyelids and opened the mouth. The high-backed ornately carved chair lie broken where he had knocked it aside rushing across the room. Light drifted down from the window. An overwhelming anguish clutched him. The Imam was not breathing.

For a second time he heard the winds of space roaring at his ears, but this time struggled to keep from being sucked up into a spiritual cyclone where he knew his identity would be scattered in a million directions and he would be lost. He would be lost. He braced against the chaos and reached far into it for a lifeline yet knowing there was none—that none existed—knowing that strength was the only virtue. The dark haze he had perceived earlier near the Imam was all around them now. He looked into it. A face looked back, a young woman's face barely visible, bruised with a sheen of sweat and blood. Parrish laid his hands upon the man. A charge of energy raced over the body in little impulses and it made him tingle. He laid his hands upon the man. There was energy and bone and muscle and he probed for the malfunction, the disease, the aberrant genes, the cancer—it was not like the girl, not like her at all with torn flesh and crimson blood, it was not that simple. There was nothing, nothing physical at all.

Then at once he knew. It came to him quiescently appearing in his mind as an apparition, as if he had figured it all out logically.

"Come back!" Parrish commanded firmly with a strong voice breathless and hoarse. He struggled to raise the Imam up cradling the heavy man with both arms. "Come back!! You hear me…I know you can hear me. Come back now!! Right now!!"

Eyelids fluttered. A throttling gasp of air. A cough. After a moment the Imam peered past the heavy lids with yellowed eyes and made small panting noises struggling against fate. He grunted, but could not speak. Astonished, the old secretary watching at the doorway fell to his knees.

"You have something to tell me, something you've never told anyone before."

"I…" Death's footsteps were still too near for the Imam to speak.

"I'm listening." Parrish assured him. "I'm listening." Softly, after a moment he bent close and uttered in great comfort and compassion. "You can tell me your sin. It's safe now."

As if from a great distance the cleric began to recite in the quiet monotony of a distressed life. His breath came in harsh staccato rushes, his gaze was weak. "They were discovered…against the Shari'ah. It was God's will. I am only *His* servant. We are pawns."

"Tell me."

"I could not help it! You can see that, anyone can. Everyone knew. They had been found out, not by me…what could I do?"

"What was it, what was it you did?"

"There were stones. Smooth stones."

"Where?"

"Against the wall. Hot, it was a hot day…oppressively hot. No air. No one could breathe. And the stones were smooth."

"When did this happen?"

"Nearly ten years ago. I was …"

"What?"

"Love cannot be hidden, it is against the law. Allah's law."

"Tell me what it is that no one knows about you?"

"I didn't believe. That I didn't believe. I was an unbeliever, yet I did it anyway. If I had of believed then I could have lived with it, but I lied... "

"I'm listening."

"The girl was only fourteen. She was discovered with a man, lying naked–naked together. This I was told by three reliable sources. Someone saw her, actually saw her with the man. No refuting it. No denial. What could I do? It s the law."

"Yes. Continue."

"She was so lovely. On that afternoon standing against the wall in the pale light...no one moved. The sentence had been passed, the *fatwa*, not by me but by the *mufti*...no one moved."

"What did you do?"

"It was I who acted first. I threw the first stone. Everyone followed my lead. They pelted her young radiance until she was nothing but a torn and bloodied mass. I did it from duty, but I didn't believe. That was my sin. It was with deceit that I killed her." The Imam broke down and sobbed uncontrollably.

But Parrish was unmoved. "What else should I know?"

"Nothing, there is nothing!" The Imam whined closing his eyes against the tears; red, faded and cowering.

"There is something else..."

With a final shuddering sob he confessed, "She was my young daughter!"

He left the Imam then sitting behind the massive desk, head in hands.

At the door the old man stood with an inexpressible look of wonder illuminating his pale, wrinkled face. "How could I believe?" he dropped to his knees. "How could I?" He grasped Parrish's hand and kissed it reverently. "They told me you were the one, how could I believe?"

"Call a doctor." Parrish replied.

VI | The Furies

THE MOON'S NIMBUS GLOWED AT APOGEE, A HALOED PEARL RADIANT against the frightful darkness of interstellar space. Beneath it lie the glittering seas reaching out from Alexandria. Night had come. Lights from freighters twinkled in the haze. Sounds were carried across the harbor on errant wind flurries: clanks and bells, groaning engines, freight shifting in the deep holds, voices of men passing. The timbers of the wharf complained as the swells rose up against them speaking the secret language of the sea that is eternal and not dependant on the technological wonders of men. Mists swirled in the air.

In the bar of the Cecil Hotel was where everything came tumbling down. It held the promise of a catharsis, yet he was deprived of release. Parrish began to shake. He felt hollow and vacant. None of it made any sense—none of it. He ignored the frustrations of his professional life and longed for personal revelation like a man denied breath hungered for air. He nursed a coffee as a surrogate to sin—it was the strongest thing available.

Suddenly, she was there. "You're with the State Department aren't you?"

Parrish struggled to fix his gaze. "Accusing me?"

"Of course not..." She had changed from the faux-Moroccan gossamer-hooded outfit he remembered seeing her wear that morning to simple khakis, a loose flowing silk chemise and a wide translucent silver blue scarf that defied description covering her head. "It's just that I was..."

"I saw you wafting through the lobby this morning."

"Did you?" She tilted her head slightly causing short blonde hair to glide in a silky wave.

"Yes." A scent of rose blended with human sweetness. "I wondered how could anyone be quite so...perfect."

She frowned. "But what I..."

"Well...are you?"

"Am I what?"

"Perfect?"

"Nonsense." She pushed her hair from her eyes, deftly slid into a chair crossing her legs and placed her hands on the table in one fluid motion. "May I sit down? "

The Cecil hotel rode on the fog's wake straddling the pinnacle between what has been and what is to come. It embraced innumerable lives, travelers who had no immediate sense of history and whose place in the world was defined solely by what each had to do to survive. Some honorable, some not—it mattered little, as long as the food was good and every whim was anticipated. The general manager excoriated the staff of one hundred and forty-four, who spoke two-dozen languages and who came from as far as fifty-five miles away to work, into a higher strata of service with the mantra, "Life is it's own reward." Meager wages, however, was his particular credo. And though personalized attention was what the hotel wished to be known for, it was in fact owned by an impersonal global conglomerate based in Cologne and was one of hundreds of properties targeted to turn a tidy profit every quarter no excuses accepted. Greed drove them to the edge of Islamic law to meet that quota and local management would have employed any device necessary, including a fully stocked bar and waitresses in fishnet stockings, if it were not prohibited by the Qu'ran.

"Show business you know." She shrugged.

"Perfection?"

Hanging her bag over the back of the chair she plowed into it. "No...I forgot my phone!"

"Expecting a call?"

"Of course." Digging further. "Perfection does not exist."

"So I've heard."

"Trust me on this one. I'm in the TV news business."

"Ahh..." He looked across the room at the bored, anxious men crammed in a booth littered with coffee cups and ashtrays—the camera crew, "out for blood?"

"Maybe, depends...the man at the desk..."

"How much?"

"What?"

"To get the information."

"What information?"

"On me."

"Oh that!" A smug smile. "Here? You kidding? Just loosened a couple buttons. Will there be any?"

"What?"

"Blood?"

"We of The State Department never speculate..."

"...but advise. So advise me?"

"Our President...you know, the one with an eighty percent approval rating…talks at length in 'realpolitik'. You know the one?"

She waited, "Be cryptic why don't you?"

"They make us study his speeches."

"Hummm…doesn't sound hopeful." She sat motionless for as long as it took the language of birds to pass between them and for the computation of the half-life of certain essential elements to be figured with certainty. "What do you really want?"

"I'd really like a drink." He rejoined wistfully.

"Boy, are you in the wrong place."

"Yes." Parrish sighed the bewildered sigh of the dispossessed in need of all life's fundamentals identical to that of the idle rich in want of nothing.

"My name is Kisa. Kisa Vanyusha.

"Parrish MacKenzie." The woman reached over and throttled his hand like an athlete, except that it was soft and lacked the coldness characteristic of men's handshakes. At least the men Parrish had met recently.

White linen, silver, crystal and a subdued ivory light made the lounge appear elegant. An ancient Steinway languished at one end of the room. Ghosts of Englishmen and waiters in black tie wove their way in between the tiled pillars that rose from the lushly carpeted floor hearkening to the time when WOGs, those other than Caucasian—including Alexandrines— were not allowed. Only in daylight could one see the yellowed walls stained by the nicotine of earlier reckless patrons and the worn seat cushions needing replacement. Discordant scales of Arabic music hung in the air from the casino where gambling was grudgingly allowed as a concession to the corporate owners in lieu of alcohol. However drinks and prostitutes could be had at any hour from some of the more enterprising bellmen who firmly believed in the mantra, "Life is its own reward," and would risk the wrath of the *Shari'ah* for some hard cash from tourists.

"Obviously," she flushed into a smile while nervously tapping her finger on the table and shifted in her chair unable to sit at rest long, "we're here for the same thing." Her eyes were a near peacock-teal blue. Fresh lipstick glinted slightly.

"Not the same reason." Parrish squinted still trying to sort it all out in his mind and she distracted him. "I really can't..."

"No...but we both expect trouble...don't' we?" Kisa hovered with shoulders hunched slightly forward until he could smell the sweetness of her breath, the warm musk rising from her body in the heat of the evening and sensed the outline of her breasts beneath the cool silver-blue silk. "I'll accept a 'no answer' as a yes."

"And you work for...?" He asked desiring and retreating at once.

"Freelancer. 'All Russian TV' gets the broadcast, 'Moskovskie Novosti' gets the online," she added with a sidelong glance and a frown. "Crew's theirs."

"Russian?"

"From Belarus."

"Perfect." He nodded sucking his coffee wary of the blonde woman whom he suspected was not entirely truthful. "No accent."

"Of course not, I'm a professional."

He placed his hands flat upon the table just to feel the cool mass of it perhaps wishing for some of its permanence. Everything was shifting; in flux, in transit, evolving and there was no stable point to cling to. None at all. "What if I didn't want to talk right now?"

"What if I persisted?" She shrugged.

"If I ignored you?"

"What if I didn't care"

"Look...I've had a bad day so far..."

"I know."

"You know?"

"Of course, I'm a professional."

"No..." Shaking his head and holding up open palms he hung suspended for a moment between this realm and the next unsure of which way it would go. "You don't understand. It's not just a bad day, it's..."

"So, get real. Go ahead, hit me."

Her scent and the sound of her voice..."What do you want anyway?"

"It's more like what I need." She exhaled with no small amount of disgust slouching back in the chair.

"What...?"

One of the cameramen materialized and stood lurking above them. "Kisa, we're heading to our rooms." He snubbed out a cigarette in the ashtray. "Hey..." he nodded at Parrish, "...meet you in the lobby, say...five AM? Should give us time to catch the kitchen setting up don't you think. Pastry chef comes on earlier I understand, but don't think anything worth shooting will happen. And we've got to see the light, it's very important I see the light in the dining room before the spot. Remember that last time—light was blue. I can't deal with that again. Makes eggs look green. Can't deal with it. No blue light. Manager said they'd do a full brunch spread for us. Sounds great huh? OK?"

"Five AM?" Parrish said. "Nice work."

"Has perks." Kisa mumbled face in hands. "This isn't one."

"So, we're OK? What?"

"OK, OK! Sure, fine. Five-thirty."

"Five! Hey..." The cameraman pointed at Parrish as he walked away. "Five, not five-thirty. See you then."

"You're interviewing the pastry chef?"

"No. Never mind. I don't want to talk about it right now."

"Blue eggs?"

"Alright. Alright. I'm The Travel Girl."

"You're what?"

She looked directly into his eyes with an unoccupied exasperation. "The Travel Girl."

"What's that?"

"You know…when I told you I was a freelancer?"

"Yea…?"

"Well, that's true but…I don't really do hard news. I'm like…a travel writer."

"A travel writer?"

"That's right. I cover destinations."

"Destinations?"

"Of course. Resorts. Restaurants. Vacation destinations. I bet you didn't know that the food here is very highly rated. Four stars, in case you wanted to know! Some people want to know these things!"

"No, I didn't know that."

"See. There. Some people want to know these things—especially the Russians. They got so sick of the black sea, now they travel like…like…I dunno! Like geese!"

"So… what is it that you need?"

"One good story. I need just one god damn great angle I can grab with both hands, sink my nails into and let it shake the hell out of me all through the media like the tail of a dog…you know? Perfect lasts until your hour is passed. Then you're…history and…you've got one chance. That's it. Just one."

"This yours?"

"Maybe. Is it?"

There was a pause in the conversation as they both just looked at each other. "So, tell me…what do you really want?"

Kisa frowned. Somewhere leaves rustled. Music from the other room suddenly penetrated the chrysalis of their conversation. A singer's bittersweet voice overcome with hunger and wishes soared out over the heads of people and into the night where a moon was serrated with cloud and no one was listening. It was a private lament: one for all the men ruined by war, for all the loves squandered before they were realized, for all the greatness desired that can never be. It was a song of coming to terms with failures, a cleansing and a self-forgiveness and a longing all packed tightly in a few moments release. Parrish could not explain how it had happened. It was as if he had fallen through the thin illusion of his life and floundered wildly until now—he found a lifeline. He could not explain it.

Later that night she stood in the dark at the broken window in his hotel room while he leaned against the door and witnessed the nude figure glowing pearlescent with moonlight. Humid wind rushed in through the gaping hole the missing pane had left and caressed her face sweeping fine blonde hair back in undulating waves. Moments before her mouth had devoured his sweetly leaving him, King of the Cynics, shattered with reaching and drawing back, wanting and denying all at once. Her taste would not leave even though he slept.

"No!" Kisa beckoned facing him from the center of the room; pale light flickered across her small breasts. The muscles corded in her arms as she struggled to push him away.

Parrish dropped weakly to his knees and leaned closer until he could smell her—the musty earth. He unconscionably wished to violate her, to absorb her completely until there was absolutely nothing left but echoes of sighs and fingerprints in the air. Lips brushed the smooth flat plain between navel and where nearly straight blonde hair ran in a river to the point where her legs met. Flesh burned him. He tasted her. Ran his tongue down through fur until he could bear it no more and slid his arms up the back side of smooth legs penetrating her wildly. She did not move against his movements, but flexed all her muscles. He abandoned himself. No words passed between them. They did not speak. Flesh moved violently against flesh. Like animals: untamed, insatiable and vulgar. Hearts raced uncontrolled. Her single moan was almost inaudible. Almost real. She cursed him as he slept while in his dreams darkness grew deeper.

Parrish snubbed out his small cigar watching the smoke's final vestige curl into the faint light. The smell of sex lingered. Kisa rolled across him and murmuring unintelligibly slid a hand deftly across his stomach down between the legs where she cupped him in her smooth palm. "I'd like to fall asleep with you inside me." Her breath made him hurt. She moved with imperceptible gentleness.

He languished between the world of men and the world of dreams. He was stricken with pain, though knew not its source—as if some agreement had been broken, some unrevealed moral code violated for which he now suffered at slumber's edge. It was the mystery that had always been in his life: The obscure demarcation between right and wrong that offered him no absolute guarantees. So he drifted on trains with no names bound for places unknown. Tawny maned lions came into his dark reveries prancing in rings with glowing eyes. Sleep that sound should have been a warning. Alarms should have sounded. One can never retreat from the harshness of life that deeply, that resolutely. It leaves one exposed and vulnerable. Parrish knew this, all of it, but had abandoned caution with her first touch.

Enormous hands gripped tightly together then released. Nervous hands. Hands grappling with the responsibility of commitment. An artist would have watched silently knowing hands mirror the spirit and dashed off pencil studies freezing the moment in time for the mood was fleeting—volatile. Far above, in the deep of the sky swirled inconsolable winds, lost siroccos in search of a cause to champion. They moaned through the tiles of the roof.

An aura of impending brilliance encircled him now spiraling upward like twin winnowing snakes trying to escape destiny. It had come with his decision. The event imparted a subtle radiance to deeply etched lines in his face that he referred to as campaign tracks—wishing somehow he had not grown older and could have escaped the dues he owed for a little longer. Like icy air it made his cheeks ruddy. Misgivings had been set aside. Forgotten. His mind was clear. Once resolved nothing between the earth and sky could change him. It was a holy mission founded on his belief that life, the awareness of being alive, was played out solely in the mind. All else in the universe materialized afterward to populate the vision. Everything came with faith.

To this end, they had all undergone rituals of purification, had bared their transgressions before Allah in an effort to achieve humility and Jibril Ben Jabbar Riyadh had recited the entire Qur'an, which he had committed to memory at a young age, before his staff without the aid of any written materials as an act of faith. Servants had not been allowed out nor any unauthorized visitors in. A story had been leaked to the press that the great General, the protector of mosques, was ill in hope that would explain the constant stream of military advisors coming and going at all hours without arousing suspicion. Jibril himself, however, felt detached, floating as he walked, euphoric with devotion. For him, it was the supreme moment. After this he would certainly be recognized as "The Commander of the Faithful", *Mufti* of *dar al-Islam* despite the wrongs done to him by his enemies and his loss of prestige by reason of irresponsible slander.

"We still have not resolved the issue of Azhara." A swarthy mustached Colonel Hasan Mawdudi sat uncomfortably attentive at one end of an overstuffed couch. White lace cloth was laid across the sofa's arms and back. One hand he rested on his knee, the other lightly on the couch.

"I know." Jibril replied rifling through a fistful of communiqués shoved at him by a spindly man in stiff pressed khaki with wet perspiration marks beneath the arms who had slipped unannounced into the room. The razor edge creases in the man's trousers cut through the air as he passed. As soon as that one departed another appeared to request a signature—his shoes spit shined in the old fashioned way: polished to a luster, doused with lighter fluid and briefly set afire, then buffed again to a hard, brilliant gloss. "I know."

"It's not as if she was your enemy."

Jibril Ben Jabbar cast a sober look in the general direction of Colonel Mawdudi, but saw nothing of the present. His point of view was shifting. He could not get a perspective on anything. Little incidentals were suspended beyond his memory and he was annoyed, for instance, to set something down and a moment later forget where it was—or even that he had possessed it. He fluctuated between the ecstatic euphoria of a holy mission and the clinging guilt of betrayal. "What man knows his own mysteries?" He mused in an effort at self-reconciliation and accepted the state as a personal transition. Social change placed extraordinary demands on men; it was a test of character, a price to be willingly paid.

A servant appeared. In one hand he balanced a silver tray filigreed with an intricate enameled design. He offered the white cup and saucer. Jibril turned on his heel and lifted the coffee with extreme care from its resting place holding it nimbly in his great maw ignoring the man completely. The heady aroma of a Turkish brew laced with cardamom made his nostrils flare in anticipation. He brushed the edge of the cup with his thick black mustache to more fully experience the bouquet. "Must be the weather." He took a first sip. "The rain and soil are quite different… minerals in the wind. African coffee will never match the beans of Suluwasi, Sumatra or Celebes. What do you think? Are you a coffee drinker Colonel Mawdudi?"

"Sorry to say I am not." The bemused colonel replied unable to hide the derision in his voice.

"Ha! That explains it then."

"Explains what?"

Jibril turned his back. "Your lackadaisical attitude toward Alexandria."

The hair on the back of the colonel's neck stood straight up. He rose deliberately, yet cautiously, and spoke through a vacant smile. "I am not lackadaisical about anything."

"That so?"

"Yes."

"There are minerals in coffee, lots of minerals. I can taste them personally but I am extremely sensitive to such things. I can feel the body absorb minerals from the air, in the wind at the shore where they are especially strong. What do you make of that?"

"That's very interesting."

"Of course it is." He stared at the younger man pensively while rubbing his lower lip with a huge index finger. "And that's precisely why we need Alexandria. Precisely. Do you question me?"

Colonel Mawdudi's ears were hot and red. "I don't follow…"

"You don't…?!" The mollified Colonel was cut short by his bark. "How can you presume?!" Jibril shouted. "Soldiers attain unattainables!" He bellowed. "Achieve unreachables! That…that is what separates them from normal men!"

"Sir." Colonel Mawdudi snapped to attention so rapidly the khaki fabric of his uniform pulling taut popped like tiny firecrackers and his eyes became empty beacons awaiting light.

"Now," There was silence while Jibril filled his chest with oxygen taking serene pleasure in the strength his body still possessed and let his anger dissipate with a long sigh, "perhaps you will tell me when this will be accomplished." Then, calmly, the white cup was raised to his lips and he drank the hot bittersweet brew.

Colonel Hasan Mawdudi, chiseled in the air as a winged Persian warrior in granite bas-relief, hated the thought of violence. The dichotomy had seeped into his fragile beliefs and, being a military man, doubt denied sleep causing a great crisis in his personal universe. This was the flaw that had kept him from advancing through the ranks any further and the one hidden weakness that Jibril perceived and was compelled to prod in an effort at rehabilitation—such as animals do to the ill and infirm of their species.

"We only await your word," the Colonel deferred responsibility to a higher authority.

"Then you have it."

"Though she is there?" His lips did not move except for the slightest tremble.

"Those who love the life of this world more than the Hereafter, who hinder from the Path of Allah and seek therein something crooked: they are astray by a long distance."

"In-sha Allah." The Colonel whispered as if a sad wind had just passed through pines overhead.

The city of the thousand minarets dominated the Nile in a raucous tumble of stone and concrete petrified where it was tossed by each successive generation. Permanent rings testified to their passings. Life was fragile at the edge of the Sahara. Millions of remorseless survivors drifted in an uneasy sleep. The moon, too, was restless in its descent. Merchant stalls at Khan el-Khalili, the caravansary built in 1382 by the Emir Djaharks el-Khalili in the heart of the Fatimid City, were sealed to the night. Canvas covering the streets rustled occasionally when an errant breeze hit. Tourists had fled. Locals, who shopped to the North and West where prices were lower, had passed oblivious through the original gate midway down Sikkit al-Badistan and some took refuge at the El-Fushwa Café on a narrow adjacent street. One could pick them out easily because only Cairenes had mastered the art of blowing aside light grounds in the foam on Turkish coffee, disguising it as a cooling gesture, and avoiding the heavy sediment at the bottom of the cup. Discos and casinos were abandoned. Cleaning crews from restaurants had evaporated. Only a few Tourist Police in their green armbands lingered at pricey hotels. Nobody was abroad that night.

Nobody except overzealous men at the compound, and they were cloaked with anonymity. In darkness events escalated. They boiled into a fever that no one had anticipated when first the plan was hatched. Men were caught up in its inexorable flow. Inside cool walls blue light flickered. Young men sat riveted to flat screen monitors—smooth faces mirroring their pale electronic glow. A flurry of messengers wove their way around agitated commanders. Cell phones were bleeping. Ringing. Buzzing. They studied images that flitted by on screens in real time, as events occurred—like a soccer match witnessed by testosterone imbued officers who chortled out their exhilaration or spat their rage between moments of rapt silence. Everything was unreal like news from another star where no one ever willingly expected to go.

It was earlier in the evening however, earlier that it had happened. Quarter past seven when the heat lingering from the day was beginning to grow tangible and arcs of moonlight began to draw tattoos on stone floors. Cairo pulsated in fervor with the rhythm of humans protesting the impossible struggle. Easterlies brushed in off the Sahara making everything brittle and impermanent. Music rose up out of the City of the Dead as cooking stoves were lit.

"They're moving." A young man sputtered adding to the muted cauldron of excitement as if faith was suddenly giving way to the undeniable.

Voices answered.

"Here we go…"

"Watch out! Cheee…! Watch out there…watch out!!"

"Fix the gain on that! Hurry!"

"Satellite lead time? How much, how much time?"

Jibril observed the indistinct images shimmering in grays and pale glowing greens. Infrared cameras captured the action and fed satellites, which they had rented bandwidth on just for this night. Figures scurried, running, blurred yet unmistakably military—their nervous movements deliberate and threatening. Over phones, officers barked orders wagging their fingers at the tiny images on screens, and though the action now was indisputable and he knew his terrible purpose was finally in motion, he could not completely come to grips with it. Jibril could not enter the virtual world since it required severing ties to this one, bonds some men had neglected to forge, but that he had welded with blood and fury.

"Why…" he pontificated to the tech officer in charge of intranet protocol, satellite uplinks and network administration, "if you can't confront a man nose to nose…close enough to smell him…well, you should question your own worth." His own faults induced knots in his stomach and caused him to reflect on vacant arenas of the past where too many times he had failed to live up to his own standards and felt remorse for things he had been compelled to do and then had difficulty coming to terms with. "A soldier should touch blood. It should be hard for him to kill. Extremely difficult. That…that is what separates him from normal men!"

A gentle tug at his sleeve. "There is someone to see you." The fat old woman was clad head to toe in a black *abeya* and *hijab*, only eyes were visible revealing all that anyone would ever know of her.

"You can see I am busy." Jibril replied without looking as if to a mate whose constant presence had evolved into a phenomenon of nature and no longer required acknowledgement.

"That may be," the woman quipped while walking away, "but he is in your study."

"Send him away!"

"He is an Imam." She taunted from down the hall.

"I don't care!"

Moments later Jibril faced the man in his study, when the woman was well out of sight, and to his annoyance trembled as he spoke staggering under the conflux of ambition and faith and guilt.

"What is it you wish Imam?"

An unruly stare greeted him from behind a tousled beard. "The will of Allah."

"Naturally," Jibril nodded unmoved. "I am General Riyadh." No answer was forthcoming. "And you…?"

"Imam Abd Al-Faraq." The cleric stood as if braced against some inner gale.

"What brings you to me?"

"A long road from the Al-Qaed Mosque in Alexandria."

"Alexandria…!" He chortled in astonishment. No one knew of Alexandria, no one outside the compound. "No offense…" his eyes narrowing to mere slits, "I would ask you to stay, but I am…" he edged toward the door hissing, "…pressed for time."

"I know. I know you are…but Alexandria cares nothing for generals. Listen!" He pointed his long finger out into the encroaching night. "Do you hear? The fortunes of battle are sand. Listen. Caesar spoke of it…a hill, sudden ground gained or lost, a lame horse, opportunity…an overlooked detail perhaps, flagging emotions, a loss of spirit…all fate even though thousands clambered to battle without question for him wishing only a salute in return. But Alexandria cares nothing for generals. Hot on the heels of brilliant victories over Pompey–who was beheaded by Alexandrines–even Caesar was nearly killed! …poisoned the water in cisterns under the city blocking its flow from the Nile. Egyptians and Roman expatriates did it. He fled to the harbor where his ship sank beneath him under the weight of the desperate scrabbling aboard to escape those on shore. There the great Caesar swam for his life. No… Alexandria cares nothing for generals."

"Is that so?" He pondered. "I sense there is a riddle here," unsure of what he had just heard, "but cannot guess its meaning and would appreciate it if you'd come to the point! *Malesh*, come back some other time when I can give you my full attention." He started for the door.

"The last thing I remember is lying on the floor of my office." The Imam clutched the bridge of his nose with two fingers and confessed. "I don't know why I'm here. I don't know why."

Jibril stopped and snatched the phone up off the receiver. It slipped in his palm, which was sweating as it did when he was disturbed.

"No!" The Imam leapt across the few feet between them and hovered with his hand inches above the General's. "Wait! I know what you think, but it isn't true, it isn't! I have spoken with Him! He has come!"

Now Jibril held the phone absolutely still. Like a great sea eagle soaring at impossible altitudes he was deafened by the roar of wind: piercing the sky at the blue edge, forsaken yet still on the hunt with eye and heart. Something had been clarified he could not name, (yet always knew was there), and then had vanished before he realized its meaning. The spirit voice that sounded for an instant…now gone. So he returned to the inner struggle against enemies he had always perceived around him. This he understood. Even in the act of ordering death he found a beautiful sadness, a sweetness that forced him to regret yet gave him pride from the strength he possessed to carry through. He had spat out like an epithet, "…I am al-Mahdi." And let it be implied to his men that he acted on the will of Allah unlike a "rightly guided man" who acted out of an intellectual understanding brought on by religious training. He wanted to be known by his men as this and then they would do the terrible things obligation demanded without complaint.

Only a short distance away Colonel Mawdudi spoke into a small cellular phone that was lost within the great hand held close to his ear. His voice was all business. Resolute like gravel yet tainted with a melancholy that had its source in an earlier life—it had been his companion for as long as he could remember. He loathed violence yet once again was using it as a solvent against the unmoving social landscape, which he had witnessed overwhelming men's best efforts—despite the ostentatious rich whom he knew were extemporaneous to real life. His was a personal mission. Change was his ensign, change at any cost. With his comrades and his slogan, he was a tribe with a flag though he struggled to find a compromise between who he really was and what crimes he would commit for his purpose. Many futile years had been consumed before he fully understood that hope was more valuable than security, but by then it was too late. If indeed there were such things as soldiers of hope, if he could only believe that…then he unleashed them tonight upon beautiful Alexandria by the sea. All across North Africa a cyclone of young men swept the hidden recesses of night. They, eager to grapple with the furies—now fuming up in roiling clouds. Some had waited their whole lives for this moment having lost track of time in the monotony of hopelessness as their existence bled from one day to the next obscuring all thought of accomplishment. For others, it was part of the great mandala as they ricocheted off whatever killing field would give vent to their rage. No one questioned the dark emotions obvious in their eyes since the beginning because no one could face them. Without understanding, there was no hope.

The crucible within which power has always turned materialized once more upon the human plain: as if by a conjurer's blackest magic, as if the veil between it and us was torn aside in the fusillade of the encroaching tempest revealing what has always been there. A thinly disguised whore painted many times in feeble attempts at acceptability— always recognizable. Men make inner preparations for its coming, even if they natter and bitch and scream and yell like crazed evangelists thumping Bibles unintelligibly on street corners when it arrives. War is welcomed as a cleansing by fire. One of the virtues. Perhaps it is still thought of as a weeding out of the genetically infirm, of the morally weak, those without the grit to be of any social value to save the rest of us from their inferior offspring muddying the blood. There are those who have taken to leaping off high bridges or buildings their feet tied to giant rubber bands; or casting themselves from airplanes diving into the wind; or braving megamillion dollar amusement park rides, where occasionally someone gets killed even though the hapless victims are strapped down and surrounded with the most sophisticated safety system career-amusement-park-engineer-gurus can devise—unlike the roller coaster bravados of the twentieth century, the wiry young man clad in jeans and white Jockey t-shirt with a pack of Luckys rolled up in his sleeve who stood to ride the speeding cars down the steepest shoot only to have his head knocked off by an unforeseen low beam. Many are tested by watching others' exploits on television. Some are challenged in their imagination only. For most though, the act of staying alive is battle enough.

But secretly, all long for the true test on the field of valor where one finds out if he has more mettle in his bosom than tongue in his head.

"Who has come?" Jibril asked the Imam mystified.

"The hidden one."

"Aughh…! A myth!" He considered the Imam with suppressed contempt boiling around him. "You've come to me with a myth! Look…" He twirled his right hand in irritated little circles above his head seeking the exact right way to put it as he replaced the phone to its cradle, "I'm busy! Far too busy for this!"

"I know you are. I know. It's a little vague to me also."

"No, that's not how it is. I am just too busy!"

The beard splayed out in a sleek windswept gray as if the Imam had been cast out of ice by the fires of nature in a storm. Unearthly eyes breached the distance between them like sly leviathans disguised as merely fog and wisps. "Azhara. She will have seen him too."

"My daughter?" Jibril ejaculated. "Azhara? Did you speak with her in Alexandria? Did she send you?!"

"No." The Imam replied. "But I know something of daughters."

"Are you part of her mischief? Allah, give me strength! Did she send you?"

"There is a man who has professed faith all his life. A man of the straight path, yet he never once realized what his covenant with Allah had truly meant. If he were to be judged by his actions—which I suppose is the only judgment possible—if you were the judge for example, what would you make of him?"

"I'd say he was worthless!"

"I confess. I never embraced the significance of my covenant with Allah, never realized it until I spoke with Him. The myth, as you call him, has come like they said he would and neither of us can deny Him—though I am as surprised as you since I never truly believed. But now… maybe I never truly believed in anything. The Twelfth Imam is not a myth…I have seen him. Touched him. So, here I am as a messenger, or perhaps I am the message itself because like you I had a daughter."

Towering above him the great general, the Commander of the Faithful, the believer-president-to-be was unexpectedly stricken with pathos for the old man—an obvious sufferer of dementia. Almsgiving, he knew well, was a pillar of the faith. "Are you alright?" He knelt beside the Imam with one hand resting on his arm. "You look ill."

"I am beyond illness.

"You are troubled. I can see that." As he drew close to the old Imam Jibril saw the dichotomy in him: that of a defrocked priest who desperately needed absolution yet was equally as anxious to lessen his transgressions by making less of those he had transgressed against so that in the end neither redemption nor justification could be had at any price. The absolute hopelessness of it propelled him as it had time and again throughout his life. "What would you have me do?"

Somewhere in the far distance, on the edge of the ionosphere where men's influence mingled with that of spirits, was a disturbance. Perhaps it was only a slight movement of electrically charged particles in those regions affected most by solar activity–immense thermonuclear explosions deep within the sun sending debris millions of miles into the solar system reaching the edge of our blue planet to slice up a sliver of the weak atmosphere for the cosmic soup. Perhaps it was the lamentation of a soul who had become lost. Perhaps it was a cry of desperation that pealed like Christmas bells in the heavens and caromed down through the murky layers of the ether into the North African night where darkness seeped into every crevasse and every heart leaving the impress of a deep and inconsolable longing like bitter almonds. And then the wind came, as if the breath of a distant phantom, to scour the ragged night where unholy warriors flew.

The compound, which had been a part of the old city long before the Europeans came or even remembered that Egypt existed, shuddered—an event that in ancient times would have brought everything to an unnatural stillness in this land, in this city of Al-Qāhirah. It would have caused children's fragile attention to sweep seeking danger, (their passage to the spirit world of *Tuat* from their last life only too near). Normally resilient men would fill the night with uneasy glances knowing that vigilance and a willingness to fight back were the only price yet stymied by their uselessness bodies. Women would withdraw preparing for the judgment they had evaded at the *Hall of The Two Truths*. They would wonder at their feelings of guilt after having been exonerated once—and their intolerance of others. They would lie awake seeking resolution for some unknown mystery that made them shudder with terror and they would ponder the meaning of help. Why did night winds bring the judges if they were purified? They must be looking for someone. So the people would have prayed: supplications would have flown on the wind to Amkhaibitu the eater of ghosts; Uatchnesert the green flame; Setqesu the bone breaker; Herfhaf, he with his face behind him; Maatifemtes, he with two eyes as knives...and all the others. Even the kings of Egypt would have rustled in their beds. Even Pharaohs.

Jibril, however, only shivered as if a tremor had passed through the ether surrounding him that he barely perceived. Yet entombed in that moment was the thought that something was terribly wrong, and had been amiss for so long no one in living memory could recall or even locate a trace of history of when it was right—nonetheless by some innate wisdom he knew as one knows beyond reason the truth from the lie. Perhaps it is only this remnant of ability in men that gives us any hope, any faint hope at all.

"What would you have me do?" He demanded irritated now by these errant longings.

"Try and stop the wind."

"You can't hinder it from blowing."

"Men are great seekers."

"They can't find things that don't exist."

"I have seen him, touched him."

"A myth! I gave up on myths long…"

"Belief you mean! You have given up on things you can't touch just as I had."

"Nonsense! I am the believer! Faith takes power from me! Now old man, out of respect for your calling I will not have you dumped into the street, though I am inclined in that direction—but you have pressed your luck so far. It is through! I am a man of the straight path, and you knew that. I am full of charity, and you knew that. Now you go back to where you came from and tell whoever sent you that I will be the Believer President and do not take advantage of me again!"

"Ohhh…he is here to destroy you." He sputtered beyond himself. "It's clear now." His eyes darted around the room a caged panther." I was mistaken." The Imam stood to leave in a flurry of black robes now anxious.

"What now?"

But the Imam fled down the hall and out into the foyer from where the plump woman in the black *abeya* had led him in. "It is written?" He called without looking back.

"This old anvil has broken many hammers!" He barked after the Imam in frustration. "Many damn you! Your myth will not be my undoing! I am the believer Imam Abd Al-Faraq you old fool!"

At just that moment Colonel Mawdudi appeared in the doorway, cell phone still glued to his palm. "Then you've heard?"

Jibril did not break his hollow gaze down the hall where the imam had vanished. "Heard? Heard what Mawdudi? Nonsense from Alexandria because you failed in your duty is what I've heard!"

"That is not..." The colonel flushed red and drew his lips into a pale, thin line, but then got a grip by holding his breath until he began to feel dizzy and continued. " Abd Al-Faraq, the great Imam from Al-Qaed Mosque is what I was referring to. You must have heard, you spoke his name."

"What? What have I heard?"

"That he died of course. I thought you knew."

"What do you mean died?"

"Earlier today. We just received word from a field commander. The facts aren't clear. Lots of confusion about the circumstances–rumor is he killed himself."

"Not possible!" Jibril ejaculated.

"Yes. It's hard to believe."

"No! That's not what I mean–I spoke with him!"

"I'm sorry sir to have assumed you'd been told." Colonel Mawdudi stiffened. "I didn't know you knew him."

"What I mean is...I just saw him! I...we spoke. He was..." But the colonel's cell phone interrupted and raising one finger before he placed the great maw of a hand concealing the tiny device to his ear he disappeared into the chaos once more leaving the Commander of the Faithful and Protector of Mosques alone.

VII | MEN WITH GUNS

"CLOSE YOUR EYES." A BREATHLESS WHISPER, THEN SILENCE. "WHAT do you see?" Said the woman. But it was earlier that the racing Saluki had come to her. Earlier than the frightened words that now faded into memory. Human thunder could be heard in the distance. A terrible sound. Her delicate brown fingers adorned with intricate henna designs painted the air and she remembered from behind closed eyes. Silver rings glinted and then suddenly were dull in the low light. Restless hands went limp at her side. "She sleeps." Said the whisper. "Help will come. In-sha Allah. Help will come." In dreams her Saluki bounded across the twilight chasing a small, wily rabbit the way it used to be.

"Azhara!" She remembered her father's booming voice. "Come here, come...come..." The ambassador from the United States, Colin Murdoch, stood before him a monochromatic statue completely motionless except for his hands, which were quivering. "My daughter," he pronounced as he grasped her shoulders so hard it hurt, "my young daughter who is leaving for the university next month will have your job! Why? Because we are held captive to witnessing your incompetent failures while you create great operatic dramas for the media to justify them—I don't know! Psychotics run amuck in the streets and you spend millions trying to understand their sociopolitical religious motivation—as if madness had a plan! That's why they call crazy people crazy! Better make your retirement plans early, she'll have your job!" And then she slept.

It was earlier still when Ishaq Sadek had followed her down the Cairo to Alexandria Agricultural road winding through the small towns of the Nile delta in the inconceivable rain. The four-lane asphalt Desert Road was faster and though 220 km long one could make it in three hours. There were no traffic rules out there and it was dark at night–no lights at all. Beginning at Giza near the northwest corner of Cairo's ring road–unsuccessfully built encircling Cairo to contain its urban sprawl–and terminating in Alexandria. Later he would wonder if she had taken the Desert Road instead and had seen the military vehicles that night if things would have been different. Surely they would have been for him. He had only been prepared for a short trip through chaotic streets pondering what a wealthy young woman might be up to in the city. If he were lucky he'd find her and a swarthy lover in some dingy hotel room and could email the digital images to his employer. Ishaq could never have imagined where the night would take him.

"Those who truly support human rights must demand secular societies in the Middle East." Azhara aflame had burned with an unexpected inner fire for the last hour on the podium whose polished red-cedar sides glowed in the poorly lit room. "I believe in the separation of religion from the state, from education, and from a citizen's identity. Religion is a private affair despite a history of its use by corrupt regimes." The night flowed like a river through the small theater-like room with impossibly high ceilings carrying moisture, as if from the Nile, imbuing everyone present with life while darkness left a tinge of foreboding. It was a nexus between what had been and what wishes these women had for the future. The air was fused with anticipation. "To impose a veil on a minor is to violate her, to use her body, to define it as a sexual object for men… the shame of inhabiting a body full of shame, a veiled body, the anguish of inhabiting a body full of guilt–guilty of merely existing. I am ashamed before Allah."

Ishaq had run the course of the long Agricultural Road from Cairo into the night tide of the delta. Headlights brushed eerily against palms shrouded with dark and mist at roadside and farmlands were glimpsed as the moon's nimbus glowed down when passing from one cloud to the next. It was unusually cold and he cursed for not having the heater core fixed when it went bad a couple years ago leaving him this rare night shivering with no heat. Mysteriously, somewhere during the journey, the disquiet had begun causing him to figure incessantly on where the hell they were going until his nerves were completely shot. Something was not right–he worried the outcome would not be as he expected. He turned when she had turned and doggedly kept behind her pressed to utilize all his vast surveillance skills to remain invisible for the entire drive. Initially he was surprised when she ducked into the old hotel, but sighed with relief and smiled at the realization the swarthy lover may turn up after all. But now his shock surprised him more. He had become inured to death and the poverty of the streets of Cairo, but not to a sea of women such as lay before him gathered to protest. From his hidden view in the foyer behind latticework and filigree he inhaled the scent of women, heard the voices of women; more women than he had ever seen gathered in one place in his entire life.

"Burqa-clad, veiled women and girls, beheadings, stonings to death, floggings, child sexual abuse in the name of marriage and sexual apartheid are only the most brutal and visible aspects of our rightlessness and third class citizen status in the Middle East!" The crowd rose in searing emotion as if wild captive birds were suddenly set free and overwhelmed Azhara in trilling and applause; Ishaq slunk down deeper into his hiding place incredulous at being drawn into this lair of unbelievers and cursing his bad luck. "Apologists for Islam say that Islamic rules and laws practiced in the Middle East are not following the true precepts of Islam." Her clear voice caromed off the bare walls. "They state that we must separate Islam from the practice of Islamic governments and movements. However, the brutality and violence meted out against women and girls are nothing other than Islam itself. Islam has wreaked more havoc, massacred more women, and committed more holocausts than can be denied with such feeble defenses. All that is needed for evil to succeed is to do nothing. It is the outrage of this century!" The room burst into a spontaneous, chaotic cheering.

It was just then Ishaq had the same uneasiness and dread he had felt on the journey from Cairo. Sounds became dull and muted. Suddenly alone. He shivered with subconscious chills. His eyes darted searching for what he did not know–only that it was tactile; the cold metallic taste in his mouth, the clammy perspiration, the vacant feeling in his stomach. The women would not cease. Would not keep still. All his senses were on alert at that moment. His keenly honed experience gripped him in its fist. He heard footsteps. Footsteps of men.

In the umbra of darkness they passed him by. Shadows racing, stealth and fury, evil on the wing. Blood surged from his thundering heart as he sank in the blackness searching in panic for escape. No one would believe him, his words would be as worthless as his life when his head was severed from his body in shame and failure in the public square for all to witness. So when they had passed he made a daring break neither looking left nor right but myopically focusing on his exit point…and he had nearly reached it too, unseen, unnoticed, nearly free when for unknown reasons he stopped cold. There was screaming. His hearing had suddenly become acute and the cacophony of the moment was upon him. Screaming. He turned and saw the soldiers falling on the women. They were tearing into them with batons and hands flailing and the women were falling on the battlefield mercilessly trampled over by the boots of men. One was drug back by her arms the aggressors tearing her blouse off hands groping, others kicking her–one young soldier jumped and landed with both feet on her abdomen with a look of absolute glee on his face. Even at his distance in the symphony of terror he could hear the scream. His eyes darted to the stage where Azhara was just caught trying to escape, captured in the fever pitch of justice fighting wildly against dark shapes surrounding her. Clothes were torn, hands flat upon her breasts, tearing at her garments to humiliate, hair yanked back so violently her mouth gaped silent without the force of an outcry, her beauty wretched into a sadomasochistic mask. A helpless rage.

Without warning the burly Ishaq Sadek with his great bush of a mustache and barrel chest was dashing through the madness clutching his ancient revolver that he had never shot, but always carried with him just in case. Now he used it to strike against the soldiers, drawing blood, pushing them aside, catching them off guard and disorienting them so some of the battered women could escape. He ducked and ran and finally made his way to the stage where Azhara was trying to stand her ground.

Many thugs pulled her hair while others volunteered slaps and slurs. In seconds her shirt had been ripped open and blood streamed from her mouth. "Help!" She screamed. Other soldiers were watching, waiting for orders. Ishaq shouted to them "They are going to kill her!" All her energies were focused on staying conscious, pulling her head up for air and down to avoid further hits. She wrapped her jacket around her body with a shoulder bag and cried again for help.

This time Ishaq leapt up and folded his powerful arms around her wrenching her from the grip of the ravenous. Two or three other women placed themselves in between him and the soldiers absorbing the blows and another wedged herself under Azhara's arm and helped spirit her away in the resultant confusion.

The cold air of the street slapped his face and he too could taste blood, his head reeling. Outside there were other soldiers glistening in the thin, floating rain the lights from their vehicles glimmering off wet asphalt. And more, up the street, cadres of soldiers lingering in tight groups nervous with anticipation, waiting restlessly and ignoring the three as they emerged bloodied and torn from the old hotel as if they were on some darker errand of destruction that reduced all else to insignificance. And so they ran. They ran as fast as they could until they were out of sight of the soldiers and then they still kept running. Ishaq felt the heat of the young woman against him, the stench of fear strong in his nostrils. She was breathing hard from shock and the other woman helped support her because she was stumbling with weakness. Finally he swept her up in his arms and the other one whose lined face caught shadows in the street lamps said, "I know a safe place, come…follow me."

Ishaq Sadek had no fear now, as the three figures became just other silhouettes in the night on some sojourn. It was a mystery why he had acted as he did and he could not understand it. Self-preservation was his best quality. Perhaps it was because of her beauty, which always made it more interesting. Or some deeper sense of humanity that had awakened without warning. Perhaps it was the truth these women were speaking, though he was loath to admit it. Perhaps it was what his client Muhammad Abd al' Rashid had said. "…she is the daughter of a very powerful man and neither you nor I would want him to know about this." And he had told him, "You can trust me."

Far into that same night Parrish cursed himself. Instinct and life were no longer separate as they had been only hours earlier. He suspected the driver the embassy had arranged; the small dark woman with black eyes and wild unruly hair that was not covered. It should have been a clue, but he missed it.

It was later when they came. Later when he woke to the struggle. The illusion of Kisa was gone. Strong hands gripped both his arms and the acrid smell of perspiration bit into his nostrils. It was as dark as insanity. He cried out—echoes from sleep—struggled to rise. Fists answered him. Twice. Three times. For a moment, everything was black. The salty liquor of blood dribbled from his mouth. Someone pulled a knit cap over his head until he could see no light. A heavily accented voice spat into his ear. "Shaddup blasphemer! We will kill you dead." Then he was dragged to his feet, head reeling from the blows and nauseous from being awakened so suddenly.

Falling to his knees he was kicked. "I can't stand..." He protested. A young man's voice warned him again and struck once more across the face. As he was drug down stairs his barefoot legs slammed so hard on each step he was sure someone would hear and summon police, but his heart sank as he remembered the hostile interviews of the day before and he scrambled to try and gain a footing. Thrown in the back of the car, he was left alone until the automobile lurched forward causing him to fall behind the seat where he became wedged in unable to lift himself with hands and feet tied. Excited voices spoke Arabic. Terse. Minimal. Parrish was breathing hard and started to shake violently worrying that he would hyperventilate with the cap over his face, afraid that if he passed out they would beat him, or maybe kill him...then he remembered it was a only a loose knit and grew angry at his buckling under duress.

"What the hell do you want?!" He demanded straining to gain control, tearing at his bindings. "What the hell do you want?!"

Someone reached down and hit him again and he felt the unmistakable sensation of a cold steel gun barrel against his temple even though he had never even touched a gun in his life. Blood spilled over his swollen lip.

The car raced through the pre-dawn streets of Alexandria toward an unknown destination. Parrish could make out blurred shapes when they passed under a street light, but little else. Certainly nothing that would help him retrace his steps. Heartbeats rose in violence and his teeth began to hurt from gritting them so hard. He fumed silently then was suddenly yanked from the car and thrown face first to the ground. Three men argued with the guard at the checkpoint who now wished to shoot him on the spot.

"I am an Ambassador!" Parrish cried out in futility, "I am from the United States Embassy in Cairo!" He was kicked again, harder than before and drug off over some dirt and gravel with one man on each arm. So much for détente, Parrish mused through his anguish.

There was a high wind racing. An unbroken and riotous wind. In the dark against a starlit sky he could see the fronds of a palm thrashing wildly and then a moment later it was still. Black against black. The city was restless. Unpredictable. He heard the rustling of the streets outside, but could not guess where he had been taken. Or why. He could smell blood, it smelled like ice, and his head ached from being hit. Breath came in uncontrolled bursts and he struggled to keep it even, to maintain a self-possession against the hysteria rising.

He longed to roar harsh profanities until he expired breathless and the force of his anger brought the walls down to entomb his captors. But most of all he wanted his freedom and raged at his impotence. He listened to the wind. Perhaps it would rain, he thought, if it were anywhere else, if he were far away. Fingers grasped compulsively at the concrete floor on which he sat with hands tightly bound behind. Bloodied wrists were all he had to show; yet he struggled eyes riveted upon the shuttered door that partitioned the rooms and hid him from their view. Parrish could hear his captors bickering in adolescent voices trying to come off as big toughs. Fear and rage flooded his perceptions.

After a while everything grew quiet. Parrish waited anxiously in the lightless room sweating a cold sweat. They must sleep, he thought, they must. Sounds were magnified out of proportion and he tried to place significance on every one hoping for some chance. Minutes were like hours.

All of a sudden the door swung open and a young man in khakis stood there only vaguely discernable in the night—a gaunt scarecrow with shirttails out and hair spilling over his ears. He knelt down and offered Parrish a cup of water, but it was pulled away just out of reach, and when his lips finally did touch the porcelain rim and he got a few drops of cool liquid the figure held what was plainly a gun up and pressed it to his head. He shut his eyes tightly, grimaced and waited. Then Parrish heard a loud click as the trigger was pulled. He hung suspended. Eyes closed. Nothing happened, he was not dead. Footsteps shuffled away and the door was shut. Parrish realized fear had numbed his senses and that he had never really been that close to death before and now for some reason it meant nothing to him, nothing at all. He could not understand why the man had done that, it made no sense, nothing made any sense.

Later, when night was at its most impenetrable and the blustering wind made shutters groan and newspapers sweep along through the street like shuffling phantoms and everyone slept locked away was when Parrish felt most alone. No one would come. He knew that now. There was no one else.

The phone rang. Viktor Jaraslav awoke shortly after three am and unconsciously answered, "Yes."

He had been on a sojourn from the human condition. Dreaming. Lost on a voyage across a feathered sea upon which the midnight sun poured its shimmering light. Narwhals glistened as they leapt high over the wake of a mysterious ship. Constellations glimmered in the far reaches reminding him of journeys in other lifetimes, which he never remembered while awake whether from amnesia or the inhibition endemic to masses of humans all living together as one gargantuan seething biological lump full of microorganisms and the fears that mortality gave him. On this ocean he had none of those concerns and so was extremely cross when disturbed.

"There is an event," a man he deemed of lesser character than he explained. Consumed with contempt for intellects that had neither the vision nor the force to deal with life and still be able to ascertain the subtle importances of things, he considered them eternal chrysalises to be dismissed.

A light snow had fallen. But now the sky was clear and a panoply of tiny stars shattered the indigo night. Brittle cold slapped the exposed faces of the homeless, of which never once had Viktor thought, *there but for fortune go I.* He could not allow himself the luxury of self-doubt for his righteousness was the rock upon which all else pivoted.

The road to the Watch took far longer than it usually did on his daily commute. Every mile, every foot, every inch he traveled gave up only with protest. His overanxious goading to go ever faster with threats and caustic remarks didn't actually make the short journey take more time, but it seemed that way to the car's driver. Outside darkened windows the reflected impressions of an egregious Washington streaked by between luxury hotels and racial inequity, between the equinox of darkness and the glint of day, between the disappointments preceding and faith in what was to come. Viktor huddled alone in the cool darkness of massive black leather seats interrupted only by the whisper of microfiltered air conditioning. He began to download information to his laptop computer over a secure satellite connection while at the same time log in to the private agency extranet. Frantic emails appeared on screen with encrypted titles such as "Situation Cairo", "Crisis Update", or simply "Coup d'état" and he scanned them hurriedly each moment gaining a clearer picture of exactly what situation was unfolding on the other side of the earth. He cursed himself over the weakness of sleep and vowed never again to allow his personal knowledge to be eclipsed by even the remotest of ambassadors. By the time he arrived at his office he had made a dozen calls sending bleary-eyed subordinates stumbling from their sleep into the cold to wake others. He raced from the car to the entryway pulling the collar of his black cashmere overcoat tight around his white neck, breath turning to little puffs of steam in the air. Exhilaration thrilled him. He lived for moments such as this

The small figure of Viktor Jaraslav disappeared inside and the car moved off into the darkness leaving no trace that anyone had ever arrived save a few footprints in the dusting of snow, though soon those too would be gone.

He descended into the building's depths like a stone that had slipped through the surface of a still lake leaving the concentric circles of his personal life to disappear. Hands fondled the lapels of his coat pulling it ever closer seeking complete immersion now that the shock of the night had erased the visions of narwhales and for some unexplained reason he thought briefly of the only woman in his history he had ever made love to. Her raven black hair and huge pendulous breasts had smothered him in a thick sexual honey that made him buckle with a raw energy from which he had never recovered.

A small group of people were huddled among computer monitors and strained their necks under the phantom landscape that glimmered with mountains and plains in eerie colors. Next to it were three magnifications. One was assuredly city streets, even though the resolution of the image left it pixilated and corrupted by artifacts. But lights could be seen moving. The lights of vehicles. Lumbering. Deliberate. A feeling of impending malice slipped across Victor's skin and despite the warm cashmere coat pulled up tight around his neck it brought gooseflesh.

"The hell are we looking at?" he barked hoarsely.

"Alexandria," a woman replied, "Alexandria by the sea."

*　*　*　*

It was earlier when loneliness came and went like a chill from a window in winter. The sun had slowly faded and Karine Russo cradled a crystal of Spanish Rioja in her hand. The thought occurred to her that she might freeze but for that one thin pane of glass. It inspired her to climb into a hot bath and soak. Later she wrapped herself in a large Turkish towel finally dropping it to slide in between the sheets after standing a moment feeling the air just to know she truly existed. Wind swayed trees outside. Snow fell silently. She slipped into the arms of Morpheus.

In her dreams Parrish came to visit–the last person she expected.

"This must be very important for you to risk your job like this?" Leering through the crack in the door.

He stood for a moment on the antique Kazak rug that graced the entryway with a hunted look as he glanced around the room like a cornered animal making sure they were really alone. "You're going to think I'm crazy."

The sudden realization of vulnerability made her nervous. She spotted the glass of Rioja thankfully left out snatching it up to help her cope. "…sit down for God's sake."

"I have to talk to you."

"I can see that."

Parrish was in evening clothes. His hair was disheveled looking like he'd past the point of needing it cut two or three weeks back. She gave him a glass of wine, which he polished off in two massive swallows and then began to explain the reason for his unannounced appearance. It was an event that Karine could not fit into any of the scenarios that explained the extraordinary, and it made her sleep tenuous and fitful.

"I have seen Death," he stated unceremoniously.

She finished off the last of the Rioja thankful for its warm hit trying not to sound too incredulous as she replied, "What do you mean?"

"It started with a dinner at the Egyptian Embassy," he began nervously. " I went to try and talk to the cultural affairs minister who's been in town since last week. You know how damn hard it is to get him on the phone–never returns calls, never responds to email, never even has his secretary…I was hoping I could corner him and get his take on this demonstration that's supposed to happen. I was trying to find out…"

"Why are you here?"

"This Egyptian woman. All in black with a black Hijab that wound down around her neck. A flawless woman. No jewelry except one gold scarab. She moved easily around the room speaking with everyone like they had some important unfinished business. I'd never seen her before. I would have heard of a woman holding an official Egyptian post. But there was something familiar about her, something I couldn't...

"You're here to tell me about a beautiful woman?"

Suddenly a bit manic, "You've got to...I have to get away!"

"I see. I see...suppose you tell me more about this."

Parrish spoke darkly. "Everywhere I went there she was...deep in conversation. I thought she was following me, but not once did our eyes meet. I couldn't tell if she was ignoring me or...like smoke. I asked some of the people she had been talking with who she was," he fell silent, "nobody seemed to remember her."

"Well, not so unusual. It was one of those diplomatic parties after all–no one really listens to anyone."

"It wasn't like that. These were deep conversations. Intense. Very personal."

"So...why are you here?" Karine moved restlessly in her sleep.

He looked down trying to put the storm into words. "I was compelled by some power...feeling anxious, almost dizzy. Then, as she was speaking with a gray haired gentleman I came up behind her, quietly, with this inexplicable apprehension. It was a party for Christ's sake...I meant to introduce myself."

"Don't blaspheme!"

"...just as I was about to speak, she turned and ran into my arms. Her breath was on me. The smell of her. I held her shoulders to keep her from falling, but she looked right at me with those black eyes and threw up her hand in a threatening gesture as if I had violated her...a surge of energy beneath that silk fabric. And hot, she was so hot. Her eyes like dark solar flares. It was electric–then she was gone. I mean...I didn't see her again. Gone."

"Erskine..." She shook her hand in tiny worried circles, "why are you so..."

"It was Death, don't you see? It was Death! I am being stalked by Death and I must leave, go far away–and you're going to send me somewhere!" He pronounced in deadly earnest. "You're going to send me tonight! Now!"

Eventide drew up around her and she pulled the covers tight against a sudden chill. Reality seemed to shimmer. In her dream she walked to the window where the cold air was seeping through. It gave her a stable point of reference. The cold was her brother. He would not be dissuaded from his desire to flee and she knew he would be worthless like this. Absolutely worthless. So in hope of greater productivity she hand wrote mission orders, as was her custom, on a sheet of paper and handed it to him. He folded it and without looking put it in the pocket of his coat then faded from view.

It was later that she dreamed of Parrish'e embassy party with indistinct images of people in small groups sitting and talking. And suddenly there she was standing in a corner with a glass in her hand. A woman in black exactly as had been described. Perhaps Parrish wasn't on the verge. Perhaps it was Death.

"You frightened one of my subordinates tonight," she stated bluntly without even an introduction.

"Really…well, if I did it was inadvertent."

"Then why did you make threatening gesture towards him?"

"Threatening? Malesh, I was just startled to see him here tonight."

"Startled, you? I don't believe it. What could startle you?"

"Why, I was just surprised to see him at all. Here, tonight of all nights. You see, I have an appointment with Parrish tomorrow in Alexandria."

Karine awoke covered with a sheen of perspiration. The sheets were damp. Cold air bit into her. Blood pooled in the middle of her body in an uncharacteristic fear as she stared out across the darkened room trying to make sense out of shapes and shadows. She switched on the light and soon saw that everything was as it had been. Then the phone rang. It was Viktor Jaraslav and he only said one thing, "There is an event."

But that was earlier in the night when the spray of stars still could be seen and the temperature was only cold enough to turn the bare tree branches into crystal filigree glittering with reflections of distant nocturnal lights. Now she raced through the nearly deserted streets of Washington in a government car that was sent for her a few hours before dawn when it was the coldest and night was at its deepest point. It was the brittle hour when homeless people went in a headlong quest for warmth save those who took the arctic windfall to pass into the next life hoping the fates would be kinder next time around. Hot air blasted out the vents and though it burned her cheeks, it felt good. Karine Russo was bundled up tight in a long black wool coat. There was steam on the windows turning the landscape into a blurred cinema of light and shadow heightening her dream like state. It was a dream where she had met Death. A dream yet it made her think about Parrish and his mission to Alexandria and how fate intertwined them all.

The night was thick with fear. Hours had passed since Parrish had managed to slip one bloodied hand free of the bindings and then the other in a fit of utter desperation. It was sudden and unanticipated and instantly his heart trilled in terror because now he knew he was committed. He would have to escape. So he waited anxiously while the rooms grew quiet and the voices drifted off into murmurs and finally to silence. Only the wind spoke. Then slowly he leaned down and worked his feet free, then waited longer scanning the darkness for movement with the cords still over him as if he were still tied in case anyone might come to check, but no one did. After long moments, Parrish stood as quickly and quietly as was humanly possible. Ears bristled with the minutiae of the night; whisperings, creaks, rustlings, every sound was absorbed, inspected, categorized all within milliseconds listening for danger. He could taste the peril on his tongue. It was metallic, like bullets and guns and speeding automobiles. Suddenly he was at the window. The hallway door was out of the question, and this opening was the only other way out. Then he was outside clinging to crumbling brick and mortar three stories up on a ledge no wider than six inches. Sweating hands made it hazardous to grip, but he didn't think about that, there was only one thought now. Slowly he inched forward, bare feet feeling every chip, every grain and loose stone. Another window was about six feet away and as he clung desperately to one frame he stretched as far as he could trying to reach it. Clearly he would have to let go and straddle the narrow ledge teetering three stories up in order to make it. Down below through clotheslines and phone wires was a cement courtyard and Parrish suddenly pictured himself sprawled out there in a pool of crimson. They say never to look down, he recalled too late, and never look back. He let go. Belly up against the brick wall scraping as he slid almost imperceptibly forward. For a moment he nearly prayed, almost succumbed to the barrage from all sides to humble himself before God, but then remembered he didn't believe in anything. Except that now he believed in survival and it enveloped him silently infusing him with a will and a passion burning deep where it had been nearly extinguished before.

Parrish ran. He ran with such inexhaustible exhilaration that he felt none of the stones, broken glass and rubble of the roadway under his bare feet as his heart screamed out in release. From the second window he had reached the kitchen of the apartment and through it let himself out into the hall. There he stumbled down stairs in the dark sure he had awakened the young kidnappers. Now he fled. It wasn't that something had changed inside him, but that events had conspired to help bring out this new person he had been evolving into and against his own volition a resurgence of meaning was taking place and as he ran he could see it clearly, more clearly than he had ever seen before. He struggled with a newfound sense of freedom.

Bounding into an intersection he suddenly froze, slammed himself up against a wall, sucked in his breath and fixed his eyes forward. Gasping he tried to make sense out of the scene. Perhaps it was police. Security for the Samūn demonstration, he attempted explanations, just a precaution he thought. Up ahead were lights. Many lights. Insignia of military vehicles could be made out. Silhouettes of men with guns.

VIII | Divine Light

A MUEZZIN'S CALL HAUNTED THE DAWN. THE ADHĀN'S LONGING SOARED above the crush of innocents that had occurred in the night on the streets below. *There is no god but God, Muhammad is the messenger of God.* A reminder to those whose faith was tested by events they could not control. Blue umber struggled with raw sunlight for dominance. Parrish languished in shadows. There was a sense of impending violence in the air. He had disabused himself of embracing the military in hopes his diplomatic immunity would keep him from harm. The dark events into which he was swept had shifted his viewpoint and left him shaken with the insight of how fragile civilization really was, how it can be disrupted by force, by terror without the slightest interference at the hands of anyone motivated by terrible impulses. His shoes and cellphone were missing and the streets had been deserted all night because of the unrest. Earlier, he had tried to find his way back to the hotel and headed toward the harbor, but there were too many soldiers, too many military vehicles roaming the boulevards so he had decided to stay put until it was light. Now he was hungry and wanted a coffee.

A hunting drone off in the distance began to trouble him. Soon he could distinguish the pulsing malevolent thunder of a military helicopter. It was circling, searching, ferreting out those who, he supposed like himself, were caught in the streets during the night when the army had arrived. He walked the silent sidewalks of dawn hugging storefronts and building entrances to keep from line of sight. Then, after two long blocks when the light of the Egyptian sun flowed through the desiccated air bringing an almost startling clarity to his surroundings, he saw them. Soldiers at a checkpoint, surly young men in uniforms. He had not expected anyone when he breached the corner and felt panic–neither had the nonchalant young men who were drinking coffee, smoking cigarettes and talking among themselves. Suddenly he was spotted and a man began gesturing for him to approach–it was unreal, as if a scene from memory that was familiar yet somewhere the connection had been lost. Parrish froze. He noticed his right foot was bleeding and then remembered he had no shoes and just watched the young soldier become more and more insistent as he soon drew the others' attention.

"God!" He recoiled. If he had heard the muffled clatter of the 30-year-old Soviet Lada as the black and yellow car pulled up beside him with its brakes complaining loudly he wouldn't have been startled out of his wits. "What are you doing!"

"Get in!" The taxi driver shouted. He yanked on the front door, but it wouldn't budge. "The back! The back…get down on the floor! Now!" Parish tumbled in and lay behind the front seat with nothing between him and the road but a piece of linoleum covering a large hole as he had done in an earlier car–only this time he hoped it was delivering him from harm not to it. The Egyptian driver pulled a squealing U-turn making incredibly big, hectic movements with the steering wheel just to hold the car in line. Parrish peered over the seat to where the meter should have been finding only an empty bracket where it had been pulled for repairs eight years ago. Then he noticed it was not only lacking a floor, but also those inconspicuous lifesaving devices called seatbelts. He glanced through the rear window at the soldiers waving their arms franticly now vanishing in the distance and wondered if he were on the right side of the glass. The old car roared through the deserted thoroughfares and he held on for all that his life was worth expecting the next instant to be sacrificed in a blinding crash.

"My name is Nizam!" The driver yelled over the hiss and roar of the car. "You picked a bad time for sightseeing!"

"I'm not a tourist."

"I'm not a taxi driver," he swerved.

Alarms sounded as they caromed through the backstreets. "What are you?"

"Meaning?"

"…if you're not taxi dri…"

"Archeologist."

"That's a relief…"

"A PhD from Cairo University."

"Why are you driving a…"

"I forgot…you're a tourist…"

"…not a tourist."

"…nobody makes money. A taxi is second income. It took me four years to get a job after I earned my degree. Now I work with the French on the underwater excavations in the harbor, but they are *Haraamiyya*– swindlers! What are you if not a tourist?"

"A diplomat. Foreign Service Officer for Political Affairs at the U.S. Embassy in Cairo."

"*Biz-zimma*–really! Are you in the wrong place!"

As the taxi fled confusion dark events of the past few weeks swirled around Parrish. He was sure the Crisis Manager had her eye on him-she who sent him on this unexpected mission upsetting the routine he had insulated himself with in Cairo. They were all watching him now; the dark disturbed eyes of Abd Al-Faraq-the great imam from Al-Qaed Mosque; the jangled, frantic eyes of the young men who had briefly held him captive and the innocent eyes of a child in the desert where it all started seemingly so long ago. "I have to get back to my room. I don't even have a passport."

"Where are you staying?"

"The Cecil Hotel."

"Ahh….Saad Zaghloul square where Cleopatra's needles stood, in front of the Corniche."

"That's it."

"Can't do it. We can't be stopped. They are everywhere. An American. No passport, no shoes…"

"What's happening?"

"Military coup…where've you been?"

"Indisposed."

"Without shoes?"

"I was abducted."

"From the Cecil Hotel?" Nazim furled his eyebrows at Parrish in the rear view mirror, but he did not reply. "We cannot be stopped."

"Why not? I've got diplomatic immunity! Let's go to the U.S. Consulate. This is a pivotal moment for Egypt-I've got to…authorities have a moral and legal obligation to respect the rights…you do know where it is?"

"Of course. On Pharaana Street, but we'll never get there."

"Why?"

"You have no shoes and no one gets kidnapped from the Cecil Hotel, it's *ahbal*–foolish…no one abducts people from a five-star hotel with its own security service the night before a military coup. They won't believe you, and you have no shoes?"

"They took my shoes so I wouldn't escape."

"It will look like you threw them, probably at the military. Throwing a shoe is unacceptable, a grave insult–belittling. Poor men wear no shoes," Nazim said. "Feet come in contact with dirt–dirt on the feet indicates the lack of social status and intellect. It's unclean. You have no passport, who will believe you?"

"Nonsense."

"Protesters wave their shoes in the air, many are lost."

"I have to get to a phone!"

"Lines are jammed. Internet is down. The Minister of Information has closed state TV. Last night I heard from friends in Cairo. Four helicopters were hovering over the Egyptian Media Production City in case of demonstrations and all private satellite channels were warned of closure if they disseminate false news or make violations."

"Look," Parrish grabbed the driver by his shirt; "I've got to get someplace where there's a working phone…do you understand? I've got to do something!"

Nizam shoved his hand away from his shirt and frowned in the mirror where Parish was looking back. "Malesh. I know where to take you."

He wondered who this taxi driver really was as they charged through the city over deteriorating asphalt streets where there were no traffic signals or center lines to constrain the daily chaos. But it didn't matter, the dusty canyons were virtually empty and only a few adventurous Alexandrians traveled out beneath the pastiche of faded Italian and French stucco buildings plastered over many times with generations of signage. Late model empty cars filled every available parking spot. Down crenneled canyons filled with balconies that had figured in the city's architecture for hundreds of years came intermittent furtive looks from one of the thousands that loomed high over the thoroughfares as curiosity overcame good sense and someone poked their head out to see for himself if they were truly under siege. Parrish rode on despair. He gripped the vinyl seats with sweaty hands. The taste of dust intruded. He scanned erratically for danger. Every muscle was straining every nerve alert. As he watched the rapidly changing landscape a sense of isolation and being far removed from home filled him with an unfathomable longing he had not felt for many years, a wanting that iced him to the bone, but instead of being debilitating it gave life and reason and passion where they had been atrophied before. It was the future, the past was nothing, it was all about desire he decided in that careening taxi. He must survive.

That was earlier when the movement of sun and earth tore the night with wind flurries and day had just begun. Now he stood on the balcony of a luxury condo high above The Corniche holding a hot tea with the tips of his fingers. The bay below was enraged with whitewater driven by unseasonable *khamaseen* winds and the churning wooden fishing boats were bright turquoise, red and yellow against the deep cerulean blue of the harbor. Seafom danced on the rocks as a broad, flat sand colored tank lumbered down El-Gaish road its diesel clatter rising above everything natural. Parrish could smell it despite the wind. The taxi driver had taken him to an elite café, which at night became a casino hosting high stakes gambling for the well heeled. Only blocks off the corniche, it was a sprawling labyrinth opening to an outdoor plaza where locals and tourists lingered savoring the Alexandrian ambiance. Not today. There were only empty tables buffeted by wind and a line of French doors shut tight with shiny brass fittings. The taxi pulled up quick and, darting looks in all directions, the driver gave Parrish caution.

"You don't want to know this guy." Nizam admonished roughly, his educated façade suddenly gone. "Don't ask questions. He's a thug. Notorious. As close to organized crime as Alexandria gets. Egypt is a source, transit, and destination country for trafficking in women and children. Wealthy men from the Gulf travel here to purchase "temporary" or "summer marriages" with Egyptian women, including young girls. He helps."

Parrish knew about the young girls. He'd learned it from a CIA fact book. Parents and marriage brokers often facilitated the arrangements. Child sex tourism occurs in Cairo, Alexandria, and Luxor; Egypt is a transit country for women trafficked from Uzbekistan, Moldova, Ukraine, Russia, and other Eastern European countries to Israel for commercial sexual exploitation; Some of Egypt's estimated two hundred thousand to one million street children–both boys and girls–are exploited in prostitution and forced begging. Local gangs are involved in all of this.

"Why the fuck am I here then?"

"He's connected. Politicians love to gamble. The military won't come here. He knows Abd al Hakim, the liberal Islamic fundamentalist, closet democracy advocate and leader of the Shura Council."

"I know who he is…"

"Then don't ask questions. You won't make it in the streets today without him. Abd al Hakim is a serious gambler."

***

They sat in two chairs shoved up against the wall. Turkish lace covered each arm. A small sandalwood table was between them upon which sat steaming cups of Karkadey tea, made from the dried, dark red petals of the Hibiscus flower. Winds driven across the Mediterranean buffeted the floor to ceiling windows and the smell of diesel exhaust from the tanks intruded.

"Get this man some shoes!" Abd al Hakim snapped his fingers and barked at a subordinate in Arabic. One of the four men who hovered around them jumped. The others had the implacable bulldog stance that quickly identified them as bodyguards. Then he turned his attention back to Parrish to respond in thickly accented English. "I understand you have been very, very upset by events, but how can I do this now? What can you expect?"

A man knelt down and helped Parrish on with some slippers. "What happened to bilateralism?"

"With a hostile Washington, I don't know," he sipped some tea, "…but at any rate it's not my doing."

"You are the Shura Council…"

"…has been suspended–Mr. Officer for Political Affairs. We are all under martial law as you have seen yourself."

"If not legitimate, whose law?

"The commander of the faithful."

"Who?" Parrish felt the drawing of a veil across an otherwise sentient conversation. He had grown inured to it after so many years in the Middle East. As if an alternate reality had been unleashed that left everyone dumb but the initiated. "Who is it then I must speak with?"

"You cannot. I myself, a childhood friend, could not sway his resolve."

"Is it worth the destruction? People are dying. Think of imports, trade…I urge you to consider carefully."

He reflected for a moment. "Jibril Ben Jabbar Riyadh. The great general, leader of one of the five armies of the faithful and a one time friend–though I cannot vouch for that friendship at this moment."

"Can you get me a meeting?"

"Certainly, but he will kill me."

"What?"

"I did not deliver the support he wanted. I am *haram*."

"How can you be a sin?"

"For all his learning–you know he is an *Hāfiz* having memorized the Qur'an at a very young age–Jibril sees things in black and white..." Just then a man leaned down and whispered something in Abd al Hakim's ear, something that disturbed him and turned his face suddenly ashen. Without a word, he leapt up and hurried off to the other room.

Parrish was left holding the tea in his hand with his imagination running free again cursing the Crisis Manager for this impromptu mission that had imperiled him. All the subordinates had vanished. He was alone, but could hear excited voices coming down the hall from the entryway and sat straight up, alert, and slowly placed the cup on the table. Electricity bristled. His Arabic was nowhere near good enough to follow the panicked voices though clearly something was happening, something that excited everybody's emotions and then it struck him that the military had found them, had breached the apartments...it was as if a premonition and he was living through pre-planned events. At once the past and future collided and whatever happened in the next few minutes would be pivotal in what was to come. He rushed into the hallway expecting to see drawn guns, flack vests and military green, but instead he was unceremoniously shoved aside by the men carrying a bloodied young woman.

Ishaq Sadek stood at the open door another young woman beside him and rubbed the scar that ran across his cheek with his thumb franticly trying to explain, "I'm so sorry, so sorry! I had nowhere else to take her. Forgive me! They are after her. Only you could help...only you...she is hurt..."

"Come in," Abd al Hakim tried to calm him, "get out of the doorway. It's all right. Of course. Come in or someone will call the police." He was sad, but not afraid of what the great general might do when he found his daughter had sought refuge with his estranged friend.

* * * *

It was earlier at the vortex of the Middle East, Europe, and Asia when the Deputy Oil Minister for Saudi Arabia gazed desperately out the 154th floor window of his apartments at the Burj Khalifa tower in Dubai, for a long time the tallest structure on earth.

It was where 12,000 day workers of 100 nationalities had sweated out in 118° heat the Hymenocallis flower, whose harmonious structure was one of the organizing principles of the tower's design; temperatures so high that ice had to be added to the concrete–poured only at night so it would not crack from drying too fast; that hinted at the onion-like domes of Islamic architecture in polished stone and burnished metal cocooned in over 26,000 aluminum silicone and glass panels hand placed by a special team of 300 Chinese craftsmen; a spiral minaret that grew slender as it rose. Innumerable tests had been conducted on Burj Khalifa to determine the effects wind would have on the super tower, its occupants and the atmospheric changes that would surely brutalize it as it rose to the clouds. During the summer season, winds known as *Shamal* become wild, gusty and unpredictable when they finally touch down at Dubai. *Shamal* whipped up the desert sand and obliterated visibility creating sandstorms that lasted for several days, as it was now. It might have been catastrophic, but as the building spirals in height set back wings provided many different floor plates stepping and shaping the tower and had the effect of "confusing the wind." Muhammad Abd al' Rashid tumbled into that confusion as he brooded over the vast Arabian Gulf to the west and the vast badlands to the east–both horizons obscured by mist and haze.

"Are you sure? Are you quite certain?" Abd al' Rashid hissed in restrained and disbelieving fury keeping his true emotions veiled.

"She has been seen. Identified by a reliable source."

The inconceivable news clouded his usually rapier like acuity and he was disillusioned at what was to come next. He spoke out of a deep well of unexpected pain. "I cannot believe it!"

"I am only a messenger."

"Still…" he whispered wistfully, "have you contacted my man?"

"He doesn't respond. No, no response, but was last seen as she escaped."

"I cannot believe it!"

Earlier still when dawn had arisen in an eerie flaming glow to the east fueled by a cyclone of sand and sent its beacons out across the Gulf tingeing each whitecap blue violet as if St. Elmo's fire rose from the waves was when it happened. He had been dreaming in indigo between cool silk sheets brown hands grasping the pillow in some private conflict when he was awakened. He was met with harsh and surreal news that was an affront to family and belief. The woman he had set the investigator on with orders to ferret out any conceivable dirt that could sully his family's name was now implicated in something far more egregious and unforgivable. Something completely unexpected. He had stumbled to his feet and numbly pulled on a long black kaftan. A servant handed him a *Türk kahvesi-sāda,* Turkish coffee–black with just a touch of cardamom.

With restraint and irony the full story was rolled out before him like a breathless pitch for venture capital by once high rollers who had lost everything in disgrace. Distasteful, full of shame and recrimination even for the tellers. Each detail had been thought out and crafted in advance and was revealed in the most delicate manner possible so as to avoid percussive consequences. No one wanted to bite the hand that gave them things they couldn't give up just yet. So they sat as if in air. Up here on the 154th floor where spirits roamed and soared in discontent with gusts of the Shamal that made common men faint and queasy so far from firm ground. Except for the chosen, those blessed with capital gains, inheritance or the consequences of wild innovative foolishness that had paid off big time; Those who possessed the vast majority of wealth and resources available on the planet leaving the marrowbone to the teaming millions to divide up between them; Those who had become so rarefied themselves that nothing could shake their confidence in existence except free falling market trajectories and unwise collusion with free falling government officials. Among the four men who sat in these stratospheric glass walled apartments on couches of the finest leathers where even the oil of a single fingerprint could leave an indelible mark there was only one of the chosen, and the others spoke to him in hushed and reverent voices always aware they were in the presence of true power.

It was as if from a seedy Bollywood drama filled with *filmi* music and sensuous dancing spotlighting the fall from grace of a once princess to the infamy of the streets–and then beyond into the terra incognito of spiritual oblivion, that realm of which the Qur'an has been the vehicle of redemption and guide to the straight path. It seemed the young beauty who ostensibly had it all–daughter of the great general, Commander of the Faithful who had demonstrated his piety by committing the entire revelation of Muhammad to memory at a young age, nurtured and cherished by family, spoiled as an only child, endowed with an impossible beauty–she who had what others longed for but would never possess was an apostate before Allah. It was tawdry. A rented hall in a rundown hotel in Alexandria filled with women insurgent against Islam. Rebels, insurrectionists, terrorists–striking at the fabric. He could never have guessed, but then people are like onions and one never knows what will be found once the layers are peeled back. This was exactly the reason it made no sense he would feel a profound and overpowering loss, but there it was.

Later, when he was alone, he had switched on the 120-inch, flat screen holographic television that had taken nearly a century to develop and watched the business news pundits give market analysis just so he could indulge himself with inner disdain for their vapid insights and weak minds. Abd al' Rashid had been known to spend six hours writing a 20-minute informal address and crafting acid rejoinders for almost any eventuality. The effect was startling and everywhere he went he was credited with being a first-class orator, a master of rhetoric made even more remarkable by his relatively young age. He knew different, but would never confide the truth that he was a writer and not an orator at all. His thought process was too refined to be in concert with the mob as an orator must be, for the people must see themselves in a great speaker and he in turn must see himself in them. Neither would ever happen because he was rarified, complex and sophisticated, a bearer of what once was called "the white man's burden", even though he was a man of color. An orator thought on his feet, in him histories and futures continually catalyzed in a never ending calculation to which he was only the messenger.

It was later, after much introspection, that he called his most trusted consigliere to his side at the window overlooking the Arabian Gulf just as the sun was glittering off into the dark reaches in a sparkling dance of nuclear fire. The man–hardened by years of submission to the wills of his masters his own desires sublimated into service and duty and obligation–heard, but could not believe his instructions. It defied all that he thought he knew about the young Saudi and he was compelled in some sort of disguised death wish to question the reasoning behind such a decision.

"Have you considered the implications?" Cold blue fire met his eyes and he knew better than to say another word.

"We will find her," Abd al' Rashid whispered.

People are like onions, the consigliere mused, and the depths beneath the layers are unfathomable to men and only revealed before Allah. Of love, he was an interloper, but could recognize its umbra all the better for being an outsider and knew it was the only power comparable to that of faith.

* * * *

A breathless whisper, then silence. Delicate brown fingers adorned with intricate henna designs upon which silver rings glinted lie still. Restless hands limp at her side. "She sleeps." Said the whisper. "Help will come. In-sha Allah. Help will come." Azhara lie unconscious and bloodied upon the snow white bed a young woman at her side. The clunking metallic diesel thuds of tanks rumbling below shook the walls.

"No one could have stopped her. She had to see the *Samūn* demonstration, had to be part of it!" Ishak pleaded, "What could I do?"

"We have to get her to a doctor!" al Hakim replied obliviously. "How could you let this happen? It's unmanly!"

"…thousands of people in the square, all of them moving at once…a human sea. And then the soldiers came in formation. They cut off the rear, no escape, and started firing. The fallen, all around us. Blood everywhere…they struck at her…" The misery at his failure knew no bounds.

"Her breathing is shallow. There is no time…" The young woman spoke solemnly.

Abd al Hakim sent one of his bodyguards into the streets for a doctor, if he was not arrested for violating the curfew imposed by marshal law, with the exhortation "We must save her! We must!"

"There is no time…she is in Allah's hands. Help will come. In-sha Allah. Help will come. In-sha Allah…" the young women chanted to herself.

"There is someone else who can help." Ishak the disgraced said looking at Parrish with a desperate expectancy sweat pouring from his brow.

After a moment, they all looked at Parrish. "Not me," he said, "I'm not the one." But that was earlier. Before he had taken the leap off the precipice, tumbled from the relative secure desperation of his own struggle between the devine and oblivion into the spirit world where he was unsure of everything–at least that was what he would call it from now on to avoid religious overtones. The thing was, in his mind, there was a war raging against the concept of religion as he had always thought of it and what had recently been visited on him. It had always been an anathema to the intellectual senses where he churned his perceptions of the world into his philosophy of the world, but now everything was thrown into question. All was now on standby waiting for the armistice.

The room was silent as the *Khamaseen* winds whistled unseen at the window and the azure Mediterranean bristled. Parrish ached for a cigarette, even a cheap, poorly cultivated Egyptian brand with harsh Turkish tobacco would do as he tried not to take umbrage at being called upon to perform like a parlor magician, a fakir, a conjurer–trying to deal with the inner rebellion at having been placed in this position against his will. "I don't know what I can do…" he protested, but when he looked at the young woman sudden memories filled him, they cascaded in on crests of waves and flooded his awareness in a revivification of some past moment–ancient memories. The shock of it took his breath away. She was like someone he had known in a far distant lifetime beyond his powers of remembrance though the faint impression still called him; fragile and complex, restless and wild it was she who had brought down the barriers between one lifetime and the next until all that remained was one long continuous thread of history pulled taut. He knew he was in a danger zone when taking a tentative step forward he reached out to the figure sprawled on the bed.

"You cannot touch her!" The bulldog-like man in the dark ill-fitting suit rose up menacingly between him and Azhara.

"Someone has to help her!" The girl pleaded, "She is too weak..."

"So, are you a doctor?"

"No." Parish admitted, "I am a diplomat."

"Then you cannot touch her! It is *haram*, against *Shari'ah*."

"I want to see how she is injured."

"That doesn't matter. *'...many are led astray by their own lusts through ignorance.'*"

"Don't be absurd Malik," Abd al Hakim rose excitedly, "let him by!"

"No." The man folded an arm across his chest, "I've heard of this one!" he pulled out a Helwan 920 semiautomatic pistol, the Egyptian version of the Beretta 92, and clutching it with both hands aimed it at Parrish's chest. "He thinks he's...but he's *Dajja*, and I will not fall for his lies!"

Abd al Hakim wedged between them slightly crouched against an imagined yet expected impact. "Don't worry, don't worry...he's just excitable..."

The attempt at reassurance fell flat. Parrish's heart beat tattoos in his ears louder than the tanks in the street realizing how much he didn't like having guns pointed at him, as had been done twice in the past 24 hours. He backed against a wall on which hung an antique Anatolian kilim from the 10th Century and stood as still as he could against the rough wool fiber though feeling the effects of vertigo. The young woman on the bed began screaming while al Hakim argued obscure points of Islamic law in conciliatory tones to his subordinate who was supposed to protect everyone, but now raged with righteous indignation as the rational conflicted with his idée fixe and he could find no middle ground. Later, he would recall the incident as a catalyst caused by extreme pressure–though he'd experienced similar phenomena in his encounter with Abd Al-Faraq, the Imam from Al-Qaed Mosque. At first the feelings of unreality crept over him quietly like a blight of white powdery mildew on crops so slow and silent it was not anticipated, everything became subdued and obscure; colors dim, voices mute. Trouble was the clarity of his perceptions was stunning, only they were as if from a distance and he was an exterior observer from another world. He could remember Egypt of the ancients and subconsciously compared where he was now with where he was then in one long glance that took in the vast panorama of tumultuous events that had coalesced into the present. It occurred to him how quickly time has passed for him to be able to remember everything so easily and then suddenly realized that it actually doesn't affect one that way as only things and objects move through space, only the landscape deteriorates, the fabric as it is used and recycled by generation after generation like the midden piles so deep in Cairo that the entranceways to old buildings were now a full story below street level. That alone is time. The people hadn't altered their view of the city; only the city had altered from their use and so had changed–how else do we measure the passage of time? Parrish knew it was a great truth, but was unsure of its usefulness or whence it had come to him in the chaos of the moment. He remembered an aristocratic young woman standing on a high, flat, stone structure in the hot desert night torchlight shining off her oiled body with dried henna covering her hair sculpted into the image of an ibis as six huge Nubians stood guard around her. The *Khamaseen* winds whistled then as they did now.

"She's not breathing!!" The woman next to Azhara shouted shrilly above the din of argument. Suddenly all was silent.

"No! You are mistaken!" Abd al Hakim replied in shock. "It cannot be!"

"She is dead and you are arguing!!"

Parrish burst forward in a blinding arc of coiled energy knocking the bodyguard flat to the floor sending his pistol careening off the wall. He landed with one knee on the bed, quickly knelt and grasped Azhara's hand, as all looked on shocked and astonished at the sudden turn of events. With both his hands he held her limp fingers and radiated with a surge of power and energy that could only be described as atomic molecular phenomena to the unbelievers, but to Malik, the bodyguard, who still lie prone on one elbow observing this primal dance from the floor an entirely different thought sprang to mind–being the most truly devout person in the room despite his blood profession where he had caused great suffering. It was *Nur*–divine light.

Without warning, from out of the silence Azhara convulsed forward taking a deep, rasping gulp of air, eyes wide, her long black hair flying wild. "I am here!" She stammered breathlessly, "I am here…" Parrish held her in his arms as she cried.

So unexpected was it that Malik was stunned completely senseless. He could not believe, would not–yet there it was before his own eyes. After a moment letting the event permeate the inner reaches where his belief dwelt he began to recite verses: "*…And We send down of the Qur'an that which is a healing and a mercy…Allah doth guide whom He will to His light*." Then he whispered, "I can't believe…Al-Muntadhir–the Awaited one."

The President of the United States sat waiting at the head of a long, glossy, obsidian conference table crowded with brushed titanium and forest green leather chairs under a glow of recessed lights softening the shadows of his face while tiny halogen spots from above created illuminated corridors that officials walked in and out of as they found their seats. A hush of anticipation permeated everything. Two marines in dress blues shielded the door. The atmosphere shimmered with power from the commanding heights where the leader of the Western World and his advisors were about to be embroiled in a crisis that would challenge their fundamental beliefs.

It was much earlier that Karine Russo was afraid. For the first time in her career control was deserting her and she questioned her ability to withstand the political backlash–she was never confirmed as Crisis Manager. But that was before, now she sat uneasily at the head of a table down deep in the Watch in a dimly lit meeting room constructed of an architectural style known as Structural Expressionism where every available space was filled with computer monitors and high definition video screens. "Why is it so damned cold in here?" The Crisis Manager exclaimed. "Electronics." Replied a young man who sat in the far corner at a booth in near total darkness except for one spindly pin-light that hovered over his workstation like a clandestine praying mantis awaiting a perfect moment for the kill. Karine turned her coat collar up close to her neck watching Viktor Jaraslov as he slouched at the far end of the table tapping his fingers on its cold surface in nervous energy–escaping, she imagined, the responsibility of the moment.

"We're not clairvoyant!" Viktor intoned with icy disregard staring at his nemesis, "just technicians and analysts–of a much higher order than those of the private sector I might add."

"I'm not questioning your ability…just why the hell I didn't get an inkling of any of this until now? Frankly, I'm a bit shocked at the lack of preemptive intelligence."

A dozen people around the table shifted uneasily in their seats with the caustic understanding that was their role, their entire mandate for existence. "Intelligence is like a chrysanthemum," Viktor replied unperturbed, "you don't know what color it will be until it blooms. Our first string of information came in a performance report from Ariel Addison. You know him…"

"Of course, Deputy Chief of Mission for the Central Middle East in Cairo."

"It wasn't until other reports were linked through our system algorithms that there was any significance to it at all. We get billions of bytes of data through here in any 24-hour period and nothing human can sort through it or make any sense of it–all runtime intelligence analysis filtered through a relational database."

She gathered her fear and channeled it into her own clear, concise language; like the language of Tundra swans that is unspoken yet buoys them on the wing from Siberia to Wisconsin in their annual pilgrimage. "So, we have another player," she spoke wistfully of migrations.

"Appears so."

"Inciting religious fervor."

"A simplification, but in a word…yes."

Watching him intently she did not speak for several moments her profile unmoved. "The military backed Islamic coup is not enough?"

"It's not that simple," Viktor explained. "General Riyadh is respected in ultraconservative quarters certainly, but he will never win hearts and minds–too much wealth, too much historical resentment towards the military. While the establishment will acquiesce, the people, especially those without shirts, will always rebel against the class he represents and he will never really ever wield true allegiance. Shari'ah yes, perhaps a coalition government, but power…no. He imagines himself al-Mahdi, but he is not rightly guided enough for people to believe."

"I don't understand."

"The *Mahdi* in Arabic means "he who is guided in the right way." In that part of Islamic theology concerned with death, judgment, and the final destiny of the soul and humankind he is a messianic deliverer who will fill the Earth with justice and equity, restore true religion, and usher in a short golden age. Inflammatory stuff. It's all about succession. The Sunnis view the *Mahdi* as the successor of Mohammad. In Shia Islam, the Mahdi symbol has developed into a powerful and central religious idea. Twelver Shia Muslims believe that the *Mahdi* is 'Muhammad al-Mahdi', the Twelfth Imam, who was born in 869 and was hidden by Allah at the age of five. It is said he is still alive but has been in occultation, awaiting the time that Allah has decreed for his return. When it comes, he promised that no one who wanted happiness would be denied and no one who had believed will be left behind. Though not part of the Qur'an it is integral to Islamic belief. Because the *Mahdi* is seen as a restorer of the political power and religious purity of Islam, the title has tended to be claimed by social revolutionaries in Islamic society. North Africa in particular has seen a number of self-styled *Mahdis*– General Riyadh being the latest."

"What is so different about our new messiah?"

"He's not a social revolutionary, or a politician–and there are miracles attributed to him that have been witnessed; events not ascribable to human power or the laws of nature, in fact perceptible interruptions of the laws of nature witnessed by more than one person. He has ignited an underground social firestorm."

"What does he want? Does he have an agenda?"

The others at the table traded surreptitious worried looks. "We don't know," Viktor replied, "but we do know that reports of *al-Qa'im*, meaning 'He Who Arises', are being texted, messaged, emailed, smartphoned and blogged throughout Egypt and subsequently much of the Middle East and has become the hottest news on all local social media overshadowing the coup d'état. This is grass roots. Completely outside the religiopolitical establishment, its…"

"That is interesting!" Karine Russo said raptly.

"Interesting," he paused on the precipice, "not quite the word I would use. It's dangerous…very, very, extremely dangerous. If we don't take immediate action we will have an inextricable political crisis that will be disastrous to global markets. I advised you before to be progressively proactive and was disregarded, now we must deal with these consequences."

The Crisis Manager sighed, folded her hands on the table and looked down; as her blood grew hot she spoke coldly. "I've told you before I don't like ultimatums. The significance of all this eludes me. What is so different about this fakir, this people's prophet performing on street corners that could cause a global crisis?"

"He is not a Muslim." Viktor uncoiled like a serpent easing himself out of hibernation onto on a hot rock in the middle of nowhere. His eyes glittered with the incandescence of hidden data only he was privy to and the corners of his mouth turned up imperceptibly, his lips almost the color of blood against pale skin. "He is an American," pausing for effect, "in fact, he works for the State Department. The Foreign Service Officer for Political Affairs posted at the Central Middle Eastern Mission in Cairo," he replied with relish.

A moment's disbelief. A dazzled expression. "Erskine?!"

"The same. Erskine Parrish MacKenzie! The coup's military leaders are also looking for him in relation with the death of a well know Imam."

Fear realized is a thousand times worse than fear anticipated. While one is lingering and gnawing the latter is full of the pain from retribution turned against oneself without recourse and without mercy by enemies one never knew one had. It was that relentless pursuit that drove most political figures who had held a position for any number of years knowing they could never turn back to the private sector once they had strode the aisles of power and had become recognized in the West

Wing by successive administrations. Retreat was impossible. Only death could relieve this terrible purpose once unleashed. It drove individuals to remarkable decisions, to measures that they would never have resorted to under more humane circumstances as The Crisis Manager was driven now before the divine wind that could annihilate her career, indeed her life, like a house of fog.

She was dressed all in black. The black silk chemise was buttoned high up her neck. The expensive black fabric of her suit glimmered and shined passing under the ceiling fluorescents as she walked steadfastly down the long hallway leading to *The Woodshed*, known to the press as the White House Situation Room. A *Sensitive Compartmented Information Facility* or *SCIF* run by the National Security Council to uninitiated staffers, the room's biggest nightmare was cyber-war–electronic malware that could penetrate the inner lobes of the national security brain. The Pentagon and intelligence agencies took elaborate precautions: The military operated what amounted to a separate, classified Internet, and nothing from "outside" was supposed to connect with it. Inside some of the most powerful individuals on earth anxiously awaited her arrival surrounded by a whisper-wall with six huge flat-screen televisions for secure video conferencing equipped with leading-edge tech links to generals, prime ministers and other global leaders making it less likely encrypted voices and images would go black at a crucial moment as had happened in the past. The staff of 40 was organized around five watch teams that provide 24-7 monitoring of international events and briefed the president daily–truth known much of their data was fed from Viktor Jaraslav's analysis, as he would be the first to admit his algorithms were unparalleled. Karine had no illusions about the extent the situation was already known. Just as she entered, the Director of Central Intelligence was beginning an operatic dialog with an overview of the latest information on the crisis.

Behind him was a door that gave access to a staircase leading to the White House swimming pool–a feature that allowed the first family to enter the cabana without crossing the south lawn that nobody thought was a security breach. A man sat at the head of the mahogany conference table with a staring-daggers gaze who had the most to lose if things went awry. Before him the table was littered with turkey pita wraps, cold shrimp, potato chips, soda and other items people reach for when stressed out. Above, on the wall behind him, was the seal of the President of the United States.

Darkness eclipsed her spirit as she agonized over the decision, but in the end there was only one course of action. She would bend the truth, despite the threat of prison time, and recommend a watchful policy, as opposed to Viktor's demands for a clandestine, paramilitary operation; because of the sensitivity of the target she wouldn't tell them everything they knew at The Watch. It would give her a chance to handle it personally and then there would be absolutely no reflection on the performance of her duty, as long as she wasn't discovered altering the facts–she still couldn't believe that the cynical Erskine was capable of the accusations. It was a calculated risk Karine accepted stoically, as Crisis Manager, when she rose to address the select clique who had sucked the decision-making process from the legislature when it came to national security issues. "As Egypt is moving forward with its political uncertainty," she began, "we should be wary of any amendments to their constitution of a particularly hard-line Islamist nature, followed by pushing for parliamentary and presidential elections and emphasize how much we would want this transition to be sustainable, inclusive, and democratic, and that we want it to succeed. Having said that, there is one clear obstacle to restoring good relations with any new leadership that we must address…" If she had foreseen the consequences of her decision that day it may have been different, but that would come later, now there was only a gnawing apprehension at hidden and ominous forces unleashed. She could not shake the image of death in the black dress with the single gold scarab and her predestined appointment in Alexandria with Erskine Parrish MacKenzie.

IX | Gift of The Nile

WHENEVER SHE CLOSED HER EYES THERE WAS THE BLUE-WHITE LANDSCAPE of the Siberian steppes with it's barren, snowy, windswept plains and vast wild lakes surrounded by fir and evergreen so deep and endless humans dared not enter for fear of being absorbed by nature in the low-light of the near arctic wilderness. It was cruel fate she had been born in a small Russian town far from any metropolis with its provincial people and parochial mindset and she cursed them all and the brown bear and fox and other creatures that inhabited her universe without permission. She had spent her life under these hidden primal influences and struggled constantly to break free to make her mark in the modern world.

Kisa Vanyusha awoke with a start staring at the clock. "хуй не путь!" She muttered to herself. Her cameraman Ibrahim Mohamed was supposed to give her a wake-up call and meet her at 5 am to interview the pastry chef; it was now 6:30. "No fucking way!" She bolted upright and then suddenly heard the diesel engines and metal treading on asphalt in the streets below. From her room at the Cecil Hotel overlooking the bay at Alexandria 15th century Fort Qaitbay was just visible across the misty sea torn with incessant Khamaseen winds. The Saad Zaghloul Square beneath her window, built to commemorate the great revolutionary nationalist, was filled with agitated people–remnants of the Samūn nationalists' demonstration now cornered by two lumbering Ramses II tanks. She couldn't believe her good luck and a surge of excitement coursed through her. "I fucking knew it!"

Like a whirlwind she showered, dressed, gathered her things and rushed downstairs where she finally found Ibrahim in the café calmly nursing a coffee his camera equipment piled at his feet. "There are soldiers in the lobby!" She exclaimed.

"No one can leave," he replied drolly. "Malesh, we can interview the chef tomorrow…when things calm down." He took another sip of his coffee.

"You're kidding, right?! You're kidding? This is the biggest story that ever happened to me! Didn't I tell you? Didn't I? We have to cover it!"

"Impossible!" He exclaimed. "Everything's under marshal law–soldiers at every exit," and took another long sip of coffee.

"That's what separates newsmen from journalists." She chided, punching him in the arm and yanking him from his seat and across the room so fast he barely had time to sling the camera equipment and bags over his shoulders. "If we run into anyone, say we're going to interview the chef!" But from the kitchen they quickly made a dash out the service entrance to the loading dock where there were no soldiers since their orders were only to ensure guests didn't leave the premises. They retrieved the rental minivan and drove it around the block, silently rolling it into position at the northeast corner of the square behind a looming, parked tour bus. Ibriham clambered on top of using the van to get there and lying as flat as he could–praying to Allah he was unseen–began filming the tanks and protesters clashing. Kisa reported the details peering from behind the vehicles on a wireless microphone.

"They're killing people!" The sudden whine of an engine. "Go take photos!" a motorcyclist screamed by while taking his finger and making a slitting gesture across his throat and then was gone. Kisa felt the shock of a chill starting at the top of her head and racing down her whole body. She knew instinctively this wouldn't end well, but being witness to an evolving melee stirred a strange excitement in her. Then a sniper appeared on a nearby rooftop wearing a balaclava and shot a military policeman. He fell to the ground motionless. The crowd quickly came under fire from the direction of the security forces. A woman who had been tear-gassed screamed, "God help us! We are unarmed!"

"Egypt is dangerously divided as what appears to have been a military backed coup during the night escalates its violent crackdown on opposition…in front of me protestors have been trapped in Saad Zaghloul Square, Alexandria, by troops backed with two battle tanks…" Kisa improvised not really knowing what had happened or how to report it. In just moments chaos broke loose in the square before her, the smell of tear gas filled her nostrils and burned her lungs, people fled from the soldiers who used buckshot and gas to disperse them before rounding them up for detention. Vans arrived filled with dark, masked military police. Reports of live rounds cracked the early Egyptian morning and people began to fall as they ran. A woman wearing full hijab cried uncontrollably on the sidewalk as someone tried to comfort her–behind was a trail of blood. Protesters began to throw rocks at the soldiers who, in response, used live ammo, shooting indiscriminately into the crowd. One man was shot in the head and dragged onto a side street. His friends tried to carry him on their shoulders, but afterwards the wounded and dead just lay where they fell near pools of blood as anyone trying to help them was also shot. Three ambulances arrived, their sirens wailing. Men began banging on the back of them shouting, "Let them through!" The soldiers turned them back and fired tear gas canisters at the men who fled. Another angry man rushed up to where Ibriham was filming and looked directly into the camera. "Is our blood this cheap? We are waging jihad now. God will have vengeance on these butchers!" He screamed above the din of battle, "the streets are full of blood!" Kisa, though rattled, shaking and nauseous continued her narrative… "In Egypt, what is a life worth?" She cried tears before her audience streaking her mascara.

But that was earlier, before they had piled into the minivan and recklessly caromed from the scene bullets shattering the rear window after they had been spotted filming. "Ibriham slow down!" She screamed after a few blocks over the roar and emotion of the moment and he finally loosened his grip on the wheel that had made his knuckles white. It was before she had met the fallen battered and bloody hiding in a café alcove seven streets away. "What's he saying?" Kisa badgered Ibriham. "What is it?"

"He's saying the military came in the night to destroy the *Masīh* and they have been sent by *Al-Masih ad-Dajjal.*"

"What does that mean?"

"It means there's a bigger battle going on here."

"Get him on camera…" Kisa exclaimed excitedly, "get him to tell you what's going on."

Ibriham set up the camera and began to ask questions. "He's afraid the military will recognize and arrest him."

"This is for Russian TV," she entreated the man, "they won't see it. Translate for me. I'm going to ask him some questions in Russian."

As the man spoke in the crowd of people jamming the café she looked into his eyes and couldn't help but fall into the slipstream. His was the ancient fire of North Africa: A brown amalgam of races that had imploded with the demise of the Pharaohs; just a man with a scraggly half beard falling from Grecian cheekbones ancestor to Alexander of the north; dark chestnut eyes with the almond shape of Arabian slavers who came across the eastern sea; the profile of Dervish nomads from the south as might be envisioned charging across the Sudanese desert through the nightmare of dust and wind on some terrible errand; and of traders who wound mysteriously through the greatest expanse of desert on Earth by unknown routes bringing blood from across the continent and beyond the western sea. Kisa could perceive the intimidating crucible of humanity though it was far from the sophisticated Western cities where she had always dreamed it dwelt when the bears and the wolves hunted her Siberian landscape–yet she could not name it because it was only an unsettled feeling. Yellow sunlight filtered into the café through the omnipresent grit in the air–the ubiquitous sand that made the Sahara shift infinitesimally encroaching a few centimeters more on the domains of men as it always had reclaiming its territory as nature always does across the earth waiting for its moment. Cities will pass because the natural world has a different clock and was created by far greater architects. Somehow all the random paths taken though the ages at once converged in this place at this time and the café was filled with these histories. She was their witness. It was destiny unfolding.

"He is explaining that everyone thinks someone special is in their midst."

"What do you mean 'special?'" Kisa demanded.

"A religious figure. Special because he's an American."

"OK, OK, so, what am I supposed to guess? This is my story! Mine! What is he fucking talking about?"

Ibriham was hesitant to go further out of some deep subconscious loyalty, even though he was not a devout Muslim it was in his blood. "The *Masīh* is sort of a messiah in mystical Islam, someone who is expected. It's not so much that it is written; it is believed–and not just by fundamentalists. It is a very common belief."

"So...?"

"Well...he says many believe he has come and is here in Alexandria and that's the real reason why the military took control. You see...think of the *Al-Masih ad-Dajjal* as the antichrist, you're a Christian aren't you? The legend goes that they will appear together, good and evil you see... he says many people have seen signs, undisputable signs...it's like a battle between good and evil for them."

"Is he crazy?"

Ibriham looked at the man, and then looked back. "No, I don't think so. He's a dentist..."

"Did he explain this on camera?"

"Yes."

"OK. Translate for me..." she turned to the man, "What are these signs?"

After a conversation between the men that seemed interminable he replied, "He says the vast majority of people who profess belief are Muslim in name only–their faith is weak, that there has been violence–the red death he calls it, there have been many Muslim tyrants, there has been a great conflict in Syria and fire from the sky in Bagdad...I think he means wars, but the most striking sign has been miracles. People have witnessed miracles. He says that's undeniable and the witnesses have been very credible that's the clincher. Reliable first hand reports."

"So, where is this messiah?"

They spent the rest of the day cruising the hollow streets of Alexandria looking for trouble, but it was quiet and without crowds more like a seaside Mediterranean town than Egypt's second largest city. Even the wind was letting up. A few business had reopened despite the marshal law edict broadcast on all local media that kept the usually impenetrable traffic minimal and some shopkeepers stood outside their doors chain smoking unfiltered cigarettes watching them drive by hoping they were customers. There wasn't much sign of the soldiers or of any more violence. Working people didn't have the margin for a military coup, hand to mouth didn't allow the time to protest or fight or roam the streets angrily when there were bills due–all that was left to the disenfranchised, the unemployed. At every opportunity they would pull up and interview whoever could be lassoed into it as hour after hour of video was shot, which she would upload to her news editors later in hopes they would compile it into cohesion, as soon as a secure internet connection was back up, meanwhile she called in reports on her satellite phone and was thrilled at the encouragement she received. It was her first real hard news story and there was no other Russian journalist in the city. It was her own personal coup–it would make her famous all over Russia–already she was a celebrity on social media there.

Over and over the same idea surfaced in people's stories, especially those from the streets not jaded by a fundamentalist propaganda outlet, but who relied on social media to keep abreast of events as they happened and thereby formed a common reality among themselves entirely separate from any organized media. There was a bigger battle going on in the mind, it was a fight between good and evil and somehow each life that had continuously grown harder despite all the political and religious promises hung in the balance.

By the time Kisa returned to the Cecil Hotel it was long past midnight. A story was forming in her fledgling news consciousness that, despite her lack of experience, resulted from an overwhelming intuition. She stood naked in the bathroom as the steam from the hot bath drew beads of moisture on her skin, clothing in a pile on the floor, dead tired and lost in thought. Then she lowered herself into the tub and stayed there soaking for a very long time sipping a whiskey from the minibar until she felt relaxed and light headed. It was later when her short blonde hair splayed across the pure white pillowcase and sleep overcame her almost before she touched down and the bears and foxes were chasing across her translucent Siberian wilderness and she ran far ahead of them for once certain in her purpose and strong in her resolve. The real story was this people's messiah not the military coup; he was on the minds of almost everyone they had encountered and true or not in their hopes as she had witnessed. People living so near the ground needed a lift from victory. Tomorrow they would find him, they would ferret him out wherever he was and she would grab the story with both hands, sink her nails into it and let it shake the hell out of her all through the media like the tail of a dog. It was irresistible now. Tomorrow she would become famous.

* * * *

There was hail pelting the ten thousand date palms where the Rashid Tributary met the Mediterranean Sea as they fled into the night. It was cold. The *khamaseen* winds had boiled up into an early spring storm even though it was still mid-winter. The river was nearly as wide as a lake at this point and riled under the weather making wooden fishing boats pound each other in the chop like a phantasmagorical drum symphony in the darkness as they passed. Though 40-miles from Alexandria to Rashid, once the three car convoy turned onto the International Coastal Road it seemed they had only just started, but now it was as if they had traveled back in time for once off the highway most of the roads were unimproved, muddy from the hail and rain and full of chuckholes. Of the 75-million Egyptians almost all of them lived in the delta cocooned by a volatile agricultural economy in the crush of a population that had doubled within 30-years. Everything was threatened. Life balanced here on a fragile ecosystem surrounded by breathless deserts.

Parrish sucked on a thin cigar and peered into the darkness trying to divine some insight into fate. Smoke vanished in drawn wisps through a crack in the window as a dark landscape fled into the night. He looked intently into the storm. It was destiny, he had decided, that determined the coincidence of events that ultimately molded a life by reason of forces and counter-forces encountered while living and what one's reaction to them was. The smallest influence could change the course of dynasties. For the first time he felt the true weight of the mass of humans struggling shoulder to shoulder against unachievable odds to grasp each his share of survival–some got the gravy, some the marrowbone–there seemed to be no rationale that explained the limitless inequities. He longed for the anonymous streets of Cairo where his happiest hours had been spent chasing after archeological artifacts of dubious origin, the only ones he could afford. He longed to be free of doubt. It was as if everyone was pushing against an impenetrable wall in life beyond which all limitations could be lifted and he, for no apparent reason, could suddenly pass through it easily. He didn't ask for this blessing, it wasn't something he'd wished for, and again he protested sub rosa, "I'm not the one…"

Despite bitter feelings Parrish found himself considering things that had never occurred to him before. Esoteric things, ideas he had no practical application for other than to clarify heretofore unexplained phenomena in life. For example, he had begun to see mental images in people's minds clearly enough to predict their thoughts and alleviate their traumas. "Knows all, sees all…" he thought and laughed at himself. It was quite simple really and he was amazed he'd never noticed it before, surprised that nobody else did.

"Rosetta," Abd al Hakim exclaimed breaking the silence that had accompanied their journey for the past hour, "that's what the Europeans call it because it was here the Rosetta Stone was discovered by French soldiers in 1799. It's in London's British Museum now, but of course you know that," he threw his elbow over the seat back, looked at Parrish and said confidentially one politician to another, "we've been campaigning to have it returned, perhaps you can help…" then he continued as before. "We call the town Rashid, locals say *Ar-Rašīd*, which in Arabic means "The Guide," one of the ninety-nine names of Allah. Wishful thinking, the name really derives from the ancient Egyptian *Rhyt*, meaning "the common people." Once our principle port and a great city during the Ottoman reign, it waxed and waned with the fortunes of Alexandria. It is known as the city of a million palms, but now is something of a backwater. They won't look for us here, and if they do…" Just then a huge rice mill slipped by looming in the darkness as they entered the town, "…nearly all the rice in the delta comes here for processing." Al Hakim added as an afterthought unable to suppress his hat as regional booster.

The ancient mansion sat across the river from the old town at Rashid on the northeast bank. Shaded and ominous, even on a rainy night, in its own compound of eucalyptus, casuarinas and palm trees it was a good distance from the dirt road that ran along the Nile over which workers from the fish farms and vast surrounding fields had traveled for five millennia. A moon tore through the clouds and Parrish briefly glimpsed its illuminated façade and then it was gone casting the landscape into pitch black again. Built in 1740 by a rich Ottoman merchant who chose these wild fields rather than the center of the city where all the other merchant houses stood because he was terrified of pirate attacks, or as legend goes because his young wife was too beautiful–Rashid has always been known for the beauty of its women. The front door covered in iron with huge cobbled nails and a bar crossed wicket above through which arrows could be slung testified that the Islamic city was founded on the more ancient site as fortification against sea invaders. Two adjacent buildings stood five stories high of molded, grouted bricks alternately black, burnt red and ivory each story overhanging the lower with inset beams and carved lintels. But the most distinctive feature was a profusion of *Mashrabiyas*, projecting windows enclosed with intricately carved wood latticework, starting at the second story and covering each opening to the highest one–delicate and beautiful, like silken masks drawn discreetly across hidden faces.

The houses had been completely restored by Abd al Hakim and were filled with minor antiquities and furnishings of the era yet with an infrastructure wired for the modern world. "Well," he would later confess, "we are an old family and much has been passed down through generations, but high office can have its rewards. My brother is the head of the antiquities police."

Parrish was in the news. He was wanted in the death of Abd Al-Faraq, the great Imam from Al-Qaed Mosque, not a suspect per se, but a person of interest strongly desired for questioning by the new military prefect. Even if it was the version of the news censored by the junta, he was shocked to see it because he was a diplomat for God's sake, an official of the most powerful country on Earth. Where were his supporters? He'd come to Alexandria on mission? He hadn't forgotten the nihilism with which he usually viewed his postings at Cairo always believing to the bitter core he was only a pawn and it didn't matter a whit if he had the intelligence of a canary or not. Any fool would do, at least anyone who would forward the official line nauseatingly developed by those chosen ones amalgamated by the group with such completeness that their wits had long ago departed. Even so he expected the department to defend him, at least publically.

He called the embassy in Cairo for the first time since he was abducted.

"Erskine?" Arial Addison's thin voice whined at the other end.

"I want to know what's being done about these news reports?"

"Where are you?"

He remembered al Hakim's warning not to reveal his location to anyone, even if he though they could be trusted, and Ariel Addison was not on that list. "Never mind where I am, just tell me…what's the plan?"

"I always knew you'd get in trouble sooner or later! Smoking. Blaspheming. I don't know what the Crisis Manager sees in you…"

It was a brief, but revealing conversation that for self-preservation if nothing else he didn't allow to continue long enough for the call to be traced. He now felt extremely isolated; much more so than before, alone he wondered what his protector al Hakim would do if he knew the State Department wasn't even working to rescue him…he decided it was better left unsaid.

Days passed and the rain finally let up to the delight of Ra-of-the-sun who had emerged from the underworld after a long hiatus, but it was still cold. Azhara had not made an appearance since they had arrived and stayed on the third floor with her friend in that part of the house traditionally reserved for women called *Al-Hadir*, the place of sleeping. Ishaq Sadek, the private detective, however was another matter all together being a garrulous man and a great source of information because he had insights into both sides of the economic divide–that of his wealthy clients, those he served, and of the poor, the disenfranchised, legion in Egypt who were his blood. They had intense conversations at the table where he would act as interpreter between himself and the cook who spoke a caustic blend of a local Arabic dialect along with regional slang that, like many places in Egypt, left Parrish wondering why he'd spent so long at the CIA language course studying the classical tongue. This was the language of blackened Nile perch, couscous, lamb and okra casserole that the Ottomans struggled with four centuries ago, but it had facilitated an empire and greased wheels that were still moving when the French and then the English came to pilfer the resources and fill their bellies on the fat of the land. Nonetheless it made it easier for Parrish not to reveal anything about himself as he talked local politics with the private eye in English who cared little one way or the other about the military coup. "Malesh," he tossed off with disdain, "the poor will always be poor, the rich will always be rich and I will always have business. The general and the politician are the same–'Mister Ten-Percent' with the hand outstretched. It's all about money isn't it? No matter what anyone says, it's all money. Look at this house," he motioned with open hands.

The dichotomy of the wealthiest ten-percent commanding a democracy as servants of the people while being rapacious owners of ninety-percent of the world's resources was a source of inner rage and unexpressed resentment. Parrish had a great solidarity with common people. It was something unannounced in his personality that dwelled beneath social veneers and even far below those strata of himself that only he was witness to and no one else surmised existed. It was an unknown child of some ancient spiritual union mired in memory, a curse that had burdened his life driving him with senseless altruism from seminary to the oil business and then finally to the State Department always preventing him from being on the inside where tacit agreements among colleagues forgave many of the imperfections and demons men are prone to and so made it easier to flourish and prosper–for he knew instinctively agreement was the glue of life and that his was a uniqueness with scarce demand in this world. Abd al Hakim came and went as his political journey now ran hot with current events, but it was only partially from duty that he maintained a public presence in the face of personal danger and partly from fear that General Riyadh would send someone unexpectedly when he would not be prepared. Especially now that he sheltered his wayward daughter. He preferred to buck up against destiny rather that to give it free rein and it would be less likely for a crime to be committed in the public eye. When he was absent, he left two of his bodyguards–including Malik who now attributed special dispensation to Parrish and even bought him clothes to wear–a housekeeper, a cook and an old man with his wife who stayed on the property and took care of the buildings and the gardens, which have grown one thing or another since the eighteenth century, in exchange for room and board all living in the adjacent house–originally built for the Ottoman's slaves. It was now restored the same as the main house–all slaves to something because of the trouble with being free; there is no where to be free to.

He had taken to walking by the river. The ancient dusty river. The river Herodotus attributed Egypt from as a "gift of the Nile" when he was here in 500 B.C. and who now resides in the country of myth. Parrish would walk north toward the Mediterranean drawn by the same mystique that carried Phoenician ships on the wind to become the greatest sea traders on earth, now dust like the Carthaginians victims of the eternal peace. At first he was consumed with cities, their pace and bumptious wavelengths electrified him with gizmos, infrastructured with ever evolving technology placing layer after layer of mechanical systems to satisfy the elemental requirements of living on this planet at the disposal of fingertips destined for higher glories than mundane pastimes like survival. All his points of reference were of cities and together they formed his worldview filled with people rushing to mysterious destinations, pursued and hectic beneath polycarbonates and glass, steel and stone and concrete wound together in a seamless macrocosm. Blurred figures flitted by, half-known identities he had struggled with, some friendly some not, and millions of the nameless who shared their common space with the buyers and the sellers and the dreamers. Urban sounds substituted for the sounds of nature as he passed lush reed beds clogged with papyrus that had been used for thousands of years to consolidate men's thoughts and set them down as history so succeeding generations would have the benefit of experience and insight and perhaps a glimmer of axiomatic truth to begin the voyage back to the garden. All this was yet a visual wash to Parrish as the chains of cities had not yet unlinked. Evolution was a gradual thing. Function monitored structure. All great truths were simple.

Parrish stood in the path of immense migrations. Across the river the horizon was spiked with fronds of date palms–"…with their feet in the water and their heads on fire", as the Arab saying goes–but overhead flew millions of birds some on the wing without rest for up to six months soaring on ancient sky trails that guided them unerringly between predestined points on the Earth as their ancestors had done without question following each a path in memory so obscured by time its origins could not even be guessed at. The Nile Delta was midway between these departures and arrivals. From as far north as Siberia and as Far east as Asia to the Sub-Saharan rain forests and the South African veldt and beyond the delta was nature's conduit and had been that way since the first bird. Disguised by the clothes Malik had bought him he felt emboldened enough to walk further each day without being conspicuous, which he had been warned against because they were looking for him, though still unaware that he moved through the spiritual firmament in which nature spoke with prehistoric languages he could not yet perceive. In his mind roiled confusion from events that had happened so unexpectedly he could not fathom them. It so fixed his attention that he did not see the birds above or hear their hundred songs around him in the river wetlands or catch the out of place flamingo launching to continue his journey to the southern banks of the Upper Nile where it will be flushed pink from the tiny shrimp it eats or see the ten-foot Egyptian cobra swimming downstream to the Mediterranean where they had been commonly spotted far out to sea. It was a mystery why the cobra swam, but all that escaped his notice.

Then one day he was sitting on the bank feeling the warm earth beneath him watching a fishing boat with a yellow wooden hull, cobalt blue gunwales and a turquoise cabin slowly fight the current as it returned from its dawn raid on the fishes the old diesel engine echoing across the distance in murmurs and muffled sighs. An otter slid silently through the reeds into the water without a ripple perhaps having spotted the cobra back from his ocean voyage when suddenly someone spoke.

"They are telling stories about you."

Parrish was so startled that when he scrambled to rise he wound up teetering on one knee staring into the dark eyes of an interloper. Like a bird flying into glass he was stunned, momentarily suspended as exquisite beauty cascaded through his consciousness that an instant before had been struggling with questions of universal law. Azahara stood before him sullen yet graceful and poised yet with an austerity betraying she was her father's daughter. "They are," he replied, "I've heard some of them even." Coming to his feet and brushing the dirt off his knees. "I'm Erskine Parrish McKenzie–we never really met" A lick of disheveled hair fell into his eyes.

A nearly imperceptible smile crossed her delicately formed lips as she ignored him shifting her gaze to the ground and walking away gracefully. "We're an ancient people Mr. Erskine."

"Parrish. My friends call me Parrish."

"Parrish…" She echoed frowning. "I am Azhara Binte Jibril Riyadh."

A sense of place descended upon him. The sounds of birds suddenly intruded on his urban cacophony resonating in layers of distances and secret social orders that are more ancient than even the Egyptians. He was instantly aware of his surroundings and all the life that permeated everything from sojourners and residents alike all harmonious in the perennial cycle that was breath and heartbeat to bird and wildebeest both migrants of vast distances. The song of the river rose as its ceaseless journey tied the landscape and people together in a bond of dependency that had been unbroken since *Merimda Beni Salama*, the "Place of Ashes," was settled nearby over 5,000 years ago.

"I don't know what you've heard, probably not much truth to it," he finally replied hoping it would dead agent events he would rather not talk about.

She tilted her head, peered at him and shot back as if a question, "Then I'll thank you for what is true…"

"I can't take the blame for everything."

"I don't know what happened either," sensing his inner storm, "but I woke and you were there. I was thankful personally. I think there is something very reassuring about you."

"Coincidence. I was concerned…just, we were all con…" he was drawn to her impossibly delicate hands with long, slender fingers emblazoned with intricate henna tattoos, "are you alright?"

"Perfectly," she drew herself more erect with inner preening. "I just thought it better…best that…" a darkness passed above them from an errant cloud on an otherwise clear day, "we are both fugitives now you know. I have crossed lines I could see plainly with full knowledge of the consequences, and you…you crossed lines only visible to those of fervent belief…you couldn't possibly have intended…the unwritten laws."

"I have a knack for these things."

"How do you know Abd al Hakim?"

"I was running from the police…the military actually'" he confessed. "Caught in the coup with no shoes I confess…it's a long story."

"Well then, I'm all ears."

"An archeologist/taxi driver introduced me to a gangster, after first advising me not to befriend him–even though I, a stranger, was about to ask a favor for which he could get jail time–who runs a casino where allegedly Mr. Hakim gambles...like I said it's a long story. We're both in the same business at any rate, the diplomatic corps. He extended me professional courtesy, and you?"

"He is a friend of my fathers, a family friend."

"Political family?"

"Yes," she said sullenly and Parrish perceived a hint of sadness. "Politics. Generations of politics. Can't you tell? Why else would I be in trouble?"

"Some things are just destiny."

"Yes, we Egyptians know of destiny," suddenly serious, "it's in our DNA. Brutality, poverty, oppression...the subjugation of women!" Parrish perceived she was even more beautiful when angry the dark emotion drawing a veil from her face to reveal something primal and raw, "...everyone thinks it's kismet, like eating sweets in the mind."

"I think people are..." he furrowed his brow and looked down river toward the piled up jumble of earthen buildings reflecting along the bank where Rashid met the Nile, "...trapped by their own lives. Trying to escape for too long has beaten them down, it makes them angry so they keep looking for a reason and always tend to find it in somebody else–it's always someone else that's the cause of their condition. Men are prone to witch hunts. That's why they're brutal, that's why they are oppressed, they are just fighting themselves and are tired and desperate, frantic and sad, even the rich can't bribe their way out–only numb themselves with pleasure. All men are losing sleep over it."

Azhara watched him soberly. "Perhaps the stories about you are true. You are a mystery."

They would meet again along the river many times as the days of hiding from the junta wore on. Parrish made it routine to walk the footpath on the eastern bank and she would appear without warning and they would speak of increasingly personal things. He drawn by her untouchable beauty, she drawn by an intellectual curiosity at the difference in their understandings and perceptions and something else; the danger of being alone with a man not her relative, which Azhara knew her father would never have allowed, and which brought her pleasure. They sought each other's company and were the only ones that it was not clear to. She was a catalyst and at some indistinct point he had begun to breathe in the essence of the place, had been gradually imbued by the mighty Nile as it ambled nimbly across a faceless desert magically bringing alive everything it touched. He smelled the humus, the untamed grasses, felt the wild tangents of animals woven into the ancient ecosystem. Life, he discovered, was dormant under the sands and had been there waiting since creation just needing a hint of it's true potential, a tiny pointer to burst forth in cascades and torrents and avalanches and great thunderous cavalcades of energy. One day he watched a Praying Mantis perched motionless on a palm frond and he began to feel heady. Buoyant. It coursed through him like an electric current as he was touched by nature and felt the power of the silence, the fury of stillness and danced at the edge of the universe for the first time in his life happy and secure in the knowledge he was heading somewhere at last. Even if driven by a terrible, mysterious purpose he still did not understand, he was heading somewhere.

X | THE EXPECTED ONE

THE BLACK HERALD HAUNTED HIM. IT HAD COME ON RIOTOUS FOOTSTEPS as he went about his ungodly business no longer restrained along with all the other demons that had been hiding in his soul when he had given the final orders to proceed. It was a timeless moment that could not be rescinded, nor recalled to memory, it was blotted out, it did not exist in his mind because the consequences were too sinister for any human to endure.

But that was earlier before General Jibril Ben Jabbar Riyadh soared above the ground with a sense of inexorable loss permeating his entire being. The primeval plain of the Delta spread out before him with colorless, desiccated earth and sand graduating into the sages and myriad greens of the alluvial fan as the main current of Mother Nile sifted through it to the sea. The air in the helicopter was stuffy, smelled like fuel, exhaust and overheated plastic and the white noise of the engine roared over every other perception. It never occurred to him that the grief came from his own hand as he drove fissures in the social structure that had endured for eons only because of strong belief and nothing more, just wisps of thought against the forces of an unrelenting universe. He couldn't afford that luxury. The other problems he had set out to solve such as reestablishing the *Shari'ah*, not enough capacity in the country to even approach feeding the inhabitants of the Two Lands, or enough work for idle desperate hands that were the fodder of extremism each more important than the errand he was now on, but these thoughts never crossed his mind either and all he could think of were his family name and what would happen to his legacy as "Commander of The Faithful" once he was gone. He loved flying, but could not now soar in spirit as he once could weighed down by deeds. Though steadfast in his religion as a true believer, right now he wasn't feeling that inspired and wondered that his faith was tested beyond the limits of what any man should have to suffer.

Earlier still the news was unceremoniously delivered to him–he who had just that day declared himself interim President, until regular elections at some far off, nebulous date, could be held; suspended the constitution and dissolved the People's Assembly and the Shura Council. Meanwhile, he knew best and would be the believer president even if he wasn't the mob's first choice. A truly great man, he believed, is exempt from the expected notions of right and wrong and social conventions and so he usually did what he pleased without regard to consensus or anything else because it was usually right. *In-sha Allah*, he would continue to be a man of the straight path, but the way he had been treated lately it would be difficult.

"It was in an old hotel." Colonel Hasan Mawdudi explained nervously standing erect in immaculately pressed khakis despite the heat of the night. "Seems she has some connection with the Arab women's rights movement organized by an ex-patriot now living in London under a *fatwa*." He was especially on-edge now that the issue of the General's daughter had come up again as a topic. He had, after all, tried in vain prior to the coup to deliver her from harm. "She was speaking to a gathering of women."

Jibril had come out into the courtyard that warm evening to find solace in the desert stars and had just taken the first sip of a strong Sulawesi coffee in an effort to escape an anxious stomach when he had been interrupted. "Truly, this exceeds credibility Colonel!" He blustered.

"It comes from credible sources." He replied as tactfully as he could hiding the tiny bit of glee he felt inside form being right in the first place. "We have no reason to doubt its veracity."

He paced and impatiently watched the confused colonel measuring his words. "And…? Surely there must be more! We knew she was in Alexandria, you yourself told me…so what is the point?"

"There is a man we have reports on," the colonel confessed. "He first came to our notice after an incident in Morocco while visiting the Deputy Oil Minister for Saudi Arabia, Muhammad Abd al' Rashid…I believe you know him…" He continued relating all the facts their intelligence service had been able to dig up. "…and he has been attributed with more than one *mu'jizah*, miracles of healing and bringing the dead to life no less! However, later he was implicated in the death of Imam Abd Al-Faraq of the Al-Qaed Mosque and is being sought for questioning. So you see, he is a man of contradictions."

"Yes, yes…I met the Imam…" Jibril replied his endocrine system signaling red alert. "Go on…go on…"

"General, I don't know how to put this…we have trouble in Alexandria."

"Plain words are best, spare me nothing."

"He is being called *al-Mahdi*. Stories are spreading like wildfire on the Internet. We believe he must be a plant to ferment dissent and social disruption–as you know the Samūn demonstrated shortly after we took over and the clash with our troops is already on global news–we believe he is an American agent and that it is a coordinated campaign to avert attention and create social disturbances."

"What brings you to that conclusion?"

"He is not a Muslim. He is a minor diplomat at the U.S. Embassy here in Cairo… and he is an American."

"An American! Really!" The sheer incredulity of it discharged volumes of emotion. "That is interesting," he said laughingly amused that anyone would think there could be a Western *Mahdi*. It was pure blasphemy, simply ridiculous; it was a statement of little faith. "Pick him up…" he chortled gleefully, "pick him up. We can certainly deport an errant diplomat!"

"We could, but we don't know where he is. And that's not all…"

"Well…what is it then?"

"Azhara. Your daughter was sighted injured at the *Samūn* demonstration and was later rumored to be with this man. This ad-Dajjal. She is missing and we believe that he has her. That he has taken her."

The impromptu flight from Cairo to Alexandria was short. They followed the long, dark ribbon of highway that ran across the burning desert like an ancient path that aliens could use as a navigational aid after their long interstellar flights. The helicopter landed in a cosmic swirl of dust and sand in the gardens of the Montazah Palace that had been commandeered for the operations center. The ornate, nineteenth century structure loomed in the moonlight with its long open arcades facing the sea. The palace was a mixture of Turkish and Florentine styles with two towers, one rising distinctively higher than the other showing elaborate Italian Renaissance design details. It was righteous, he mused, that it was in military custody as a symbol of power. "Everyone needs to know who's the master on the throne of the Pharaohs," he had told them in his instructions for taking the city.

General Jibril Ben Jabbar Riyadh stormed through the corridors with the audacity of a rampaging bull elephant and every subordinate he passed snapped to with uncompromising fury and he left rows of soldiers teetering in his wake speculating at the cause of his rage hoping they hadn't inadvertently done something to incur this wrath. At last he settled in the office of Khedive Abbas II, the last of the Muhammad Ali Dynasty rulers to hold the Khedive title over Egypt and the Sudan. In seeming moments top local commanders and civilian officials stood at attention before him though it was now four in the morning.

Azhara had been the only light in his life, which was sometimes bitter yet always focused in the direction of duty and unrelenting self-promotion in order to stay at the top of the greasy pole that was politics. It was always she that softened the moral compromises of leadership he had been forced by his position to make for the greater good that left him emotionally desiccated and devoid of any human feeling for long periods of time. He had always felt that somehow his daughter was compensation given him by Allah for his sacrifices and the long stretches in the void, compensation far greater than the myriad of women he lay sweating with in moments of passion and lust rolling his seed to them under the cloak of darkness where he prayed it would remain. He had wanted her to follow him as a leader of the people, even though he knew from the start she would never equal his religious genius he had sent her to the best preparatory schools, the finest universities until the knowledge took root and she became an intellectual force of her own. The *ulama* had warned him against having a daughter educated; "Female education is against Islamic teachings and spreads vulgarity in society…it inculcates Western values…" He vigorously defended her and told them the Prophet said *"Can those who have knowledge and those who do not be alike? So only the wise do receive the admonition… The person who goes forth in search of knowledge is striving hard in the way of Allah."* Confusion overtook him this night when he was most vulnerable reeling from the stress of conquest and the necessary crimes he had committed accompanying it. Now, in the dark hours, he wondered if they were right and if his own blood had turned apostate.

"This is *jihad*! There will be no peace until everyone confesses there is no God but Allah..." he began pacing before them eyes downturned to hide the flames. "*Al-Masih ad-Dajjal*, the False Messiah exists...he is here now among us. I was warned, but had not the faith to believe then. I could not believe, even though an imam came from the other side of life to warn me. Now he has taken my only daughter." The General pontificated for over an hour lifting his massive arms in dramatic supplication and weaving his intricate knowledge of the *Qur'an* with his own brand of populist politics and military discipline until all present were in a frenzy of politico-religious fervor. "People are beginning to call him *Mahdi*, but he is *Kafir*' a disbeliever and is a curse against Islam! The mission I am charging you with is to find him and defeat him before he can gather his followers. It is *jihad* I am asking of you!"

A sweeping, frantic yet organized search began branching out in a naked web from the Montaza Palace. All units briefed. All civilian police recruited. The story was leaked to the international press that Erskine Parrish McKenzie was being sought for questioning in the death of the imam from the Al-Qaed Mosque, and that he, General Jibril Ben Jabbar Riyadh, "The Protector of Mosques," had risen in righteous fury to track down the perpetrator of an un-Islamic crime the authorities had missed and that was only one reason why there had been a need for the military coup. "To take the reins of power from those of little faith," he was quoted as saying to the press, but in his heart he prayed it would shift the focus from his daughter's betrayal of Islam and in the confusion that followed exonerate her for youthful indiscretion no matter how many lives he had to take to accomplish it. "*...let them find harshness in you, and know that*

God is with the God-fearing."

It was a conquered city swept by dreams and wind. All bets were off. All plans unhinged. All waited in the wings to see what fortune would deliver them. Fatalism was endemic to Alexandrians with their long history of rebirths from ashes. It wasn't what was seen in the streets, but what was left unsaid that held all breathless before dawn as the muezzins performed the *Azan* from every minaret their voices blending into one lament crying for the moon.

Earlier she ran. Perspiration from the warm night air made her silk blouse cling to her stomach as she rounded a corner and slammed her back against a wall listening intently for the slightest sound. She gasped for breath. Sweat ran into her eyes. Footsteps echoed. They were still coming. Pursued, she fled. But it was earlier still that flight had begun from the confinement of a hot, sleepless night into the mean streets where life was cheap and survival wasn't guaranteed.

It had all started in her hotel room. Kisa was leaning up against the balcony rail to cool off in the darkness. A short black rayon kimono hung loosely over her bare shoulders. She had just showered and now moonlight bathed her in ivory iridescence. Streets far below were silent. The air conditioning was on the blink for a whole section of the building and, despite cooler temperatures outside, it was steamy in the confines of the hermetically sealed room–they called it a suite, but it wasn't even big enough for two people. A scarcity of maintenance engineers due to the martial law edict was the reason given; so she waited it out unable to sleep anyway in her condition and exasperated had slipped outside on the balcony for relief. When she was like this, she could never sleep. Alcohol just made it impossible, so she avoided it altogether as it set pictures alive in her mind, sensual images she didn't know the source of and would rather not face especially when she was like this, in the grip of some kind of carnal energy that crawled up out of her solar plexus, saturated her senses and strained against all human decorum to be released in violent, physical passion. She gazed out over the Corniche and roared inside with a restrained ferociousness at the North African night.

Suddenly there was a knock at her door. "I've got something," her cameraman Ibrahim Mohamed exclaimed guardedly trying to keep from being overheard.

She pulled her loose wrap tight and let him in. "What's so damned important." She plopped down on the bed folding her long, smooth legs up under her like an insect, lit a cigarette in frustration and looked at him antagonistically.

He just stood there smiling for a moment in his ubiquitous vintage U.S. Army M65 olive drab Field jacket. "That first night…you know, when they came, after the military had arrived…it was under marshal law, right? Everyone knew it, right?"

"I suppose…" she replied skeptically taking a long drag on her cigarette trying hard to resist his enthusiasm.

"Then, I thought to myself," he said smugly, "it shouldn't be so hard to find an American loose in the streets. Where would he go? What would he do?" Hands flew in animated flight clarifying his meanings. "So, on impulse, I just spent the last four hours talking to taxi drivers."

"Four hours." She nodded accusingly. "Taxi drivers…"

"That's right. Logically, why would this foreigner have his own car, driving it with military all over the streets…and I found a guy, a guy who said he picked up an American just after dawn that first day. An American with no shoes. Roughed up. Disheveled. I couldn't get much out of him, but he knows more that he's telling that's sure. Sent up red flags."

"What makes you say that?"

"Wouldn't look me in the eye...told him we were Russian press, that we wanted to tell the true story to the world...."

Kia was interested now. She sat straight up on the edge of the bed. "So, you think it was our guy?"

"Yea."

"I'm ready to...but, why? Why do you think that?"

"I just do. Nobody else was on the streets; most of the drivers weren't even working." He shook his head slowly and pondered his own conclusions for a moment and shrugged. "What've we got to loose?"

"Right!" So, where'd he take this American?"

"El Salamlek Casino. But there's something else, he said be careful... the owner's a gangster and involved in 'summer marriages,' selling young Egyptian girls for sex. He's notorious."

The moon and stars littered the pristine sky. Sea mist furled in the warm air with memories of trawlers sitting heavy in the darkened bay awaiting their next day's journey out on the brine where silver fishes roamed in unknown numbers. The smell of the catch on old wooden decks waxed and waned with hints of breezes on the unexpectedly warm night, which often came after a storm when fluctuating pressure zones rolled ominously across the Delta. Ibrahim hovered menacingly on one arm against the bricks. Kisa stood under him back against the wall trying to look unobtrusive, like lovers, to get the lay of the place. She could smell his sweat. The Casino's arcade of Belle Époque brass trimmed doors lined up under phosphorous street lamps across the street adjacent the ancient Shallalat Gardens in the Al Shatby neighborhood where the original Hellenistic defensive walls could still be seen. The park, though over manicured with lit up walking paths, was a glade of palms and grasses giving relief from the bleak, lifeless canyons of the city. But tonight it seemed sinister. Anonymous automobiles slid up and departed from the casino's entrance leaving a burning mystery as to who would be patronizing the notorious gangster known for selling young girls, especially when the city was under siege.

"What the hell are we going to learn out here?" Kisa fumed impatiently and dragged Ibrahim off by the hand. Soon, after telling the maître d' "…just waiting for someone…", they stood at the long antique varnished bar under tiny illuminated spots that made everyone look semi-glamorous. The casino was spread out beneath a vast infrastructure of low slung lights that isolated every gaming area to itself while the long row of slot machines stood at attention each with one arm raised. The sparse crowd was subdued, but Kisa could see the whole layout from the bar that was stationed near the entrance where parties could congregate and strategize their attack on the tables and impulse drinkers could be snared coming and going.

"We are tourists," she told the barman.

"From Russia," Ibrahim added.

"Who is the owner?"

"You want high stakes? That man over there. Talk to him." He pointed across the room to a stout, middle-aged man conversing with a blackjack dealer who had close cropped black hair meant to minimize a bald spot, a belly tucked into his buttoned jacket and a strong, square bulldog jaw."

"No, no…just curious…friends back home," Kisa replied and watched the man as the night wore on surreptitiously making conversation with Ibrahim wondering why the American wound up here.

Cigarette smoke filled the air. The lilting din of the crowd was melodious with Arabic phrases she could not understand and pierced her inner world with alternating sharp then minor movements as conversations rose and fell like breathing. Smells of cumin, garlic and saffron wafted from the kitchen mingling with those of alcohol, lime and beer. It infused her with a culture alien to her own established points of reference and the foreignness of the place in which she was an interloper made her feel self conscious and suddenly more observant of the casino's murky landscape. That was why she noticed the tall black man. He had Ethiopian features and was dressed all in black. An elegant man, he approached the casino owner and after a brief word led him over near the door. There an Arab appeared from the shadows in a white *thawb* with a flowing black, gold trimmed, wool *bisht* robe and Kisa knew immediately he was not just anyone–one of the few trivial minutiae she did remember about the Middle East was that the *bisht* was not a common garment. Not in a nightclub. Not anywhere. It was reserved for special ceremonial occasions, or for men of importance. She watched intently and elbowed Ibrahim in the ribs so hard he spit out an ice cube from his drink.

"We're leaving," she muttered heading for the entrance. In the darkened foyer, behind another party on their way out near the potted Kentia Palms she suddenly turned and embraced Ibrahim. He shocked at the lean heat from her body. Stiffened against her right hand toying with his hair at the neckline. "What's he saying?" She whispered hoarsely into his ear; demanding, impatient. "Dammit, what's he saying?"

"Who?" Ibramim replied holding her at the waist up for the game and without anywhere else to place his hands.

"The Arab! The man in the black *bisht*," she growled, "I can't understand that lingo…" pressing him closer for emphasis. "He's an official! He's important!"

A moment passed. "I can't hear much. He's looking for someone. He's repeating the name 'Azhara,' and…I hear 'Abd al Hakim' that's all I can get. He's asking questions about…can't hear him," he said as the Arab, the black man and the casino owner left through the entry doors.

"God…! You're no fucking help!" Kisa shoved him.

"What? I don't get…"

Outside they slowly walked passed the stout, middle-aged man with close cropped hair and a belly tucked into his jacket flexing his strong, square bulldog jaw as he talked to the Arab and the statuesque Ethiopian, but couldn't pick up any more. From the shadows they watched the silver car pull away, then it was quiet.

"Azhara…" Ibrahim questioned. "Isn't that the name of the General's daughter, mastermind of the coup? I think I heard it on the news at the hot…

"That man was an official," Kisa ignored him as if thinking out loud, "a Saudi. This place is a hotbed. I'm going back inside."

"Don't you want me to come?"

"Find that taxi driver. Get what else you can out of him. See you at the hotel later."

She had three vodkas at the bar. One after the other. Straight, no chaser. Beads of perspiration appeared on her forehead. Kisa had seen places like this in Russia, she had worked in dumps that were worse, but that was before she transformed herself into the Travel Girl in a maelstrom of self focused discipline that she still teetered on the edge of. It was in an earlier incarnation when she was a broke teenager bumming around a small town a hundred and twenty miles from Moscow where she had been reluctantly born. It wasn't the family problem; parents were doctors and both had good positions at the state hospital and were, by all standards then, middle class. They had a nice apartment. A car. Had sent her to university where she studied linguistics, which she hated. All they had was trouble with her; tantrums, moods, depression then mania…her mother would bring home psychiatric drugs to calm her, to make her fit in when all she felt was a certainty that destiny was holding out on her. It was just that she hated everything her parents stood for–routine, provincial lives that had suffocated her from the instant she awoke to the fact she lived outside the mainstream in a cultural backwater filled with peasant stock, potatoes and borsch. But then she discovered guys and they were crazy for this lithe, blonde, Arian goddess of the streets and she told everyone; "The guys are crazy for me I guess, but I don't give a shit. It's all for my career." Only then her career was men. Young men, old men, married men…the last of which beat her silly when she went to see his wife after he had refused to buy her a coat she wanted. One day she seduced her mathematics teacher, unzipped his pants and played with his penis right on his desk at the front of the classroom when nobody was around. Then he would buy her things. Take her to lunch. Later came the drugs. The sitting in the park at the center of the "podunk" town drinking cheap vodka with the toughs. Kisa; thin, wiry Kisa could out drink many of the boys and sometimes woke up in their beds missing the memory of the night before as well as all her clothes. They did drugs, bought drugs and sold drugs. It was the only business opportunity outside the black market, which the older crime gangs had a vice grip on. The Russian mafia ran the national networks. But drugs, that was how she met her first real gangster, that was how her life had changed inextricably.

It had been a bad time for her. Hadn't seen the parents for a while and the last boyfriend who was supporting her from his drug dealing had beaten her and trashed their apartment smashing almost all the dishes and anything else that could break and then blew. Was gone. Disappeared. He was mad because he found out she had slept with another married man and called her a slut at the top of his lungs as he slammed the door off its hinges. She had only wanted more than he could give. Now hungry, with a bruise still visible on her right cheekbone she had dressed to the nines, put her young flowering body to use with a tight dress and lipstick, high heels and a leather jacket then went to see a man about a job. She got it at a fast-food place owned by an American chain, but hated it so much that she left after only one day. That's how she reinvented herself and became a stripper. An exotic dancer. The man, the owner was a lot like the casino owner she watched tonight, only more raw, less refined and brutal in thought and deed. He would be her sponsor if she promised to work hard, not complain and make customers happy. "It's all about money," he had told her, "we're in business for money. Nothing else matters."

The first time she took her top off on stage felt silly. It was cold. Lights blinded her and she could not see the audience and the music was so loud it made her ears ring, so she had a couple shots of vodka and then it was all right. After a few nights she forgot about the audience and just did what she wanted certain she was sexy as all hell...sexy as all get out. "The guys are crazy for me..." But all that ended when the owner came into the back room one night and, gripping her arm so tight it left a bruise for each one of his fingers and his thumb, let her know that she wasn't doing enough to make his customers happy. "You can make some money, I pay you commission for each one. You can touch them, but don't let them touch you." It was the beginning of the end of her reinvention of self, her transformation from street urchin to woman. He did pay her, for every private dance with some troll-like, anonymous man in one of the bare bones side rooms where the bouncers could watch them and make sure nobody touched the girls. Kisa quickly discovered that wasn't where the money was. Men wanted more, they wanted everything and weren't embarrassed to ask for it and she wanted money so she started pushing their boundaries, driving them up the wall...the very next night she cautiously turned her back on the bouncer while performing a private dance and took a man's exposed member in her mouth just as he released his seed. She couldn't believe she'd done it. Couldn't believe it, but there it was and all the vodka in the place couldn't wash it away nor erase the indelible experience that had been branded in her psyche forever so she never went back. Never returned.

Now the memory burned her. "You need a girl?" Kisa eased up to the stout, middle-aged man with close cropped hair.

He frowned at her, distracted, annoyed. "Cute," he said bluntly.

"I'm looking for work."

The man nodded sternly. "Good for you. What makes you think I need a girl?"

"I'm Russian."

"Real blonde?" He glared at her luridly. "Does the carpet match the drapes?"

She wanted to kill him. "What do you need?" Men had always been crazy for her, but she never could form an emotional bond with any, just using them as sex objects when she was climbing the walls as she had been earlier that night. Necessary, but disposable. "I can do that. I'm experienced. Men are crazy for me."

"I'll bet they are…I had another girl like that. Didn't work out. She let the men do whatever they liked, but neglected the money. Didn't get paid. Besides, you're too old." He turned away.

"Look…I need help. I'm Russian, ran out of money and I can't get out of here. Someone left me. I know you can help me."

"How do you know?" He asked now suspicious.

"I heard you helped an American the other night," she exclaimed innocently enough hoping that it would get his attention and he would reveal some vital information "you and…" thinking fast she remembered the name Ibrahim had overheard, "Abd al Hakim."

This time he really frowned and squared off toward her flexing the muscles of his bulldog jaw in rhythmic pulses as he gritted his back teeth. "Where did you hear that?"

"A taxi driver."

"Well…he was just looking for a good tip. He saw you coming, that's common on the streets of Alexandria. You better get out of here now if you're not a paying customer. I don't need any girls." Then he walked away without looking back.

Outside, Kisa stood nonchalantly at the entrance freshening her mandarin red lipstick in a vanity mirror, looking behind and being paranoid. There were no more cars. The thoroughfares were very quiet. Nobody was abroad. What she didn't see when she walked down the street was a man who came out of the casino, paused a moment and then flagged a car from the military pool containing two soldiers. There was a brief conversation then they spread out menacingly into the night, the three of them, wraithlike.

The city held its breath. She could feel silent longings all around her emanating from darkened rooms in darkened buildings, soaring out on the thermals into the shot spray of stars scattered across the sky like a hat full of diamonds. It was the same where she had come from. The air was thick with wishes. Nobody had the life they craved, money was scarce, everyone lived on government promises and hope that wore thin when nothing changed. Happiness was as elusive as economic mobility in a calcified society where supply far outstripped demand and the result was just making ends meet from cradle to grave. Kisa tasted these things, they were tangible in the air like smog and rain and mist and had fled all her life to escape them, but wherever she went there they were awaiting her arrival. As a result, she had unfulfilled longings of her own brooding over her existence.

The warm night held her in its embrace with no respite even though it was nearly four a.m. and her footsteps echoed drum like off stucco and stone as she started back to the Cecil Hotel. At the end of the block was when she first noticed it; after she had stopped to check her smartphone map to be sure she was heading the right way. Someone else was out that night. She heard them walking, but could not see anything when looking back–the sounds stopped when she stopped, started as she moved on. Hurriedly, she crossed the street to the *Shallalat Gardens* hoping to lose her stalker or at least escape to the well lit footpaths if necessary and for a few moments heard nothing so was relieved. But there it was again and a pang of fear speared her seasoned defenses. Just then, up ahead were silhouettes. Two men crossing the street. Then came footsteps again from behind. Looking back she just caught the movement in the turbid light. Trapped was the worst feeling she could imagine. Adrenaline surged through her as she ran headlong into the park now hearing many footsteps following in the distance. A clatter of footsteps. Heavy racing feet of men. Pursued, she wove in and out of the light as the dirt path made its way through palms and grassy lawns trimmed with shrubbery and beds of annuals closed up for the night. Perspiration made her silk blouse cling to her breasts as she splayed up against a wall listening intently–a huge, ancient, rough hewn stone wall. In 332 B.C. Alexander the Great, King of Macedonia envisioned Alexandria atop the limestone spur between the Mediterranean Sea and the flat bed of Lake Mareotis. It was then the wall was built and now a surviving part of it towered above her in darkness foreboding, but no longer protecting from enemies. She gasped for breath. Sweat ran into her eyes. Footsteps echoed. They were still coming. In the semi dark she fumbled for a handhold and found a railing, cold galvanized steel, and she followed it to a flight of steps at the bottom of which was an opening leading to a chamber. Climbing into the dark window she threw her leg over the cool stone and slid down into the cavern until she was holding on just with her fingers and still her feet had not touched down. The sounds were coming closer. She let go. Down she fell a few feet and crumpled to the floor. It was pitch black except for faint ambient light coming from the opening above her. On her hands and knees she crawled into the blackness hearing repercussive echoes of each movement and gasp for breath making her realize it was some vast chamber she had entered. Her fingers reached the edge on each side–it was a stone beam, a lintel spanning the void whose depth could only be guessed, but she knew no good would come if she fell and so kept moving slowly forward until she reached what appeared to be a cross beam with a pillar at its center then crawling around it to the side away from the high window. There she curled up and held her breath.

Suddenly a beam of light burst through the window above. It arced down into the darkness and swept along the stone path she could now see–dusty gray-brown from some distant prehistory. Light hit the pillar; she slowly moved her foot in closer and instantaneously realized she had dropped her scarf and that's how they had found her and stopped breathing altogether. She cursed herself for dropping the scarf. Sweat from her cheek fell against the stone. The men were talking in low Arabic murmurs as they searched for her and she cursed that abrasive language that she never understand and its impenetrable depths always seeming to hide the malicious intent of swarthy, darkly menacing people. Then she cursed the night and wished she were back out on the balcony of her room at the Cecil Hotel. After hovering for an eternity, when they finally left, Kisa did not breathe again for the longest time. Her mouth was dry. Throbbing heartbeats pounded in her ears and she was tired. Infinitely tired. So tired all of a sudden that she slept as she lay in the starless, moonless, dusky, shadowy cavern of which she knew nothing and whose woof and warp was a complete mystery to her.

It was the sun that woke her. A bird chirped and its voice echoed. She gradually opened her eyes amazed to see a vast, underground cathedral three stories high supported by four rows of columns shrouded in darkness balancing precariously on delicate arches, which linked the rows rising out of the deep. Light filtered in from a hidden array of sources painting the cistern in mottled, yellow hues as if a pre-Raphaelite painting exposing its depth and breath. Kisa lay there taking it all in as if some prescient knowledge imbued her with the history of the place, of those who had come before and died and many who almost met their end here as well.

In 1422 Ghillebert de Lannoy wrote to Henry V of England, *"Underneath the streets and houses, the whole city is hollow...there are conduits roofed over with arches, through which the wells are filled up once a year by the River Nile."* Alexandria, the pearl of the Mediterranean, lay superimposed on a city of cisterns the streets of which are subterranean canals–over 2000 once existed. Ancient when Caesar renovated them in the year 40 B.C. and even more ancient when they were poisoned with seawater during the siege in the year 48 B.C. when he and his troops nearly perished. They had been used for 8-centuries until a tsunami flooded them with salt in A.D. 365. A traveler in 1634 counted 500, but when Napoleon invaded Egypt there were only 400. Sometime between 1710 and 1712, Francois Paumier, a member of the third order of St. Francis, exclaimed with admiration, *"there is nothing more beautiful and complete than the vaults; nothing better constructed than their apertures; nothing more superb than the pieces of marble with which they are surrounded."* Vanished wonders by the 20th Century, many later resurrected by archeologists as cultural treasures.

It was here Kisa lay transfixed, barely awake, staring through a filter of dreams at centuries of brilliantly confused architectural elements; finely carved ancient capitals that had been reused as bases to support shafts of Aswan granite topped by Ionic bases of white marble that were now capitals, and the Corinthian capitals of the Roman era with finely chiseled acanthus leaves made of marble from the Princes' Islands. She breathed in the thread of humanity and felt the profound brotherhood to which she belonged and it almost obscured the events of the night before, except for the excitement that boiled inside that she now knew where to find the Messiah of The Streets.

But it was later at the Cecil Hotel when she knocked on Ibrahim's door and he stood before her in his shorts, hair disheveled and wild rubbing sleep from his eyes when she told him, "I know where he is!" And handed him a coffee in a Styrofoam cup.

"How do you know?" He mumbled not really sure what she was talking about.

Kisa barged into the room. "I stepped on a cobra, and he bit."

"So, where is he?"

She whirled. "Find Abd al Hakim and we'll find the American Mahdi."

* * * *

Moonglow hit the sea and shattered into a million glittery pieces tumbling relentlessly through the impenetrable velvet night. Cirrus clouds riding the jetstream radiated with the faintest blue violet smoldering of the departed sun. The throb of the rotors was muted and sublime as Karine Russo raced before the wind at nearly 240 miles per hour–almost double what other helicopters could do. The only light was the luminescence of the fly-by-wire instruments. Far below the dhows and trawlers plying the Mediterranean's murky depths trembled in her wake as if a ghost ship were passing on a mission more profound than anything only one life could justify. She hadn't slept in over 24 hours and felt ragged longing for the dreams of ringed mountains rising far beyond the tree line with immutable rock faces heavy with ice and snow and of the ceaseless winds like those that raged not three feet from where she was sitting now buckled into a military aircraft. Suddenly weightlessness flooded her senses as the vessel dove down upon the water until it fled just 20-feet above the surface where they would remain until landfall to avoid detection. That was the signal. They were leaving British airspace far off the island of Cyprus. She had been briefed. It was expected, and yet her apprehension grew. It had all begun with her handwritten orders.

The man seemed to have brought the cold with him. It was an omen she failed to recognize. Dressed in an ill fitting suit with a shirt buttoned at the neck whose collar was too big. His hair was cut close so that the light shone off his scalp and the large boned jaw was set like granite into his lean, determined face. He was holding a note, which he folded and placed into the pocket of his coat.

"I'm going to need your absolute commitment, you know...the event horizon is at the beginning of the mission, we're at the point of no return now."

"I understand." Her first thought was that there must be something not stereotypical about him because she never trusted anyone who appeared to be who they were. Perhaps, she mused, he was a fundamental Methodist who went to secret meetings twice a week preparing for the arrival of aliens. Anything would do, just something to prove he was real and not a robot. "I am quite committed as anyone that has worked with me can testify and frankly, I'm not used to being patronized." She exuded power and could almost feel the deliciousness of it like the anticipation of sex. "So let's knock that off and we'll get along fine."

Unfazed, the man continued. "You will be working with a select team of specialists who will get you in and get you out. You're not used to working with people like these; highly trained and highly motivated, like fine racehorses, purebreds. I'm going to need your absolute commitment."

She called in a favor from a friend in operations at the CIA and had gone to extraordinary measures to keep it all hush-hush. Nobody at State, especially not Viktor Jaraslov, knew anything. Her friend had returned her call on his personal line–there would be no official phone records–and had initially balked when she told him what she wanted even though he owed her. "Layers," he had said wearily, "this involves layers." That she didn't understand until later, much later when he began to introduce her to an odd mix of strange individuals who lived outside the framework of the civil servants she was used to being around. At first they seemed normal enough, but it was as if there was a parallel universe where they all secretly dwelt only emerging to make arrangements like those she was making with them now; a shadowland, living their lives in counterpoint to civilized people and then retiring into oblivion nobody ever knowing their accomplishments, their catastrophic failures or their longings. In their eyes she saw the unmistakable sign of this alien landscape without exception, in each one, identical. The look of it was unearthly and unsettling and brought into question her own preconceived ideas about life and how it was supposed to be, what one was supposed to do and how one was supposed to act. It finally dawned on her that her friend was setting up an extraordinary team to accomplish the extraordinary mission she had selfishly requested, but it still set her on edge. *Layers*, she thought, *this involves layers*.

Each day for two weeks they met in a Brazilian café to avoid any suspicion and she lingered over empanadas and caipirnha, Brazil's national drink made with hard sugar cane liquor called *cachaça* and lime, meeting the corespondents of her clandestine mission one by one and going over the granular details. Slowly the picture began to evolve of how she would be flown undercover into a hostile Alexandra Egypt, extricate Erskine Parrish McKenzie before he enflamed Near East relations beyond repair and had become such a liability to the Department that the CIA would be directed to handle him by rendition. Assistance has long played a central role in Egypt's economic and military development, and in furthering a strategic partnership, and nobody wanted to jeopardize that investment. There was something else however, something personal. It had always confused her why she held any feelings at all for Parrish, he was a rebellious employee, an iconoclast nobody really understood or even had the inclination to try, yet an unnamed quality about him drew her close despite her best efforts to remain aloof, an unknown quantity, an unrealized potential. The emotion she felt was undeniable. It was out of these impenetrable depths motivation came to undertake the clandestine mission alone, off record, sub rosa.

The long flight from Washington to the British RAF Akrotiri airbase located within sovereign land on the island of Cyprus was made longer due to the lack of amenities on the military transport her spook friend had appropriated for her compact team. They landed and were immediately whisked to a pad where a helicopter was in final prep for departure. Introduced to the pilot anonymously as a State Department Official she quipped looking at the craft that would fly them into Alexandria, "It's pretty small isn't it?"

"Maybe," he replied stiffly lights from the field reflecting off his shiny, polyester flightsuit. "Don't let its size fool you. It's a next generation attack helicopter with excellent low speed capabilities yet allows high speed flight with no configuration change."

She just looked at him pleasantly nodding. "Translated to layman's terms?"

"Fast as hell!" He grinned the best he could without moving any of the muscles of his face and showing no expression whatsoever. "It's so advanced it can reach speeds of over 230 mph, nearly twice any other helicopter."

"Which means no one can catch us." She semi questioned squinting up her eyes to contribute to the gravity of the technical discussion.

"Better," he gloated, "no one will even know we're there."

"That's reassuring…very…"

"It also has a low acoustic signature reducing the liability of detection and acquisition by the enemy and allows for decreased ingress and egress time, which gives a significantly greater chance of mission success," he continued in practiced military monotone. "It is equipped with twin coaxial counter-rotating main rotors, in place of one main rotor and a tail rotor," he added confidentially, "and a pusher propeller for less vibration and long-range, hot and high hover capabilities–a barrier to conventional rotorcraft and of great advantage in the heat of the desert where we are headed. Can reach over 10,000 feet in 100-degree temperatures. Simply the best multi-mission capable aircraft we have. Makes you proud to be an American doesn't it?

"Of course," she nodded. "Hot and high hover capabilities. "

The coast was visible as tiny clusters of lights along a dim demarcation between earth and sky. Alexandria glowed in the distance. Destiny was in their sights. She felt the heady, surreal intoxication of danger as they streaked across the Mediterranean headlong into the turmoil that defined the continent of Africa. The gravity of it was thick and irresistible as it had always been to Europeans drawn by avarice and greed and the innate quality of manifest destiny that falsely inhabited them. Within its borders lie one fifth of the world's land mass and nearly the same of its people and a huge percent of all living species made their home there. But of poverty, it was the irrefutable master and the spawn of political chaos like that into which she was bound. Africa was the symbol of an endangered earth.

The craft swept in with silent whooping from the north and Karine Russo with two stout companions had barely touched their feet on the ground when it swooped away and was gone. Soon the silence was profound and the intense sense of loneliness permeated as she realized they were alone in a strange, hostile land. Out of the surrounding date palms a black and yellow Alexandrian taxi pulled slowly up across the fields with its lights extinguished driven by an Egyptian with a PhD from Cairo University named Nizam–the discovery of a CIA field operative who also had the idea that someone must have seen the American. With a plume of dust and precious cargo he set off for a secure location in Alexandria. The night was dark. The lingering breeze searched for someone to embrace with flows and eddies. The stars were their only witness.

XI | Listening to Silence

Out on the edge of oblivion where the continent ended and the sea began and life was most challenging, people flourished. Perhaps it was the rush of humanity hard pressed against the remorseless Mediterranean, the endless motion countering the static sea–it was a buffer to unfulfilled expectations that tumbled up touching the shore undulating in breathless hopes and hungers, sweat and desire. Voices mingled with the howling sirocco that bore down on the Sahara moving cities of sand each year grain by grain, changing the maps cartographers had belabored over as testament to man's dominance of nature, to man's conquest of the planet until all living things were in jeopardy of extinction. The wind laughed at men and made a mockery of their maps. Dreams were scattered and lost in this wild collision and sometimes never found again, but other times they lured with irresistible fatal voices and their clues lingered in the mind and in the air as hope against despair. Wise men listened to the silence while fools slept. When that faint music was no longer heard, death would not be far behind; for wealthy and poor alike these things hold true. Truth laughs at kings.

Kisa awoke. She listened to the waves lapping against the sides of the yacht and caught a glimpse of stars through passing cloud layers and then they were gone. The boat rolled silently with the swell in the harbor. She breathed in the deep and sea creatures great and small languished within her boundaries. A salt smell filled the air. Everything was musk and indigo, and then she was asleep again living only in the moment never once thinking of how she got there or what the consequences might be. It was a grand release.

She had been pursued by darkness all her life. It gave her little rest and coerced her into responsibilities she had no wish for. Darkness and light. This was the dichotomy she struggled with, the constant unbalancing of good and evil inside that compelled her to do irrational things she later regretted with a fury, things she would never talk about with anyone, as if they had never happened, that became stronger with time instead of fading and the shame of moral violations drove her to acts of the same nature in justification of her choices like the string of married men she had been involved with. Somehow she felt it was just all very human and conflict was simply part of the baggage one assumed by being born into this life, but fantastically she always had hope, there was always the search even though many crossing her path were secretly merchants of chaos and to their last breath would deny anyone redemption. Though she was suspicious of those who never flaunted the light, who were charmed and free of troubles, serial optimists, bon vivants; she never freed herself from the illusion of hope.

"Isn't that the man we saw?" She exclaimed with enough excitement to startle Ibrahim to his senses.

"What man?"

"That one," grasping his arm and pointing to a tall, swarthy, enigmatic figure in the flowing black *bisht*, "over there."

"The Arab?"

"Yes," she resolved just then, "I'll bet he knows."

They had spent days trying to get a line on the politician Abd al Hakim, but he had gone underground and no one was talking, everyone was tight lipped, fear in all eyes and besides government offices were closed. There was no access to public records, not even real estate titles and they were just returning to the hotel after another fruitless search when the Saudi appeared with a small entourage in the twilight smoking a thin cigar exuding an umbra of wealth and sin despite the façade of the straight path.

That was how it all began, but later Kisa was poised at the bar in the Cecil Hotel with perfect posture on a stool nursing a fundamentalist substitute for a cocktail and missing the jolt of vodka or even the smooth burn of brandy looking out over the harbor at Alexandria in the shimmering eventide. He with the dark wandering eyes sat in a corner with colleagues being pandered to by the staff, one for each person at the table, plying the carpet like sharks for tips and the benefit of good public relations with the uber-rich and the future income and prestige that it would bring the hotel. It was the credo of the manager and all employees adopted it or were given walking papers because there were plenty of men without shirts in Egypt and employment was never secure. She could see him in the mirror and had already decided even if he hadn't glanced in her direction more than once. *Men are crazy about me,* she mused sensing the danger, being that much more determined. He had something she wanted.

She turned to face him placing both elbows back on the bar and then took his measure, absorbed him as if a row of vibrantly blooming orchids in a garden letting his living essence wash over her until she got the gist of him, the sense of him, the perfume of him. Muhammad Abd al' Rashid's keen eyes flickered like lantern flames and he too paused to face the young blonde woman across the room whose look burned into him until they were locked one upon the other. The walk from here to there took only moments though it was mesmerizing in its performance and Kisa stilled the room with secret primal messages mingling the spirit with the animal, long legs brushing against silken fabric.

"You can help me," she announced gliding into an empty chair at his table acquiescing, but only slightly, to the others.

He nodded and narrowed his eyes with an imperceptible smile. "I would be honored."

The two other men at the table became suddenly impatient and looking at one another, raising their eyebrows in tacit consent, rose from their chairs. "I'm sorry we can't do business tonight," one coughed up patronizingly as men do when another needs something only they can give, "…on such short notice…" In normal circumstances the roles would be reversed, but now was the time for throwing one's weight around.

"Perhaps tomorrow…" the other rejoined buttoning his coat.

"Yes, tomorrow. I will have something for you tomorrow," and then with formality concluded they left.

"You see…?" al' Rashid exclaimed.

"Of course." Kisa replied. "They have something you want."

"How do you know?"

"I'm in the news business," she tossed off.

"Ahhh…a correspondent?"

"That's right. 'All Russian TV' gets the broadcast, 'Moskovskie Novosti' gets the online. I'm the only Russian here. I'm covering events."

"You mean the coup."

She glanced out the window at the night flurries. The vast distances brought feelings of alienation as she sat at a table on the northern coast of Africa trying to dissect a culture far different than her own and struggling out of her depth chasing her first real news story. "What is a Saudi doing in an Alexandria under siege on a night like this?" She smiled hoping to connect.

"Business," he narrowed his eyes suspiciously, "business."

Kisa just looked at him expectantly, "Shall I guess?" tapping her finger nervously on the white linen tablecloth.

"Oil business."

"Oh," she mugged satisfaction. "I would have thought government."

"Then you'd be right. I'm the Deputy Oil Minister for Saudi Arabia."

"I knew you could help me!" Intrigued, she smiled, "It must be easy for you to get in and out, you must know a lot of people?"

al' Rashid slipped one of his thin, crooked cigars out of a gleaming silver case and had just barely placed it to his lips when the tall Ethiopian she had seen him with earlier appeared holding a flame to light it. His skin was so black it was almost blue and glistened in the glow. "I hope you don't mind if I smoke." The Arab inhaled deeply. "It is an indulgence." The black man glared at her.

Kisa ignored the looming servant. "Abd al Hakim for instance," she continued nonchalantly, "do you know him?"

"You mean the latent liberal leaning conservative and onetime Shura Council leader?" He smiled in his tragicomic way. "We've met, but no...I don't really know him."

"But perhaps you know where he is?"

"In hiding I suspect. Got on the wrong side of General Ridayah before the coup, before the junta, even though they were old comrades. Fancy his standing now. No friends in politics."

"Well..." Kisa replied petulantly, "that's not exactly the answer I was looking for." It was only then she noticed the ineffable aloofness of the man who sat across from her. The enduring mark of wealth, good genes and insufferable intelligence.

"I'm looking for someone myself. Someone of importance. Someone that a correspondent might get wind of." He paused for a long moment surveying her for any obvious flaws. "Perhaps we can help each other."

He spoke to her of a young woman in the third person as if she were a character in one of the wildly popular Egyptian soaps about who everyone dished like they were real people. Azhara Binte Jibril Riyadh, he told her confidentially with a promise to keep it a professional secret, daughter of the great general behind this coup d'état. There was intensity she felt, a fury to this man and a brittle, intellectual edge that defined him as one with his own path no matter how devoted he may seem in public. Kisa studied his refined features as he talked; the long, aquiline nose; the lips whose delineated edges were turned down slightly at the corner giving him a tragic look even when he smiled surrounded by the dense, black mustache and goatee endemic to the Saudis. But his eyes were the most telling; dark, brooding and so keenly intelligent nothing of value would pass unnoticed. There was something personal about this young woman he was searching for, not love or even desire, but something personal and it elicited long dormant emotions in her.

"My name is Kisa. Kisa Vanyusha.

She found herself feeling sympathy for this man to whom no whim went unsatisfied, who probably never had a physical need in his life unfulfilled unlike her own existence marked by want and unanswered yearnings. Perhaps it was the pressure of having to deliver on the first big chance in her career and finding only dead ends and confusion in the aftermath of the military coup that an otherwise experienced reporter would be able to deftly plumb sending back dispatch after dispatch of insight into the region's struggle, but it was at that point she decided she would possess him. Men had been a familiar commodity since she was a girl. They were crazy for her and it was a currency she used frequently.

The harbor lights were muted and subdued by a fine mist that rose off the water. The yacht rode on its back. It was, he explained, secured in lieu of a hotel while he was in Alexandria because he felt more comfortable staying aboard, but Kisa suspected ulterior motives as she welcomed the first alcoholic drink in a month relishing its burn. Hundred and fifty year old cognac splashed into crystal snifters and left her light headed as she pulled him down on her and kissed him so deeply, so viciously like an animal searching for his current, his essence, that she drew blood. The flow was palpable. It left the room thick and honey sweet as they rolled in heat and perspiration. She stood then by the window in the cocoon of bubinga wood paneling and let her thin dress slip to the floor. Starlight sliced through the racing clouds and painted her body with an irresistible luminance while fishes and creatures innumerable haunted the depths beneath her feet. Halfway to the stars they touched. Her blonde hair moved in waves as fingers swept into secret places. Her small breasts touched him. She arched her back to meet his hand.

Al' Rashid wanted to know her, to truly know her, to deliver her to the ritual and absorb her delicious agony, but it was the moral ambiguity that possessed him most and as much as he was driven to pleasure, he was equally withdrawn from it. The conflict fixed him in time so that all women become less individual and simply sexual commodities one very much like the other to satisfy his carnal urges with impunity. He had always felt there was something fundamentally wrong with having a body that demanded sexual satisfaction and had tried all his life to be a man of the straight path and sublimate his desires as the mullah had suggested, but at last had succumbed to demons more elemental. His yachts were the buffer between this steamy world and that of his social milieu. So it was that on the floor of the main salon he, scion of desert kings, head of the great oil cartel, Oxford educated and Islamic bred buried his face in her sex with abandon until her knees buckled and she collapsed to the floor with a single moan.

"No," she cried and pushed him away, "damn you…" she surrendered. In the lost Egyptian night two figures hurled themselves into the moist caldron abandoning all pretense and struggled against one another flesh to flesh in an ancient primal dance that knew no name. Al' Rashid thrust deeply into her overcome by a bestial spirit never whispering, never a word while he held her in the grip of his lovemaking. Kisa undulated against him, impaled by lust, possessing, enveloping and wrapping her skin against his satisfied that for this brief time she owned the enigmatic, swarthy, brooding young man completely and afterwards, nothing really mattered.

The unexpected comes without consent. So it was that two people lost their foothold in an ancient bay on the northernmost shore of the Dark Continent in the small hours of the night. Both now puppets to the Fates, the sparing ones, by whom the thread of lives are spun, measured and cut. Fine armed daughters of night; one sings of things that were, the other of things that are and the last of things yet to be and neither advice nor consent will influence the outcome.

The dreams would not let Parrish sleep. He stood on the balcony with the wooden *mashrabiya* thrown back smoking. The song of the river permeated all things in the delta. Wisps rose with the dawn. Fishing dhows had already set sail. White flamingos took wing after a rest to continue their long migration to the upper Nile where they would consume the tiny, pink river shrimp and take on their rose color. Morning breezes brushed his face as the day awoke.

With his exile, he had time for the changes in his life to come into full view. Struggle though he might he could not fully understand one stable element, one touchstone except that the world he'd always known was not what it seemed. Life was illusory and though he could not yet see behind the apparition, he knew something was there. But it was earlier that he stood in the Abu Mandour Mosque arguing with the mullah. After his three-mile walk to the south where Azhara had warned him not to go because the presence of any American on the dirt road along the river would cause suspicion, but he wanted to avoid her that day and knew she would be looking at the usual place–her dark beauty distracted him and she was not anywhere he should go.

It had appeared on a small sandy promontory just after sunrise across the river from the fish farms. At the foot of a hill on a tiny peninsula of the Nile stood a tall, aged, white building trimmed with gold, the parapet of its walls indented like point lace, one onion dome in its far southern corner and a minaret of rare elegance rising clearly over twice its height. Dark intricately designed tiles framed its entrance and ran to the top with three circular windows covered by carved wooden shutters that overlooked a dirt courtyard. Across the river an army of date palms marched north to the town of Rashid whose low buildings rose above the tree line in a jumbled panorama. Light was still soft, defined shadows were just beginning to appear, the air held a subtle coolness and moved in currents and eddies when suddenly a *muezzin's* call scintillated across the dawn as it had for centuries. A resonant voice rose from the sand and reeds and mist like a spirit soaring in transmigration caught in between the real and the imagined. It stopped Parrish cold in his tracks. Seconds later a chorus faintly echoed from up the river as all the minarets of the town flamed to life at once singing the *adahn; Allāhu akbar, Allāhu akbar. Ash-hadu an-lā ilāha illā allāh.*

"I have never lived before!" The mullah replied antagonistically with open hands. " We are born…anew!"

All through the night impressions had violated Parrish's consciousness without consent and swept away any last remaining social reserve. Filled to overflowing with blood and passion, yearnings realized and hopes crushed they invaded heartlessly with vivid strokes rendering past experiences in details so complex and incredibly random he knew he could not be imagining them. The pain and the wonder. No creative mind was that agile. No improvisation that labyrinthine. It was as if all one had to do was look through the thin veil haphazardly tossed between lives to suffer the full impact of lifetime upon lifetime of memories down the eons arranged in perfect linear progression with every remembrance cherished or reviled just waiting to appear. It chilled his blood. Little wonder why people did not want to remember. Could not admit their past. It was forbidden history. Earlier selves. Incarnations whose transgressions could never be atoned for even in a thousand lifetimes. The past. The endless chaos struggling to survive in a relentless universe. It was best forgotten.

"We do not believe in past lives," the mullah continued his grey eyes sparkling with rage, "as Muslim's do not believe they have had a past life. We have one…one life on earth. It is a 'test' in which we should live according to the teachings of the final prophet Muhammad–after that we have a second eternal life. After that…"

"Do you ever feel that you have been somewhere before, somewhere so familiar that you know details impossible otherwise?"

"Of course. Everyone has. Tricks of the mind, that's all. Imagination, nothing more."

"Wouldn't you like to know when?"

"The answers are all in the Qur'an."

"…another reminder that we're just not good enough," Parrish muttered.

"Whenever a Muslim recites the Holy Qur'an, those in heaven see him in the same way that those on the earth see stars shining in heaven."

It had begun after prayers. The few who had attended inside left. Parrish was anxiously walking around the mosque alone kicking up dust, subconsciously studying its architectural details and, after concluding it had been built sometime in the eighteenth century, noticed small objects in the sand. He knelt and inspected one. It was a pottery shard. Rolling it carefully in his hand he judged it to be from pharaonic times and the discovery eased his anxiety and left him feeling elated.

"There is more here too," a voice suddenly interjected, "gold coins, lamps and other objects have been excavated–we are rich in history at least." The cleric pointed to a nearby slope. "True believers say the holy dervish Abu Mandour supports with his shoulders the mountain of sand that threatens to overwhelm the mosque. It would be a terrible loss, don't you think? We call it the 'Hill of happiness.' You're an American aren't you?" The mullah, who had just led prayers, loved to talk and was so delighted to find a foreigner that he invited him for tea. Inside they spoke of many things, for over an hour they talked. Parrish asked about Rashid, the discovery of the Rosetta stone for which it was famous and the beautiful, restored merchant houses while being evasive about himself, but the mullah, though garrulous, seemed to be harboring a hidden agenda. He was sly. His eyes betrayed him.

Parrish wasn't really paying close attention. Everything was shifting, in flux, and points of reference he always had that helped define who he was were gone. New ones had not yet arrived. It wasn't like it was supposed to be. Looking at the swarthy, middle-aged man across from him whose bony cheekbones drew lines down his face he wondered if the marks around his eyes were from laughter or anger.

"What is faith?" He asked.

"Belief." Came the instant response.

"And you, for example, what do you believe?"

"There is no God but God and Muhammad is the messenger of God." The mullah answered curtly.

"But," Parrish shook his head, imploring, "do you observe things for yourself?"

"We have the Qur'an," he replied confidently. "All of life is contained within it. It helps us understand and when we follow its precepts, things go better. Simple."

"My problem is this, I'm seeing things that fall outside what I've learned. Spiritual phenomena I guess you'd call it. Makes me feel a little crazy. What would you do if you observed things that fell outside the teachings of the Qur'an?"

"There are no such things."

"There are many. Have you lived before this life for instance?"

"Of course not."

"Then what do you do with your memories?" He asked wistfully. "I can't seem to stop mine…"

The mullah raised his eyebrows and pursed his lips, face flushed. "I have never lived before!"

"…I can see clearly, that's my problem. I can see beyond the veil. It's not that I want to, it's just happened…and I…just thought you might be able to help…"

"We can't wonder about these things. It causes trouble. You should consider other things."

"Anyone can question. Nothing should be taken at face value."

"Look," he exclaimed, "this is what faith is! Faith and blasphemy. On the one side are mysteries beyond our comprehension essential to living and on the other are paths that lead nowhere. It's reliance that there are greater powers, higher intellects. It's symbolic logic, a pattern for life to follow–otherwise…you're just too busy trying to figure things out to get on with it. Faith is all about survival; the Prophet has already gone there and has written the Qur'an so we do not have to question."

"I believe only what I can know."

"Blasphemy is denying the truth. No one can live without hope. Would you deny hope?"

"Is the junta bringing hope?" Parrish was suddenly hot. "I understand General Riyadh is a devout Muslim. How much death and martyrdom before hope is achieved?"

"Hope is earned. It is not a gift. It is a struggle."

"The world was built on the backs of free and cheap labor and they all believed in the struggle. Something that only paid off for the rich. They believed in lies. Everyone should question belief. Everyone!" Parrish just stood and looked at the mullah as if departing from this world for the next, as if all bridges had been destroyed and there was no way back. "It should be required!" Then he walked out the door.

"You are the one aren't you?" The mullah called after him. "You are the one!"

They began arriving late that afternoon. Only a few at first, so Azhara thought they were itinerant workers from the rice fields or date farms who frequently traveled the roads along the river in search of work between jobs. But they were not; they were people of the storm. By the following morning there was a crowd of about a hundred and as the day wore on more came in a small, unrelenting stream of footsteps. Some brought bags or pots of food; some small folding chairs or blankets that they used to stake out a territory for themselves; some stood alone and others congregated in small groups all surreptitiously looking up at the house for any signs of activity; women kept to themselves and tended to the children they had been forced to bring because no one else was available to look after them; some had the pale, desperate expression of those beyond salvation who travelled through life as passengers, victims of any whim the universe or its masters doled out; some wore the bright countenance of expectation as if they had an inside line on winning the lottery; still others the strident, demanding stance of activists, but all of them had one thing in common. Strong young men with the sleeves of their t-shirts rolled up. The weathered dentist recently arrived from Pakistan. Shopkeepers from the stalls in the center of the old town Rashid who preyed on tourists, restaurant workers and field hands, mechanics who overcharged, housekeepers who were underpaid and others who lived day to day, hand to mouth in an incredibly massive society that never could employ the bulk of its workforce. Cairo was the biggest city in Africa and Egypt the continent's crown. They all believed in each their own way that some essential understanding was missing in their lives, something that acted as an unknown influence, something beyond the veil keeping them down, holding them back and they all wanted the truth and would go to any lengths to get it and though none could tell exactly what that might be, each was certain he would know it when he heard it. Each longed for it to be revealed. So they kept coming and soon Azahara went down the long drive from the house to find out what they wanted.

"We must leave." She exclaimed breathlessly rushing into the house.

"What do you mean?" Parrish asked peering out the window.

"We *have* to go…! I'll get the others…"

"Wait a minute!" He grabbed her arm, "What's going on?"

"You," she gave him that look she had, the implacable one, "they're all here to see you."

"Me?!"

"How did they find us?" al Hakim's bodyguard Malik tumbled into the room his Helwan 920 semiautomatic pistol drawn Ishaq Sadek shadowing close behind.

"A local mullah. Seems he had a visitor yesterday morning…I told you not to go down there! Small towns…everyone will know by tomorrow."

"The military. They'll be here before tha!" Ishaq interjected.

"Grab what you can," said Malik, "Ill get the car ready."

"Wait, where can we go…" Parrish cried anxiously, "Isn't it better if I negotiate with…?"

"Negotiate?" She glared at him incredulously. "My father doesn't negotiate."

* * * *

It was later, while everyone scurried around frantically preparing to flee, that Parrish had slipped out of the house and walked the long drive to where the people were congregating. It was only by chance that Malik spotted him from the upper window and furiously ran after him driven by his word to al Hakim that no harm would come to the American. "Wait!" He yelled in disbelief, "Wait!" But it was too late. He would never understand what complex reasoning had compelled the foreigner to ruin everything when he was safe and being delivered. But it wasn't belief in something tangible, not empirical logic or anything that Parrish could have justified. The action was a pure leap of faith. It had welled up from years of suppression and confinement in which all his beliefs and aspirations were smothered by the chains of earning wages and having to serve lesser minds in the process. It was act of personal liberation, or as close to it as one could get in the material world where all of life was a paid for experience in one way or another, an invisible hand guided him and he did not question it closely. When Malik finally caught up with him people were crowding around, reaching out, touching him and all of them with questions, beseeching, imploring, demanding.

Parrish shouted over the din of people speaking so fast he could not understand, "What are they saying?"

"They all want something." Malik replied hand inside his coat on the cool handle of his pistol.

"Tell them I'm not the one," he waved his hands at the crowd and shook his head. "It's not me," he shouted as if speaking louder would bridge the language gap, but the crowd only swelled, became louder.

"They don't believe you. They think you're just testing them."

Frowning he faced them with more resolve. "That woman…" pointing to a strong, wiry figure in a headscarf, "what's she saying?"

"She says she is tired of struggling. Nothing gets better, nothing changes…is exhausted, can do no more…"

"Tell her she is doing the wrong thing. Going in the wrong direction. Tell her to find out who she really is and then follow that path." He quickly scanned the assembled people. "What does that man say?"

"He complains that others are out to get him, that they are spreading rumors and trying to destroy his reputation, but they are all wrong–he knows what they've done."

"Tell him to write down everything he is afraid they will find out about him, every misdeed real and imagined…then send it to them. Tell him a man of truth cannot be hurt… What is that young man asking?"

"He doesn't know what to do. No ambition, he feels apathy. He is lost."

"Tell him to find out what he wants to have more than anything else in life. That will guide him in what to do."

For over two hours Parrish grappled before the growing crowd losing ground, inching backward trying for a spiritual foothold, finding none. The questions came in a torrent as if an endless river had been tapped, as if a cornucopia of discontent and confusion poured from the well of souls where voices of the living mingled with those of the universal dead awaiting judgment. The voracity of it was overwhelming. Some were covert intent to expose a weakness and inflict harm, but most spoke out of earnest distress and anguish, out of personal ruin that gnawed away at lives like a hidden cancer causing pain and unhappiness and displacing the hopefulness they once knew. It was the interminable misery of the human condition that crushed against him and they longed only for the touch as confirmation of belief in an omnipresent invisible God whose will was as mysterious as his directions for living. Few had success to show for their elusive faith and there always seemed to be something else, some new tenant they had failed at, some obscure line in the scriptures forgotten, some other sin they had inadvertently committed or some payment due. It was an ancient skirmish.

A mysterious power gave him the presence of mind and insight to act without self-inspection as he usually did and he flew on wings unknown. Though with each desperate plea he was able to envision the cause and offer solutions, trying at resolution to lives he had never known just as he had with the girl in the desert by the side of the road so long ago, a realization slowly began to come over him in the swirling dust on the path near the banks of the Nile that changed the way he looked at everything. It wasn't like the girl, or the imam at the Al-Qaed Mosque, this was a grander dynamic. This was at the borderline where desire and consequence boiled over, where dreams and disabilities canceled out each other until nothing was left except indelible fingerprints where once someone had stood. This was the source of human longing; what deep purposes lie there unexplored would remain forever a mystery. It was crushing in its immensity; he could not bear the burden. It occurred to him that healing was an individual thing and though he still didn't understand his gift, dealing with the dysfunction of humanity in all its living chaos was nearing divine and he was not the one. "I am not the one..." he uttered silently. Parrish looked over a sea of faces that now stood transfixed before him each with their own unique history and hard luck story to tell and he was overawed finally, at this interminable moment grasping with painful certainty that his transformation was complete and he was no longer just the Assistant Foreign Service Officer for Political Affairs posted at the Cairo mission, no longer Erskine Parrish Mackenzie, but a new man. Homo novis.

There was a hidden face in the assembly. A freelance journalist who had been hoping to cash in on events surrounding the coup had just got wind of the crowd gathering at the house of a prominent politician across the river from Rashid. The following morning an inflammatory article appeared in many of the independent news outlets, "American Mahdi shielded by Shura Council leader Abd al Hakim."

East of Alexandria near the terminus of the Desert Road from Cairo Karine Russo paced anxiously before the bay windows in a rented villa on the beach. The smell of fried fish, fava beans with olive oil, cumin, garlic and Turkish coffee filled the air as she stared out at the brilliant turquoise Mediterranean shimmering in the North African sun. The wind was already whipping up whitecaps. Streets had been nearly vacant the entire drive from their landing place the night before, only a few solitary souls haunting the dark reaches–some waifs of shattered lives others menacing as they roared by in the black and yellow Soviet Lada taxi indifferent to any other suffering than their own. She moved impatiently in white cargo pants while mentally trying to navigate the impenetrable Islamic lifeways of her confused surroundings–the inability to hold still made all the more insessent by a complete lack of sleep. She had spent the night worrying and mulling over suspicions about her companions who had not been any too anxious to fill in the details of exactly how they were going to find and extricate Erskine Parrish MacKenzie. "We have inside contacts," she was told with the unmistakable attitude of "…a need to know basis only," though wondering if she didn't need to know, who did? They were not forthcoming and it was a red flag. Her navy blue military style sweater had patches on the elbows and on each shoulder for insignia of rank and was warm, far too warm and out of place for a bright Egyptian delta day like the one presenting itself and was a signal that she had never really left the beltway where snow and ice surrounded her and was the only place she felt at home other than in the ringed mountains of her dreams.

"Read this!" One of the surly CIA men exclaimed in disbelief slamming an Arabic language, Egyptian opposition newspaper down on the breakfast table in front of her with a loud smack. He was appropriately named "Jack" and probably recruited, she imagined, from one of those stultified Ivy League schools at which point he became fixed in time and now looked like a jock approaching middle age whose mother still bought his clothes.

"I don't read Arabic?" She replied under her breath.

"It says," he exclaimed with exaggerated inconvenience, "*American Mahdi shielded by Shura Council leader Abd al Hakim*…someone found him for us."

"Where is he?"

"We're on the cell to our contacts right now," he replied enigmatically invoking the need-to-know barrier that caused her great anxiety. "Abd al Hakim is a well connected politician with a house in Rosetta…we're sort of in a day-late-dollar-short scenario if you get my drift."

The rented car rolled to a stop in a small cloud of dust off the dirt road across the river from Rashid adjacent al Hakim's compound. They had made the trip from east of Alexandria in less than ninety minutes. Several military vehicles blocked the entry gate and a few nervous soldiers milled about as crowd control. Karine slouched down in the back seat hoping the headscarf she wore lent enough anonymity to keep her from attracting attention while the two men in the front looked at each other sardonically and Jack punched in a speed dial number on his cell. Watching the gates she was surprised to see an officer suddenly answer a call and then look directly at them, startled she slunk down further, when he hung up Jack bounded out the door and walked with confident bulldog strides across the dirt to where the soldiers were standing. Yasser, a native Egyptian in the front seat, looked back nervously and said, "If anyone asks, you're my wife."

The sun bore down on them like a heavenly spotlight as it rose to apogee in the cerulean blue streaked with cirrus clouds signaling a coming storm. In the city she would have perspired, but here Karine began to sweat like a man unaccustomed to being in the field and not dressed properly. Bicycles and motorcycles littered the ditch bending the long, dry grasses beside the road and a few cars were strewn haphazardly parked, but most had come on foot and their dusty prints had been absorbed into the woof and warp of the trail that their ancestors had travelled since the pharaohs. Naked feet and nut brown faces. Pilgrims seeking salvation. Suppressed by an iron hand. Just as always, she mused, the only real changes in the world were things and the technology to make things, people were pretty much the way they had been as if the past was just a blaze of industrialized madness and when the market wore out everything vanished into one of the mysterious epic extinctions that loom over all human endeavor like a scythe goading everyone forward least they fall behind and be consumed by history's turning of the soil. Men were constant gardeners. It was the perennial seeking of something new that left old questions unanswered.

All of a sudden her door was yanked open with a rusty squeal and she looked up to see a young man with his olive drab sleeves rolled over his biceps, a glossy sheen covering his grimacing face. Yasser chattered madly in Arabic to a soldier outside his window also demanding he get out of the car. In a moment they stood at gunpoint, erratic soldiers barking commands, fingers on triggers.

"What do they want?!" She asked insistently trying at the same time to appear calm, mustering a slight smile as a disguise.

"I'm handling it…" Yasser exclaimed presumptively trying to shut her up, "…tell them you're my wife!"

"I don't speak Arabic…"

"*Ma⊠áa-ya!*" He yelled pointing to Karine, "*Zawah!*"

"*Ma⊠áa-ya!*" She repeated.

"No, no! You're saying 'my wife.'"

Karine was only slightly frantic when Jack returned with the Egyptian officer and plopped his arm around the shoulder of her interrogator. "It's OK." He smiled confidently. "We're leaving." Later, in the car, on the road back to Alexandria he explained that Parrish had escaped just before the military had arrived and was presumably heading west toward the lakes. "He is with a young woman. The district will be crawling with military. They're just awaiting reinforcements to start the chase. I'll make some calls. We'll find them."

"…but isn't that why we're in Egypt?" Karine impressed on him making no effort to hide her displeasure. "Explain to me again, why are we going back?"

"He has taken the daughter of the General. It's not safe here."

*   *   *   *

It was much later that Ishaq Sadek was again summoned by Muhammad Abd al' Rashid on matters personal and confidential. They were to meet on the yacht in the harbor under cover of night. He had been manically racing around Rashid and other close in Delta towns searching for leads as to where the American and Azhara had escaped in the few days since he managed to evade the consequences of being in the wrong place at the wrong time. How they had vanished without him knowing he chalked up as just another riddle in the dust along the Nile. Thankfully, he had once done a professional favor for a military official by exposing the sexual liaisons of a woman the man had eyes for consequently saving said family dishonor and great embarrassment. It had been some of his best photography. Their milieu, which despite any liberal political leanings, was ultra conservative and packed with hardliners when it came to matters of sex. Though against his code, he had called in the favor due and consequently was permitted to leave without question much to the consternation of several agitated, testosterone imbued soldiers,. But now his heart leapt in his throat and he sweated coldly at the prospect of confessing to his client he had lost the trail of the exact young woman he had been hired to shadow—in fact that the trial had grown cold. One incident was all it took to ruin an illustrious career and he had witnessed many colleagues flame out for that very reason. Reputations lacerated beyond recognition.

"I have no words," Ishaq began. The swirl of the harbor night, the scents of the sea and the eternal motion of the swells intoxicating him. He had been ferried out to the yacht by the tall Ethiopian in a small, wooden runabout with polished mahogany decks, brass fittings and an inboard motor that murmured in the water like talking drums. Whether it was the ocean or the unfathomable wealth of the man before him who lived in the rarefied environs of the commanding heights that made him feel giddy was unclear. Living so near the ground only life and death are certain.

"When I returned, she was gone," al' Rashid stated with a hint of confusion in his voice that was only the veneer of a darker storm that brewed within his confines. He drew pictograms in the air with his long, brown fingers as if diagramming the mysterious incident in an attempt at clarification, perhaps hoping the grip upon him would lessen, "…that's all I know," but then dropped his hands to his lap in frustration. The Ethiopian brought him a drink and small crooked black cigar on a silver tray. All he offered the detective was a look that turned him to cold blue steel.

"I have lost her trail," Ishaq interjected skittishly in an attempt to mollify his employer, "I confess…but it's only temporary. It's just one of those…nearly all the best things that have ever happened to me have been unexpected." Desperation rose in him boiling up out of an inbred fear of the streets and the self-abnegation that went along with failure not to mention that it was the only thing he knew how to do. "It's part of the business…setbacks can bring new opportunities." Hunger motivated him to improvise.

al' Rashid was unmoved and looked through him like he wasn't there. "She must be found." A strange fascination had taken hold of the Arab that was forcing him through the chrysalis ready or not and on the other side was something familiar yet forbidding that made him reach and pull away all at once.

"Believe me, I have never failed a client before. It's just… circumstances…the American, he was unexpected, but as I said we should look at this as an opportunity."

"Yes. I can see that now. This would never have happened…"

"…she did escape, if she had of been arrested I would never have gotten to her."

"…it may be as they say."

"…I barely got out myself," sighing with relief at the Arab's tacit agreement, "and if it were not for a former client, a very grateful one I might add, I would be in jail right now, tortured…even dead!"

"The salt air, that's what does it. I absorb it. I breathe in its living substance and a particular astringency brings my emotions to the surface. Don't you feel it? The vast space of the open ocean is like the ether to me, plains of tranquil distance that give me room to be as I truly am and not as I must be, not as I am supposed to be and this is my reason to lie at anchor offshore. Human nature cannot be denied, don't you think? Faith and desire are one, wouldn't you say? Even the Qur'an corresponds to the true requirements of man's nature." In his mind the push-pull of swirling emotions began to crystallize until he could almost see who he really was, almost grasp it, but just as he was nearly there, it was gone and all that was left were the remnants of who he was supposed to be in shattered pieces dictated by the socio-religious and family constraints he had been born into. Desire mingled with profit and loss statements, longings blended in with market forces and prices. He needed justification if he was to break out and have once small corner of his life that was truly his. "The sword has two edges…the Prophet said, *'These are the words of Him who has the double-edged Sword. To him who overcomes, I will give some of the hidden Manna.'* *Zulfiqar*, the sword of heaven. It may be a sign, his coming; it may be as they say. She must be found!"

Ishaq's face drained of color afraid the elegant, young Arab had been driven senseless with loss. "Let me tell you I have been sweating blood to find them and have combed towns surrounding Rashid in the last few days. No trace. Azhara Binte Jibril Riyadh has simply vanished…but it's just a matter of time…if you'll…"

"No. No…her name is Kisa Vanusha. Russian. A correspondent. Freelance journalist from Belarus and she works with an Egyptian cameraman, Ibriham Mohamad–he was easy to trace…works here all the time."

"Kisa Vanusha?"

"Yes," he replied with a hollow look. "Find her."

"But…who is she?"

"It's like I said."

"What of the lady in question, Azhara?"

"*Malesh.* Leave her to her father. Her will locate her and the American, but you must get there first. Kisa has foolishly chased after the story, she is here covering events…there has been a misunderstanding. The General will not allow foreign journalists. The man is a fascist, a religious fanatic, a liability…she is in danger. Great danger. I am trusting to your discretion… but find her."

"I may have difficulty…"

But Muhammad Abd al' Rashid wasn't listening anymore. He had turned to gaze out at the Mediterranean sleeping in the womb of night. The memory of their sexual tryst would not leave him. It trembled in his memory. Whether love or lust it had satisfied some deeply personal, essentially primal urge that he had always denied yet unconsciously longed for. The dichotomy defined him. It was the reaching and never touching that had left him empty, until now. Emotions flooded his senses and swept him away in their wake–he with the keen, intelligent eyes. They had breached meticulously devised barriers behind which he hid from the real and violated his inner world like a fifty amp current leaving him racing before the wind. He ruminated on who was to say what is sacred and what is profane and how perhaps the truth was that men were indeed islands and though their shores may mingle one with another, sands upon sands, their interiors were unfathomable and as individual as each star in heaven.

XI | Into The Abyss

THE MUFTI FROM CAIRO ARRIVED AT TWILIGHT ON THE SECOND DAY. HE roared up in a late model convertible raising dust devils behind each tire wearing mirrored, aviator sunglasses that reflected the whole panorama right back at anyone who looked him in the eye. He was still shaking from the ordeal barely escaped from by this windfall trip. The whole town had been waiting with a brittle anticipation anxious to put the salacious business behind them because news of an incident this notorious traveled fast in the backwater of the Delta where everybody was a farmer or depended on agriculture and in some way or another was connected. It was life on the edge. Only a slender margin determined who would survive and who would not. The whole social structure had always existed on the brink of chaos as it did everywhere living was so hard and religion was the universal twine that held it all together. Even the slightest ripple could unbalance the collective equilibrium and send lives reeling irreparably. Nobody was willing to take that chance so he had been called in at the first sign of controversy. Things like this just couldn't be ignored.

A renowned archconservative, he represented the authority of the al-Azhar Mosque–the first mosque established in Cairo, city of a thousand minarets. Founded in 970, it was the second oldest continuously run university in the world and benchmark for Islamic studies and *Shari'ah* law interpretation worldwide. The *mufti* was summoned at the frantic demands of a local *imam* who lobbied hard for the scholar so he would not have to judge the matter himself and be responsible for unforeseen consequences. His memories of the man were luminous; a religious prodigy, an apprenticeship under the Grand Mufti of Egypt, himself a contender with considerable political clout and he had generated an expansive reputation that far exceeded his own constituency. He was a cause célèbre in the stultified world of Islamic scholars and for that reason no one, not even his wife, actually believed he would come to the dusty, provincial town in the Delta and derided the imam for aggravating an already inflamed situation with the idea.

But the request hit the mufti at the exact right moment. Though the news had not reached the outlying Delta yet, a scandal had erupted in Cairo after a sex tape that appeared to show him committing adultery with an unidentified young woman was leaked. About 60 angry protesters rallied outside the Mufti's office that Wednesday to show their outrage over the sex romp video. Demonstrators shouted that he should give up his credentials and resign his position, as he had no moral right to them. The chagrined mufti desperately tried to explain the clip, which had to be removed from the Internet by his lawyers, to a ravenous media by saying that it showed him and his second wife. Nobody thought to ask who was filming them or why. "Polygamy is legal in Egypt," he responded authoritatively. "Many wealthy officials have multiple wives," but he didn't mention there had been previous legislative attempts to outlaw the practice and a huge women's resistance movement. A member of the Egyptian parliament had even filed a lawsuit over a feminist article questioning why polygamy is allowed for men in Islam but not for women. It was true, in

Islam men can marry four women at the same time–if they can treat them all equally, but he only had two so felt extremely victimized by the unfair attack. It never occurred to him that women in more traditional parts of the Arab world can suddenly find themselves after years of marriage with few or no rights if their husband chooses to take a new wife. Of several he had asked to be his second wife, one shot back at the proposal, "…after all this waiting, I can't marry half a man!"

In an impromptu interview, he told a Ministry of Information official at the state owned Media Production City that the video's release may have been another political move that was orchestrated by the head of the country's commission for religious affairs. "They simply want to replace me with a more compliant cleric and take control over the country's organization of the hajj pilgrimage to Mecca," not mentioning that the muftiate collected $20 million every year for it. He also didn't bring up that he was under investigation on suspicion of evading taxes on money taken as bribes while organizing the hajj trip quota system and of laundering those funds through illegal businesses.

Hoping that General Riyadh and coup leaders would help him, he claimed that elements in the government were involved in a plan to intimidate him, an Islamic scholar of impeccable reputation and a man of the straight path, into leaving his duties. He pointed out that other muftis had resigned early amid similar alleged corruption scandals and even been kidnapped and beaten. He insisted he was innocent of all wrongdoing and just a scapegoat for the now fallen civilian government.

With all this trouble brewing he accepted the call for his professional services with great relief as a message from Allah. "Of course I'll come my old friend," he had patronized the provincial imam who claimed to have studied with him at al-Azhar even though he had no memory of it and was certain the man was lying to get what he wanted, "I will be glad to see you again." He was burning rubber on the desert road out of Cairo in less than an hour grateful for the reprieve from public crucifixion. *All things come with faith,* he thought as the desert wind tossed his hair in the convertible streaking down the highway with Egyptian sun glinting off the mirrored surface of expensive aviator sunglasses.

* * * *

But that was later, days after a pursued Parrish and Azhara arrived in the small village of Shakhlubah on the southern shore of Lake Burrulus. It rose mirage like from the hundreds of square miles blanketed by small fields of sugar cane, cotton, maize and above all rice as a pastiche of irregular mud brick buildings crowding the shore on both sides of a wide irrigation ditch where it collided with the lake. Lateen rigged feluccas lined the banks awaiting a rag-tag army of fishermen who set sail each dawn onto the glassy waters to scoop up leaping mullets, sole, eels and the prize Nile Perch that can reach 6-feet and over 300-pounds. It smelled like dust in the late afternoon light. Nothing moved except for an occasional dog, pickup truck or small motorcycle interrupting the scene as if a fresh brushstroke across a completed painting. Rolling into town through the outskirts they passed without noticing an anonymous building gutted by fire. The trembling walls were a missed omen; it was a clue to the undercurrent they had just been swept into once the bridge over the canal had been crossed.

It all began with a young woman. A Coptic Christian who, as a non-Muslim, was unveiled and barefoot in the dust. Sectarian violence had a long and celebrated history in the region and peace was punctuated with intervals of mindless barbarity resulting in internecine carnage beyond anyone's ability to bear. As a consequence, revenge had a long memory. Especially when the fish had stopped running in the lake and the

Government was rationing grain. But recently an itinerant, fundamentalist imam had been igniting the Muslim men of the village by urging them to abduct, enslave, and sell non-Muslims as a Shari'ah approved way of making a good living. "If only we can conduct a jihadist invasion at least once a year," he hissed, "or if possible twice, then many people on earth would become Muslims. And if anyone stands in our way, we must kill them or take women and children and confiscate their wealth. Such battles will fill the pockets of those who struggle in the paths of Allah." The young woman was abducted and never seen again–Copts retaliated and in the ensuing melee 12 people were killed. Two days later a makeshift bomb exploded in front of the once tiny Coptic Church killing all inside. Only the dust had settled. Everyone was on edge.

Azhara had covered her head the moment they entered the village as if some telepathic command had been received and looking at Parrish said, "Don't talk to anyone." Like an earlier century, everything moved slower. There were no inns or lodges. No cafes. It was a rural enclave where fishermen from the lake mingled with farmers from the fields. Azhara ferreted out a small house overlooking the water a man was willing to rent to her and Parrish, her husband, on the short term. He needed the money. It was primitive. Three rooms and a small oil stove. They settled in at dusk and pulled the curtains tight.

Parrish did not venture outside for the first few days. He sat in a wooden chair and looked through the window facing Lake Burullus and the clusters of reed islands close to shore across the brackish mud flats that reeked of the sea. Further out were the armadas of sleek hulled feluccas gliding along a glassine surface where the mist obscured the horizon line until it was a frosted gradation of pastel aqua, ultramarine and pearl with a hint of salmon refracting a rose colored sunrise. Flocks of lateen sails slashed the skyline all at the same angle as if they were pure white birds lifting off for places unknown. Cool, moist air rolled onto the shore where it quickly became desiccated by the breath of Egypt, restless under the weight of history. He needed time and the landscape provided. A profound change had come over his life, something completely unexpected and inexplicable. It left him light headed, but focused. Where once anger had colored his perceptions and dictated his reaction to all difficulties now there was a bristling energy and a drive to be on the leading edge where culture, invention and speculation each acted as a catalyst upon the other enkindling brand new worlds. He was at once the same yet different, himself only more so. This was not a mental state or anything he could glibly explain and the fact that the malingering self-inspection infecting him with a grim persistence for so long was now missing escaped his notice entirely because he was no longer looking at himself trying to figure it all out. He was looking at life. All things appeared a little new, more crystalline, clarified. Colors were brighter. He had a new perspective on everything.

He watched the mystery of Azhara as she came and went busily gathering up what they might need until a plan came to them and revealed their next move. For the present, anonymity was good enough. She brought back some Turkish coffee and sugar on the first day and then strong French cigarettes–not the small cigars he loved, but good enough. He was happy she had her priorities straight and it was not until the second day before any real food was brought in. It was miraculous, he thought, that she had managed to hang on to her money after their ordeal–a trait of the rich he mused, her pockets must have been stuffed with bills though he couldn't imagine where. Later she fried up fava beans, fish with spices and some vegetables explaining, "My father learned to cook from the best chefs in Lebanon, taught me everything I know! What do you say to that?" She was not entirely perfect. Her teeth were a little crooked and she was not blessed with perfect symmetry, but she was endowed with a huge physical life force that was purely genetic as if it was something she wore over her deeper qualities. Hair as black as night tumbled down almond, panther like skin and even darker, alluring eyes. Parrish marveled at her and speculated if she was immune to being so closely observed as beautiful things often were–like a large captive cat restless and fine and dangerous, but still completely wild her eyes flashed with inner light, voice sparkled as a haunting, lyrical, lament in an Arabic mode that resurrected long dormant emotions. She had impossibly graceful hands still tattooed with intricate henna designs. He didn't know what he felt, drawn like Icarus ascending on foolish arms.

Azhara, at the same time, was watching the brooding American with mysterious powers who commanded her attention against her will. She who at times covered her eyes hiding from the real was now dancing on the edge; pursued by her Father's soldiers, an outlaw in fundamentalist cliques and afraid she would miss her destiny if it all continued too long. Still, it may have been providence that their paths crossed because she knew something was happening though she didn't know what it was. Religion was like breath, it had been engrained from birth and she took it all for granted until a new social consciousness began to spontaneously grow in her like a shark capable of virgin birth. It was the inability to reconcile medieval dogma with human rights that led her to apostasy and that was the point religion became mere superstition–ideas obscured in symbolism as if in code, parables of common sense for the illiterate and misanthropes. Then Parrish happened. Out of nowhere. Was he a messenger? Was Muhammad truly the messenger of an unaltered and final revelation of God? The experience had invoked questions that ran deeper than she had ever ventured before and shook her fixed ideas until she trembled. So it was a shock to discover the emotions that seeped to the surface without her consent like sap from the roots of trees, like seedlings dormant for generations only to sprout with a chance deluge beyond volitional control; speaking a language more primal and visceral that that of humans and engaged in conversations dealing with the destinies of generations. When she drew near him breath quickened. With his look her eyelids became heavy. A mere touch and she heard the music of lifetimes and sexual energy welled up inside her on its own accord. All of it confused her yet she could not deny the attraction that came from the ancient unspoken ritual.

Blue sky slowly surrendered to encroaching darkness dissolving into heaven when at last the final vestiges of human civilization gave way to the primordial and revealed our true position in the universe; poised on the precipice of the vast and merciless. Gazing out across this infinite landscape one could see the nuclear fire of stars igniting in the cosmos with a luminous dazzle greater than ten thousand of our own galaxies whose light journeyed so long to reach us that when we of earth and loam caught its glimmer it had already died and its ashes had scattered to the solar winds. Somewhere between our prying eyes and those flickering lights spirits soared on the edge of oblivion clinging to unfulfilled longings and wishes just as we do on the ground, only theirs were so much grander than ours, so much more like our dreams. In between those breathless whispers and our soft beds was the migration. The constant motion. The coming from somewhere heading someplace else. Each following a map in the head. They streaked silently across the moon leaving no trace, vanishing into the night from which they came and allowing men to lie in their sleep undisturbed and feeling superior certain they were the masters of it all. But above the millions flew on long distance errands inconceivable and hidden from us as they circumnavigated the planet buffeted constantly by ferocious winds, driven by the rain, pelted by the sleet, torn asunder by sheets of lightening and dynamic cracks of thunder that would drive any mere man to madness. Yet on fragile feathers they flew impervious to the immense distances, unafraid and steadfast into the mystic, into the limitless. No one has been able to explain migrations; they are a mystery riddled with scientific theory and ponderous erudition, but will forever remain a secret of the wild man is thankfully not privy too. Over the small house nestled up against the salt marshes of Lake Burullus raced 500 species of birds including wigeons, shovellers, pochards, boots and whiskered terns, thousands upon thousands at a time breaking the air with their wings striving for silent running as a master rower in a skull feathers his oars striving to slice the water imperceptibly without leaving a ripple. Only perfection with each stroke will do. If one embraced nature as a world of universal law, a world apart, a world build on perfection then he would be able to live in that silence and hear the quiet thunder of flapping wings passing far above, but as it is in this life embroiled in conflict shadows in the night were their only witness.

On the morning of the fifth day Parrish awoke to sea mist and sunlight filtering through the window. The smell of coffee wafted over him. Rising, he pulled on his trousers and walked sleepily into the main room where he poured a strong cup of dark brew and turned to the window looking out over the ubiquitous lake where dawn haze and distant fishing boats swept before him in an ancient tableau. A flickering movement out of the corner of his eye caught his attention. Turning his head slightly a sudden vision made him suck in his breath. It was so unexpected he froze and watched unable to move, entranced by the forbidden, wanting to flee and wanting to remain at the same time–desire and repulsion fighting within. There in the early light Azhara stood completely naked, hovering timelessly as if a mirage just outside the back door facing the salt flats, reed beds and shimmering expanse of water heavy under the weight of morning vapors. Above her head she held a large vase and tilting it let the water run down the nut like flesh of her nude body leaving rivulets and drops glistening like jewels on her flesh. Maroon nipples grew erect on small, tawny breasts, arms raised in lithe surrender to nature. Wet, ebony hair glistening back against her head, dew forming on the fur beneath her slightly rounded belly. She glowed with an endowment like fruit hanging heavy from a tree at the perfect ripeness longing to be picked, desiring to be sacrificed, to be eaten as destiny demands. She quickly grabbed the sheet covering herself and flitted back inside closing the door behind her without a sound. Then there was the silence of first light again the whole incident lasting but a moment in the great stream of time. Still Parrish did not move waiting for the current to pass through him and the sensation that coursed in his veins like honey heated to the boiling point. He breathed and took a sip of the coffee, the carnal urge rising up and threatening him fearing what he might destroy if he gave in to it. She was the most beautiful creature he had ever seen.

Parrish finished dressing and without a word walked out the front door for the first time since they had arrived hoping the embrace of the chilly waterscape would help him flee the intruding passion. Unseen and malingering another pair of eyes watched as well. Someone who chanced upon the scene in one of those random coincidences that makes up the very essence of living and dying. He had been late that morning having overslept and was taking a short cut through the reed flats to reach his boat and get out on the lake before the few fish available for the day's catch were swooped up by the competition. He too had been shocked immobile, transfixed, and stared dumbfounded with disbelief, invisibly, both feet stuck in the mud unable to grasp at first exactly what he was looking at. It appeared to be a naked woman, but the sight was so incongruous, so out of place that it took the entire moment and until long after Azhara had ducked back inside for him to fully realize what he had just seen.

"...nude woman!" He thrilled to himself in disbelief. A wave of deeply repressed sexual sensation shook his body nearly buckling his knees with its sickly sweetness and was so enticing and daring and forgotten that he immediately flexed all his muscles at once in a divine effort to repress it. He remembered a phrase from the Qur'an, *"Oh children of Adam! Do not let Satan seduce you, in the same manner as he got your parents out of the Garden, stripping them of their raiment."* Then, seeing Parish, a non-Arabic white man walk from the house he muttered, *"Shaitan!* I see *Ibis,* the devil!" He resolved right on the spot to expose the dual sins of fornication and being with a non-Muslim man—so in the unlikely event the two were married he would still have grave charges to bring. "It is *haram....*" he mumbled relishing the image of the nude female that lingered in his mind and contemplated if it was this evil on the shore of the lake that kept the fish away as a sign of Allah's displeasure. He knew he had been chosen out of all the men in the Village and the thought buoyed him above the disappointment of catching nothing the entire day. He knew this because he was a personal friend of the man who owned the small house on the shore and he would make it his duty to reveal the crimes taking place under his nose, on his property, behind his back. Later, when a boat mate asked him, "Why are you smiling with no catch?" He responded, "You will see."

Down the narrow few blocks between mud brick houses Parrish escaped toward the estuary collar turned up in anonymity, padding footsteps echoing off walls. When he reached the channel connecting the far off Nile, he turned north toward the lake both hands thrust in his pockets with a narrow focus. There were a few boats still strewn along the shore that had not gone out with the disheveled fleet at daybreak, wide, flat, feluccas lolling half-beached in ripples some with fishing nets rolled neatly prepared to cast off at a moment's notice. Nobody was around. All

the houses were still asleep without any signs of life save a few wisps of
smoke from tin chimneys and all along the shore for as far as he could see
there was no one–no one until he spotted a hunched over figure sitting
in a boat up ahead with his back turned. Parrish stopped and considered
for a moment whether he should continue and chance discovery, but felt
strangely compelled, almost predestined to be where he was and had a
slight premonition of lifetimes fleeting by hearing the winds of space in his
ears. Then, when he was nearly upon the boat, the man suddenly turned,
startled with a desperate expression of excruciating pain in his face. It was
then Parrish saw it. Cradled in his arm was the dark, unmistakable shape of
a gun and even if he hadn't seen it the aura of death hung heavily. The butt
of the stalk was wedged into the floorboards and he was holding it steady
with his foot, the muzzle of the barrel pointing at his head not a foot away.
His finger was on the trigger.

Parrish stood absolutely still raising his hands quietly palms toward
the man in admonition and whispered, "No!"

Like the center of a spinning wheel, a beginning or an ending, the
pinpoint on which a top whirls, like the place where a pebble touches
down on still water concentric circles forming all around it, like the instant
between breathing out and breathing in, like loving completely then losing
everything in a heartbeat, like moments when living hangs in timelessness
and all things are in motion except oneself caught in an inescapable
spiral, an equilibrium between worlds–one of light, one of shadow. The
man floated, clinging to the idea of life on nearly imperceptible gossamer
threads so fine and fragile. He looked up with a three-day growth of beard
and black rings around his red, tearful eyes hollow cheeks gaunt and
drawn in the gray morning light sweating in the cool air. Parrish knew this
place; it was somewhere he had been before. He recognized the signs, had
rambled down these crooked streets into darkness besieged by demons.

Then he spoke in his best Egyptian Arabic. "It's when you look and nobody looks back that you understand there is nowhere to be free to. You only take your burdens with you, one life to the next. It's then you find out who you really are." He inched forward with his hand outstretched. "Talk with me a while."

The two men faced each other fully intent on a course of action, poised like paper silhouettes against the ever changing landscape of reeds and rushing water and endless migrations that crossed invisible highways in the stratosphere for which no man had a roadmap. Clouds metamorphosized out of thin air and drifted away, wind flurries came and ruffled the waters face and then moved on, rushes beat out a rhythm like wrinkling paper along the shore as purple swamphens led their young brood out into the open river to swim with the big billed, russet colored shovelers and Egyptian cobras heading out to sea on one of their mysterious voyages. Iridescent dragonflies buzzed by as the sun came up upon the scene–Amun-Ra the hidden one revealed, King of the Gods. At last the man wearied and unceremoniously set the gun down on the deck sad and defeated, but not ashamed. Parrish sat down beside him and they began talking. Slowly a picture evolved of a hard subsistence life dependent on the vagaries of an exhausted nature where all necessities came hand to mouth with only a meager profit to buy needed supplies, materials for repairs and anything else for one more morning of casting the nets. Where a man was only as good as his last day's catch his worth was fleeting. Ephemeral. There was no equity in experience. Only in strong arms and backs, blistered and sunburned, dirt under the nails, bringing home the bacon, getting up when you've fallen and running twice as hard, twice as fast, never giving in...never. Until the fish stopped running and the kids got hungry and the wife disheartened before her time. He despaired that there hadn't been a sustainable catch in months, that he and many in the village had no alternative and the inability to feed his family and to feel any self worth, any value, any place in the world had gone with the fishes. They talked as the sun rose in the sky and warmed their shoulders. When the first of the small fleet of pale turquoise and white, red-hulled feluccas began straggling into their harbors along the river, they were still talking and continued until the light was straight up and there was barely a shadow on the ground. Then Parrish rose and the sun streamed from above him setting his hair ablaze.

"Tomorrow, there will be fish," he said with great finality. "Tomorrow the fish will return," and then he walked away back into the narrow streets to the small house hidden on the edge of the salt flats of the great northern Egyptian Lake Burullus. He had almost forgotten the vision of Azhara early that morning, but the memory lingered close to the surface. He left the dusty streets of the village behind and crossed the fields toward the bungalow they had taken refuge in when suddenly a shocking sight before him made his blood run cold. There were men standing at the door of the house, many men—he ran toward them as fast as he could all the time knowing it wasn't near fast enough.

* * * *

The next morning a fleet of feluccas broke the dawn mists with their tattered lateen sails running before the wind. Tired fishermen driven by hope alone with as many sets of steeled eyes faced the unending bargain with nature in which they seemed to come out on the losing end, as if the universe sought out each man's secret weakness. He had not told anyone of his encounter with the enigmatic American, he was too ashamed and besides, why should others suffer a fool's errand? He didn't really believe anyway—had discovered long ago words are cheap. People will say anything. When they reached open water the boats spread out like giant mosquitoes standing on the lake reflecting in the mirror like surface without a ripple. Nets were cast. It wasn't long before a cry was heard out among the vessels, a shout that carried effortlessly on the slight breeze. The first net had been hauled up heavy with fish and joyful men let their joy be known despite the code of silence on the fishing grounds–the glint of the sliver catch shining over a great distance for many to see. Other nets were pulled in too and they also were laden with fish–mullet and sole, sand smelt and eel. Suddenly emotions were high and empty nets were cast again into the brine and later gathered filled with wiggling, squirming life struggling to be free. Throughout the day nets were being filled and recast and boats began to sit low in the water their holds stuffed to the point of sinking. The man felt gladness, he felt delight and unexpected jubilation and let out whoops of exuberance with the others as he piloted his boat toward land sea foam splashing over the gunwales it was so burdened down astonished that he had been on the brink of annihilation just a day ago and if not for the American would have missed it all. There was not even the slightest hint of doubt in his mind that it was a miracle just as he had read about in the holy Qur'an, but never once ever imagined he would witness. He felt suddenly blessed. Then he remembered the stories, the stories filtering out of Alexandria of a Mahdi, rumors he had disregarded as useless, quasi-religious nonsense until now...and he was euphoric as the boat came to rest on the shore at the edge of the village where the buyers, who had already gotten word of the bonanza, waited. The man could hardly believe his good fortune even though there it was exactly as the American had said.

The mufti paced before the group of Village men. Dappled sunlight trickled through palm leaves outside rustling slightly with errant breezes causing illumination in the large, stuffy room to vacillate like those of two minds inside.

"The Qur'an was written as a testament because we cannot always know the right thing to do," the mufti explained patronizingly, "especially in such a case. We cannot be swayed by sympathy–that is a detour on the straight path. *'This is clear insight for humanity and guidance and mercy for people with certainty.'* The Shari'ah is absolute on the subject."

The imam who had invited the mufti sat gloating at his left hand, the very same man who had been invoking a jihadist invasion to abduct, enslave, and sell non-Muslim women. A dozen other men sat around them. "Her sin has been witnessed," he added.

"I would like to know more about the circumstances," an older man said.

"They have violated my house! What circumstances...? Who will rent it now?" Replied the landlord.

"...that house isn't worth anything. It was a windfall someone gave you money...we should use it for firewood..."

"She was naked, and that's the truth. Naked in the house with the American. What else?"

"Then why did you look at her?"

"Didn't the prophet Muhammad, praise be upon him, reveal *"If it had not been for the favor of Allah upon you and His mercy, you would have suffered..."*

"They are non-believers! He, a Westerner...and blasphemes pretending to be the Mahdi and she...apostate...infamous! *'Those who reject our signs, we shall soon cast into the fire.'* She turns women against Islam and is doubly blasphemous because her father is reputed to be a pious man. My wife wouldn't even sleep with me after rumors of her meetings…"

"Wait…wait…wait…we have never done this in our village!

"…I don't want whores and *shaitan* keeping the fishes away. '…*slay the idolaters wherever ye find them.*'"

"Will you kill them? If no one was with you, would you do it–blood on your hands alone?"

"What kind of a question is that?"

"You should be thankful for the memory of a young woman with no clothes–like a ripe flower. Look at you…an old wrinkled olive…your days with women are through…"

"It is the Qur'an that holds us all together. The true word. If one grain of sand is pilfered from the shore you may not notice, but is it not less? Isn't one sin all of ours?"

"He is right. Our job is not to debate the law, but simply to determine if they violated it. We are not responsible here for the rationality of it…the law is beyond the internal phenomena of conscience…"

"I agree. It is a question of honor…the reputation of our village…it doesn't matter if it's rational or not."

"Honor demands action…constant vigilance…" The room mumbled in a collective show of agreement.

"…but still, what was the context?"

"Guilty! Guilty! They are both guilty! Sin knows no context. It's black and white. Do you want justification? Let's decide so I can go home…" the man exclaimed tapping his left leg impatiently on the ground. "We all want to go home."

"This is about people's lives not your dinner getting cold."

"Alright…alright! The evidence is irrefutable." The imam finally said. "The woman was seen indecent. We have a witness here." The fisherman who had witnessed Azhara and Parrish stood up his whole body nodding with his hands outstretched in supplication looking each person in the eye. "The man has committed the worst kind of blasphemy leading people…I say we put it to a vote." He looked sheepishly for approval from the mufti from Cairo not wanting to appear too bloodthirsty.

"But he's an American…"

"All the more reason," the mufti interrupted, "we must show that the West is not influencing our belief." The imam nodded thankful he had not lost face. "We will vote now."

Hands were counted. More arguing ensued until long after the sun had left the sky. In the end the men wandered out into the moonlight exhausted from the turmoil of indecision and began the long walk home in the dark each feeling that the intricacies holding such problems in balance are too complex to fathom; each suffering the burden of righteousness; each still of two minds vacillating even though the votes had been cast afraid they had done something they would regret the rest of their lives. All but the imam who realized a profound satisfaction at the verdict reached behind closed doors without even the accused present. Nobody slept well that night save him.

The next morning Kisa and her cameraman Ibrahim Mohamed arrived just after sunrise. It was only chance that brought them. They had been searching the lake district ever since Parrish and Azhara had been exposed at Rashid by the inflammatory newspaper article. *Shakhlubah* was the only village south of Lake Burrullus and she was following a hunch, eating the last of the croissants brought from the hotel and holding a cup of cold coffee. Just a few fishermen were heading out and their boats appeared like lonely sentries on the placid water of the lake. They pulled the car off into a field just outside of town and as they made their way on foot people could be seen gathering in the distance. Many people.

"C'mon," she nudged Ibrahim, "keep out of sight! Shoot anything you see–we'll edit later."

"I've got three battery packs!"

They padded anxiously through the dirt and crept around corners hugging the low building walls trying to appear nonchalant, but standing out like diamonds on a black man's finger unsure of what to expect in this rural backwater. Soon all six blocks had been crossed between the fields and the river and they spotted a junction up ahead where dirt streets crossed and formed a small square. It was rapidly filling with people straggling in from all directions. As they approached, Ibrahim climbed some stairs to a second story landing of a house that appeared to be vacant for the moment and Kisa nervously followed.

"What's going on down there?" She spoke in a hushed tone.

Ibrahim raised the camera viewfinder to his eye and, wiping the sweat from his eye, extended the zoom lens. "...something."

"Is that a hole? Are they digging something up?"

"No." A long moment ensued while he struggled with the equipment to get a better view.

"So...what?"

"It looks like burying...they're burying something."

"What is it?"

"A woman."

Kisa wrestled the camera to her eye and exclaimed, "God...! It's Azhara! God...! They're burying her!"

"Just to the waist. It's a ceremony...see the white beards? Village elders..."

"God...! What d'ya mean 'ceremony'?"

"*Shari'ah*. It's a sentence, a punishment being carried out."

"Punishment?"

"Looks like a stoning."

"No...they don't do that any more! God...! Do they...? They can't..."

But Ibrahim was no longer listening. He had lifted the camera up on his shoulder and steadied his hand in the strap leaning against the wall to keep it from shaking. A red light began blinking on and off.

"We have to do something!"

He was a silent witness. "Tell the world..." he said in muted anger torn between the compulsion to act and his mission to document so that others would act, "I am not a soldier."

Azhara was dragged flailing across the dirt square bound hand and foot wind sweeping away the dust. Her wretched face covered with sweat and smudges alternating between rage and supplication, black hair completely undone tossing madly in the air. The whites of her eyes flashed brightly across the distance and her cries pierced the morning all the way to the secret landing where Kisa watched and Ibrahim filmed in utter helplessness sick with rage.

"What is she saying...?" Kisa pleaded.

"She is calling them medieval dogs. Islamic butchers, and spitting on them."

"God...! That won't help!"

Held in the shallow pit just long enough for other men to shovel dirt over her until she was immobilized from the waist down, Azhara finally stopped her futile struggle and glared at her oppressors defiantly hands secured behind. Her thoughts raced as if navigating city streets jammed with caroming traffic determined to come through despite the odds, all her schemes, her plans and wishes lay naked now unearthed and incomplete burning from all the wasted time and purposelessness that was the plague of a well do young woman with time on her hands. She seethed with unfulfilled dreams. A semicircle of brutish figures formed around her next to a pile of jagged rocks gathered up the night before. No one moved, everything was silent except for Azhara's cries.

"Brothers," the mufti finally broke in, "this is your community, it is not my place to throw the first stone."

"We have never done this before."

"Can't you cover her face..."

" She is giving us *Ayn ⬛ārrah*, the hot eye! The Prophet said, *'The influence of an evil eye is a fact...'* God has willed it.

"Recite your verses. That will protect you."

"I am not afraid, " the imam strutted out before the group. It is unmanly to be afraid, especially of a whore!" He picked up a large chunk of broken basalt. "Who among you is too faint-hearted to defend Islam?" The others to a man sheepishly picked out a rock from the pile and one was feebly tossed in the direction of Azhara, but it missed. "We must do better than that," the imam muttered with a deep resonating malevolence as he raised his hand and cocked his arm as he had seen baseball players do on television immediately mimicked by the others. Suddenly, his jaw dropped, eyes squinted red and he buckled at the waist as a wave of pain crossed his face like a shot. The stone dropped from his hand and he yelled in agony staring at his palm blistered, burned and still smoldering. In the same instant, the other men dropped their stones and let out anguished bellows and a few rolled in the dirt like animals trying to rid themselves of fleas on a hot Egyptian afternoon. Their palms were raised acrid with burnt flesh, red and split, waving in the breezes. Their cries echoed like a pack of hunting hyenas out across the village paths forewarning of a powers greater than their own. Azhara stood bewildered, cast iron and frail.

"What's happened?! What is it?!" Kisa implored.

"Dunno..."

"Did you get it? You getting this…?!"

"I'm live…close ups!"

"Get down, someone will see!" You getting all this…?"

"Their hands are burnt?"

"What?!"

"I can see it through the lens. Burnt red, cracked, blistered… *In-sha Allah!*"

"That's impossible…! What…"

"In-sha Allah!"

Just then a small military vehicle pulled out of a side street into the square with a plume of dust. Three soldiers leapt out landing squarely on the ground assault rifles cocked high on their shoulders at eye level, fingers on triggers, faces grim. Frantic shouts were heard as the men in the semicircle were forced to their knees–some with the help of gun butts thrust into the backs of their legs–and most onlookers scattered shrieking in all directions. Then another dusty vehicle arrived and still another followed by a truck that disgorged more troops into the street. Pandemonium gripped the village as people fled helter-skelter while Kisa and Ibrahim cowered on their perch, engrossed and isolated from the chaos below capturing events as if immune from catastrophe. When the dust had settled a shiny midnight blue, luxury sedan pulled up into the fray and the driver jumped out opening the back door saluting crisply clicking his heels sharply and standing motionless at attention. A large, taut man covered in military insignia and sporting dark sunglasses with tortoise shell frames in an officers hat heavy with braid and scrambled eggs emerged and commanded everyone's attention as he surveyed the scene bearing all the weight the head of the Supreme Council of the Armed Forces was entitled to–even though he always thought of himself as the "Commander of the Faithful." Scowling at the soldiers across the yard who had just finished excavating Azhara from confinement he walked purposefully up to her. Jibril Ben Jabbar Riyadh confronted his daughter and had to suppress the tears that welled up in his eyes. Showing weakness, he knew, was the first step to losing ones way on the straight path and becoming part of the mob.

"Daughter," he said, "I have come to take you home." And he ushered her off to be swept away by the midnight blue, luxury sedan where Azhara collapsed into the great man's massive arms tears flowing like the Nile flood, finally breaking down, crumbling inside, deteriorating at the core from unrealized dreams.

Moments later Parrish was brought out with a swarthy soldier at each arm. He wretched loose and paused glowering down in front of the cursed imam; who could not look him in the face and trembled while he nursed his damaged hand in pain awed at what had happened, in terror at being found out afraid of what people would do to him if he let them be free, but overriding all these considerations was the pervasive idea that the American really was the guided one who arises, the hidden imam emerged from occlusion and he, a religious man, had crossed paths with destiny and the burn on his hand was the mark of sin. He hissed "Mahdi" to himself in mock penance as Parrish disappeared inside the small military vehicle with the three soldiers and vanished down the road in dust and diesel whine.

The mufti had managed to slip away unnoticed with the first sign of commotion and was burning rubber on the desert road back to Cairo grateful for the reprieve from public crucifixion. *All things come with faith*, he thought as the wind tossed his hair in the convertible streaking down the highway with Egyptian sun glinting off the mirrored surface of expensive aviator sunglasses. The local imam who had reeled him in however was not so lucky because the military men left behind had very exacting orders to get to the bottom of the affair and meet out appropriate punishment, or as General Riyadh put it "divine retribution." It wasn't long before all fingers were pointing at the man who many felt was too much of a fundamentalist for anyone's good and the opportunity to shirk responsibility and rid the village of a social menace all at once was too delicious to pass up. The imam was summarily "disappeared" only to be found later that afternoon shot dead lying by the boats where Parrish had told the fisherman that all men were sailors and that the fishes would return on the bank of the canal leading to Lake Burrulus, shot dead lying on the grasses and young green reeds bursting with life.

A crowd had gathered around the body, which attracted the camera eye of Ibrahim and Kisa—who cursed her bad luck for not having filmed the execution because they had been forced to hide from the military. Each person was overflowing with conflicting felings of relief and abhorrence as they hovered morbidly around the body a few women trilling into the air when unexpectedly a girl cried out, "Aya! Look...! Look...! It's Aya!" All eyes turned to the shore. There an ephemeral, young girl was emerging mysteriously from the water. She was dressed in a black abaya with a hijab covering her head. "Aya!" They cried one after another, "Aya!" Sobbing with astonishment and fear and joy all at once. The girl came up from the water to the shore and smiled gently as if glad to be home and sad to have ever left, but no one would embrace her afraid she was a djinn or at best a *ruh*, a soul because that would contradict Islamic teaching that once a person dies he never returns until judgment. Though each knew of *hadiths* and stories of the dead communicating with the living through dreams, none had even heard of the dead physically visiting the living unless of course the *Imam al Mahdi* had truly visited them and this was part of the plan. The villagers became frenzied seeing that by the time the girl reached them her garments were completely dry as if she had never been submerged in the canal. As if she had never left. It would not be until later, much later, that Kisa would discover this was the same Coptic girl who had disappeared when the interreligious trouble began in the village two weeks before their arrival and had not been seen since, presumed dead until now resurrected upon the shore as Lazarus of the Four Days had rolled away the stone.

"Do you see that...?" Kisa pulled on Ibrahim's arm.

"Stop it, you're jiggling the camera..." as he moved in on the crowd to get the money shot.

"...we're going to get the Pulitzer!"

"Quiet..."

"Get in closer...I want to ask her some questions. We'll be the first people to ..."

Later, Kisa could not recall what had happened next that set the small crowd chasing them. It all changed in a flash. Perhaps it was that they had witnessed the mystic for which no one had concrete answers and the villagers were afraid, or that they were just as xenophobic as urban Westerners and had to vent their outrage at death and rising again because it assaulted their beliefs. Or events had simply stressed them to the breaking point. They ran for their lives into the dusty street stumbling under the burden of the equipment that Kisa was ready to die for since without the untold story they now possessed her life would return to the humdrum of the Travel Girl interviewing morose, two-bit chefs at middle class resorts. Now that she had sunk her teeth into a major breakout news event and was the only broadcast journalist on the case a vicious tenacity arose that scared even her in its ferocity. Feet padded along the narrow lane like marathon runners, echoes of footsteps pursuing from behind raising their heartbeats to dangerous levels gasping for breath seeking escape, but as they caromed around a corner a group of surly men from the square stood right in front of them and they froze in their tracks. Kisa's ears pounded as blood coursed through her veins and rivers of perspiration stung her eyes making it hard to focus when suddenly Ibrahim slammed her back against a wall. A rock whizzed by landing in the dirt kicking up a small cloud. Then the pursuers appeared from round the building and were on top of them, instantly too close—she could smell their odors, bodies and cumin and fish and began to feel faint.

A gunshot rang out into the clear Egyptian sky. Roosting birds took flight. Women threw up their arms cowed and shrinking back. Men turned to flee then caught their cowardice mid-stride and reluctantly looked back to face fate. Burly Ishaq Sadek rubbed the scar that ran across his cheek with his thumb then stroked his great bush of a mustache and stood barrel chested between hunters and prey.

"*Salaam aleikum,*" he said quietly leveling the ancient revolver at his waist toward the crowd.

"*Wa aleikin as-salaam,*" Ibrahim replied mystified.

"I think he's on our side," Kisa whispered.

"With a gun…?"

"Why do I always seem to be meeting women this way?" Ishaq rejoined. "Let's go now…someone wants to see you."

The phone rang just as the last vestige of light left the sky with only a magenta streak whispering across the Mediterranean horizon. It was detective Sadek calling and Muhammad Abd al' Rashid pressed the personal cell to his ear without a word listening intently in the dark. He had been waiting with anxiety in the womb of the ancient harbor at Alexandria on the yacht crafted with carbon fiber and rare woods joined ingeniously without the use of any metal fasteners. It boasted an art collection created by a Persian curator who had access to the world's black market whose subterranean corridors were overflowing with centuries of pilfered treasures. Eight different types of marble adorned the cabins much of which was quarried at the same place Renaissance masters Bartolommeo Brandini, Donato di Niccolò di Betto Bardi and Michelangelo di Lodovico Buonarroti Simoni found stone for their masterpieces. Below deck sat four gleaming German diesel engines powering a triple jet propulsion system of 30,600 horsepower capable of 80 knots on calm seas. Decks of mahogany and teak were intermittently covered with hand-knotted, antique, silk Beshir carpets. On the seabed beneath him lay Cleopatra's palace where she and Marc Antony were entombed forever. But of all the treasures the enigmatic al' Rashid had access to the words he heard on the phone were the most valuable. "She is safe," Ishaq reported. "I have her."

XIII | The Hidden Pillar

IN THE NIGHT RESTLESS SNOW FLURRIES PELTED THE OFFICE WINDOWS AS a brutal Arctic cold front descended demonstrating that no one is above nature. He sat hunched over a large, nineteenth-century partners' desk crafted from the timbers of the British Arctic Exploration ship Resolute that was a gift from Queen Victoria in 1880. Lights were dimmed and most had left hours ago except for security–including the Secret Service men who hovered out on the veranda even in inclement weather, his secretary just outside the door and a few other ambitious staffers or those too disorganized to get their work done during the day. He poured over the State Department's Morning Book given to him earlier containing the National Intelligence Daily, the Morning Summary, diplomatic cables and intelligence reports with particular attention to burgeoning developments in the Middle East–intensified by recent events in Egypt, which he noticed with relief few deaths were attributed to. "...praise Jesus," he muttered to himself certain that the fundamentalist general Riyadh was prone to bloodshed by reason of Islamic fervor. He had strong convictions on the subject because he had committed large sections of the Bible to memory in his youth, could still recite them at will and had been considered a religious prodigy. Shooting his cuffs he unbuttoned his coat letting down now that he was alone and extremely tired having started work just after 5:30 am. He believed clothes made firm impressions and held former Chief Executives in great disdain with their polo shirts, khakis and jeans for the damage they wrought on the prestige of the office. It was part of the Fabian quality he aspired to and he had never grown to hate business suits as his father had with his fifty years of starched collars.

"Just remember that there are many important people who work in the White House, and you're not one of them." The Duty Officer said as he hurried down the long hallway his associate struggling to keep up, not get too winded and be ready for the impromptu, coherent, professional conversation with the President. "Let me do most of the talking."

The President's secretary stood at the door. "There are two alphabet boys from the Woodshed here to see you."

"Why didn't they call? …it's late."

"Important. They say it's important," and the two squeezed into the office.

"Sir, the Foreign Service Officer for Political Affairs at the Central Middle Eastern Mission has been arrested."

"Where's the Crisis Manager?"

"That's just it, nobody seems to know."

The three men perched on facing couches and spread out reports on the low table in between. The Duty Officer took the initiative his training as a Navy Lieutenant demanded, bold, aggressive and complete in all details to date delivered with measured tones taking great care to impart precise information without any inflections that would give away personal feelings, because he knew coolness under fire was an attribute of command and that it was best to check egos at the door. He played the disk they had obtained of an All Russian TV news broadcast showing

Foreign Service Officer McKenzie being taken into custody by soldiers. "But look here..." he said, "...watch." The scene shifted to earlier in the village square, the semicircle of men, a woman half buried in the ground and the dropping rocks with grimaces of pain–zoom shots on hands with first-degree burn marks. Snippets showed the military storming in, releasing the young woman and spiriting her and then Parrish away. Next, handheld camera shots focused on a body lying in grasses by a river surrounded by a small crowd–then of a young girl mysteriously coming up out of the water onto the shore and people falling at her feet as if in worship, but when the crowd turned on the cameraman it ended all the while a Russian newscaster's voiceover droned on.

"What do you make of it?"

"Russian TV says locals are claiming miracles...just got the translation minutes ago."

"So, I am in the loop...where is this place?"

"Northern Egypt, a small Village on the southern shore of Lake Burrullus–just south of the Mediterranean coast. The newscaster says there have been three miracles attributed to your Foreign Service Officer there..."

"Yes, we had rumors before about this man that I thought had been put to rest...apparently not. A 'clear obstacle to restoring good relations with any new leadership' as I think the Crisis Manager described it...she was to handled him personally...he's her staffer..."

"...as I said, nobody knows where she is at present. Grapevine hearsay is she went off on a CIA sanctioned mission to Egypt, but none have been authorized at all. Zero. We checked thoroughly. The situation remains we have a U.S. State Department official arrested by an illegitimate military junta...and some pretty serious religious overtones that could destabilize our already delicate relations. Another damn jihad or something...!" The

Duty Officer held his breath, furled his brow and stared down at the table instantly regretting that he had been so candid.

"Sir," the assistant NSA intelligence analyst finally broke his silence to help his boss save face, "the fact is we've got to avert a crisis. We don't expect the major news services to pick up on this story for a day or two since it's an off line piece, but when they do...we've got personnel from State in foreign custody and Islamic nationals attributing certain religious phenomenon to him that could escalate retaliatory violence globally. Could be a firestorm."

"We don't know who all these people in the video are yet," the Duty Officer asserted "but Russian TV reports he's raised the dead for Christ sakes, like a fucking prophet! What will happen when this news hits mainstream Middle East media?"

The President gazed across at the two men with steel gray eyes for a moment. "Thank you gentlemen," was all he said and soon was alone again in the Oval Office. He stood and buttoned his jacket then picked up the phone and pressed one key. "I want the National Security Advisor, Chairman of the Joint Chiefs and CIA Director Miller to meet me in the Sit Room in 30 minutes and I don't care where they are. Notify Mission Ops were kicking off an operation tonight...and tell those two alphabet boys to be there too. Oh...and instruct the Secret Service to find Karine Russo, apparently she's been lost."

* * * *

On a low plateau east of central Alexandria overlooking a white sand beach on the Mediterranean the Al-Haramlik Palace at Montazah was burning bright with revolutionary fervor. The contingent returning from the village south of Lake Burullus drove up the long drive lined with Belle Epoch streetlamps and crossed the secure perimeter where the great

General, Commander of the Faithful, surrendered to the ornate building long used as a center of government believing it granted succor to him for his unconscionable acts as a military man. He had bitterly come back with an apostate daughter and a false prophet both an assault on his faith, but strangely felt relief. Khamaseen winds whipped up the sea into a rage of whitecaps glimmering under cover of darkness as contradictory emotions roiled deep within his umbra.

But that was earlier, before his conversation with Azhara. He had summoned her hoping for some justification that could explain away all that had happened and expected to be greeted with the soft, compliant eyes of the daughter he secretly cherished beyond anything else, but instead was met by a complex woman of heart and mind.

"Make me understand'" he said reaching for a thread. "Enlighten me."

She was slow to respond, thoughtful. "I have seen things I never before thought possible," as she recalled witnessing inexplicable events. "I don't think I understand them myself, but they have changed me."

"How so?" Jibril paced anxiously across the room cast in the low, warm light of antique lamps left over from the last Sultanate of Egypt fretting whether it was only the fates determining important events in his life and not adherence to the sunnah, the well trodden, the straight path. Or perhaps his influence over the dynamics of life was waning…if so, he had many things to account for though he wasn't prepared for such moral failure just yet.

"I am tired of living in the land of invisible women."

"But I have given you everything…!" He feigned exasperation throwing up his hands.

"Not in our home…" she gathered her thoughts while her eyes grew cloudy. "It is a place where mosques are our prisons and Islamists our jailers. I refuse to give up Islam to the Islamists…I could not see that before. I saw all Muslims as the same, the umma–the collective community, but I perceive now there is truth and there are lies and the problem is distinguishing between. Islam and those who follow it are two different things. Islam is not its people."

"You have become your own woman…"

"Islam can be a political ideology that preaches violence and applies its agenda by force–but I find beauty in the Qur'an and great wisdom…I don't find subjugation or justification for evil…why such contradictions if we all read the same scriptures unchanged for 14 centuries? Isn't that the point? Aren't you 'The Protector of Mosques,'"

"There's a difference between truth we can live by and human nature. Men are weak in spirit. We people are a bit…vulgar. Perhaps some things shouldn't be inspected so closely…"

"Islamists are trying to challenge the legitimacy of all other voices and I'm tired of being challenged."

"Well…is that all?" He shrugged and cast his eyes cat like aside. "Malesh…and what of love…? What of good cooking…?"

"I believe in women's rights. Human rights," she stated emphatically.

"Daughter," he said looking down at his left shoulder as if to see an angel writing down his haram act, "great contributions have been made by Muslim scholars and artists. Islamic civilization has taken its place among the great cultural achievements of human history. None of that would have happened without original ideas…it doesn't make you an unbeliever to assert your own viewpoint or to be intellectually strong, that's why I sent you to university…and you are my daughter after all." He spoke from the heart without regard to deeper consequences, and furled his brows in defiance of nature for he knew he had sinned overlooking apostasy and then added in a conciliatory tone, "We will tell everyone you are not an unbeliever."

Azhara gazed at him for a long time "I intend to marry the American so do not harm him!"

"In-sha Allah," all the more devastated by this revelation. "Then you have an appointment in Samarra, but Allah is the lord of all men's ways." Praying for forgiveness he resolved not to be so lenient on the blasphemer. Appeasing one's own blood was one thing, but some things cannot be recovered from.

It was a test. Just as he had been tested and never once flinched from all the forces life unleashed or let his grit be dissolved he would now put it to another and see what his mettle was made of. Only this was different. For two days he reeled from his daughter's pronouncement, just when he thought the issue resolved and he had completely exonerated Azhara–he'd even consulted a professor of theology and chair of Islamic Studies at al-Azhar University–he went away with a flea in his ear. To marry a non-Muslim was an obstacle, but a false prophet...this was something entirely of a different cloth, he was guilty unseen of blasphemy and the thought of his daughter...or that she had been in private with him... there was a point beyond which rationality ceased to exist supplanted by a righteousness that manifested as raw unrestrained rage. God help those on the receiving end of his fury, and there had been many in is long military career, but this was more delicate and needed an adroit touch to keep from alienating his daughter whom he prized above all things. So he devised the test as a masterpiece of interpersonal relations in the belief that trusting Americans is like trusting water in a sieve. *I will eat him for lunch before he eats me for dinner,* he thought...*a fool always hangs himself if he is put at ease.*

Jibril Ben Jabbar Riyadh, the Army of the Faithfull's great general supervised every aspect of the food's preparation and those items he didn't actually cook himself personally made sure adhered in excruciating detail to the very exacting recipes he had collected starting with his stint in Lebanon as a young man studying under the finest chefs. But it was all to be very casual, nonchalant, hush-hush…so when the American was brought down to meet with him nothing was suspected, nothing seemed out of the ordinary and even the elaborately prepared food was made to seem like an afterthought. Therein lay the genius, he mused, because some of the best recipes in the Middle East were from street food found in vendors' carts or stalls to be eaten without ceremony.

"You don't look like a prophet."

"Hunger does that…"

"Ah…hunger!" He snapped his fingers and trays of delicacies were brought in by orderlies in crisp, khaki uniforms and laid on the huge, low table between them. There was Red Sea fish *shaour* in a delicate spice for *sayyadiya*. Many different kinds of *mezze* with flaky pastry shells such as *kunafi*, shoelace pastry filled with sweet white cheese; also *sambusek*, triangular pies filled with spiced meat, cheese and spinach; and pita bread with *mouhammara*, a mixture of ground nuts, olive oil, cumin and chili to dip it in. Turkish coffee sat in a silver pot rich and sweet along with a *sheesha*, the water pipe he used to smoke dried fruit through after the meal.

Jibril used the food to engage in small talk as Parrish, famished after days without proper nutrition, ate like it was his last meal never suspecting that it may be just that. "Excuse my manners, it's just that it's so…"

"…delicious?" Jibril interjected hopefully.

"…exquisite is more what I was thinking." Parrish stuffed his mouth full. "I haven't had food like this since dining in downtown Beirut eight years ago. You must have a superb Lebanese chef."

"Yes…he ties, he tries," surprised and bemused the American understood truly refined cuisine, but his pleasure overridden by a darker motive.

"I haven't had a good meal in…"

"What is your post at the embassy in Cairo, mister…?"

"McKenzie…Erskine, call me Parrish. Foreign Service Officer for Political Affairs."

"Of course…I knew that…" The general launched his massive body off the couch and began pacing unable to keep still. "…and what exactly are you doing in my country?"

"Situations," he paused with a furtive look in his eye sensing the predator. "It's all about situations. Interpret and advise on Middle East issues–decipher events as they relate to our interests…"

"I don't believe you are CIA like some of my more enthusiastic advisors, but indulge me…"

"No, no…" he replied modestly to allay suspicions, "just keep my eyes open, assess the impact of political developments here on the U.S. and make recommendations…" he glared as if at some private irony, "not that they're necessarily followed…think of me as the black sheep of State. I try to help my government communicate with…you for instance."

"I'm honored," Jibril responded coldly, "but you've been crossing lines I think. You have been wanted for questioning in the death of the imam at Al-Qaed Mosque. Did you know that?"

The sudden chill in the room invoked an urge for self-preservation beyond his volitional control. "…dead…that was a surpri…yes, I've heard the news. I was trying to reach the embassy and got targeted."

"There are rumors…you seem to have a following."

"I'm not the one…"

Jibril delicately picked up a china cup in his massive paw. "Coffee?"

"I haven't been myself for some time…"

"Tell me, what exactly happened on that road north of Safi…they say you healed a girl?" Sipping the thick saccharine brew laced with cardamom.

"A mistake, rural people..." events again swirled around him, "I don't believe she was injured in the first place, just scared...she had the blood of another's on her..."

"Yes, the people...I have a great covenant with them. Don't mistake an inhabitant of the countryside for someone with an intellectual disability, we are a tribal people and intrinsically different than you in the West. We are also a religious people, Allah guides us in all things with the words of the Prophet, peace be upon him. We are not a people of war and camels, but of spirit."

"I was kidnapped. That's how this all began...wanted some prisoners released, I was a bargaining chip."

"Abducted from a high security five-star hotel? I have my sources and there is much about you that doesn't make sense. My daughter seems to like you, I myself haven't made up my mind just yet..."

Parrish felt cornered. "I'd just like to contact my embassy..."

"The more modern we are the more complex we become–don't you find that so?"

"Personally I am a student of antiquities..."

"Yet all great truths are simple," he continued eyes glazed in reverie. "I find this a mysterious contradiction because it seems to condemn all evolving technology; medicine, engineering...indeed progress itself. So it places the scientist on the one hand and a religious person on the other. It is not a question of belief, but of faith."

"There's a fine line between fundamentalism and fascism. In the cauldron of a truly free society an invisible hand balances ideologies. I believe it's personal choice..." He was racing now, a deafening roar filing his ears as he was pressed forward into a responsibility he had no wish for.

"We cannot trust our lives to these 'rural people' as you call them, can we? For a fifth of the world's population, Islam is both a religion and a complete way of life. The Holy Qur'an and the Sunnah provide the framework for Shari'ah, the sacred law of Islam, which governs all aspects of the public and private, social and economic, religious and political life of every Muslim. Do not underestimate us. We number in the billions. The Qur'an is our invisible hand!" He towered in righteousness. "Muslims have religion always uppermost in their minds, and make no division between secular and sacred."

"Many fear this…but I…? Just a public servant, not the one to judge these things."

"Look at it this way," he sermonized with a didactic condescension, "the most sophisticated person is still yearning to discover 'The Way'…but to where? To what end? Some turn to money, some turn to love and some to drugs–still others to religion…all people have these needs, fundamental needs, but are lost. People are lost, don't you see? There may be more than one straight path, if so I have not found it. There may be more than one final prophet if so I have not found him. People require this wisdom to refer to; it is humanity's treasure. To mislead is sinful, we call it haram. If something is haram, it is so no matter how good the intention is or how honorable the purpose is. What you are doing is *haram*!"

But Parrish was seeing through him as if all was now being revealed. "You have given up haven't you?"

He gasped with indignation. "I…'The Protector of Mosques?' Nonsense! I don't claim to be 'The Awaited One', simply a believer. It is you who have blasphemed…! You are causing social unrest!"

"I just helped where I needed to…never asked for this burden of dreams…! I'm not the one! I'd give anything to be back in Cairo chasing down antiques…but there's no turning back for either of us, is there? You've given up on any power except the force you command…perhaps

I've come to help you have stronger faith in the unseen."

Jibril seethed. "Faith! The Prophet tells us, peace be upon him… 'Powerful is not he who knocks the other down, indeed powerful is he who controls himself in a fit of anger', so I will not have you executed for blasphemy. Asserting a belief contrary to Islam is equivalent to the denial of God and his unity. No, I will let the others do that after you go on trial for everyone to see. I will expose you!"

"I think you will have a revelation that will change your mind. In fact, one is already here…"

"How could you know?" The general shouted enraged. "…aughh! There it is again! No one knows the future or the unseen except God… it is the sin of sihr, sorcery! They are calling you Mahdi, but you practice cheap tricks just to win attention! You are a charlatan and I will expose you before the people and end this charade and I will be the 'Believer President.'"

At that exact moment an aide entered and crisply saluted raking his back straight and clicking his heels. "Excuse me…" he announced, "there is someone here to see you."

"What? Me, without an appointment? Who is this someone?"

"She claims to be the U. S. Under Secretary of State for Political Affairs." He handed the general a business card. "Her name is Karine Russo."

∗　∗　∗　∗

It was earlier that her suspicions began. It was after the long trip back from their unprofitable adventure in Rashid that she realized how loosely the mission had been organized and started to feel insecure, like she was associating with cowboys not professionals trained at The Farm in Virginia. She never got their 201-files to verify identities and now wondered if her go-between had been economical with the truth. They were entirely too secretive for her, the one who had initiated the exfiltration operation, and were supposed to be subordinates, but instead patronized her sullenly raising hackles on the back of her neck. Karine Russo didn't like her prerogative bucked and never negotiated until an enemy was brought to his knees at which point she showed great empathy. To challenge her was futile, she was always ripe for a fight and their mistake was underestimating a woman in their misogynist bluff. Emails were also telling. She had not retrieved any from her phone because nobody was supposed to know where she was–and there were plenty of the usual variety, but an inordinate number from Viktor Jaraslav caught her attention. He almost never sent her messages, but as soon as she was on mission…there he was like a burr under the skin. It gave her a headache and caused irritating concern about his motives, as they were never what they seemed and always self-serving verging on egomania. She began to believe he was trying to triangulate her position using satellites if she were to respond and so kept the phone off.

Days passed since they discovered Parrish had escaped with the general's daughter into the Lake District, the army in expected pursuit, and she had cooled her heels in the house by the sea anxiously awaiting word as the operatives came and went chasing down leads from "blind dates with friends", as they called it. Then everything changed. They came careening into the house one late afternoon like Pamplona bulls and began hurriedly packing equipment.

"What's happened?" Karine demanded.

"We've found your man."

"Where?"

"The military have him in their headquarters at Montazah. He's been arrested."

"Arrested! …Christ! Now what?"

The operative connected with someone on his mobile and turned away to speak. He said only two things she could make out, "Al-Haramlik Palace. Lunar," waited, as if for confirmation, then hung up.

"What are you doing?"

"Reporting in," he replied furtively.

"To whom?"

"…just keeping in our logistics lines. We've got to move now!"

Minutes later she was hurtling recklessly down an anonymous street with only her small shoulder bag. There was a stone in her shoe and it began to hurt–vulnerable to any passing danger, praying she could reach a main thoroughfare and flag down a car before they noticed her missing. It was impulse. Like taking your hand out of fire. Her heart hammered. The decision was made in the breathless seconds that determine success or failure in a crisis. While the two men had been distracted checking and packing equipment, like a white bird she had flown. The obscure message spoken by the burly man in the house that he didn't want her to hear and lied about sounded suspiciously like betrayal. That was not on the menu. The wind streaked the sky with cirrus clouds painted crimson against the deep cerulean blue. Karine Russo didn't like her authority challenged. It seemed like forever until she reached a main highway, and longer still before a black and yellow taxi responded to her frantic hails.

"Al-Haramlik Palace." She said to the driver's surprise, and they roared off toward Alexandria.

The small boat landed on the beach at Montazah just as the

sun disappeared over the horizon. Kisa was jumpy–the military was everywhere. Ibrahim hoisted the camera onto his shoulder and she followed him breathlessly up the embankment onto the King Farouk Bridge. Cobblestones rolled beneath her feet, the ornate terra cotta pillars towered above with huge, baroque, metal lamps silhouetted against the sky–thankfully dark due to the unreiable power grid. It was silent. Nothing moved except waves. No one could be seen. They started off toward the trees looming in the dusk beyond which was the Al-Haramlik Palace surrounded by the Montazah gardens lush with palm groves, agave and grassy meadows where tourists used to glide in better times. Al' Rashid's yacht lay anchored among the other pleasure boats in the small harbor and when the polished mahogany runabout took the party ashore, it was like being hidden in plain view. No one would expect visitors by sea, but just in case al' Rashid sent along Ishaq Sadek, the detective, with a pistol. "In-sha Allah…" he had finally uttered in exasperation after trying everything to dissuade Kisa. "Nothing can stop her."

They crept silently along the darkening road that traced the curve of the shore leading to the palace. Its towering pinnacle could be seen in the distance lights twinkling yellow against the haze sentry to another time. Palm groves grew more ominous as the day faded. Every sound and nuance caught Kisa's attention though she didn't hear the silent wings of the ten-thousand birds passing high above following designs more essential than those of men, but that was because nothing else existed right now, this was all there was. At last she was beginning to feel like a citizen of the world escaping the chains of anonymity and utter hopelessness in which the vast majority of people live out their lives. It didn't matter that the news reports she generated were ephemeral, virtual things that wafted through the collective consciousness with only one byte of information among the millions of megabytes consumed daily by populations desperate for excitement in their uneventful lives. Merely a blip for short attention spans. She was unconcerned that the profession was littered with burnouts famously saturated with alcohol so they could persist in churning out the pulp necessary for the media every waking hour. Those things didn't matter. She laughed at them. The byline mattered. Recognition and fame–celebrity mattered. And money; the root, the source, the holy grail of accomplishment. If she had money and fame she would no longer be that skinny kid from the small town in central Russia with no future. She would lose the feeling of nonexistence that haunted her and that nothing could wash away except for hot, mindless sex–and even that was only temporary. As she walked along the road and drew near the sequestered military headquarters her headiness became intoxicating. She would scoop the world and just the thought of it made her weak in the knees.

As they came over the rise an unexpected sound met their ears. Crowd sounds. People milling about talking and laughing and arguing. A great shift of anxiousness descended as suddenly the palace lie before them some hundred yards off ablaze in lights as if every room was filled with industrious revolutionary soldiers plotting another overthrow. A crowd gathered outside the high metal gates far down the long drive lined with Belle Epoch streetlamps. Kisa exploded with delight, it was better than she could ever have imagined. "Something's going to happen!" She cried out loud. Ishaq Sadek glared and tightened the grip on his pistol.

They plunged headlong into the crowd mingling and gregariously questioning everyone they met. Ibraham shadowed Kisa camera at the ready after she had admonished him passionately, "Capture it all! Don't turn it off for anything–it's history! God! It's history!" A cacophony of voices erupted most speaking English, but some in the grip of a desperate anticipation let loose replies to her questions in soaring, staccato Egyptian Arabic that left her frustrated, frantic to comprehend and so she grabbed al' Rashid's detective demanding, "What's he saying? What's does it mean?" She asked the same questions, "Why are you here? Why have you come?" The tide of people soon became a flood as night fell and more hopeful arrived. The flood a deluge. They were of all social strata from the streets to the offices, the homes and universities all finding common ground at this one isolated moment coming together, daring to believe in a world filled to the brim and overflowing with disappointments and vanquished dreams with a collective yearning, a final effort, a last chance for their innermost beliefs to be confirmed. One phrase dominated their impassioned replies, "Al Mahdi."

"Allahu Akbar! Al Mahdi!" Came cries out of the crowd. *"Allahu Akbar! Al Mahdi!"* A distant voice echoed in response. Kisa saw in all eyes what betrayed the common thread in this parfait of humanity; it was faith that had brought them, faith that had drawn them from their own comfortable seclusion where each had constructed barriers pretending a private world secured by walls of homes, businesses, classrooms where they were safe from the assault of a relentless, merciless universe that sought out weaknesses in men's souls leaving them festering in the half light of hope. *"Allahu Akbar! Al Mahdi!"* With each call and response the swelling of the crowd grew as if an inner jihad was being awakened and nothing, not even the increasingly nervous soldiers amassing at the gates to the palace, could put it back to sleep again. Kisa was caught in the far off storm where haze and restlessness mingled, where purpose and redemption rushed in as motive and alibi. She trembled with excitement.

Suddenly, a flickering light caught her eye. Hovering out past the far end of the huge palace in darkness it lit up momentarily in the sky and then was extinguished as if an omen of the apocalypse. By this time the front gates were swarming with people and crowds trickled down the long, metal bars of the security fence all edging closer to the glittering edifice looming across the grassy courtyards where their captive was being held. "Down there!" Kisa yelled at Ibrahim, and he instantly swung the camera around to focus in. "Up in the air, beyond the trees," she pointed, "…do you see anything?"

Ibrahim extended the zoom as far as it would go and struggled to keep the view from shaking so much that everything became indistinguishable. "Yes…" he shouted, "…there's something…I can't tell what. Could be military, a jet–but it's gotta be way off, or a helicopter…"

"That's it!" She cried. "Common'…!!" She yanked his sleeve so hard he almost dropped his equipment. "They're moving him!"

Even Ishaq Sadek jumped. Hyper alert, he was enveloped with an uncharacteristically extreme anxiety brought on by the manic crowd and the frenzied woman al' Rashid had charged him with protecting remembering philosophically, "Beauty has many takers."

Running, they made their way through the thinning crowd just in time to see it swooping down through the trees almost completely hidden stealth-like in the darkness. There was not even a sound due to the low din of the people, but regardless it was nearly silent as if a phantom apparition. Instinctively all three crouched down preparing for anything, Kisa behind Ibrahim, hand on his shoulder as he trained his camera on the unfolding drama.

The throb of the rotors was muted and sublime from its low acoustic signature, as it had swept across the Mediterranean Sea at nearly 240 miles per hour from its base at Akrotiri on Cyprus. The odd twin coaxial counter-rotating main rotors soon became faintly visible as it hovered over the tree line momentarily as if a bird assessing a threat. It had no lights and that should have been a dead giveaway.

* * * *

Two strange, intense men entered the dim office unannounced. They had been dispatched late in the afternoon from another building inside the beltway after a series of data coincident events crystallized and an urgent call was made from Langley, Virginia. Viktor Jaraslav was too engrossed watching satellite images of events on the other side of the world to notice them at first, but with then sudden realization he was being observed calmly severed the network connection and stood with the composure of a cobra rising to a fakir's flute. "Pamela?" He pressed the intercom while looking directly at the interlopers, "Who are these men?"

It was later he followed them up the winding stairs and secure elevators from deep within his lair at the Watch where he personally assumed immunity for all his actions would be automatic because in the end he was always right about national interests. Staffers gawked at him in shock at the specter of the high brought low and with the sudden realization there had been a shift in power. During a short ride in the back seat of the government car he held a handkerchief to his mouth aghast at the unsanitary conditions he had been placed in where many others had left their biological calling card by way of the deadly pathogens he abhorred. However, when he was told his arrest had been ordered by the President himself and was part of a global operation initiated just days before he was relieved to be the center of things again where he was happiest. Furtively pulling his cell from the breast pocket of his coat he composed a final text, an epilogue, then pressed, "send" before he pulled the sim card from the phone to clean it of all incriminating data. The message raced through the cyber-ether on its way to Karine Russo whom he had always butted heads with as The Crisis Manager, but now felt great nostalgia for as she had been one of the few worthy adversaries he'd ever had.

"We know you've retained some cowboys for an unauthorized mission...we just don't know what it is. That's why you're here, to bring us up to date."

"How did you form this conclusion?" Removing the handkerchief from his mouth just long enough to speak.

"Routine, just routine. Akrotiri. The RAF air base on Cyprus… British probe into kickbacks on the base from local contractors led to the arrest of the commander. In the ensuing investigation documents were turned up that eventually led back to…you. Aircraft requisitions. Phone records. You were very messy…"

"Well, I'm not used to this sort of thing…not a field agent. Somebody had to act in the national interests, everything is so calcified that nobody can take responsibility to do what's right…that's the trouble with democracy, everyone's equal."

"You can start by telling us where the Under Secretary of State for Political Affairs is…"

*   *   *   *

Emotions were climbing the dark ladder as wild rumors were born like eddies in the wind amongst the volatile crowd and then dissipated again while soldiers nursed the triggers of their semiautomatics overwhelmed at the prospect of having to slaughter their own to turn back the tide of unrest. The cries of *"Allahu Akbar! Al Mahdi!"* came more frequently and the mass of bodies shifting against the gates made the sentries more agitated. It was the stillness of chaos, the precious interval of moments when the mob could go either way, when events were delicately balanced in an equilibrium of forces and nobody was their master regardless of the best intentions on both sides of the fence. The critical mass had been reached and the event horizon crossed. All bets were off.

Karine Russo raised the porcelain and silver demitasse cup of Turkish coffee to her lips and tasted the heady brew. "Thank you," She sighed peering inquisitively at Parrish who sat dumbfounded across from her. "I've been under some stress lately, this helps." She unconsciously looked at her cell and opened the recent text message that had just come though. "Good luck," was all it said, but originating from Viktor Jaraslav she knew it had hidden meanings she'd like to know more about. "Why?" she typed and pressed, "send" not knowing it was too late and her message was lost in cyberspace.

Jibril listened to a situation update whispered in his ear by Colonel Hasan Mawdudi and an anxious shadow crossed his face, "I'm not surprised you're in Egypt, but...here? No entourage?"

"Taxi. I took a taxi." Composing herself as the realization of imminent danger started to creep in and chill her. "You have quite a crowd outside."

"We were just discussing the situation..." He scowled.

"General Riyadh," she began in the disarming cadence of international protocol tinged with the brittle edge that often swayed things her way, "I am here for two reasons. First to repatriate my Foreign Service Officer for Political Affairs to our consulate in Cairo, he is a sovereign U.S. citizen with diplomatic immunity...I can't impress on you enough the damage arresting our..."

"We will need to discuss that...officially, in private session. For now he's suspected of civil and religious crimes...the second?"

"To warn you."

"If you think...!!" He struggled to maintain composure remembering the lines from the Qur'an. "...I don't respond well to threats."

Night fell completely. She tried to explain her worst fears outlining a scenario that involved some undefined operation aimed at discrediting the interim militarily government and calling into question its legitimacy before the international community without revealing her own clandestine mission. "...or possibly your assassination. We, a country founded on revolutionary ideals, are part of a global economy, nothing happens anywhere without affecting things somewhere else." None of it would have mattered; none of it if she hadn't the conviction a rogue mission was in the works that could set back Mid-East relations by decades. Just what it was, she wouldn't speculate, but advised placing troops on high alert with orders to handle any situations with extreme delicacy. Nobody wanted chaos. In the back of her mind the thought lingered that somehow this had the stamp of Viktor Jaraslav on it.

It was all a test, he thought, as they bantered political rhetoric back and forth far into the night without gaining much ground, neither side truly trusting the other. He knew instinctively only with trust could there be any peace or stability. Parrish, however, was in tune with universal constellations and braced himself with the unknown certainty that everyone's faith would be tested that night; the General's professed belief in Islam, Karine's confidence in evangelical democracy and his own faith in himself that had been lost for so long its sudden reemergence still left him bewildered. And it was later that it happened. In blue shadows heralded by the crack of a gunshot. The crowd swelled in the distance. Footsteps rang in the halls.

Ibrahim's camera had barely caught the movements as shadow figures flitted across the grass on the dark side of the Al-Haramlik Palace, but he could see where the helicopter had landed some distance away–a deeper shadow in the darkness–its rotors still moving itching to be on its way again. It was so stealth, no one else in the crowd had noticed. Ominous silhouettes rappelled up the sides of the building.

Inside black-cloaked figures shimmied down from skylights and vulnerable roof top doors and flitted along the outer arcades entering unguarded windows. In minutes twelve special-ops members of an elite direct-action raid force were in the building undetected and began a pre-planned search based on the original 1932 floor plans from King Faud's personal architect. Methodical and relentless, each man had already chosen death and once that specter was eliminated they were like enraged dogs afraid of nothing. Pain became just another perception. Bodies expendable. They were consummate fighting machines far superior to the common soldier who still had desires in life, a woman waiting somewhere, something to live for. Covered with carbon-fiber-reinforced polymer thermoplastic armor and fitted with low profile, AN/PVS-33 night vision goggles featuring ghost-image intensifiers and high light cutoff protection they owned the night. Within 3-minutes they had isolated Jibril's crack revolutionary guards to the lower two floors, where trouble had been expected and all the firepower was amassed–now useless. Passages secured. Guards summarily eliminated one at a time with muffled shots, knifed or garroted from behind. The remaining three began the descent into darkness of the top story, to the target, to where the General was meeting with Parrish and his unexpected guest, the Crisis Manager. The night sang with the whistling Kamaseen wind and the crowd roared in holy furor as events escalated beyond spiritual tolerance.

Suddenly, all lights blacked out. Shots echoed from a nearby hallway. Jibril instantly grabbed his 50 caliber, semiautomatic, stainless steel pistol with polymer grips and crouched down. "Get behind me!" He ordered securely holding the most powerful handgun the world.

"It's me..." Colonel Mawdudi rushed into the darkened room weapon dawn, "...and Azhara..." the two figures were silhouetted by filtered moonlight as they sprinted toward the others, "...we have intruders from the roof!"

"Not the crowd?"

"No...someone else. Airlifted...they're fully equipped, looks like special ops...commandos. A third party...they've sealed off lower floors…"

"They're after you!" Karine blurted out to the General. "I knew something would happen!"

Outside the helicopter had been spotted and the news ignited by the rumor that the military was spiriting *al Mahdi* away to a secret location where he could be eliminated burst through the throng like fire. The mob exploded with incendiary fury and leapt up on the sixteen-foot fences shaking their foundations and making them sway a hundred yards at a time. The reinforced sentries now backed by rows of troops retreated from the gates and formed a line some distance away, face shields pulled down– searching back and forth between the teeming mob and the suddenly darkened palace not sure where the enemy was, or who the enemy was– the situation as delicate as nitroglycerin on a house of cards.

"Don't go near the windows!" Colonel Mawdudi said taking the lead, "They're on the arcade…we have to get out of here…" and he led them to a door at the far back of the room inside of which was a long, narrow, windowless servants' hallway. They filed through the small door one at a time trying to hear anything over the sounds of the teeming crowd in the distance. Footsteps creaked on the hundred-year-old yellow oak flooring and the only light was from the moon's illumination into the room where they'd left the door open behind them. Like racing to oblivion they hurtled into the darkness along the passage that ran the length of the building and was originally meant to give servants private access to all rooms so the elite would not be disturbed by their presence, but when desired one would appear as if from nowhere to cater to privileged whims. Now it was a lifeline. When it stopped, there was another door and just as they had disappeared into it the light at the other end of the hall was blotted out as three figures chased in hard pursuit. Up the spiral stairs in total darkness they fled, not a word was spoken. At the top the colonel broke down the locked barrier and suddenly they all tumbled out on the roof awash in ivory light caressed by the Kamaseen winds. To the east where the deserts lay was a blood stint in the sky from roiling sands, to the north raging whitecaps on the Mediterranean glowing white with phosporescent algae beneath the haloed moon. Looming to their left was the huge, baroque tower designed in the Turkish style that soared up into the night while directly in front lay a two-storied penthouse building behind the lesser tower facing the courtyards at the front where the churning masses jostled and chanted *"Allahu Akbar! Al Mahdi!"*

As one they made a crazy dash for the ramped stairs climbing the rooftop apartments and had just made it to the second tier when three men appeared below. Wood and plaster splintered. Shots muted by silencers sliced the midnight air. They hit the decks Jibril and the Colonel frantically returning fire, but Parrish, out of some uncontrollable survival impulse raced ahead to the top and ran out on the mezzanine veranda. Suddenly, all three men in black turned toward him and let out a barrage shredding the walls and windows. Just at that moment the twin coaxial helicopter with counter-rotating main rotors appeared rising like Icarus from the rear of the palace blowing gusts of hot wind and debris. It was a darker shape in the darkness with one tail rotor facing backwards; two rear stabilizers turned down at the middle and a weapons pod on each side of the fuselage and stuck terror in everyone because it was extremely quiet and unlike any craft they had ever seen. The marauders continued to go after Parrish ignoring the others and as the aircraft began to land it's side door slid open revealing the other intruders that had just been picked on the grass below.

"Why do they want him?" Jibril shouted incredulously at Karine Russo. "Him of all people?" Clearly observing the total lethal force directed at Parrish now pinned down at the opposite end of the landing from the door. "Isn't this your operation? Why do the American's want him? I thought it was me...you told me I was the target!"

"I don't know..." Karine yelled as she flexed all her muscles and dashed madly up the stairs reaching for the door shouting, "Erskine! Erskine!" But as it was forced open she slumped down in a lifeless heap blood gushing from her back silent, motionless in the fury, cut down mid-stride.

Then out of the chaos there was more gunfire–loud, stacatto reports from many rifles...an automatic storm filling the air with noise and confusion like a mad, psychotic carnival. However, when the raiders had been lifted off the ground the soldiers had broken through and now poured out onto the roof in a vicious firefight with the cornered commandos. The three men in black ran for the helicopter, but only one was pulled in the side door before it lifted away...the other two cut down where they stood their bodies lacerated and torn apart with bullets. Suddenly, the aircraft was belted by a ferocious gust of wind and radically shifted sideways forcing its main rotors to hit the high tower just below the ornate capital of the minaret. Instantly it rolled ninety-degrees and with an ear busting, piercing crash of metal against stone it slammed into the tower with such tremendous force that the column broke like a twig and the helicopter slid screeching down the wall, shattered the edge of the roofline as it collided then tumbled flaming to the ground where it hit with a massive, sonic-boom like explosion engulfing everything in a fireball that shot 500-feet in the air and littered the promenade with metal pieces, jet fuel and huge chunks of the building. The top third of the high tower, that had been an architectural landmark of the delta for over a hundred years and was considered by many a baroque masterpiece in the Turkish style, tumbled down the three stories of the palace to the ground where it broke into hundreds of pieces raising huge plumes of dust that rose and mingled with the smoke and fire of the catastrophic inferno.

Parris knelt over the lifeless body of Karine Russo in disbelief. He felt the cold shock to his core never realizing the bond that existed between them, until it was broken. The thought that he must do something shrieked inside. Then, laying his hands upon her felt flesh and sinew and bone and probed for the trauma…in his heart was panic, in his eyes were bitter tears.

Great roaring cavalcades of voices, thunderous, tumultuous voices rose up from the seething crowd below now enraged because of the violence and many believing their *Mahdi* had perished in the flaming crash of the helicopter and had been taken from them after they had waited over a thousand years for the world to be filled with justice. They had come out of absolute faith, and even those who doubted were now converts and climbed the fences surrounding the palace so that in places those fences began to collapse. Troops in the yards around the great structure braced themselves and raised their automatic rifles aiming at their brother citizens. Acting for the common good cleansed some of sympathy; fear of violent death motivated everyone else.

"There will be blood…!" Azhara stood above him and placed her hand on his shoulder. "She is gone, there are others who need you more…"

"I…I can't, I'm not who you think I am…"

"Listen…" The roar of the crowd below shook the building and iced their bones. It was no longer a chorus of chanting, but a cacophony of rage and impending violence about to erupt, an impossible pressure seeking release. "There will be blood!"

Parrish rose looking darkly at the lifeless body strewn like chaff at his feet, his heart once again raking the jagged pinnacles beneath the lowest depths where men, once they had reached that farthest point, never returned. Then, without warning he fled up the steps. Up through the outer veranda winding his way among the openings and little flights of stairs to the top of the lesser tower facing the front of the Al-Haramlik Palace where the troops were standing before the hordes who had just broken through the collapsed fences crushing each other in their chaotic rush to nowhere. Suddenly, all the lights came back on and it caused the crowd to pause as one, like the suspension of belief in a play had been interrupted and all looked up to see real life. The enormous building was lit up like a beautiful glittering arcade the glow of the burning helicopter casting its flickering shadows and floodlights hitting the façade and shining on him way up there standing among the pillars of the portico at the top of the tower beneath the sloped, terra cotta, four-cornered roof. First one and then another and soon a chorus of others spotted him and pointed shouting: "There he is! There!" Up there! In the tower! Look! Look!" The restless, agitated crowd cheered en masse and roared and yelled and screamed as emotions ran rampant into the wild night.

Parrish raised both his arms in a defiant, uplifting stance and mirrored all their emotions right back at them. He shuddered with the moment and thrilled at the unexpected power he now held in his hands awed by his terrible purpose awakened by some unknown force. "I am not the one!!" He shouted as loudly as he could desperately trying to turn back time. "It's not me! I am not the one!!"

But they didn't hear him. *"Allahu Akbar! Al Mahdi!"* Came the scattered response of a few dozen voices.

"I am not the one!" He yelled. "It's not me!"

"Allahu Akbar! Al Mahdi!" Now a few hundred joined the refrain. *"Allahu Akbar! Al Mahdi!"*

The great general, Commander of the Faithful stood behind his beloved daughter Azhara both watching the American, of whom he had still not made up his mind–but the fact that he had been targeted for his power raised esteem for the man in his eyes. He had many scars from many battles. These things happened and no longer bothered him, but of belief…it was the void into which he had plunged as a young boy hoping that someone somewhere would catch him. That was a pillar of his faith, complete submission to the unknown, but now he saw a man who held everything he himself had ever aspired to in his hand yet denied it all and somehow it reconfirmed his hopefulness.

The people raised their right fists in unison, their voices in gigantic crescendos of unshakable belief…*"Allahu Akbar! Al Mahdi!"*…the people who had come here for no other reason.

"Allahu Akbar! Al Mahdi!" Within minutes the whole of the mass of people as a single living organism began chanting in a thundering chorus that shook the ground beneath their feet.

"Allahu Akbar! Al Mahdi!

"Allahu Akbar! Al Mahdi!"

"Allahu Akbar! Al Mahdi!"

Sunrise tore the sky in a crimson shattered brilliance as sand lifted by the Kamaseen winds hung in the distance. Overhead the great migration continued unseen as birds spoke their secret language in flight waiting, only waiting for men to have their day and pass into the ashes of history as all things do in the natural world. It was their hymn to the dawn and ran deeper than any of the cities below, which were losing the battle inch by inch as the Sahara slowly reclaimed its own.

Parrish gazed out the window of the third story embassy office in the Garden City district south toward Old Cairo, Al-Qāhirah the

Conquorer. He picked up a small figurine from his desk, a seated female figure carved out of a hard black stone with iridescent flecks of quartz. The jewels that once were inlaid and the gold now missing, only the discoloration remained from where they had been. He ran his fingers across the exquisitely detailed rings and curls of the hair each forming a perfect symmetry and the sublimely proportioned face watching him from across the centuries. For once he felt like he belonged and looking out across thousand-year-old Cairo where in the melodious corridors of slums hopeless humanity made music with their voices he was glad to be home.

Suddenly, there was a knock on the door under the raised emblem of an eagle enclosed in a circle with the words "Department of Sate" at the top under which in a smaller, understated serif typeface was inscribed, "Deputy Chief of Mission for the Central Middle East."

"I'm all packed…just wanted to say goodbye," Ariel Addison said his usually pale skin now flushed. "Sorry, I'm a bit breathless…been lifting things…not used to…I just wanted to say, good luck."

"Thanks…"

"…God knows you'll need it–those news reports from the Russian reporter couldn't have helped you much, but I always knew you'd make good," he wheezed out begrudgingly as an act of contrition, "I had my eye on you."

"I remember…"

"It's inscrutable you know…they say all men are the same under the skin, but nothing seems to change does it? Like ever spinning spirals…"

"It's funny Ariel, I've never been more optimistic."

"Events have happened haven't they, the whole place is shot with superstition…they're different than you and I you know, just different… just tribes with flags…be a shrine to you before you know it!"

"Faith…Addison, faith. That's what binds us…we all have hope in something we can't yet touch, don't we? It's the one thing there's a word for in every language.

"…maybe…maybe," he demurred with a covert grace, "but explaining faith is like trying to catch the wind."

As he disappeared down the corridor he brushed past another who had come with high expectations for the ship of state. She stood in the amber glow of the doorway unsure of who he really was, someone she could love or like "God-intoxicated Man," Pharaoh Ikhnaton would he try to usher in an new age in a sublimely tragic effort. Parrish looked into her eyes.

"Are you ready?" She said as he took his place in the great Mandala.

GLOSSARY

A GLOSSARY OF ARABIC TERMS

abeya - Robes women wear in some parts of the Muslim world including North Africa and the Arabian peninsula.

Abu al-Abbas al-Mursi Mosque - The most historic and most beautiful mosque in Alexandria. It was built primarily in 1775 over the tomb of a Spanish scholar and saint, Abu El Abbas El Mursi (1219-86), and stands on Mosque Square overlooking the eastern harbor.

ad-Dajjal - Arabic for "The Deceiver"

adahn or azaan - In Islam, the call to prayer five times a day, usually by a muezzin from a minaret. From Arabic adhān, from adhina to proclaim, invite. Allāhu akbar, Allāhu akbar. Ash-hadu an-lā ilāha illā allāh. (God is greatest, God is greatest. I bear witness that there is no deity but God.)

Adhān - Or azan (as pronounced in Afghanistan, Iran, Pakistan, Bangladesh, India and Turkey), is the Islamic call recited by the muezzin at prescribed times of the day summoning Muslims for mandatory prayer. The root of the word means "to permit"; another derivative of this word is udun.

Allahu Akbar - Although the phrase "Allahu Akbar" is a common phrase used by all Muslims in various situations, including the Salah (obligatory five prayers a day) and has even been used in the past by some non-Muslims as a show of support for the protesting Iranians, it is widely associated with the Muslims who shout it whilst engaged in Jihad. Many people claim it is simply the Arabic translation of a common English phrase meaning "God is great!" Lane's Lexicon, the most revered and scholarly dictionary of the Arabic language, confirms the majority view is that "Allahu Akbar" refers to Allah being "greater". Muslims have also used it historically as a battle cry during war.

Al-Muntadhir - "The Awaited one" is a messiah-like figure in Shia Islam, sometimes referred to as the Mahdi, but distinctly of a Shia tradition.

al-Qa'im - "He Who Arises" a name for Mahdi in Shia Islam.

bisht - A traditional Arabic men's cloak popular in some Arab countries. It is a flowing outer cloak made of wool, worn over the thawb, but the bisht is soft and it is usually black, brown, beige, cream or grey in color.

bokra - A colloquial response that means "tomorrow", and implies that something will be done some other time than the present.

cardamom - An aromatic spice, a member of the ginger family, used to flavor Arabic coffee.

Dajjal or Al-Masih ad-Dajjal - An Islamic figure similar to the Antichrist; means "liar" or "deceiver". is an evil figure in Islamic eschatology. He is to appear pretending to be Masih at a time in the future, directly comparable to the figures of the Antichrist and Armilus in Christian and Jewish eschatology.

Dar al-Islam - "Abode of peace" as realized by an Islamic society. Opposed to "dar al-harb", abode of war.

fatwa - The interpretation, legal opinion or decree issued by a mufti on a fine point of Islamic law or on new situations or questions.

hadiths - Traditions. Muhammad's habitual behavior as recorded. Regarded as a manifestation of the will of God, these hold a stronger moral weight than the accumulated practices of the community in the right way to act.

Hāfiz - Someone who knows the Qur'an by heart. Literal translation: memorizer or Protector.

Hajj - An act of obedience to God's command as expressed in the Qur'an. Commonly the annual pilgrimage to Mecca required of all Muslims at least once in their life.

halal - An Arabic word meaning "lawful" or "permissible. Permitted lawful activities.

haram - An Arabic term meaning sinful. In Islamic Jurisprudence, haram is used to refer to any act that is forbidden by God, and is one of five that define the morality of human action. Acts that are haram are typically prohibited in the religious texts of the Quran and the Sunnah. The category of haram is the highest status of prohibition. Islam teaches that a haram (sinful) act is recorded by an angel on the person's left shoulder. If something is considered haram, it remains prohibited no matter how good the intention is or how honorable the purpose is. A haram is converted into a gravitational force on the day of judgment and placed on mizan (weighing scales).

harim - To the extent to which a family was wealthy, powerful and respected it would seclude its women in a special part of the home, the harim. Openly active women were of poor families.

hijab - Veil or head covering worn by Muslim women in public. The traditional head scarf worn by women as a sign of Islamic identity and faith.

hijra - In 622 when Muhammad was not accepted as the messenger of God in Mecca, he left for an oasis settlement 200 miles away called Yarthrib, later known as Medina. While the word symbolizes the flight from Mecca, it implies the seeking of protection by settling in a place other than one's own.

Iblis - Iblis is the personal name of the Devil who is mentioned in the Qur'anic account of Genesis. According to the Qur'an, Iblis disobeyed an order from Allah to bow to Adam, seeing Adam as being inferior in creation due to his being created from clay as compared to him (created of fire). As a result he was forced out of heaven and given respite until the day of judgment from further punishment, so he endeavored to turn others from the straight path by enticing them with temptation and sin.

imam - An Islamic religiopolitical leader. An imam is an Islamic leadership position. It is most commonly in the context of a worship leader of a mosque and Muslim community by Sunni Muslims only. In this context, Imams may lead Islamic worship services, serve as community leaders, and provide religious guidance. It may also be used in the form of a prefix title with scholars of renown.

iman - "Faith". Religious belief or conviction in the fundamental doctrines of Islam.

In-sha Allah - If God wills it; or- if God is willing.

Islam - Submission or surrender to the will of God. Believers in the Qur'an and the faith engendered by Muhammad's revelation. The Arabic word 'Islam' simply means 'submission', and derives from a word meaning 'peace'. In a religious context it means complete submission to the will of God.

iwan - A large circular arched door, which spread westward into the Arab world from Iran.

jallaba - The traditional flowing robed costume of the Arab.

jihad - To strive in the way of God, (to follow Islam): Defense of the faith: To fight in order to extend the bounds of Islam

kafir - "Unbeliever". Infidel. One who is ungrateful and rejects the message of Islam.

Khamaseen - A dry, hot, dusty local wind, blowing from the south, in North Africa and the Arabian Peninsula–known in Europe as a sirocco. From the Arabic word for "fifty", throughout the Levant, these dry, dust-filled windstorms often blow sporadically over fifty days, hence the name.

Mahdi - The "guided one'" Shi'is of the main branch held that the line of imams, descendants of the prophet through his daughter Fatima, had come to an end with the twelfth. In 874 the twelfth Imam of a Shii Islamic community disappeared. It was then believed that he was only in hiding and would return as a messianic figure at the end of the world to usher in a perfect Islamic society. The Mahdi. In the absence of the hidden Imam, though he communicated regularly with them, the community was to be guided by the religious experts who would interpret God's will, Islamic law.

majlis - In Arabic architecture, the main reception room leading off of a courtyard.

malesh - Literally… "never mind". A common phrase in Cairo used as an effort to change the subject.

Mashrabiya - Latticework wooden shutters to windows often used to enclose hanging balconies across the Arab world for privacy from the street.

The word "mashrabiya" comes from an Arabic root meaning the "place of drinking," which was adapted to accommodate the first function of the screen: "the place to cool the drinking water." The shade and open lattice of a mashrabiya provided a constant current of air, which, as the sweating surfaces of porous clay pots evaporated, cooled the water inside.

Masīh - is the Arabic word for messiah. The word Masīh literally means "anointed one"

mu'jizah - The Arabic word for miracle. It stems from the word ajz, meaning something that incapacitates, cannot be resisted, unique.

muezzin (mu'adhdin) - A public crier who calls out the times of prayer from a high place, usually a tower or minaret attached to a mosque.

mufti - A mufti is a Sunni Islamic scholar who is an interpreter or expounder of Islamic law, (see shari'a.) A muftiate is a council of muftis. Muftis are experts in Islamic law qualified to give authoritative legal opinions know as fatwas. Within Islamic legal schools, a mufti is considered the pinnacle in the hierarchy of scholars because of the advance training required out of the individual inspiring to be a mufti. Originally, muftis were private individuals who gave fatwas informally, regulated their own activities, and determined their own standards of the fatwa institution. A mufti could also be defined as an individual well grounded in Islamic law.

mullah - An Islamic cleric, often considered tradition bound.

Muslim - An adherent of the Islamic faith. One becomes a Muslim by saying 'there is no god apart from God, and Muhammad is the Messenger of God.' By this declaration the believer announces his or her faith in all God's messengers, and the scriptures they brought.

qawwali - Literally "utterance". Devotional music of the Sufi Muslims, the mystical sect of Islam, intended to elevate the spirit and bring both performer and listener closer to God. The mouthpiece of divine power. In the communal, ritualized setting of a Qawwali session members of the audience are often brought to a state of trance-chanting, swaying and clapping, even falling into physical convulsions.

Qur'an - The word itself means "recitation". The word of God as revealed to Muhammad ibn Abdullah between 610 and 632 and written in Arabic. The sacred scripture of Islam.

Ramadan - A strict fast during the month in which the Qur'an was first revealed. It is one of the pillars of Islam. All Muslims above the age of ten are obliged from eating and drinking, and from sexual intercourse, from daybreak until nightfall. The only exceptions are for those who are too physically weak to endure it, those of unsound mind, those engaged in heavy labor or war and travelers.

salaam aleikum - A common Arab greeting... Peace be with you. The response is, Wa aleikin as-salaam... And on you be peace.

samūn (Simoom) - (Arabic: samūm; from the root s-m-m, "to poison") is a strong, dry, dust-laden local wind that blows in the Sahara, Israel, Jordan, Syria, and the deserts of Arabian Peninsula.

Sayyid - (Arabic: meaning Mister) Sayyid is an honorific title, it denotes males accepted as descendants of the Islamic prophet Muhammad, who is the descendant of Ishmael and Abraham- through his grandsons, Hasan ibn Ali and Husain ibn Ali, sons of the prophet's daughter Fatima Zahra and his son-in-law Ali ibn Abi Talib.

Shaitan - Shaitan is the equivalent of Satan in Islam. While Shaitan is an adjective (meaning "astray" or "distant," sometimes translated as "devil"– it can be roughly translated as "Enemy," "Rebel," "Evil" or "Devil."

Shamal - A northwesterly wind blowing over Iraq and the Persian Gulf states (including Saudi Arabia and Kuwait), often strong during the day, but decreasing at night. This weather effect occurs anywhere from once to several times a year, mostly in summer but sometimes in winter. The resulting wind typically creates large sandstorms that impact Iraq, most sand having been picked up from Jordan and Syria.

Shari'ah (Shari'a) (also Shari'ah, Shari'a, Shariah or Syariah) - The Islamic legal code based entirely on the Qur'an and regarded as divine law. Translated literally from Arabic it means 'the road to a watering hole"...hence the path to God. It is the Arabic word for Islamic law, also known as the Law of Allah. Islam classically draws no distinction between religious, and secular life. Hence Sharia covers not only religious rituals, but many aspects of day-to-day life, politics, economics, banking, business or contract law, and social issues. The term Shari'a itself derives from the verb shara'a, which according to Abdul Mannan Omar's Dictionary of the Holy Qur'an, connects to the idea of "spiritual law" (5:48) and "system of divine law; way of belief and practice" (45:18) in the Quran.

Shi'i Muslims - Those following descendents of Ali, Muhammad's cousin. Shi'ism. Perceived as an underprivileged minority who carry a sense of being oppressed and wrongly governed.

sihr - is the Arabic word for magic or witchcraft. Sihr is so called because its means are hidden or secret, and because the practitioners of sihr deal with things in secret which enable them to perform illusions to confuse the people and deceive their eyes, and to cause them harm or steal their money, etc., in a secretive manner so that in most cases nobody realizes what is happening. Hence the last part of the night is called sahar, because at the end of the night people are unaware and they do not move about much. And the lungs are also called sahr, because they are hidden inside the body.

Sufism - The Arabic equivalent to the word' mysticism', which is tasaw-wuf, from which comes the anglicized form 'suf'. A mystical sect of Islam.

sunnah - The way of life prescribed as normative for Muslims on the basis of the teachings and practices of Islamic prophet Muhammad and interpretations of the Quran. The word sunnah plural sunan is derived from the root sanna meaning smooth and easy flow (of water) or direct flow path. The word literally means a clear and well trodden path.

Sunni Muslims - Those following the line of the first Caliph, Abu Bakr, the Prophet's best friend. From sunna, meaning habitual behavior of the community in what is right and survival- mores. Specifically, the Prophet's habitual behavior, which is considered to be a manifestation of God. Sunnism. Conservatives of the Islamic world, they represent a majority of the population in most places but Iran, Iraq, Lebanon and Bahrain.

tariqah - Sufi mystical brotherhoods that have been historically active, along with ulama associations, in nationalist struggles. In the late 20th century these were replaced by Islamic activist groups with non-clerical leadership.

thawb - A thawb or thobe is an ankle-length garment, usually with long sleeves, similar to a robe. It is commonly worn in Arab countries. It is normally made of cotton, but heavier materials such as sheep's wool can also be used, especially in the colder climates of Iraq and Syria.

ulama - The body of informed and concerned Muslim religious scholars.

umma - An Arabic word meaning "nation" or "community". It is a synonym for ummat al-Islamiyah (the Islamic Nation), and it is commonly used to mean the collective community of Islamic peoples. In the Quran the ummah typically refers to a single group that shares common religious beliefs, specifically those that are the objects of a divine plan of salvation. In the context of Pan-Islamism and politics, the word Ummah can be used to mean the concept of a Commonwealth of the Believers.

wahiya - The bosses of Cairo's trash collection racket.

Zabbaleen - A term that means, "rubbish collectors". Early in the 20th century Muslims from the Western Desert had developed a business collecting Cairo's garbage. When Coptic Christian from the South arrived in the city in the 1930's, the Muslims sold them the rights to collect and keep the trash. Routes are passed down from father to son sustaining them, yet holding them in social bondage. They earn no money, only the right to keep the trash and scavenge a living from it. As late as 1987 there were over 25,000 Zabbaleen. They live in the Muqattam Hills, a barren plateau east of and overlooking Cairo.

Zulfiqar - Shia Muslims believe that when the prophet Muhammad was nearing death, he appointed his son-in-law Ali as his successor, and handed him his sword named Zulfiqar to his young cousin Ali. By most historical accounts, Ali used the sword at the Battle of the Trench to cut a fierce Meccan opponent and his shield in two halves. No one had dared to fight him except Ali, who killed him with one powerful blow. It is said that the sword came down from Heaven as a gift from Allah and it is seen as a symbol of honor and martyrdom.

Books by Michael Jeffery Blair

EXIT POINT

THE ARCHITECT OF LAW

SUDDEN RIVERS

MICHAEL JEFFERY BLAIR is a novelist and writer of fiction and non-fiction. He is also an award-winning designer and media artist. He has created communications for many of the world's great companies and is the principal and creative director of a design firm based in Los Angeles specializing in marketing communications for which he has garnered dozens of national awards. His work has been published extensively in the U.S. and Europe. He has been involved in the theater, written several stage plays and a collection of poetry entitled "Fisher In The Abyss." His novels include "Exit Point," "The Architect Of Law" and "Sudden Rivers" and his editorial work has appeared in the New York Times and other publications.